THE JANUS DECEPTION

A NOVEL

THE
JANUS
DECEPTION

A NOVEL

JOHN
F. BAYER

BROADMAN
&HOLMAN
PUBLISHERS

NASHVILLE, TENNESSEE

0-8054-2439-3

Published by Broadman & Holman Publishers, Nashville, Tennessee

Dewey Decimal Classification: 813
Subject Heading: FICTION
Library of Congress Card Catalog Number: 2001035090

Library of Congress Cataloging-in-Publication Data
Bayer, John.
    The Janus deception : a novel / John F. Bayer.
       p.   cm.
    ISBN 0-8054-2439-3 (pbk.)
    1. Chemical warfare—Research—Fiction. 2. Americans—Mexico—
Fiction. 3. Conspiracies—Fiction. 4. Soldiers—Fiction. 5. Mexico—
Fiction. I. Title.
    PS3552.A85868 J36 2001
    813'.54—dc21

                                  2001035090
                                    CIP

1 2 3 4 5 6 7 8 9 10 05 04 03 02 01

DEDICATION

Dedicated to the doctors, staff, and
patients of the
Veterans Affairs Medical Center
Memphis, Tennessee

ACKNOWLEDGMENTS

This book was written with the help of many people, some who were friends and some who became friends in the course of my research. To everyone, I say thank you. I hope I have left out no one. All contributed, and for that I am grateful.

Thanks to:

The Department of the Navy and Captain Ann E. Rondeau, Commanding Officer, Naval Support Activity, Mid-South (NAVSUPACT), Millington, Tennessee.

Pam Branch, Public Affairs Assistant, Naval Support Activity, Mid-South, who gave of her time to provide critical details of the day-to-day operations of Naval Support Activities, Mid-South.

The Department of Veterans Affairs (VA), Washington, D.C., and to Veterans Affairs, Regional, Nashville, Tennessee.

Mr. Kenneth L. Mulholland, Jr., Director, Veterans Affairs Medical Center, Memphis, Tennessee, for his help, support, and understanding in the writing of this book.

Special thanks to Ms. Willie M. T. Logan, Director, Public & Consumer Affairs, Veterans Affairs Medical Center, Memphis, Tennessee, without whose assistance this book would have been less than what it is.

To Dr. Sarah A. Carter, Chief of Staff, Veterans Affairs Medical Center, Memphis, Tennessee, for her invaluable insight and especially her willingness to share her philosophy of patient care that makes the VA what it is today.

To Tommy Davis, Chief of Security, Veterans Affairs Medical Center, Memphis, Tennessee, for his input into the inner workings of the VA.

To Mike Higginbotham and Mark Raburn of the Counter Spy Shop of Mayfair, London, for their input into the workings and capabilities of electronic surveillance devices used in this book.

To Rhonda Jobe and Dr. Wendy Gunther of the Regional Forensic Center, Memphis, Tennessee, for their time and assistance.

GLOSSARY

AWOL-Absent Without Leave.

BDU-Battle Dress Uniform. Replaces traditional fatigues.

BUPERS-The U.S. Navy Bureau of Personnel.

CNO-Chief of Naval Operations.

DEA-Drug Enforcement Administration.

FLIR-Forward-looking Infrared. Infrared detection system.

GPS-Global Positioning System.

HMMWV-Highly Mobile Multipurpose Wheeled Vehicle (see humvee below).

Humvee-Replacement for the Jeep.

Klick-short for kilometer.

MAD-Magnetic Anomaly Detector. Used by aircraft to detect metallic objects.

MANSAT-MANSAT SATCOM communications terminal developed by Ferranti International from a design originated by the Royal Signals and Radar Establishment. Provided full-duplex, capable of being carried and operated by one man. A self-contained satellite communications system for tactical warfare use.

MC-Medical Corps.

NAVSUPACT-Naval Support Activities, Mid-South. Pronounced, Nav-soo-pack.

NBC-Nuclear, Biological, Chemical.

NCIS-Naval Criminal Investigative Service.

NCISRA-Naval Criminal Investigative Service Resident Agent.

NSA-National Security Agency.

PA-Posterior/Anterior. Traditional chest X-ray.

PCS-Permanent Change of Station.

Rub' al Khali-South Saudi Arabian desert.

SAS-Britain's Special Air Services regiment. Britain's special operations unit was formed in the western desert during WWII. This unit was disbanded after the war and reformed in the early 1950s as the 22nd Regiment to combat Communist terrorists.

SATCOM-Short for satellite communications. Communication systems utilizing orbiting satellites.

SOC-Special Operations Command. A combination of Special Forces, SEALS, etc., combined under one operations umbrella.

SOCSOUTH-Special Operations Command, Southern Command. SOC contingent headquartered in south Florida, whose operations zone includes Central and South America.

SOFA-Status of Forces Agreement. The contract under which the U.S. military operates in other countries.

SOUTHCOM-Southern Command. Formally headquartered at Fort Clayton, Republic of Panama, now operating from Florida.

TDY-Temporary Duty.

PROLOGUE
1998

Tierra Quemada, Mexico
Monday, January 12, 1998
5:30 A.M. Local Time

The boy shivered in the predawn cold of the high desert. He threaded his way gingerly through the darkness of Tierra Quemada, avoiding the sharp spines of the cactus, keeping an eye out for the odd sidewinder that might already have begun its search for food despite the morning chill.

Today was a day of firsts for the boy, and he wanted to be certain he made no mistakes.

As soon as he delivered the goats in his charge to the high pasture some 10 kilometers from his village, he would return to Colinas Verde and the joys of the celebration that would take place there.

Even as he herded the goats toward the scrub pasture, he could still remember the smells and the sounds as he had left the village earlier this morning. The village women, including his mother, had already begun the cooking, and the odors of boiling chicken, freshly ground corn tortillas, and fresh *salsa verde* had filled the high plateau air. It would be a celebration to remember.

The boy stumbled, his mind quickly returning to the task at hand as he picked himself up and brushed away the small pebbles embedded in his right knee. He could not see in the gray darkness, but by the feel of it, he had cut his knee. It didn't matter; nothing could ruin this day for him.

The forty-odd goats were tracking directly toward the high pasture his father had designated for the day's grazing, and the boy was content to follow in their tracks. The quicker he got the goats to the pasture, the quicker he would be back in Colinas Verde; and the quicker he returned, the quicker he could begin enjoying his day of firsts.

The village of Colinas Verde was three hundred years old today—not old by Mexican standards—but the celebration would be one that none of the few hundred inhabitants would forget. The food would be abundant and *sumptuous.* That was the word the priest had used, and even though the boy did not know what it meant, he had seen the gluttonous pleasure on the priest's face and knew it had to be special.

The priest would be there too. Normally, the small village church hosted the itinerant priest every seventh Sunday, but the boy knew that where there was a celebration and free beer, the ruddy-faced priest was sure to be.

That would be one of his firsts, the boy thought. His first beer. He could hardly wait to taste the golden liquid that seemed to have such power over most of the men in Colinas Verde. Even the priest thought the beer was special. After Sunday morning mass, he was the first one to arrive at the small cantina across the town square from the church.

PROLOGUE

In front of him and the rest of the village men, a line of brown, long-necked bottles would appear on the ledges of the cantina's glassless windows, like fence posts freshly cut and lined up for future use.

Today would be his day to join the ranks of those who so proudly contributed to that line of bottles.

It would also be his first day to kiss Maria Sanchez Orozco, the dark-eyed beauty who lived three doors down from his own house and seemed to delight in taunting him with a smile that made something inside him creep, and crawl, and tumble. In the last few years, his feelings for Maria Sanchez had been transformed from a childish dislike to feelings he could not explain. Sometimes he lay awake at night, thinking of her.

It was all planned. The kiss would take place behind the ornately decorated grandstand, which even now sat in the middle of the town park. After a few beers, he would lure Maria beneath the grandstand by informing her he had a secret to tell her. It was not an elaborate plan, but it did not have to be. He was certain Maria would be a willing participant as long as she had a legitimate excuse to be beneath the crepe-paper-covered grandstand with a young boy who had had too many bottles of Corona beer.

It would be a glorious day, as soon as he delivered the forty cursed goats in his charge to the high pasture.

Dawn was breaking, and the predawn chill would quickly be replaced by a high-desert sun that would beat down on the land unrelentingly.

The land had been well named: *Tierra Quemada*—the "burned land." There were no trees to provide protection from the sun. The landscape resembled pictures of the moonscapes his teacher had shown his class in one of the thick books she kept on her desk. The boy was not certain he believed that the *Norte Americanos* had actually set foot on the moon. After all, the same pictures could easily have been taken right here in Tierra Quemada. The small, flat cactus, a food staple his mother prepared as *nopales,* dotted the landscape. *That* might be the only difference between Tierra Quemada and the moon.

The boy still remembered with amusement the *gringa* missionary who had come to the village once. The fair-skinned woman had thought the nopales with boiled yucca had been something called green beans with potatoes, and had scooped a mound of the flat green nopales onto her plate. The first bite had told her the jalapeño-spiced nopales were not the beans she had thought they were. The boy had laughed so hard he had thought his sides were going to burst.

Besides the low flat scrub brush and cactus, there was little to see—if you did not count *el castillo,* which was just now coming into view in the west.

All the boys called the place *el castillo*—the castle—because of its construction. The castle was surrounded by an industrial fence topped with gleaming razor wire. The building itself was taller than any in his village by at least ten meters. There were windows only on one side. Three walls were solid masses of concrete painted white to reflect the sun. Four *torres esquineras*—corner towers—loomed over the land-scape, standing like solitary soldiers on guard. Chimneys topped the structure, adding another twenty meters to the height and giving the fortress the appearance of a squat, square, four-poster bed standing in the midst of a dusty soccer field.

The rising sun was beginning to paint the white sides of the fortress with its yellow rays. Soon, when the sun rose higher in the sky, it would be all but impossible to gaze at the white flat sides of the huge building.

The boy hurried the goats along. Some were slowing, content to graze on the existing foliage rather than trek to the further pasture, and the boy was anxious to return to Colinas Verde. The celebration would be starting in a few hours, and he wanted to be there. He especially wanted to be there for his first beer and the kiss he would steal from Maria Sanchez Orozco.

PROLOGUE

As the boy herded the animals west, skirting the castle, a strange smell began to drift in on the early morning breeze. It was faint at first, nothing more than a brackish whiff carried from the castle compound. Odd smells were not uncommon coming from the strange building. Once, just such a smell had killed most of the vegetation around the complex. The authorities had been summoned that time, but little had been done to stem the foul odors.

This time the smell had an even stranger quality about it. There was something in the air that burned the back of the boy's throat and caused his eyes to water. The goats even seemed to sense it. The herd had stopped, unwilling to advance any further on their own.

The boy made his way between the balky goats, pushing and shoving, shouting at the stationary animals, trying to force movement from them. At this rate, the boy knew, he would be late for the start of the celebration.

The burning increased and the boy stopped to rub his hands across his watering eyes. The action only made the effects worse.

The goats had completely stopped. They no longer grazed on the sparse vegetation. They seemed confused, disoriented. Some bleated. Others just stood.

The boy felt bile rise in the back of his throat; he wanted to throw up. The goats were sitting down, keeling over, as the horrible smell increased.

They were dying! The goats were dying before his very eyes!

The boy felt panic rising to meet the bile in the back of his throat. How could he explain the death of the goats to his father?

More goats keeled over, their thin legs jerking in death spasms as white mucous poured from their mouths. The boy's eyes were watering so much now he could barely see. His throat burned unceasingly.

The smell hovered over the area, a thick mass that was invisible yet deadly.

The boy saw the last of the goats roll onto their sides and die before his watering eyes. He wanted to do something, but he realized he no longer had control over his legs. He wanted to run, to escape. It was impossible.

The boy felt his legs collapse beneath him as he shut his eyes and let a deep blackness replace the yellow rays of the morning sun.

The invisible cloud of death moved gently on the morning breeze toward the village of Colinas Verde.

Colinas Verde
Monday, January 12, 1998
7:00 A.M. Local Time

The village came to life with the rising sun; dawn was a time of renewal. The red, early morning sphere would change to yellow in a matter of minutes, and later to a white hot desert sun that baked the surrounding countryside. The chill of the desert night could not dampen the enthusiasm of the village inhabitants. Today was fiesta day, a day of celebration and praise, and Colinas Verde was set to take full advantage of the coming festivities. Three hundred years was a milestone in any civilization, and such was the case for this tiny village that sat on Mexico's high plateau, more than three hundred miles north of Mexico City.

Already children swarmed the dusty streets, and the smell of cooking filled the air. The odor of frying onions, peppers, and meat wafted on the early morning breeze. Freshly made corn tortillas rested in mounds by every vendor stall, awaiting fried vegetables and meat, along with the freshly prepared red and green sauces.

The small town square was decorated in joyous colors, particularly green, red, and white, the national colors of Mexico. The Mexican Eagle—the flag emblem of Mexico—soared from a large banner strung from the steeple of the Catholic church to the corner grocery across the street. Colored garland lined every doorway and window frame. Strings of lights swooped between buildings and trees, prepared to light the gaieties long into the night.

Music rolled and pounded from massive stereo speakers set in doorways around the town square. The rhythms would be replaced later in the day by live musicians whose guitars, violins, and trumpets would announce the official beginning of the celebration.

Gaming booths were being assembled in the middle of the square's park area. Everything from bingo to wheels of chance was beginning to dot the colorless landscape. Prizes of every kind were being stocked in the booths: stuffed animals and small piñatas for the children, homemade foodstuffs and fabrics for the women, and beer for the men.

Juan Antonio Hernandez, the mayor of Colinas Verde, strolled around the town square, his large hands clasped behind his back. It was his responsibility to see that all the activities were coordinated so one aspect of the celebration would not detract from another. It was not a difficult task. By the early afternoon, he knew, the men would have had enough beer not to care about such mundane things, the women would be gossiping among themselves, and the children would be busy sipping a first beer, stealing a first kiss, or just being children. Random *futbol*—soccer—games would be springing up on the village's dusty playing fields. Those who were able would amble over to the fields to watch the contests, not really caring who won, or by how much, content only with the competition.

Juan Antonio waved to the proprietor of the only fabric store in the village before continuing on his rounds.

Large, galvanized metal tubs—tubs that would tomorrow return to their use as horse watering troughs—were being placed in strategic locations around the square. Huge mounds of ice filled the tubs, and Juan Antonio knew he could even now dig beneath the ice to find cold bottles of *Corona, Dos Xs,* and *Sella Roja* beer, donations from the various companies to the fiesta. The beer banners were going up now, strung between trees, their colors adding to the festive air. Canvas pavilions, also donated by the beverage companies, were being erected on every available plot of dried earth.

For Hernandez, this was the culmination of several months of work. There was little enough to do as mayor of Colinas Verde. His principle occupation was that of the only *abogado*—lawyer—in town. Even that did not require his full attention. Few people, except for certain larger landowners, needed an attorney, so Juan Antonio supplemented his income as the official representative of the government in Mexico City. Whatever was required by *Los Estadoes Unidos de Mexico,* or *El Estado de San Luis Potosi,* he did. From collecting taxes, to notifying relatives of the death of a loved one in some distant state, Juan Antonio served. The various functions provided a living for him, his wife, and five children, but there was no recognition to go along with it. Therefore Juan Antonio Hernandez relished the approaching fiesta with anticipation. This was his day, his village's day.

People were everywhere now. Children streamed through the streets. Some clung to their mother's dress tails, others—the more adventurous—sprinted among the buildings, booths, and canvas pavilions, playing a version of "chase." Men clustered in small groups, talking among themselves. Women dressed in brightly colored skirts and *blusas* sought out each other in the shade of the almost leafless desert trees in the center of the town square. Music blared, but no one listened.

The first hint of trouble came from a group of men standing near the corner of the grocery store across from the church building.

When the first man fell to the ground, those nearby laughed.

"Tempranito," one man laughed, indicating it was too early for his companion to be so drunk as to pass out in the town square. His *compañeros* immediately supported him in his assessment. Then another man grasped his throat. He tried to speak, but words would not come.

The men laughed, thinking the actions a poor rendition of what had just happened to the other man. The laughter escalated as the second man hit the wall behind him and slumped to the ground. Only when blood appeared around the man's mouth and nose did the others realize something was dreadfully wrong. By this time other men in the group were clawing at their own throats.

Juan Antonio Hernandez saw the commotion at the corner grocery and wandered in that direction. It was too early in the day for the men to be so inebriated. This would surely put a damper on the festivities, particularly the speech he was scheduled to deliver at noon. He would not be cheated out of his glory, fleeting as it was.

More men were now on the ground near the grocery. Others in and around the square were beginning to react in a similar manner.

Several men who were putting the finishing touches on one of the canvas pavilions fell to the ground as Juan Antonio approached. The mayor made a mental note to chastise the company for sending such men as their representatives.

The Honorable Juan Antonio Hernandez barely had time to record this last thought when the pain hit him. His throat constricted as if an unseen pair of hands was choking the life from him. His eyes began to burn and water. In seconds he could not see the corner of the grocery where he had been heading. His legs felt like overstretched rubber bands. He willed his hands to wipe the tears from his eyes, but his arms would not obey even the simplest commands. Then, as if by some magic, the street scene was replaced by the burning blue sky above him, and Juan Antonio wondered how such a thing was possible. The last thought before the mayor of Colinas Verde died was that he had somehow fallen onto his back, and he had better get up before he embarrassed himself.

The entire village of Colinas Verde died in much the same manner as its mayor. No one was spared, including the dogs, cats, and various vermin.

The Rub' al Khali
The North Yemen—Saudi Arabia Border
Thursday, January 22, 1998
4:30 A.M. Local Time

Specialist Jerry Wallace (E-4), USAR, grappled with the wheel of his humvee, all the while cursing the turn of events that brought him out into the desert night the day before he was due to rotate back to the States.

Seated next to Wallace was Second Lieutenant Brian Anthony. To Wallace's way of thinking, the Lieutenant—the "El Tee" to the members of Second Platoon, B Company—was all right as a person but lacked some of the basic leadership qualities necessary to lead the patrol out into the southwestern Arabian desert. But this was Jerry's last patrol with Anthony, and he could live with that.

Wallace focused on the narrow road ahead. Not really a road, he thought, more of a camel trail, and even that assessment was generous. A narrow, winding corridor of sand and rock threaded between high outcroppings of jagged rock in the high desert of southern Saudi Arabia.

The light beams of the humvee's headlights cut a swath in the desert night no more than fifty feet in front of the vehicle. Night in the desert swallowed light from whatever source.

Behind Jerry Wallace's humvee followed four more, plus a single five-ton truck, carrying the remainder of Second Platoon. The patrol had been on the schedule board for a month, so the excursion was not a surprise. The fact that Sergeant Rick Bashear had come down with some kind of upper respiratory infection was the real fly in the ointment, to Jerry Wallace's way of thinking. Bashear should have been the driver for Lieutenant Anthony. With Bashear in the dispensary, it had fallen to Wallace to drive the lead humvee on the patrol.

Well, thought Wallace, at least it gave him something to do the last day. Better than waiting around the barracks for the truck that would transport him to Riyadh to catch the C-17 transport back to the States.

Wallace grabbed at the wheel of the humvee as the front tire twisted on a desert rock. The road was almost nonexistent now, and he had slowed the vehicle to no more than a crawl. With his mind centered on the manila envelope he'd left lying on his bunk back at the barracks, slowing down was the prudent move.

The manila envelope held the one thing that meant more to Wallace than all the military pay in the world: his PCS orders. Permanent Change of Station orders were coveted by the men of Second Platoon, B Company almost as much as ice cold beer after a long day in the desert, something that had to be consumed sparingly and judiciously in the Muslim country.

His orders transferring him to the 380th Medical Company of the Army Reserve Training Center Naval Support Activities, Mid-South (NAVSUPACT), in Millington, Tennessee, were an answer to prayer as far as Wallace was concerned. He was from Indianapolis, and NAVSUPACT was no more than a seven- or eight-hour drive from the central Indiana city—six hours and fifteen minutes if you wanted to challenge the Illinois State Police.

"We're coming up on it, Jerry," Brian Anthony said.

The comment jerked Wallace back to the chill of the desert night. "Right, El Tee," Jerry answered, braking the humvee to a stop.

"It" was the midpoint of the patrol, the turnaround point, as indicated by the rocky outcropping coming up on the right side of the humvee and verified by the GPS mounted in the humvee.

The patrol was one of several that took the men of B Company out into the southwestern desert of Saudi Arabia, near the border with North Yemen. It was argued by the commanders that the patrols were effective training excursions, but Jerry Wallace couldn't see it. Neither could most of the other soldiers of B Company. What was the value of sending an entire platoon of men on a hundred-mile round-trip exercise into totally unoccupied desert, only to turn around at some arbitrary point and return? Oh, he had heard that rebels from North Yemen sometimes strayed over the border, but that was understandable. No one really knew where the border was. What were the rebels going to do? Steal some Saudi Arabian rocks and sand and carry them back to North Yemen? No, on balance, the patrols didn't make a whole lot of sense.

"Wait here for a second, Jerry," Brian Anthony ordered.

Jerry rested his arms across the steering wheel of the humvee; the remainder of the vehicles braked to a stop behind him. In less than thirty seconds, First Sergeant Emil Zorren joined Anthony beside Wallace's humvee.

"What's the scoop, El Tee?" Zorren asked. Zorren was in his late thirties, a burly Greek from New York who had been in the army all his adult life. A massive handle-bar mustache adorned Zorren's broad face and was the butt of jokes back at the barracks, always when Zorren was not present. Emil Zorren stood just under six feet, weighed in around 220 pounds, and sported a fifty-one-inch chest atop a thirty-two-inch waist. No one, not even officers, questioned whatever First Sergeant Emil Zorren had to say.

"A little change this time, Sarge," Anthony answered his top non-com. "We're supposed to check out a point about five klicks southeast of here," he said, pointing to a map he'd spread out on the hood of the humvee and illuminated with the red beam from his flashlight.

"I make it half an hour at the rate we're going," Zorren added.

"Sounds about right. Have the men take a break and have some coffee, and we'll be on our way."

"Got it, El Tee," Zorren acknowledged and headed back in the direction of the other vehicles.

"Sort of strange, isn't it, El Tee?" Wallace asked when Brian Anthony was once again seated in the humvee.

"Yeah, Jerry. I don't know what the brass thinks might be out there, but I guess we'll take a look-see."

"Don't like these changes, El Tee," Wallace said, not looking in the direction of Anthony.

"You've got your PCS orders, don't you?"

"Laying on my rack ready to go. Supposed to catch transport in Riyadh at fifteen hundred hours."

"I'll get you back in time, don't worry."

"Worry never crossed my mind, sir. What's to worry about out here?"

■ ■ ■

The Rub' al Khali, the southwestern Arabian desert, glowed in the thick darkness. The Bedouins called it the "Light of Allah." Yehya Homaid was not so sure about that particular description because he, unlike some of his comrades, did not believe in Allah. He did know that whatever caused the phenomenon, it only added to the discomfort caused by the cold that ate into his bones. Yehya preferred the heat of the desert sun to the cold of the desert night.

Yehya glanced to his right, toward his companion, Ahmed Badaani. Ahmed was snuggled down in the old, worn, down sleeping bag he carried with him wherever he went. Yehya chastised himself for leaving the warmth of his own sleeping bag too early. He had been awake for almost two hours, waiting. The patrol schedule was emblazoned on his mind; the soldiers would not appear for another half hour or so. But Yehya had not been able to sleep; so he had risen, leaving the warmth of the down cocoon, and sat at the base of the rocky promontory, waiting. During that time, he had reviewed every aspect of the current assignment.

It had been Ahmed who'd insisted the assignment had been one for fools, which meant Ahmed saw no ideological virtue in the job, nothing to advance the cause of the great Allah. Ahmed was a believer. Yehya had scoffed at his friend, calling him an old man. Ahmed had acquiesced, but not before registering his complaint.

Now, as Yehya Homaid peered above the slight rise behind which he and Ahmed were hidden, he was beginning to think his friend was right.

At the very least, what they were doing could be construed as a diplomatic incident by the Saudis. At worst, they could get killed. Should the latter occur, the fact that their bodies would be misidentified as being members of the SOLF—the Sultan of Oman Land Forces—provided little comfort. While it was true that the Omanis occasionally violated their border with Yemen, it was seldom that they ventured this far west. There was an understanding between the Saudis and the Omanis, so Yehya was certain their being dressed as SOLF soldiers would not hold up under close scrutiny.

While it was true the border between North Yemen and Saudi Arabia was, at best, an undefined boundary, changing as often as the shifting sands of the Rub' al Khali, it was also true that the Saudis considered this particular portion of the boundary sovereign Saudi soil— holy land—to be protected with lives, if necessary. That made it the perfect spot for the ambush.

With that in mind, Yehya checked the Austrian Steyr AUG 5.56-mm rifle he carried. He then adjusted the single length of cloth that formed his headdress and shifted his webbing harness. The Pakistani-produced webbing was a cheap version of its British equivalent, and the areas beneath the webbing were already chaffed and irritated. Yehya Homaid would be glad when this day's task was finished.

Yehya retrieved a pebble and tossed it in Ahmed's direction; his friend stirred within the sleeping bag. "Time for final checks," Yehya said quietly, knowing sound carried in the cold desert air. And while he had not yet heard the clatter of diesels, he was taking no chances.

"It's all right," Ahmed muttered sleepily from inside the sleeping bag.

Yehya Homaid felt an instant of anger flare within him. Even if Ahmed was usually right about the more mundane aspects of their job,

PROLOGUE

it still bothered Yehya that he was seldom accorded the respect to which his rank was entitled. It bothered him even more when Ahmed ignored orders that were designed to keep them both alive.

Yehya picked up a larger rock and threw it at the amorphous mass that was his friend. "Check the mortar, Ahmed," Yehya ordered, the edge in his voice communicating his displeasure.

"OK, OK. Don't get in an uproar," Ahmed said. "But I'm telling you right now that it's fine."

"Check the sighting and the baseplate carefully," Yehya said, disgust tingeing the order. He turned back to the glowing area that lay before him across the desert dunes and low, rocky mountains. In a few minutes he could hear Ahmed going through the checks on the Soviet-made 81-mm mortar behind him.

He and Ahmed had packed-in the mortar over the rugged terrain two days earlier. It had been an arduous task, and Yehya still had the bruises across his back from carrying the heavy weapon over twenty kilometers. But it had been necessary. The American army maintained a periodic radar sweep of the area, and the presence of aircraft might have compromised the assignment. Or so he had been told.

"Finished," Ahmed said behind Yehya's back.

"Good. Come take over for me while I have something to eat. According to my watch, the patrol should be passing this way in less than a half hour."

"This could get us killed," Ahmed grumbled. "At the very least, if we're caught dressed like this we could face life in prison, and I don't particularly care to spend the rest of my life in a Yemini prison."

"Nor do I, my friend," Yehya responded. "Preparations have been made. You know that."

"If you're talking about the suits and the masks, how do we know they will stop this stuff? We don't even know what it is."

Yehya said nothing. It was Ahmed's nature to moan and grumble, but this time, he thought, his friend might well have raised a valid point. How did they know the protective suits they had been issued would stop the chemical contained in the 81-mm mortar shells? Would the gas masks function properly? What about the two radios they carried? Were the frequencies they had been given valid? After all, not even the radios had been tested yet. Would the prearranged helicopter appear to whisk them away from the attack site?

As to the primary question Ahmed asked: what *was* the stuff in the shells? Yehya wondered for the millionth time.

Yehya checked the rudimentary instruments they had brought with them: temperature, wind direction, humidity, etc. . . . . He recorded the findings in the small notebook and stuffed the book into his pack. The one thing that had been stressed above all else was the information contained in the small, cheap notebook. It was vital information and one of the reasons he and Ahmed were being paid so much money. That and the fact that they were about to kill a lot of people.

■ ■ ■

Lieutenant Brian Anthony raised his hand, and Jerry Wallace slowed the humvee, bringing it to a stop just short of a large rock outcropping that glowed in the desert darkness. First Sergeant Emil Zorren had been right. It had taken right at thirty minutes to traverse the last five klicks.

"What's this all about, El Tee?" Wallace asked when he'd stopped the car.

"Beats me, Jerry," Anthony answered. "Orders."

Wallace grimaced. "One of the guys said it was just another exercise."

"One of the guys would be wrong, then," Anthony answered, consulting the map beneath the faint red light of his flashlight. "There was a report of a border intrusion. That's all I know right now."

"That should be a problem for the Saudi Nationals, shouldn't it?"

"To my way of thinking, yes. But those decisions are made at a policy level, not a tactical one. We just do what we're ordered to do."

"Right, Lieutenant," Wallace replied, letting Anthony know he was displeased by addressing him as "Lieutenant."

The response was not lost on Anthony, but he ignored it. He couldn't blame Wallace. He knew he was thinking about the flight he was about to take out of Riyadh, and he couldn't blame the young man. He wouldn't mind being gone from Saudi Arabia himself. And he was certain the rest of his troops were thinking along the same line. It didn't make a lot of sense to send out an entire platoon of Army soldiers to check on a border intrusion in an area where the border was not even clearly delineated.

Anthony folded the map and turned to Wallace. "That's the objective over there," he said, pointing toward the southeast. He grabbed at the microphone on the dashboard of the humvee and spoke into it. "Sarge, come alive back there. We're heading southeast. I don't like this. Make sure all the men are 'weapons ready.'"

"Got it, El Tee," the response came back almost immediately.

Anthony smiled. He felt secure just knowing Zorren was riding two cars back. While Anthony knew he was technically in charge of the patrol, he also knew beyond a shadow of a doubt that "Sarge Zee," as the troops called him, was the tactical master. If ever shots were fired in anger, it would be Zee who would take charge.

Anthony held on as Wallace gunned the humvee over the rugged terrain, following a general southeast direction, keeping the all-drive vehicle on as smooth a course as possible.

The shout from the radio that came on minutes later shocked Lieutenant Anthony to the core of his being.

"Incoming!" the shout blared from the radio speaker of the humvee. The voice was that of Emil Zorren, but Anthony had no idea what his Sergeant was talking about. "Incoming" meant the patrol was taking fire, but Anthony had no idea what type or from where. He heard and saw nothing.

The first mortar shell exploded fifty yards short of the patrol line. *Lousy shooting* was Anthony's first reaction to the shell falling short. His next thought was *Who, in this forsaken and forlorn land, is firing mortar shells at a U.S. Army patrol?*

The next transmission from his sergeant instantly told Anthony why the shell had fallen short.

"Gas masks!" the words came through the speaker.

Anthony felt his stomach roll at the words. It was all happening too quickly. He pulled at the gas mask that was standard issue in the Middle Eastern countries where the army operated, and in less than two seconds he was listening to himself breathe within the protective mask.

A second mortar shell exploded. This time the pyrotechnics of the gas shell showed that the mortarmen had lowered their aim and had delivered the shell forty yards closer, almost on top of the patrol.

Anthony felt a surge of fury race through his system. Whoever was behind the attack would pay dearly, he vowed. He also congratulated himself for having the foresight to go "weapons ready" when he did.

Orders were flying. The troops were scattering in response to a prearranged design. Wallace, Anthony noted, was fighting the wheel of the humvee, directing it toward the explosions. The tactic would put the vehicle upwind from the explosions and thus out of range of the gas. Other humvees were turning in the same direction. Anthony could hear the rattle of the two roof-mounted M-60 machine guns as the gunners let loose a covering barrage in the presumed direction of the attack.

There was no smoke, no indication that gas had been released from the shells. Anthony was thankful the desert air had been cold when the patrol had begun and all the men were wearing thick clothing against the chill. The same clothing would protect them against the effects of the gas.

PROLOGUE

The humvees were now advancing on a small rise no more than a hundred yards away, charging at the highest closure speed possible. The two M-60 machine guns were still chattering, their bursts now more controlled. Anthony thought he heard something, and then he was sure. He'd heard the sound before, most recently back at USARSO—U.S. Army, South—at Fort Clayton, Republic of Panama. It was the sound of a helicopter. Not just any helicopter, but a UH-60 Blackhawk.

Who in the border area has Blackhawks besides the U.S. Army? Anthony wondered to himself. Wallace held the humvee on its course, straight for the distant rise.

"El Tee. You hear that?" the radio crackled.

Anthony recognized his Sergeant's voice, even through the distortion caused by the gas mask. "Sounds like a Hawk," Anthony said into the radio.

"Nobody's got Hawks down here, El Tee. Nobody 'cept us, that is."

The radio went silent as the M-60s continued to fire. Anthony could see the target now, and the gunners were kicking up dust and rock along the top of the ridge just in front of them.

They were fifty yards away now, almost on top of where the first mortar shell had landed. The gas masks were doing their job. The platoon was rolling through the terrain as if nothing had ever happened.

Then the humvee just to Anthony's right faltered, fell behind, and twisted in the desert sand. The vehicle flipped over onto its roof. Anthony could not tell what had happened.

"Wha . . . ?" Anthony turned to Wallace as his own humvee began to fall from its line of advance.

"Sun . . . thin's wro . . ., si . . .," Wallace stuttered. The humvee's left front tire twisted on a rock, and the car plummeted onto its side.

Anthony reached out as if to support the toppling vehicle with his own hand. It was useless, he knew. It happened in slow motion, painfully slow, slow motion.

He glanced to his right as his humvee toppled, just in time to see two more vehicles crash into each other. The five-ton truck was nowhere to be seen. The last thing Lieutenant Brian Anthony saw before he died was the light-colored sand of the Rub' al Khali rushing up to meet him.

■ ■ ■

Yehya Homaid watched the humvees and the truck just on the other side of the rise where he and Ahmed Badaani waited. He could just make out the occupants of the vehicles, but it was enough to know that every man in the patrol was dead or dying.

He felt a tap on his shoulder, and Yehya turned to gaze into the eyes of his friend.

"The helicopter approaches," Ahmed said through the protective mask he wore.

Yehya nodded and abandoned his position. He scribbled some quick notes in the all-important notebook and followed Ahmed down the back slope of the rise to where the helicopter would land.

The UH-60 Blackhawk swooped in low like a predator from the skies. Yehya and Ahmed had the 81-mm mortar packed away. There would be no signs left to indicate who had killed the soldiers. As the helicopter landed, the two men rushed for the open cabin door. Both stopped short when a single man appeared in the doorway, a Steyr AUG rifle held menacingly at the ready.

"You have the notebook?" the man shouted to Yehya over the sound of the rotor wash.

Yehya handed the book to the man, and the man examined the notes, nodding his approval.

"Well done. There is one more sacrifice we must ask of you," the man said as he raised the rifle. Two three-hot bursts erupted from the rifle, and Yehya Homaid and Ahmed Badaani died in the cold of the Rub' al Khali.

PROLOGUE

The man with the rifle motioned to the pilot of the Blackhawk. The pilot twisted the collective and pulled hard, and the helicopter rose in the cold air, leaving the dead and dying to themselves. Later, if all went as planned, another patrol would find the bodies. The dead would be shipped to the United States and another phase of the project would begin. The man wondered if the sacrifice was worth it, but then he remembered how much he was being paid, and all twinges of conscience left him.

Colinas Verde
Friday, January 23, 1998
5:00 A.M. Local Time

A cool morning breeze blew in from the Sierra Madre Occidentals, sweeping over the high plateau of the Mexican state of San Luis Potosi in the district of Tierra Quemada and the dead village of Colinas Verde as if the blustering wind was trying to blow away the horror that had engulfed the tiny village.

General Abraham Solis Zedillo watched the face of the American colonel with fascination as huge yellow bulldozers worked to level the village in the distance. A choking cloud of yellow dust rose, proof that Colinas Verde would cease to exist at the end of the day. As he furtively glanced in the colonel's direction, he wondered how he could have been so wrong about a person.

Days ago he had placed the call that had put in motion all that he saw before him. One of the calls had been to his Pentagon control officer, the colonel he now stood beside. He had detested having to call a mere colonel, but now, as he watched the stolid face of this officer, chills ran down his spine.

There was no emotion in the thin face, no evidence of compassion, no sense of loss. The colonel stood well over six feet tall. His blond hair, almost white, Zedillo noticed, was shaved almost to the scalp. The skin beneath was tanned. The uniform was impeccable. Even in the early morning desert, the uniform creases were knife-edge precise. Cold blue eyes gazed out toward the distant village of Colinas Verde. To General Abraham Zedillo, it was the most unemotional gaze he had ever seen in his life.

"How long?" The words were unusually soft and lithe. Not the tone he would have expected from *el coronel,* Zedillo thought. The meaning was anything but.

"The engineers tell me it will be finished by the end of the day. There is much to do, even with all the equipment your army has supplied," Zedillo answered.

The colonel nodded his understanding. He continued to focus on the distant cloud rising from the desert floor. Every test result indicated that the cloud of dust was not lethal, but the colonel stood upwind nevertheless.

From the time of the first call he had received from General Zedillo, it had taken time to airlift massive quantities of equipment to the village of Colinas Verde. Five Air Force C-17s—the Air Force's newest and most capable transport aircraft—had been put on immediate standby, loaded with enough heavy equipment to level a small city, and flown to the now-dead village. The equipment had not been the normal green-painted equipment used by the U.S. Army but had been specially reserved equipment, painted the familiar yellow of the equipment manufacturer. The primary reason for the paint scheme was to disguise the involvement of the U.S. Army in the total annihilation of the village of Colinas Verde.

"The plant?" the colonel asked.

"Already leveled and buried," Zedillo said without taking his eyes off the distant yellow cloud of dust. "This is the last," he added with a touch of sadness in his voice.

"Good," the colonel said dispassionately. "I am sure you understand the importance of this, General," he continued. "We must be certain no one is the least bit curious about what went on here. The contingency plans that are in place will be put into action immediately after the equipment is airlifted out of here. Is that understood?"

Zedillo felt distaste for this American officer boil up into his gut. It was not that this man was a mere colonel and he was a general. It was not even that the man was American and he was Mexican. Modern realities and SOFAs had a way of mitigating those factors. It was that this *person* showed virtually no emotion at the destruction and death that lay before them. A village had died; *people* had died, and as far as Zedillo could tell, this was no more than a military exercise for the soulless colonel. Not that Zedillo, himself, was that sentimental, but these people had been Mexican, and he felt a certain, if distant, kinship.

"I said, *is that understood,* General?"

"Perfectly, *Colonel,*" Zedillo responded. "The fires will be set in"—Zedillo consulted his watch—"five hours."

A thin smile appeared on the colonel's face. "Good. That will take care of this village and the plant. No one will ever know what really happened here."

"No one but God," Zedillo muttered quietly.

The colonel's smile broadened. "And there is nothing he can do about it," he replied instantly, his gaze never leaving the yellow-stained horizon.

Once again Zedillo felt a chill race through his body. He himself wasn't *that* religious either, but he did have a healthy respect for Deity, something he knew this colonel would not understand.

The plan to which the colonel had alluded was simplicity itself. El Niño, the ocean phenomenon off the west coast of South America, had caused all sorts of weather anomalies in the past months. Even now, fires burned on Mexico's high plateau. The smoke from the Mexican fires could be seen as far north as the midwestern states in the U.S. Texas was particularly hard hit by the effects of the firestorm, with as much as 70 percent of the state under air-quality advisories.

Young children and older adults were advised to stay indoors. Firefighters from Mexico, Canada, and the United States battled the out-of-control blazes with little success. Another fire would hardly be noticed and would offer a valid reason for the total destruction of a chemical plant and a small, backwater village like Colinas Verde. If, that was, the question ever arose.

"I am told the plant has already been relocated," the colonel said.

"It will be in a new industrial park in the Mexican state of Queretaro, south of here," Zedillo answered. "It will take a year to construct the plant, but it will be state-of-the-art, and security will be better."

"I suppose the delay is to be expected."

The colonel's tone of voice, Zedillo noticed, was one of resignation, as if the delay was the result of some form of stupidity or laziness on the part of the Mexican people. Nothing could be farther from the truth. The plant would be on-line in less than a year, producing an even more lethal version of the same chemicals that had killed all the people in Colinas Verde. Had the plant been built in the United States, it was entirely possible that the preliminary designs would never even have been approved. But such things worked differently in Mexico, and the plant would be built, and quite possibly, others would die because of it.

■ ■ ■

As the huge yellow machines erased the last remnant of the village of Colinas Verde, one pair of eyes, hollow and sunken in a sunburned face, looked on. A single tear rolled down the weathered cheek, and the jaw clinched tightly as the men and machines went about their business.

"Todo lo puedo en Cristo que me fortelece," the thin lips uttered in Spanish. *I can do all things through Christ who strengthens me,* were more than words. The short Bible verse would be the only comfort for the boy in the coming years as he sought retribution. The years would

be as hard and desolate as the desert that now surrounded him, but the boy knew he would survive to find his own revenge. That was a promise he'd already made to himself, a promise that would come back to haunt the people who had done this thing. The sunken eyes closed briefly, blinking back more tears, and then closed to sleep the sleep of exhaustion.

BEGINNINGS
2000

CHAPTER ONE

Naval Support Activity, Mid-South
Millington, Tennessee
June 12, 2000
0900 Hours

Jake Madsen gently rubbed his temples with his fingertips, trying to force the pain and throbbing from his head. It wasn't working.

Madsen, a lieutenant commander in the United States Naval Reserve Medical Corps, was beginning the second week of the yearly two weeks active duty required of all active reservists. The previous week at Branch Medical Clinic had been spent much as he anticipated spending the upcoming week, assigned to the 0800-to-1000-hour sick call for the military personnel at the Naval Support Activity, Mid-South. Included with the navy active duty personnel were contingents of active-duty Army Reservists, Tennessee National Guardsmen, and Naval Reservists who filtered through NAVSUPACT on a predetermined schedule during the summer months. After sick call, Jake would take his place in a small cubicle within the Health Services Department of BMC, treating non-life-threatening illness among the same military members.

Jake reached for the bottle of aspirin on his desk, downed two of the tablets without water, then opened the medical file on the desk before him.

Another summer cold probably. That was the most serious illness he had treated the previous week, and that was what he expected to treat this week. It was just as well. Summer colds, minor scrapes, and an occasional strep throat were about all he could deal with at the moment.

"Next patient is ready, Doctor," the navy hospital corpsman said, sticking his head into the treatment room.

Jake looked up and said, "Send him in."

"Uh, . . . Commander . . .," the corpsman hesitated.

Jake met the young corpsman's gaze. "What is it, Jamie?" he asked testily, not in the mood for games. He was immediately sorry for his tone of voice. Jake liked the young corpsman from Indianapolis. They had been working together since Jake came on active duty last week, and most of the acceptance he felt at Branch Medical Clinic came from Jamie. After all, reservists were reservists. Active-duty personnel made a conscious effort to avoid most reservists, doctors included. Jamie Parker's welcome had been a breath of fresh air for Jake, and he appreciated it.

"Doc, I could get in trouble for this . . ."

"Come on, Jamie, spit it out," Jake said, leaning back in his chair, his arms behind his head.

Jamie Parker took a step into the examination room where Jake sat. A desk with two chairs, an exam table with a disposable white paper cover, and a supply cabinet were the only furnishings. Pale green walls scrubbed spotless, along with several medical posters that someone had deemed appropriate completed the decor. The room was functional and not much more. The glare of the florescent lights added a fitting touch of the impersonal to the room.

"Doc, I could get in a lot of trouble here," the young corpsman began again, pointing to the chart that lay before Jake. "Captain Dean isn't here this morning, and he always sees this next patient . . ." Jamie shifted his weight from one foot to the other, then continued. "But Jerry needs to see someone, and I guess you're it."

Jake opened the chart before him and quickly scanned the information. Name, rank, serial number, unit, and commanding officer were all there, but little else. The normal medical history sheets were not attached to the chart. A single, lined, blank sheet was stapled to the information sheet to be used by Jake to record his findings during the exam. Nothing else.

"What's the story, Jamie?" Jake asked, surprised at his own interest. Very little had interested him for more than a year now, since his wife, Kathy, had died.

Kathy, the love of his life. Jake felt the familiar sense of loss mingled with an almost overwhelming sense of guilt at the thought of Kathy. There was a physical ache in his stomach. The ache had moderated somewhat over the past months, but it still reminded Jake how much he had loved his wife.

Kathy had been everything to him, his reason for living. He could still see her short brunette hair bobbing in the breeze as she danced ahead of him on their all-too-infrequent walks near their midtown Memphis home.

Home might have been a bit of a stretch, Jake conceded, recalling the large brick house. He and Kathy had purchased the house on North Parkway between Evergreen and Hawthorne Streets as a fix-up project. Jake had been doubtful, but the house had been a real buy, just what they had been looking for. Jake had completed his active duty service in the Naval Reserve in 1998 and had begun his career in the internal medicine department of the Veterans Affairs Medical Center in Memphis. They had wanted their own place, so they bought the house and started fixing it up themselves. Despite the limited time they had had to work on the structure, it had been one of the happiest years of Jake's life.

Until that day in August. Jake felt the all-too-familiar cramp attack his stomach once again, and he had to make a conscious effort to force Kathy from his mind and concentrate on the next patient, the one about whom he knew nothing.

Jamie Parker took another step into the examination room and closed the door behind him. "This is Captain Dean's patient. All of us corpsmen have instructions that no one sees the X-file patients except him."

"X-file patients?" Jake almost laughed.

"The ones indicated by the red X on the outside of the chart folder," Jamie said.

Jake flipped the folder closed and examined the outside. "I don't see anything."

"Captain Dean keeps the files under lock and key in his office. He probably took them with him down to Pensacola. He's the only one who ever sees them."

"What's special about the X-files?" Jake asked, feeling foolish for having used the title of a popular TV show in a medical context.

"No idea, Doc. It's some kind of special study or something, but Captain Dean never confides in us. I'm not sure any of the other doctors even know what's going on with the X folders. That's what the captain calls them. Doesn't like any of us calling them the X-files, but, hey, you gotta expect that. Right?"

"Right, Jamie. But if the captain is so particular about these patients, then why am I seeing this"—Jake checked the name on the folder—"Sergeant Jerry Wallace?"

"Jerry's a friend of mine. We met at the Helmsman Club one night. Played pool, that sort of stuff. He's from Indianapolis, too, so we hit it off. He's the supply sergeant for the 380th Medical Company over in Building 751."

"Army Reserve?"

"Yes, sir."

"What's his problem?" Jake asked.

Jamie hesitated for a moment. "I don't know. That's one thing we never talk about. Whatever it is, he's pretty closemouthed about it, almost like he's got orders not to discuss it. Only sees Captain Dean for sick call, and there're no open files on what treatment he's receiving. That's why you don't have a history sheet in his file."

"So why isn't Captain Dean seeing him, if this is a special case?"

"Captain's not due back from Pensacola until this afternoon. He's at the naval hospital this week. Meetings and such. Don't forget, BMC is part of Naval Hospital Pensacola's health care delivery system."

"What's Jerry's complaint?"

"Not much more than a cold, I think, but he seems to get them pretty regularly. He's miserable right now, and I told him I'd get him in to see you. Shouldn't take you too long."

"Are we going to get into trouble because of this?" Jake asked, a slight grin splitting his face.

Jamie smiled. "Not on your life. Just write what he needs in the blank chart and let me fill any prescription from our stock here, and we should get by with it. I'll be sure the chart doesn't get filed," the corpsman said with a grin.

"OK, Jamie, send him in."

"Will do, Doc," the young corpsman said as he left the examination room. Then sticking his head back in the exam room door, he added, "And thanks."

Jake Madsen watched the young man from Indianapolis leave, and his memories flooded back with a vengeance. With the memories came the headache.

Just over a year ago, Jake remembered, life had been good. He had just turned thirty-three years old, married his childhood sweetheart, and was beginning a new job. Everything he had ever dreamed about was coming true. Most importantly, he had Kathy. Life had been beautiful, made all the more so by Kathy with her radiant smile, short brunette hair, and the odd spray of freckles across her nose. Now she was dead, and it was his fault.

Jake let his head fall into his hands, his elbows resting on the desk. The headache was pounding now. Life was no longer beautiful, and Jake Madsen suddenly wished he were dead.

■ ■ ■

Sergeant Jerry Wallace, USAR, felt ghastly, but that was not unusual. He had felt the same way, on and off, since that patrol back in Saudi Arabia. He could not be sure that all his symptoms were entirely physical ones. At times, especially at night just before he dozed off, he could still see the dead and dying men of Second Platoon, B Company, surrounding him in that forsaken desert near the Saudi Arabian border with North Yemen. Of the forty-odd men who had been on that patrol, only he and two others had survived the attack. Jerry was not so sure that was a good thing.

Right now, like most weeks, his head was splitting. At odd times, light seemed to mutate into multicolored, almost bizarre, shapes before his very eyes, transforming themselves into jagged spikes of light. Today it was difficult to breathe as well. His chest felt as if some giant were squeezing him with all its might.

As supply sergeant for the 380th Medical Company, it was his responsibility to see that everything that was needed to take the company to the field was available at any given time. The Three-Eight-Oh, as it was known, was an army reserve company, staffed by reservists for the most part, but buttressed by the permeant staff over in Building 751. Most civilians didn't know that for every reserve unit in the military, there were "active reservists" making certain that the "weekend warriors" had everything they needed to respond successfully to a call-up at a moment's notice.

A flash of pain streaked through Jerry's head; his eyes felt as if they were about to explode from their sockets. He'd lived with the pain since that day in the desert, and he wondered briefly about the other two men who'd survived the totally unexpected attack. Another wave of pain forced all thoughts from his mind except the possibility of getting some relief from Captain Dean.

Captain Dean was Jerry's guardian angel. Since coming to NAVSU-PACT, the captain had taken care of him. It made him feel like he was more than just another reserve weenie, that he was someone special. The captain had been adamant about Jerry seeing him and no one else, and that had been the way it was—except today. Jamie was telling him that Captain Dean was down at Pensacola, and he would have to see the duty doctor on sick call. That was all right with him; he just wanted the pain and lights to go away, to be free of the torment that haunted him during the day as well as the night. And he wanted to take a deep breath again without feeling he was being held underwater.

A sharp twinge beneath his left arm, just inside his armpit, reminded Jerry of the only time he'd been to Naval Hospital, Pensacola.

It had been in mid-1998, just after his arrival at NAVSUPACT. After the attack in Saudi Arabia, he, along with the other two survivors from Second Platoon, B Company, had been air-lifted to the hospital in Wiesbaden, Germany, to recover from the effects of what could only have been an unprovoked attack. His transfer orders had been expedited as soon as he was feeling better, and his transfer to the Three-Eight-Oh had brought him to NAVSUPACT, Mid-South. Captain Dean had taken over his treatment. Back then, the lights and pain had only just begun, but his chest had hurt terribly. Part of Captain Dean's treatment had been to send him TDY to Naval Hospital Pensacola. There, the doctors had gone over him with a fine-tooth comb, and just before leaving the hospital to return to NAVSUPACT, a small incision had been made under his left armpit. It had been an exploratory surgery—a biopsy—minor in every way, he had been told, and the results would help determine future treatment. It had sounded plausible to Jerry, and he had returned to Memphis two days later.

But something was strange. After the surgery he had always felt that something was not right, as if something had been excised from his body, or even more strangely, that something had been added. The twinge was back today, and since he was not going to see Captain Dean, maybe he would ask the doctor about the unusual feeling in his chest wall.

"Jerry," he heard his name called. Looking up, he saw Jamie coming toward him.

"Doctor Madsen will see you. Come on."

Maybe the new Doc will find something, Jerry thought as he matched pace with the hospital corpsman.

■ ■ ■

William "Bill" Dean, Captain, USN, MC, flexed his jaw and opened his mouth to equalize the pressure in his ears as the C-20G began its approach into the Millington Municipal Airport.

That the navy had seen fit to transport a mere captain in the C-20 was indication enough of the magnitude of the problem represented by the files he carried with him. Normally the aircraft was reserved for the Secretary of the Navy, the Under Secretary of the Navy, a few select Assistant Secretaries, the CNO, and, if they were extremely lucky, blessed, or chosen, a few full admirals. The C-20, a Gulfstream IV that had been converted by Electrospace Systems, Inc., to serve in an electronic warfare role, had cost the taxpayers of the United States more than $43 million. At the moment the aircraft was configured for personnel transportation, but Bill Dean had heard the crew mention that esoteric equipment such as the FLIR, MAD, and Advanced Nose Radar were still installed in the plane. As a medical doctor who had never been a naval flight surgeon, the acronyms meant nothing to him.

The pilot banked the Gulfstream to the left, following the normal approach pattern into Millington.

Years earlier, when Naval Support Activity, Mid-South, had been Naval Air Station, Millington, this same runway had served NAS Millington and had been off-limits to all civilian aircraft. Naval Air Station, Millington, had been a training facility, dedicated to the education of the navy's future airmen. But as surely as taxes and death will eventually take their toll on a person, reorganization will strike the military, and the training facilities had been moved from western Tennessee to Pensacola, Florida. Naval Support Activities, Mid-South, was now home to naval support organizations, the largest of which was the navy's Bureau of Personnel (BUPERS), where more than 30 percent of the base's personnel labored to keep up with the entire contingent of sailors on active duty.

Bill Dean saw the flat landscape streak by the Gulfstream's round window; the wheels touched down with a definitive thump that reminded Dean that naval aviators were all trained to fly from the decks of aircraft carriers, and landings on those floating cities were always "aggressive." To navy pilots, a carrier "trap" was the equivalent of a controlled crash. Dean hoped the Gulfstream's undercarriage was reenforced sufficiently to handle the added stress of "navy-style" landings.

The white aircraft taxied to the terminal building, and Dean released his seatbelt and made his way to the exit, his heavy briefcase in his right hand and his small suitcase in his left. Of the two, the briefcase was the more important. It was not really a briefcase, Dean corrected himself subconsciously, but a version of the flight bag all career pilots carried their flight charts in. The difference was what was contained in the case: five thick medical files, all identified by a single red *X* in the upper right corner. The corpsmen at Branch Medical Center laughingly referred to them as the "X-files." Dean wondered if they would be so cavalier if they knew what the charts actually contained.

The Gulfstream's engines idled, telling him that the pilots were waiting for him to exit the aircraft before they continued on to Andrews Air Force Base, the home base of the navy plane.

"Thanks, guys," William Dean said as his foot hit the first step of the Gulfstream's foldout staircase.

"Any time, Captain," the lieutenant/copilot responded.

A car with *U.S. Navy* painted in small letters on the door was waiting. Dean got in.

"Officer's country, please," he told the driver. He would go home, have a shower and breakfast, and then go to the clinic. *What could possibly happen today to make already miserable circumstances worse?* he wondered. And then he remembered it was only Monday.

United States Embassy, Mexico City

John (Juan) Francisco Ortiz looked forward to the coming week in Mexico City. From his office window in the United States Embassy building, he could see that a heavenly west wind had swept through the city and, for a brief moment, had whisked the ever-present pollution of the world's largest city into the waiting stratosphere.

Ortiz watched the traffic moving along Paseo de la Reforma, the most famous street in all of Mexico. Green-and-yellow Volkswagen Beetle taxis vied for position along with small and large buses, and other normal Monday morning traffic in downtown Mexico City. The trees lining the boulevard had a particular sheen to them this fine morning. Perhaps, Ortiz thought, it was because the pollution was missing for a change. Even the trees and shrubs and flowers knew enough to enjoy the all-too-infrequent reprieve.

"Get the fax from Erickson?" Albert Bell asked Ortiz as the former came through the office door and flopped down in the only comfortable chair in the office.

John Ortiz smiled. "The one about Nuevo Laredo and Juarez?"

"The same," Bell answered, propping his leg over the arm of the chair.

"It's about time the good guys won one," Ortiz said.

"And we won two this time."

"Three if you include shutting down the truck line here in Mexico." Ortiz referred to Mexico City simply as "Mexico," as was the habit of the Mexican nationals. "There was enough stuff in those trucks to keep most of the States in dope for the next six months."

"Not anymore," Bell grinned.

Ortiz smiled at his partner. This was the reason he had joined the Drug Enforcement Administration. The DEA had just shut down one of the largest cocaine operations in all of Latin America. Most U.S. citizens knew of the Cali and Medellin drug cartels in Colombia, but few realized the massive quantity of drugs that passed from Mexico to the United States over their common border. The Mexican Mafia was equally adept at drug smuggling and probably twice as ruthless as the South American cartels.

The sting operations that had just been concluded successfully had been over a year in the planning. A coalition of DEA agents, agents of the Mexican Policia Judical Nacional (known simply as the PJN), the FBI, and the Ejercito Mexicana (the Mexican army) had executed "Operation Border Limit," and in the process had confiscated more than a dozen tractor-trailer rigs carrying the white powder.

Removing a dozen eighteen-wheelers from the road was in and of itself reason enough to be satisfied with the operation, Ortiz thought. Since the North American Free Trade Agreement (NAFTA) had been ratified, trucking companies had sprung up like anthills in the desert. On those rare occasions when he had to drive to the Mexico-Texas border, Ortiz made it a point to drive the toll roads, or the *cuotas* as they were known in Mexico. Even if he had to pay the exorbitant tolls himself, it was better than competing with the huge trucks on the two-lane *libres,* the toll-free roads, which were narrower, in worse condition, and clogged with local traffic. Even driving the cuota required ten hours of hard driving to reach the border from Mexico City. There was no telling how long it would take using the libres.

The only good thing he could think of concerning his infrequent driving trips to the border was that he looked, acted, and talked like a native Mexican, which he was not.

Born in Hollywood, Florida, of a Cuban/American father and a sixth-generation displaced Englishwoman, Ortiz had grown up speaking Spanish and English with equal ease. While his Spanish had the flavor of the Caribbean, the tendencies toward slurred words and especially the "dropped *s*" at the end of sentences were mitigated by the educated English of his mother. His Spanish came out sounding more like that of Columbia, Costa Rica, or, to John Ortiz's good fortune, that of Mexico.

John Francisco Ortiz was his given name. It had been an easy transition from "John" to "Juan" while working in Mexico. Truth be known, most of his DEA companions thought his given name was Juan, and he had not discouraged that thought in any way. It was safer.

"So what's next?" Albert Bell asked.

"This," Ortiz said, sliding a single piece of fax paper over to his partner.

Bell read the single paragraph and whistled. "So, the show's not over yet."

"Maybe not. According to that, we may still have a connection between the States and Mexico."

"I thought that's what everyone wanted when they passed this NAFTA thing. More cooperation. More interaction," said Bell. "Well," he continued, tossing the fax back on the desk, "that's exactly what they got, and it's making it twice as hard on us as it was before they passed the thing."

"Tell me about it," Ortiz agreed. "But we'll check this out anyway. Get started on it. The normal contacts in the Ministry of Economics, over at the *Bolsa de Valores,* and the Ministry of Health."

"Health?"

"Sure. This is a pharmaceutical company, *ain't* it?" Ortiz said, tapping the fax with his finger.

"Listen to you. Your mother would have you by the hair if she heard you say *ain't.*"

"Yeah, but she ain't here," John Ortiz laughed. "Let's get to it."

CHAPTER
TWO

"Doc, this is Sergeant Wallace," Jamie Parker said as he ushered the army sergeant into the exam room.

Jake finished reviewing the basic information before greeting the soldier: age, weight, height, blood pressure, pulse, etc. When he looked up, however, what he saw shocked him.

Sergeant Wallace, according to the records, was twenty-four years old. The man who had just entered the exam room looked twenty years older than that.

His cropped hair seemed to grow in patches over a thinly stretched scalp so pale it reminded Jake of his grandmother's skin just before she died. Wallace's ashen complexion was heightened by the harsh white lighting of the exam room. Light blue eyes peered from sunken hollows surrounded by reddened tissue, giving the young sergeant the appearance of a Halloween jack-'o-lantern with large cranberries for eyes. Wallace weighed no more than 160 pounds on a six-foot frame, further contributing to his stark appearance.

"Thanks for seeing me, Doc," the young sergeant said, sniffing and rubbing the sleeve of his BDU across his nose.

"Jamie tells me that you normally see Captain Dean?"

"Yes, sir. That's the way it's been since I left CENCOM."

"CENCOM?" Jake repeated. Since beginning his two-week active-duty stint, he still was not accustomed to the army acronyms. He was familiar with most of the navy's, but the army spoke a different language.

"Central Command, sir," Wallace answered. "Technically, I was stationed in Germany, but my company got further afield than that."

Something in the way Wallace said the last statement caused the hair on the back of Jake's neck to stand on end. His medical intuition told him there was a story behind the sergeant's simple declarative sentence—one that Jake felt directly pertained to the current health of the young man.

Jake's own pulse began to elevate as he took Jerry's wrist and felt for his patient's.

"What do you mean by 'further afield'?" Jake asked, monitoring the pulse with his watch, hoping the young sergeant would not notice that he was taking longer than the corpsman had earlier.

"You know, Doc. Outside Germany. CENCOM pretty much has a wide range of responsibilities."

"Give me an example," Jake said, dropping Wallace's wrist and reaching for his stethoscope while pulling the sphygmomanometer's blood pressure cuff from where it hung on the wall-mounted instrument.

Jerry Wallace rubbed his sleeve over his running nose once again. His eyes were burning now, and he was having difficulty breathing.

The "underwater" feeling had returned. "Doc, I don't feel so good. Captain Dean usually does a few tests and then gives me some stuff to make the feeling go away."

"What feeling, Jerry?"

"Like, you know, when you got a really bad cold or the flu or something. Sort of like being underwater. Hard to breathe. Lights flashing. That sort of stuff," the young sergeant answered.

Jake's heart went out to the young man who sat before him. Wallace's pulse was rapid and his blood pressure was depressed. It was difficult to tell exactly what was going on without a history, and that was the one thing he did not have. Wallace's succinct explanation of what Captain Dean usually did seemed like a plea for relief, one that Jake could, under normal circumstances, ignore until his examination was completed. But the sergeant's circumstances weren't normal, were they? Jake was shocked by his conclusion. What made these circumstances different? He was not sure.

Jake scribbled notes on the blank sheet in the folder and moved his stethoscope to Wallace's chest to listen to his lungs. What he heard shocked him. He had listened to enough chests filling with fluid to know that Jerry Wallace was in dire straits. It sounded like the distinctive rattle of advanced pneumonia. But what kind? Pneumonia was a generic diagnosis. What had caused the affliction? Bacteria? Virus? Foreign bodies? All were possibilities, and he needed to pinpoint the cause quickly. The first test would be a PA and lateral of the chest. Maybe the traditional chest X-rays would tell him something.

"Jamie," Jake called to the hospital corpsman.

"Yeah, Doc," Jamie answered, coming around the corner and entering the exam room.

"Get me a PA and lateral, quick, and then draw some blood."

The corpsman's eyes went wide. It was not the order for the tests that alarmed him, but the tone of voice Jake Madsen had used. It had only been a week, and Jamie was still unfamiliar with all the nuances of this reserve doctor, but the tone of voice spoke volumes.

"I'll need an X-ray order, Doc."

Jake grabbed a small pad on his desk, wrote out the order, and handed it to the corpsman.

"Come on, Jerry. Let's get you down to see Bayou Benny."

"Bayou Benny?" Jake repeated, amused despite his alarm over Wallace's condition.

"Benny Terrence. Chief petty officer down in X-ray. He's from some podunk town down in Louisiana. Right on the Mississippi River. Just about the best X-ray tech I've ever seen."

"OK, Jamie. Get Sergeant Wallace down there and tell your swamp-fox chief I want that film ASAP. Then get the blood drawn and take it to the lab. Send Jerry back down here to me when you're through with him. Got it?"

"Got it, Doc. Won't be but a few minutes. Come on, Jerry. Let's go."

Jake watched the two young men disappear from sight as they headed for the X-ray department of Branch Medical Center. Jerry Wallace was twenty-four years old, Jake remembered. Jamie Parker was what? Maybe twenty-one? *Probably* younger. They were the men who defended America. Men? Was a nineteen-year-old a man? Where had he been at that age? Certainly not in the military. He had been in college, and Kathy had been with him. They had both been eighteen, she only three months younger, and they had eloped, much to the consternation of both their parents. He loved her so much.

Suddenly Jake wanted to throw something, anything. He wanted to lash out at some unseen being that had induced the pain he felt deep in his soul. God? Maybe. God would be the logical choice. He controlled the universe, didn't he? And Jake's universe had gone haywire. No matter what Jake did, no matter how much he analyzed what had happened, he always came back to the same conclusion: Kathy had died, and he had killed her.

■ ■ ■

"Bayou," Jamie Parker called out when he entered the X-ray department. "Hey, Bayou, I need a PA and lateral ASAP."

"Bayou" Benny Terrence stepped into the small alcove off the X-ray room proper. "You don't have to yell," the chief petty officer yelled back at the young corpsman. Anyone listening to the initial exchange between the two navy corpsmen would have thought a battle royal was in the making. But, as Jamie Parker knew, that was the way it was with Bayou Benny.

The X-ray technician was a large, jovial man with dark hair that he kept clipped shorter than even navy regulations called for. At five feet four inches, he seemed to waddle around Branch Medical Center. First impressions of the man seemed to indicate he was anything but athletic, probably as coordinated as a puppet whose strings had become entangled. However, anyone making that assumption soon realized their grievous error.

Chief petty officer "Bayou" Benny Terrence wore the insignia—the "Budweiser," as it was known to the men who wore it—of a Navy SEAL. He was one of the friendliest corpsmen in the clinic, but Jamie knew he was also one of the most competitive—and one of the meanest, given the right circumstances.

Jamie had observed those right circumstances during an intramural football game between BUPERS and the medical and dental clinics of NAVSUPACT. One BUPERS player had made the mistake of taking a cheap shot at the X-ray technician, and Terrence had come back to the huddle muttering under his breath. When it happened a second time, he had come back cursing. At the end of the next play, however, the BUPERS player was on the ground screaming and holding his left leg. When a doctor told Terrence to get the man to the clinic to X-ray the leg, the chief petty officer had said, "Ain't no need, Doc. It's broke."

"How do you know, Terrence?"

"Cause I broke it. He ain't gonna take no more cheap shots."

Jamie Parker smiled every time he recalled the story.

"Say you need a PA and lateral. What doc?" Terrence asked.

"Commander Madsen. The reserve doc who's doing his two weeks here," Jamie answered.

"Give me the order."

Jamie handed the X-ray order to the technician and watched as Terrence entered some information in his X-ray log.

"OK, Wallace. Up against the wall over there." In a few minutes the job was done, and Terrence pulled the large X-ray plates from their holder on the wall. "I'll get this in the developer."

"Thanks, Chief," Jamie called back over his shoulder as he escorted Wallace from the room. "I'll be back to get it as soon as I draw blood and get Jerry back to Commander Madsen."

The phone in X-ray jangled just as the two men left the area. Jamie escorted Wallace to another room where he drew the blood needed for the tests, and then took the army sergeant back to Jake Madsen's office.

"X-ray coming up soon, Doc," Jamie told Jake. "Got the blood too. I'll get it to the lab, then swing back and pick up the X-ray."

"Thanks, Jamie," Jake said to the back of the retreating corpsman.

The doctor turned his attention back to his patient. It seemed as if the young sergeant had deteriorated further in the few minutes he'd been away.

"How you feeling, Jerry?"

"Worse, if that's possible, Doc. I don't remember it ever being this bad." Wallace rubbed the sleeve of his uniform across his nose once again, trying to stem the seemingly unending flow. This time, visible even through the camouflage pattern of the BDU, there was the dark stain of blood.

Jake felt an instant of alarm. "Get up on the table, Jerry," Jake ordered.

Wallace did as he was told.

"Let's get this uniform top off." Jake began unbuttoning the large buttons and helped the soldier shrug out of the uniform top first, then the army green undershirt. Jake began a more comprehensive exam, working slowly and deliberately, not wanting to miss any signal.

When he examined Wallace's left side, he noted the small scar beneath the army sergeant's armpit.

"What's the scar, Jerry?" Jake asked, once again wishing he had access to the young man's medical history.

"They did that down at Pensacola the one time Captain Dean sent me down there. Said it was some kind of test or something."

"Biopsy?" Jake furnished the word.

"That's it. A biopsy. Never told me what for. But to tell the truth, Doc, the thing's been bugging me ever since they did it."

"How so?" Jake asked.

"Just bugging me, you know. Like maybe they took something out, or put something in that's not supposed to be there. That sort of thing."

"Any pain? Sharp or dull?"

"Naw, it's not that. It just feels . . . different."

Jake gently palpated the area. From the looks of the scar, it was less than two years old. Jake could still feel hard, dense tissue beneath the small white incision. What had they done at that hospital? What type of biopsy had been performed on the young man? Jake was working blind, but he planned to take care of that. He picked up the phone, punched one of the buttons across the bottom of the instrument, and spoke, "Corpsman Parker, return to examination room number three, please." Jake heard his call go out over the clinic's public address system. BMC was not a large facility, but its elongated symmetry made the paging system necessary. It would not take long for Jamie to return, Jake knew. In the meantime, he continued the exam.

■ ■ ■

Hospital Corpsman Jamie Parker heard the page just as he entered the X-ray department. He decided to grab Wallace's X-ray before he hurried back to room three.

"Chief," Jamie called out. This time there was no gruff answer to his shout. Jamie remembered the phone ringing a few minutes ago and realized Terrence had probably been called away. The X-ray department was not one of the busiest departments at BMC. Jamie could hear the film developer humming in the next room, so he entered and went to the machine. A PA-sized film was laying in the bin and a lateral was coming out. Jamie checked the film numbers against the X-ray log. It was Jerry Wallace's. Without looking at the film, Jamie stuffed the two exposures into the X-ray jacket on which Terrence had already written Wallace's name with a thick, black marking pen and headed out the door, beelining it for exam room three.

■ ■ ■

Jake had done all he could for the moment. Lying down seemed to relieve some of Wallace's discomfort. Why, Jake could not determine, but since that was the case, he left the young sergeant where he was on the exam table.

Jamie came through the door. "Sorry it took so long, Doc. I had to pull the X-ray myself." The corpsman handed the sleeved film to Jake.

Jake took the film and placed it on the desk. He had more important concerns at the moment.

"When is Captain Dean returning from Pensacola?" he asked the corpsman.

Jamie felt an instant of alarm, but said nothing. "Today or tomorrow, I think, Doc. I can check and see. Why?"

"Because I want to talk to him about Jerry's condition."

"Commander, you know what I told you. Jerry is Captain Dean's patient, and orders are that no one sees him but the captain. If you talk to him, he's going to know that I disobeyed a standing order. This could get real dicey, sir," Jamie said worriedly.

"I'll tell Captain Dean I saw Jerry in the waiting room and took it on myself to examine him. But I need to talk to the captain when he returns."

"Come on, Doc. Give me a break. The captain usually gives Jerry some stuff and lets him go back to work. You could be opening a real can of worms, here, sir."

Jake felt an instant of fury flare within him. He recognized the feeling as one he had not felt in quite some time—concern for another human being. That, he reminded himself, was an emotion he had not experienced since . . . since Kathy died.

"Just leave a note for Captain Dean, and let's get Jerry into a ward bed right now. I want him where we can keep an eye on him. I'll start him on medication, oxygen, and an IV. I want him monitored every fifteen minutes. He's got fluid in his lungs, and I don't want to aggravate the situation with too much fluid. And call the lab and tell them I want that blood work yesterday."

"Commander—," Jamie Parker started to say but was abruptly cut off.

"Now! Corpsman," Jake ordered abruptly.

"Yes, sir, Commander." The word *Commander* was spoken with a hard edge to it, indicating Jamie Parker's displeasure at the turn of events.

"Sorry, Jamie," Jake relented. "Jerry's about as sick a soldier as I've seen since I've been here. I'll cover you with Captain Dean. That's a promise."

Jamie grinned. "I'll get Jerry into the ward. You're right; he is worse than I've seen him. And I'll check on the captain's return as soon as I get Jerry settled in."

"Thanks, Jamie. I'll be back to check on him after sick call." Jake wrote a prescription and handed it to the corpsman. "Get him started on this too."

"Aye aye, sir," the corpsman said, throwing Jake a mock salute.

"Get out of here," Jake laughed, despite his concern for Jerry Wallace.

CHAPTER THREE

NAVSUPACT
June 13, 2000

Sleep had not come easily for Jake. He rolled over in the strange bed and let his eyes focus on the morning light coming through the single window in the room. As he had done since commencing his two weeks of active duty, he had to remind himself where he was and why he was there.

Jake had taken up temporary residence in what NAVSUPACT was now calling Estocin Hall. In reality, it was the Bachelor Officer's Quarters. During Jake's time in the navy, every BOQ had been known only by the three-letter designator. Here, he had discovered, it was known as simply, the Q.

The Q was situated just off Navy Road, with Branch Medical Center to the southwest. Jake could have walked if he had wanted to, but he'd discovered quickly that he did not have the energy. He had driven every day, and today would be no different.

Before calling it a day yesterday, he had looked in on Jerry Wallace. The soldier seemed to be holding his own. Maybe the medication Jake had prescribed was having some effect on the pneumonia. He had left orders with the night corpsman to continue the treatment and call him if any change occurred. There had been no call, and Jake was now anxious to get dressed and check on the sergeant.

He also had not heard if Captain Dean had returned from Pensacola. He had left word that he be notified, but there had been no notification during the day; and when he'd left Building 771, headed for the Q, he'd forgotten to ask. Captain Dean lived in Officer's Country, just west of the Q. Perhaps he could find Captain Dean's housing unit.

As quickly as that thought came to him, Jake dismissed it. He checked his watch and jumped out of bed. He was on sick call again today and only had about a half hour to get there. He would have to shower, shave, throw on his summer-weight white uniform, and hustle to the clinic.

In the shower a few minutes later, Jake remembered the X-ray of Jerry Wallace he'd tossed on the desk in the sick call exam room. He'd forgotten about it. It was not like him to forget such an important treatment factor, but he had. The blood work had come back from the lab showing only nominal abnormalities, ruling out a bacterial origin for Wallace's pneumonia. Viral tests took longer, but for some reason, Jake was confident the problem was not viral. What did that leave? Jake tried to think, but thinking was one of the things that bothered him these days. He had so much trouble concentrating after Kathy . . .

Jake stepped from the shower and again felt a sense of lostness. This place was strange, alien in some way, he thought. He could have stayed at the house on North Parkway in Memphis. NAVSUPACT was only a few minutes' drive up Highway 51. But the house on North

Parkway had been his and Kathy's home. It represented the union of two minds and bodies and souls. And that union had been destroyed for an eternity.

Or had it been? If he believed Kathy, they would see each other in heaven. That was Kathy. Religious to the core. Not a squishy, sentimental religion, but a satisfying, rational one. Jake had occasionally accompanied Kathy to the small Bible church a few blocks from their house. It was not that he believed what the preacher touted from the pulpit. It was simply a matter of following Kathy wherever she went, and if church was where she wanted to be, that's where Jake wanted to be also.

"We messed up, you and I, God," Jake said softly as he stared at himself in the mirror. His eyes went to his watch. He'd just lost ten minutes thinking about Kathy and the house on North Parkway. He would sell the house. And the more reasons he could find not to stay there until the sale was consummated, the better that would be. Too many memories; too much pain.

Jake pulled his uniform from the closet, dressed, and headed for the medical center. His mind went to the X-rays he had forgotten yesterday. Where would they be now? In Wallace's chart? Stashed away in some other file? They most certainly would not still be lying on the desk in the sick call exam room. This was the navy, and nothing was left lying around at the end of the day. No, some corpsman or nurse would have snatched the film and filed it away. That would be his first chore for the day.

And then there was Captain Dean. He wanted to talk to Branch Medical Center's boss about Wallace. Jake had been frustrated yesterday at his inability to treat a severely ill soldier because he lacked the proper information, a simple patient history. And while he was at it, he just might ask about the "X-files," as Jamie Parker had called them. What was that all about? Why did Captain Dean maintain sole possession of such critical files?

When Jake walked out of the Q and got in his Jeep Cherokee, he was feeling better. The day looked brighter. This day had purpose, at least for a few hours.

■ ■ ■

Good days, Captain William Dean thought, seemed to be an oxymoron. If it was day, there could be nothing good about it, and if there was any good to be found, then it couldn't be a new day. New days brought problems whose solutions evaded discovery. Every day was more and more difficult.

Dean had arrived at BMC just before 0600 hours this morning. Yesterday, after returning to NAVSUPACT aboard the Gulfstream, he had intended to put in an appearance at the medical center, but he had taken care of some personal business first, and time had gotten away from him. By the time he realized the hour, the clinic had been closed. The duty staff would have been there, of course, but there was no reason to disturb them after a long day.

Now he sat at his desk skimming the previous day's reports and initialing the various logs kept by the different departments. This was one of the things he least enjoyed about command responsibilities: the paperwork. What he needed was another Medical Service Corps officer to relieve him of the more mundane chores of command. *That* was something to look forward to. He'd made the request at Pensacola. He would have to see what happened.

Bill Dean scanned the various reports with a trained eye. He was accustomed to assimilating huge quantities of information in a short time. No one got through medical school without that ability, and he had done better in his classes than most. He scanned the reports from the support functions of the clinic, the various lab reports, and the X-ray departmental log. One name on the X-ray log jumped out at him.

Dean felt a thumping in his chest followed by a sharp intake of air. He examined the entry closely. The film control numbers were there, along with the types of film, the time of day, and the doctor who had ordered it. These particular X-rays had been a PA and lateral chest—routine chest X-rays of Jerry Wallace, (E-5), USAR.

Dean checked his watch. It was just a few minutes before 0800 hours. Already the enlisted corpsmen were busy setting up for the day's work. Most of the doctors would be in the clinic too. Dean checked the doctor's name on the X-ray log one last time: Madsen, Lt. Commander, USNR.

Dean pressed the call button on his telephone and waited until the reception area out front answered. He told the corpsman who answered the phone that he wanted to see Dr. Madsen immediately. He was informed that the doctor was not yet in the clinic, but that the corpsman would give him the message as soon as he came in.

Bill Dean slammed the phone down and glanced at the only other log he'd not reviewed. The ward admissions log had three names listed. Dean could not believe his eyes. The first name in the log was that of Jerry Wallace.

Dean sprang into action. Maybe there was time to mitigate the damage, damage that could easily cost him his command—or even his life.

First, he must get Wallace out of that ward. He could have him admitted to a local hospital. NAVSUPACT, Mid-South, had contractual agreements with several of them.

With Wallace in a local area hospital, if that was required, he could run down the chest films that had been shot yesterday and destroy them. The difficult task would come when he talked with Lt. Commander Jake Madsen. Madsen, he remembered, was one of the reserve doctors fulfilling his two-weeks active duty here at BMC. Maybe the conversation wouldn't be so bad, after all. He was a captain—the equivalent of an army colonel—and Madsen was nothing more than a reserve lieutenant commander. But first he had to get Wallace out of the ward—and fast.

■ ■ ■

Jake pulled out onto Essex Street and headed for the medical center. He had fifteen minutes to get there. He decided to take a quick turn through Officers' Country and look for Captain Dean's housing unit. He turned onto Elrod Loop, driving slowly, reading the small signs in the yards that indicated the occupants of particular houses. Captain Dean did not live on the Loop. There were only a couple more streets, but when Jake checked his watch, he realized he'd taken more time than he'd intended.

He headed for the parking entrance to Building 771. He'd barely make sick call. Maybe the captain was already there. That would be a mixed blessing, he realized. Technically, he was late for the 0800-to-1000 sick call. For that, he could be chewed out by the captain, but at least that would be the beginning of a dialogue.

■ ■ ■

"How are you doing, Jerry?" Captain Dean asked the young army sergeant who was just finishing his breakfast tray.

"Pretty good, Captain. Sorry about going back on our agreement. I was feeling pretty lousy yesterday."

Dean smiled. "That's all right," he said, retrieving the chart that hung on the end of the bed. "Looks like everything has stabilized. You would probably like to get out of here, right?"

"To tell the truth, sir, I do have some stuff I need to do. We've got some reserves coming in next week for training."

"How about I get you back on your medicine and let you go?"

Wallace's face beamed at the prospect. Whatever the sick call doctor had done had made him feel a whole lot better, and the prospect of going back on his own medicine that Captain Dean would give him brightened his prospects considerably.

"Sounds great to me, sir. Should I get dressed?"

"Go ahead. I'll arrange your dismissal and get the medicine myself.

You can go back to work tomorrow, but today I want you to go home and let the medicine take effect for the rest of the day. OK?"

"Whatever you say, sir. You're the doctor," Wallace said, getting out of bed and pulling his BDUs from the locker next to his ward bed.

William Dean strode from the ward, his mind operating overtime. In less than two minutes, he had Jerry Wallace checked out of the ward. He returned to his office and retrieved the medicine for the sergeant. Less than ten minutes later Wallace was on his way home. One problem down. Next were the X-rays.

Dean wondered if he should make the call he knew he would eventually have to make. Perhaps after talking to Lt. Commander Madsen, he would have more to tell the man in Pensacola. Whatever he learned from Madsen, he could pass on to the men down there, knowing that the same information, in the form of an encrypted tape recording, would eventually make its way to the D-ring of the Pentagon. The prospect was disconcerting. Dean decided to put off making the call a little longer.

■ ■ ■

Jake missed the quick turn-in to the medical center's parking lot. He continued down Essex Street with the intention of doubling back, but then, as always, thoughts of Kathy intruded. What had caused the thoughts to return this time? Jake wondered. Then he knew.

He needed to get to the house on North Parkway, but first he wanted to tell the corpsman who ran the check-in desk, and also the other doctor who would be handling sick call this morning.

The Med Center parking area was only marginally filled. Most of the cars were ones he recognized as either those of corpsmen or doctors who worked in the building.

Jake pulled into one of the designated spots used by the center's doctors and headed for the door. First he wanted to find Jerry Wallace's

X-rays. The film took precedence over what he wanted to retrieve from his house on North Parkway.

"Doc," the corpsman behind the desk said as Jake entered, "we got patients. Commander Dixon is working sick call this morning, but he says he needs you."

"Look, Bradley," Jake began, glancing at the name tag on the corpsman's chest. "Tell Commander Dixon I've had a sudden emergency in Memphis. Tell him the water lines at my house burst last night, and the plumber called me. I've got to get home. I'll be back as quickly as I can."

"Water pipes burst? Doc, it's the middle of the summer!"

"Yeah, I know. Inconvenient, isn't it? I've got to find some film shot yesterday, and I'm out of here."

"What film?" the corpsman asked.

"Just a chest and lateral on that patient I admitted yesterday. Forgot to read it, and I thought I'd take it with me on the way in."

"That reminds me, Doc. Captain Dean is in this morning, and he said he wanted to talk to you as soon as you got in."

Jake almost stopped in his tracks. No doubt the conversation would be about Wallace.

"Is it about Wallace?" Jake asked.

"Can't say, sir. He just said to let him know as soon as you got in. I think he was sorta angry."

Jake thought for a moment. If Dean was angry about the Wallace case, Jake's being late for sick call would provoke the captain further. That would lead to a prolonged conversation behind closed doors. Jake was in no frame of mind for that.

"Where would I find the X-rays I left in one of the sick-call exam rooms yesterday?" Jake asked quickly.

"Probably in the same room. Look in the bottom right drawer of the desk," the corpsman answered.

Jake headed for the exam room. He could hear voices in the adjoining room. That would be Commander Dixon treating a patient. The waiting room had had no more than half a dozen waiting. There was no urgency that he could see.

Jake entered the exam room, went to the desk, and pulled the drawer open. There were various files, but only one folder large enough to contain the chest X-rays. Jake pulled it out; it was Wallace's. He headed back through the waiting room area, heading for the exit.

"Doc," the corpsman called again. "What do you want me to tell Captain Dean?"

Jake ignored the question and pushed out the door of Branch Medical Center, almost sprinting for his Cherokee. He tossed the X-ray in the passenger side seat and headed for Navy Road and Highway 51, which would lead him back to Memphis. He had to get to the house this morning and find the one thing Kathy had left him that really was a part of her.

Jake checked his watch. He planned to take no more than an hour. Maybe an hour and a half at the outside. That would put him back in the clinic by 9:30 at the latest. If the traffic didn't clear out, though, he would be later than that, and he knew Captain Dean's wrath would be in direct proportion to the number of minutes Jake was late in returning to the clinic.

■ ■ ■

"He what?" Captain Dean demanded.

"Said he'd be back as soon as he could. Commander Madsen said the plumber called and his pipes had burst in his house. Said he had to get there," the corpsman repeated to his commanding officer.

Dean fought to control the rage he felt welling up within him. He needed to talk to Madsen ASAP, and the young whelp had walked out on him. He would deal with Madsen when he returned.

What he needed now, with Jerry Wallace out of the ward and on his way to his apartment in Millington, were the X-rays that were shot yesterday. That film could be the single most damaging piece of evidence should it come to light.

Evidence? What was he thinking about? The film could only be evidence in a court of law, couldn't it? And *that* was something that would never be allowed. No, the X-ray would never reach a courtroom. But that did not in any way diminish the need to get the film back and destroy it.

"Bradley," Captain Dean began, "get me Chief Terrence in X-ray and have him come to my office. Tell him to bring any chest films that didn't get read yesterday." Dean didn't think it possible, but there was the outside chance that the film had not been read and was still in the possession of the senior X-ray technician.

"Chest film, sir?" the corpsman behind the desk asked.

The captain felt a chill snake over his body at the way the corpsman asked the question.

"Yeah. A PA and a lateral. You know something about them?" Dean asked.

"Commander Madsen went into the exam room and came out with a film folder. He said something about some film he'd had shot yesterday. I told him it would probably be in the desk. I guess the one he came out with was the one he was looking for."

Dean felt his anger reaching the boiling point. Was everyone else in the whole world incompetent? He was dealing with morons here. Of course, that was not the way Pensacola nor the Pentagon would see it. *He* would be lumped in with the morons and dealt with accordingly.

Dean ran through the possible contingencies in his mind. He could send someone out for Madsen. After all, the lieutenant commander was technically AWOL. He could have the Tennessee Highway Patrol, along with the Memphis City Police, put out an All Points Bulletin for Madsen and have him picked up between Millington and Memphis. At the very least, he could give the police Madsen's address in Memphis and have them there waiting for the young doctor. But any of those actions would defeat his one overriding need: secrecy.

No, his only option at this point was to wait for Madsen to return and have a very private conversation. In the meantime, he needed to make the phone call he'd hoped to avoid.

Dr. William Dean, USN, walked to his office and shut the door. He dialed the number with an 850 area code and waited for the phone to be answered. When it was, there was a wait until the 128-bit encryption device signaled that the call was now secure. Dean began speaking slowly, hoping to communicate a sense of control he did not feel.

To top it off, he hated talking to computers.

CHAPTER FOUR

Luck, and plenty of it, Jake Madsen realized, was what he needed if he was to get back to Branch Medical Center within a reasonable time period. *Reasonable,* he'd already defined, was that time frame within which he could most logically defend himself against the ire of Captain Dean. That time frame was quickly fading.

Jake pulled into the slightly uphill drive next to his brick house just off North Parkway. He jumped out of the Jeep and raced into the house. He knew exactly what he was looking for and exactly where it was.

He rushed up the stairs leading to the master bedroom. There it was, on the table next to the side of the bed where Kathy used to sleep.

Jake picked up the thin volume and raced back down the stairs. He'd left the engine idling, so he shifted into reverse as his hands fumbled with the seat belt. In seconds he was charging back down North Parkway.

The light at Bellevue and Jackson changed to red, and Jake braked to a halt. Only then did he remember the X-ray he'd previously thought so important. If they were *that* important, why hadn't he taken the time to examine them? They were nothing more than normal chest X-rays, after all. He knew he would find the abnormalities that had caused Jerry Wallace's problems yesterday morning, but that was to be expected. They were the X-rays of a very sick young man.

A sick young man Jake had failed to check on this morning. The oversight bothered Jake.

He reached over and pulled the X-ray folder from beneath Kathy's book. The light was still red. He pulled the film from the folder and held the first one up to the window.

His first reaction on seeing the film was that "Bayou Benny," the crazy Cajun X-ray tech, had really messed up the film. What he was seeing was not possible. The lobes of both lungs showed clearly, as did the shadow of the heart. The same juxtaposition of lights and darks was there, conclusive indication that Jerry Wallace did, indeed, have fluid accumulating in his lungs. But that was not what surprised Jake.

He moved the film and looked through the window of the Jeep Cherokee; he could just make out the traffic on the northern leg of I-240. Maybe there was something in the background shining through the film, producing the phenomenon he was seeing. But there was nothing, not a thing that would produce the abnormality on the film.

Jake held the film up to the light again. It was still there. He grabbed the other film, and quickly examined it too. The same abnormality was present.

Horns began to blow; the light had changed to green. Jake headed out onto the I-240 leg that would take him up 51 to Millington. The X-rays lay on the seat beside him. What was on the film? He'd seen similar films in the past. Similar but different. What was different about this one?

Maybe *this* was what Captain Dean wanted to talk to him about.

■ ■ ■

Bill Dean could have predicted the bent of the conversation with the man in Pensacola. He could not have, in his wildest imagination, have predicted the action that was about to be taken. Expecting to file a report via a voice-linked computer, he'd been shocked to have a human intervene in the conversation.

Dean held the phone and listened to what the man was saying. He felt hot flashes course through his body, to be replaced an instant later with equally chilling ones. His hands sweated; the one holding the phone became slippery. His breathing, he knew, was erratic, and he hoped that the sound of it did not translate well over the encrypted phone lines. In the end, he knew the man in Pensacola was right. Sometimes the right to choose the correct course of action was governed by the circumstances. Such was the case, but that did not mean Bill Dean particularly liked it.

"Stage four," Dean answered, reacting to the question the man on the other end of the phone had just asked. "If he follows the pattern like the others, he probably has four to six months."

Again Dean listened, finding himself involuntarily nodding his head at what the other man said. Nodding? Did that mean he was in agreement with the man in Pensacola? Had it come to that? And if he had reached the point of no return, how had he arrived at it? Had he thrown away everything he'd ever believed in?

"There's one more problem," Dean said into the telephone. "The doctor who saw Wallace yesterday took some chest film. From all I can find out, he's got the film with him right now." Dean waited for the reaction he knew was coming.

The man in Pensacola spoke for less than a minute, but it was a minute that made Bill Dean's blood run cold in his veins. Had he heard correctly? What kind of person could order the death of two men as casually as he ordered a pizza or hamburger? Captain Dean was beginning to understand the depths to which he had sunk.

He was brought back to reality by the humming and clicking of the handset he held in his hand. The encrypting device had gone off-line. The man in Pensacola had hung up. Dean put his face in his hands and exhaled. He marveled at the cruelty that man, any man, was capable of. He was especially mortified by the depth of his own brutality—brutality that was motivated by his own advancement.

In his eyes, William Dean, U.S. Navy Medical Corps, was now no more and no less than a murderer.

■ ■ ■

Sergeant Jerry Wallace felt better as he left the Branch Medical Center ward. The medicine Captain Dean had prescribed for him was working. Already he could breathe easier, and the pain was subsiding. He was happy that the captain had not been angry with him for coming into sick call and seeing that other doctor. The other doc had been kind and caring, but only Captain Dean knew what kind of medicine really brought relief.

Jerry left the NAVSUPACT complex, heading for the town of Millington and the apartment he rented with two navy petty officers who worked over at the navy's BUPERS. Both the other men would be at work, so he would be able to get some rest before they came back in the afternoon. As an E-5—a buck sergeant in the army or a second-class petty officer in the navy—he was entitled to special, on-base housing, but like many single sailors and soldiers, he chose to live off-base. The nightlife in Millington was pretty restricted, but Memphis was only a twenty-minute drive south, and it had everything. He particularly liked the atmosphere on Beale Street and the Memphis-style blues played in the clubs there.

Jerry coughed once, and pain struck at his lower abdomen and back. It felt as if he'd strained some muscles. It was not as painful as a pulled muscle but just enough to know that something was not quite right. Jerry took another swallow of the medicine Captain Dean had given him, all the while concentrating on his driving. He'd arrive home soon, crack open a beer, and slump into the recliner in front of the television. In the course of only a few minutes, he knew, he would put the beer aside and fall asleep with the ESPN Classics channel broadcasting a football game from ten years ago.

■ ■ ■

The man in Pensacola had no choice. They had come too far to allow discovery of even a portion of the experiment. Besides, the steps to be taken were delineated in the procedures manual in front of him. He lifted the phone and dialed a number in Washington, D.C. Termination procedures were strict and had to begin with the man sitting in the office in the D-ring of the Pentagon. Of course, the man in the D-ring would probably not answer the phone, and the call would be intercepted by some form of voice mail.

The phone jangled and was answered on the third ring. While the man in Pensacola waited for the 128-bit encryption device to connect, he wondered about the two men whose names he had in front of him: Sergeant Jerry Wallace, USAR, and Lt. Commander Jacob N. Madsen, USNR, MC. The addresses were also there. Bill Dean had told him he'd sent the sergeant home for the day, and Madsen was out of the clinic for the moment but should return within the hour. The encryption device connected, and in less than two minutes, the man had relayed the information, and the phone line went dead. He'd been right; the encrypted phone transmission had been made to a voice-mail link. Exactly where that link was, the man was not sure, but he knew action would be taken.

Border between Ecuador and Peru
400 Kilometers Southeast of Quito

The pilot of the single UH-60 Blackhawk brought the big helicopter down on a steep approach angle, keeping his eye on his touchdown spot on top of the mountain. The helicopter settled to the ground with a resounding thump as the pilot literally drove the craft into the ground rather than try to flare the aircraft in the high wind that swooped up from the valley below. The pilot was experienced, but he didn't like the mountain winds generated by the severe topography of the Andes Mountains near the border of Ecuador and Peru.

Three passengers leaped from the rear of the Hawk and headed for a small collection of tents located just below the mountaintop—the command center for the small contingent of peacekeepers assigned to Operation Safe Border.

It was a strange amalgamation of soldiers, much like all the others had been. The observation team was tasked with keeping an eye on potential hostilities that could erupt at any moment between the two South American counties.

The arrival of the three men, who had just set foot on foreign soil for the first time in their military careers, concluded an effort that only a select few knew about.

Most United States citizens, if asked about the involvement of the U.S. military in foreign countries, could easily name the several Middle Eastern countries and the handful of Asian and European countries where American forces operated.

What most people did not know was the extent of the involvement in Central and South America. Some people remembered Nicaragua and President Reagan's surrogate, Ollie North. They might even make the connection between the CIA and Guatemala and Honduras. Operation Just Cause in Panama still aired on the History Channel from time to time. But there was almost total ignorance when it came to the massive continent south of the Isthmus of Panama. Despite that fact, of the countries in South America, there was not a single one in which the U.S. military had not had some sort of influence, whether direct or indirect.

Operation Safe Border was a direct commitment of manpower and machinery. The observer force consisted of contingents from Argentina, Brazil, Canada, and the United States. The contingent from the United States were all members of SOCSOUTH, SOUTHCOM— Special Operations Command, South. SOCSOUTH had previously been housed in a warren of offices below the elementary school on Albrook Air Force Station in the Republic of Panama. With the culmination of the treaty that had turned the Panama Canal over to Panama on December 31, 1999, SOCSOUTH had moved to Miami, Florida, much to the relief of virtually every member of the force.

The logistics of the move had thrown the transfer of the personnel selected to Safe Border behind schedule by more than a year. It had taken almost six months of constant wrangling and transfers to achieve the proper mix of manpower at the small base in the Andes. But now the necessary assignments had been made. Each of the men now assigned to Safe Border was single. None of the men of Safe Border had any primary relatives to raise unwanted questions about what was about to occur. Some had first cousins, and one even had a brother whose estrangement had been verified before the soldier's assignment had been approved. None had children. There were no fathers and no mothers; no one to later make claim on the bodies. The men of Safe Border were as much "loners" as could be found in the U.S. Army. And for that, they would die.

The death would not be pretty.

CHAPTER FIVE

Mexico City, Mexico

Mudanzas Mundial, S.A. de C.V. was located just inside Mexico City's *Circuito Interior* in the central section of the city, close enough to make the interior roadway accessible, but far enough away to discourage interlopers. *Mudanzas,* literally "World Movers, Inc.," if you translated the company name into English, was a legitimate moving company, dealing almost exclusively with moves between the United States and Mexico.

Having begun in 1863, when the company used horse-drawn wagons to move French army officers into Mexico City, and a year later, Emperor Maximilian into his palace, Mudanzas had a long history of service.

Service that, when it was profitable and expedient, went against the desires and wishes of the Mexican people themselves.

Today the company moved diplomats, oil company executives, manufacturing vice presidents, and such between Mexico and the United States and Canada. Germany was the third-largest client behind the U.S. and Canada, a fact that could not be forgotten with all the Volkswagens on Mexican streets. Although Volkswagen of Mexico was officially a Mexican industry, exchange of personnel between the two countries still took place. For Mudanzas, the Germany connection had been the perfect entrée for Mudanzas' most profitable commodity: cocaine.

And, John Ortiz reminded himself as he pulled his Mexican-built Mercury Mystique into the nearest parking garage, if you burrowed into the organizational chart of Mudanzas, you did not have far to go before you found the parent company that had purchased Mudanzas ten years before NAFTA had passed. The parent company of Mudanzas was Chemicos Norte Americano, S.A. de C.V. Chemicos had purchased Mudanzas ostensibly to provide transportation between the NAFTA countries. John always wondered how companies such as Chemicos had known NAFTA would exist ten years later. The fact was, they had known, but he would leave that problem for another day. Chemicos, in turn, was a wholly owned subsidiary of North American Chemical Research, Inc., whose home office had relocated from a small New Jersey town just south of Trenton to Memphis, Tennessee. The usual justifications had been given to the residents of New Jersey: weather, taxes, wages, etc.

Ortiz knew all the reasons. He'd heard them before and, at one point in his life, had actually believed what corporate America said. But that was in the past, pre-NAFTA. A very distant past.

Ortiz accepted the parking ticket from the lady working the booth in the garage and walked out into a beautiful Mexico City morning. The only blemish on the day was the fax he had received earlier that morning and now carried in his coat pocket.

If Mexico City ever succeeded in ridding itself of its pall of pollution, Ortiz thought, it would truly be a heaven on earth. At over seven thousand feet elevation, the temperature seldom ranged higher than the mid-twenties Celsius. John smiled at the thought. He had been in Mexico long enough to accept the metric scale for temperature. What would that be in Fahrenheit? Somewhere in the neighborhood of eighty degrees? And that was for a high in the summer. Winter was sometimes uncomfortable because most Mexican homes did not have heating systems and the temperature could reach into the thirties (Fahrenheit). The air was perpetually dry; the relative humidity rarely rose above the 50 percent mark, making every day pleasant except for the pollution. Today, John was thankful, even that had been driven out by the west wind. *Yeah,* he thought, *if they could just rid themselves of the air pollution and purify the water too.* Either would be welcome. Both would be a miracle.

Ortiz turned the corner and walked toward the large warehouse that occupied an entire block. His task this day was no more than exploratory. He wanted to check out the Mudanzas warehouse for possible entry portals, and, conversely, escape portals. Nothing more than that, at least for today.

If the information he had just received on Mudanzas (and by association, Chemicos Norte Americano, S.A. de C. V.) was accurate, he and Al Bell would soon be up to their necks in one of the largest investigations they had ever undertaken as DEA agents assigned to Mexico. The only other thought in Ortiz's mind as he enjoyed the sunshine and crisp morning air was that the operation he foresaw could easily be the most dangerous he and his partner had ever participated in.

Branch Medical Center
NAVSUPACT

Jake pulled his Cherokee into the parking lot of Branch Medical Center, noting as he did so that there were now more cars parked here than there had been when he left. A chill raced up his back as he reached for the small book he'd retrieved from his house in Memphis. Why had he abandoned his duty at the clinic to go after this book? And what about the X-rays that lay on the seat just beneath the book? There was an anomaly on the film. Whatever it was, one thing was evident: something had been implanted in the young sergeant's body, placed there by a medical team at Naval Hospital, Naval Air Station, Pensacola, Florida. And whatever it was, Jake wanted to know about it.

He picked up the book and opened it. He had watched Kathy read the small New Testament many times in their years of marriage, always wondering what it was about the book that seemed to give her so much comfort. Whatever it was, it was a comfort he wanted, one he needed.

There were several paperclips attached to the tops of some of the pages, and Jake flipped to one of these pages. Kathy had made notes, scrawling comments in the available space in the margins of the Bible. There were underlined passages too. Passages that coincided with Kathy's notes in the margin.

Jake read the first underlined passage he came to: "I can do all things through Christ who strengthens me." It was a verse from Philippians, and Jake felt his heart beat just a little faster as the meaning sank in. The note to the right of the passage, written in Kathy's compact handwriting said, "I claim this promise for Jake." The date next to the note coincided with the time he'd been struggling in medical school.

Jake felt the tears on his cheeks before he realized he was even crying. That was Kathy, the Kathy he loved. But what did it mean? What was the promise Kathy had claimed? And for what purpose? To what end?

Jake wiped the tears away and reached for the X-rays. It was time to face Captain William Dean and endure whatever punishment was meted out for his temporary absence.

■ ■ ■

The pass was grabbed by the wide receiver for the Florida Gators, or was it the Florida State Seminoles? Jerry Wallace hovered just at the edge of consciousness, letting the medicine prescribed for him by Captain Dean go to work. Along with the two beers he'd just downed, the medicine had produced a slight buzz in his head, and his eyelids were getting heavier by the minute. He had forgotten who was playing the game on ESPN Classics, which didn't bother him a whole lot, he had to admit. The feeling of euphoria was one of the best he'd ever had. The medicine, he thought, must have been a little stronger than the last prescription he had received from the captain. Of course, the warning label on the bottle had cautioned against mixing the medication with alcohol, which, to Jerry, was nothing more than an invitation to do that very thing.

Muted cheers erupted from the television set, indicating that something had just occurred in the game. The excitement on the screen barely registered with Jerry as he felt his eyes closing, inexorably pulling him from a blissful state of semiconsciousness into total unconsciousness. It was the same feeling he'd had when the doctors down at Naval Hospital Pensacola had done whatever it was they had done to his left side. His hand moved slowly to the small scar left by the incision. He rubbed it gently, being careful not to aggravate the scar and cause it to itch, which had happened in the past.

The last thing that registered on the senses of Sergeant Jerry Wallace in this life was the gentle smell of cinnamon wafting from the air freshener plugged into the wall next to his chair. *One of the other guys must have bought the thing,* Jerry thought incongruously. It hadn't been there earlier.

■ ■ ■

The man sat in his car just outside Jerry Wallace's apartment in Millington, Tennessee. He was uncomfortable, not only because of the

midsummer heat fueled with high humidity, but because of the proximity of the apartments to the fire and police station of Millington.

The message he'd received less than an hour ago had been
emphatic, demanding action within the hour. He checked his watch.
He was seven minutes inside the required time period. The necessary
information had been relayed to him electronically, the method of exe-
cution flexible with two provisos: it had to look like an accident, and
the body had to be destroyed.

The man had listened as the pertinent information was quickly
relayed to him, all the while smiling to himself. He had performed the
same services for the same men many times before, and each one had
been successful. Same men? He smiled at that. He'd never actually
seen the men, had heard only one voice, and most information was
transferred via the beeper he carried on his belt. As far as he was concerned, he was working for a ghost.

There was no reason to think this particular job would not end as
successfully as all the others. And if success was its own reward, then
success in his business was even sweeter. Sweeter to the tune of
$100,000, the amount of the contractual agreement between him and
his . . . what? Employers? Of course, the man reflected, it might be a
difficult contract to enforce in a court of law, but then there were other
methods, weren't there?

It had taken nothing more than rapid response to put himself in
position to complete the assigned task. As usual, with haste, there
was always the possibility that something could go wrong, but the
technique he was using had several advantages. It was a technique
he'd devised several years ago. The idea had come to him when he'd
been attending, of all things, a home show in Memphis's Cook
Convention Center. The method had been absurdly simple and ridicu-
lously effective.

Now the man listened as Jerry Wallace began to snore softly. He
adjusted the squelch control to eliminate background noise, and

reduced the volume on the RX-U500 pocket receiver built by CCS International, Limited, of London. He could hear the football commentators from the television as clearly as if they were coming over his own car radio. The transmitter was an STG 4400 WMTX-U, built by the same company and highly modified by the man to fit within the innocuous-looking case now plugged into the wall in the apartment's living room. The literature claimed reception was crystal clear at up to three hundred feet, but the man had used the device many times before at a quarter mile. As long as there were no steel reinforced concrete walls to penetrate, the small listening device functioned at a level almost beyond belief.

He waited another five minutes to be sure there would be no movement from his intended victim. When none was forthcoming, the man reached for a small device that looked exactly like a remote garage door opener, which it was. He depressed the "open" button on the remote control, knowing he was well within range of the device he'd plugged into the wall socket next to Jerry Wallace's recliner. The fact that Wallace had chosen the recliner to go to sleep in was an added advantage, although the device would have functioned perfectly with Wallace in any room of the apartment.

The instant the remote control button was depressed, a small circuit, scavenged from the power section of a garage door opener, activated, sending an electrical pulse through a liquid capsule, releasing enough potassium cyanide gas to prove lethal anywhere in the apartment.

The man heard a single gasp propelled over the small transmitter embedded in the electrical plug-in air freshener he had installed in the apartment. The air freshener device had several advantages, not the least of which was the tendency for police and fire investigators to overlook the common device as an assassination tool. Under normal circumstances, the entire device was usually destroyed, or at least damaged to the point that it did not rouse the interest of fire investigators.

The fire. That was the next thing. The man picked up another garage door opener and pushed the "open" button on it. Modern technology was wonderful, he thought as he heard a small *pop* over the CCS receiver. The sound told him that the second circuit he'd installed in a second air freshener case had ignited the small amount of flammable liquid contained in a slightly smaller capsule. The second remote control transmitted on a different frequency from the first one that had released the cyanide gas. Air fresheners were the perfect delivery device. Small yet common, with their own source of electricity, and large enough, if one was judicious with the available space, to contain the necessary circuits and capsules to not only kill but to dispose of the evidence.

The man would wait a few minutes to be sure all went as planned, but the technique had never failed, and the proximity of this victim to the air freshener virtually assured success.

The last thing the man heard over the small transmitter/receiver was the shrill blare of a smoke alarm activating within the apartment. He smiled. It was too late, he knew. The flammable liquid had already ignited the wall. The fire would destroy not only the body, as required, but the source of the fire, as well.

The man started his car and headed back to Memphis, eager to report yet another success. The Millington Fire Department would respond to the call, but the apartment building was old brick over a tinder-dry substructure that would go up like a fraternity bonfire. If there were others in the building, they too might die, but that was not his concern. They were in the wrong place at the wrong time, and there was nothing he could do about that. The building even predated the fire codes requiring fire walls between apartments. The entire structure, along with the body, would burn quickly. The man would take his money and spend a few weeks at the casinos in Tunica, Mississippi. Maybe, he thought, as he made his way south along Highway 51, he would splurge and head out to Las Vegas.

Ecuador-Peru Border

The small patrol, concealed in the jungle, had watched the helicopter land, disgorge the new members of the observer force attached to Operation Safe Border, and leap back into the air. For them it was a signal.

The leader, a man in his midthirties, motioned for the others, mostly younger men who thought that membership in the Shining Path rebel movement of Peru brought with it confirmation of manhood. The man glanced over his shoulder at the young men. They would have grown up quickly in the mountains and jungles of Peru if they had had the opportunity. But that opportunity would elude them; today their lives would end, sacrificed to a greater cause.

"Move the weapon to the side," the leader instructed in a harsh whisper.

"*Si, Jefe,*" the nearest man-boy answered, moving off to fulfill the demand of his commanding officer.

"You others, over with the weapon," the leader ordered. The wind had picked up, coming from behind them. The wind was a mixed blessing, the leader knew. It would deliver the munitions quickly into the camp of the international observer team, the pigs of the earth, but it could just as easily carry the voices of his team up the mountain to the same hated enemy.

"Jorge, move up with the others. And tell them to put on the masks as I showed them. Tell them to move on around the ridge. I will give the order to fire."

"*Si, Jefe,*" the boy obeyed, scampering off to join the team.

The leader watched through his binoculars as the small team assembled more than a quarter of a mile to his right. A sudden pang of conscience struck him; the boys would have been good team members, good rebels, ever willing to obey orders, to fight, and to die for their leader. But then, that was what was being asked of them today, wasn't it? To die?

The team was busy assembling the weapon they had brought up the mountain with them, an antiquated, yet still effective, American army 60-mm mortar. There was, thought the leader, a certain irony in killing U.S. Army soldiers with one of their own weapons, regardless of the age of that weapon.

The leader trained his binoculars on the Safe Border observation camp. Men were moving around freely among the tents that had been erected on the mountaintop, joking and laughing in foreign languages on foreign ground—ground on which they did not belong, thought the leader.

It was difficult to tell the Americans from the Brazilians, the Brazilians from the Canadians, and so forth. Every man in the camp wore only what the U.S. Army called BDUs. To him, they were *los uniformes de la selva,* the uniform of the jungle. Nothing more than black T-shirts, camouflaged pants with large pockets, and jungle boots. He should be so fortunate as to have such clothing for his men, but then, that was what this mission was all about, was it not? If all went well, this single attack would provide equipment, clothing, and provisions to carry on the struggle within his country. And if he had to sacrifice a few raw recruits to achieve a great victory, then that was all right, was it not?

A movement from the right caught his attention, and the leader retrained the optics of the binoculars on the team beneath the ridge. The boy nearest him waved, indicating that the mortar was in place and ready for firing.

"Fools," the man uttered under his breath. Youth was nothing if not fatuous and idealistic. Both were attributes that could cost you your life in the mountains.

The leader raised his hand, holding it up with his fingers spread apart. As he counted down, he lowered one finger at a time, until no more fingers were showing, and time had run its course.

The low frequency *whump* of the mortar was lost in a sudden swirling of wind, but the leader knew the first of three mortar shells had been fired. He watched as the assault team dropped another mortar shell into the nearly perpendicular tube, the second exploding from the tube even before the first had landed. The team fired the third shell just as the first landed fifty meters short of the nearest observer tent. The third was in the air before the second landed.

The second shell fell to earth less than ten meters from the first; the third even closer to the first than the second.

The leader trained his attention on the observer camp. Men were scrambling in all directions. The shells had fallen far enough away that the explosions had done nothing more than awaken the observer team members who had been sleeping within the tents.

Those who had been awake had already identified the direction from which the mortar shells had come. Some of the soldiers were working their way toward the area where the mortar was set up. The leader could see that the soldiers were armed with some type of machine gun. He'd never seen one such as this, but he could feel his blood run cold at the sight of the small, silenced barrel that protruded obscenely in the mountain light. Another small group of men were working their way toward him, and for a moment, he wondered if he'd been spotted. Then he realized this group was doing exactly the same thing as the other group, only from another direction. Both groups were executing flanking moments, moving in from both sides of the mortar position.

A hideously loud gun shot made the leader jump. Movement from his mortar team caught his attention once again. He could see one man down, another waving frantically.

The observer team commandoes—for they were commandoes of some sort, the leader now realized—moved with the fluid motion that comes from endless hours of training. But they were faltering, he could also see, as if an unseen barrier had suddenly been erected in front of them, which it had. Already two members of the observer team were on the ground, and others were dropping their weapons and grasping at their throats. Some, knowing what was happening, began racing for the tents. The leader knew what they were doing. There were gas masks in the tents, and the commandoes who had invaded his country were trying to get to the masks. It would do no good. Gas masks could only delay the inevitable. Perhaps painfully so. The men, he knew, might have a chance if they could scramble into the full protection of the NBC suits that covered them from head to toe in an impermeable shield, but it was already too late for that.

More shots rang out. Somewhere nearby was a soldier with a .50-caliber sniper rifle, and he had located the men of the mortar crew. There was no protection for the men now. The man watched as, one by one, the boys he'd led up the mountain died.

In less than three minutes it was over. The man lifted his head, unaware that he'd involuntarily looked away from the carnage on both sides. The mountain was quiet; the wind rustled the tree limbs and tall grass, but nothing more. The men of the Safe Border observer force were all dead, he knew. Whatever chemical had been loaded into the three mortar shells had been deadly almost beyond belief. He had never heard of such a weapon. Not one that could be fired in high wind on the mountaintop and still be 100 percent effective. It was a frightening thought.

The leader rose from his position. It was strange, the man realized, being alone and yet not alone. There was an aching within him, a well of compassion no amount of logic would ever be able to purge. But he had made the deal, offering his men for the supplies necessary to continue the struggle. The price had been high but worth it. His Shining Path rebels would be funded and supplied for the next few months at a level that, before this slaughter, could have only been imagined.

The leader retrieved his binoculars and turned to retrace his steps down the mountain. It would not be very long before other troops in other helicopters would arrive. Surely someone sent an urgent message to the home base in Quito. It would take several hours for the trip from Ecuador's capital to the mountaintop; and in that time, the leader knew, he would be well away from the dreadful sight, collecting the blood money that he and his men would operate on in the coming days.

As the rebel leader stepped from his hiding place, a sharp crack echoed over the mountain; he never heard the sound.

The sniper carefully placed the custom-made Whetherby 7-mm magnum rifle in its case and closed it. He checked the area to be certain he'd not left any sign of his presence, and then started down the mountain. As he moved through the jungle, he wondered when it would end, or *if* it would end.

He thumbed the beeper on his belt, knowing the small device would relay all necessary information. Technology was wonderful.

CHAPTER SIX

Jake Madsen had endured the harangue of Captain Dean for the past half hour. The young doctor sneaked a peek at his watch, marveling that the tirade had only been going on for a scant thirty minutes; it seemed like an eternity. What made it worse was, Captain Dean was right.

"Never, in all my time in the military, has one of my doctors chosen to disobey my orders in such blatant fashion," Captain Dean said, with his back to Jake.

Jake sat in one of two chairs facing the desk of the commanding officer of Branch Medical Clinic. The office was not large, but then Dean was a doctor, too, and while the office was comfortably appointed, the captain spent as much time as he could with patients. The office afforded him a place to complete the paperwork he found both vital and boring.

For Jake, the size of the office was of particular interest at the moment. He would have liked to crawl under the chair, the desk, anything he could find.

"What would you suggest I do about you, Dr. Madsen?" Captain Dean asked.

The question caught Jake off guard. He had been exposed to dressings-down during his time on active duty, but nothing that compared to what he was experiencing now. For a moment he was not sure if the question was merely rhetorical or if the captain was indeed asking him his opinion. He said nothing.

Captain Dean turned back to face him, and Jake realized the captain did not require an answer to the question. It was just as well because Jake didn't have one.

"Dr. Madsen," Dean was saying, "I am going to relieve you of duty here at BMC. You have a few days left on your two-week active duty schedule, but I can't use you here. Perhaps the Reserve Manpower Center can find another spot for you; however, I doubt that. There's not enough time. You live in Memphis and work at the VA. My suggestion is that you go home and wait for your reserve unit commander to contact you. Is that clear?"

"Perfectly," Jake answered between clenched teeth.

"And one more thing. We seem to be missing a PA and lateral you had shot on Sergeant Jerry Wallace. I need those X-rays."

A warning flash went off in Jake's mind. He was not sure what it was he had seen in the film; but whatever it was, it was something Captain Dean did not want revealed, something strange enough to warrant the fear Jake now saw in Dean's eyes. And whatever it was, Jake was equally determined to root it out.

"You had no right to treat Sergeant Wallace, no right to shoot the X-rays, and no right to withhold the film now," Dean said.

Jake felt his anger boil to the surface. He'd taken about all he cared to take. "If I shouldn't have been treating Sergeant Wallace, like you say," Jake shot back, his voice rising, "then his primary physician should have been here. That's you, isn't it, Captain Dean? You should have anticipated problems with your patient, but you didn't. That's what this is all about, isn't it? You were down in Pensacola, and one of your special patients needed you. I treated him because I'm a doctor. I was the doctor on sick call when the sergeant came in. You weren't. I don't ask a person in pain if he can wait until someone else shows up to treat him. I treat him. That's what I do. And that's how it works at the VA. Maybe you should try it sometime." Jake could feel his anger building, his words tumbling out. Somewhere in the exchange, he'd risen from his chair. He no longer felt like cowering before this doctor/administrator.

"As far as the X-rays are concerned, I have no idea where they are. There must be something on them you don't want me to see, but that's your problem, captain. I don't have the film." Jake felt not the slightest embarrassment at the lie. The film was still on the seat of his Cherokee. For some reason he'd left it there, and now he was glad he had.

"Madsen . . .," Captain Dean blustered. Jake cut him off.

"And where is the sergeant, by the way?"

"That's none of your concern."

"I had him admitted to the ward for observation. At the very least he's got a form of pneumonia. Possibly some pulmonary fibrosis too. I was waiting on the film to check that out, but I could hear enough in his chest to know that much." Lying was becoming easier, Jake realized. Part lie, part truth.

"So you didn't look at the film at all?"

"Not yet. And I suppose I will never see it, will I?"

Dean said nothing for a moment, then rejoined, "I had the sergeant released from the ward. He's on a special medication. I gave him a new supply and sent him home. His condition is treatable. He'll be fine."

"And I'm out of here. Right?" Jake said.

"Go home, Commander. Go back to the VA. I don't care what you do, just get out of my clinic. I'll be making a full report to the Reserve Center, but I don't want you back in this clinic as long as I'm here. Is that understood?"

Jake straightened and, contrary to navy protocol that prohibited saluting without a hat or inside a building, flipped a salute to Captain Dean, completing the salute before Dean could understand the mockery attached to the act. Jake stormed out of the office, but he had a stop to make before leaving Branch Medical Clinic.

■ ■ ■

The Millington Fire Department pumper truck was on the scene in less than five minutes. A second alarm, put in by the fire captain on the scene, requested a snorkel truck so the fire could be battled from above as well as from below.

The roof of the apartment building where Jerry Wallace lived was fully engulfed. The fire had spread quickly upward, but because of a newly installed sprinkler system, the fire had not spread laterally.

The snorkel truck was on the scene six minutes after the second alarm had been put in. Firemen scrambled over hoses laid out in the street. Smoke billowed from the building's roof. Despite the sprinklers, the fire had found the path of least resistance and was racing through the attic of the old building.

Firemen clambered to the roof, venting it with axes and chain saws. Water poured into the building from the man-made breaches, smothering the flames from the top down.

Less than twenty minutes after the automatic fire alarm had sounded, the fire was nothing more than a smoldering memory. One apartment had been damaged, along with the roof of four others. The Millington Fire Department had performed a miracle.

Now, as the fire inspector followed three firemen into the apartment where they thought the blaze had begun, the four men found what they always dreaded in these types of fires. A body, charred badly but still intact, sat in a burned-out recliner against the far wall of the apartment.

"Captain," one of the firemen radioed. "We have a body."

"Stokes on the way," the reply came back, referring to the rounded metal stretcher used to transport victims.

The firemen watched as the fire inspector worked his way around the room, tentatively moving around the body in the recliner. There was a sense of propriety in such a place, and the inspector was respecting that.

The inspector moved around the chair, noting as he did so that the plug-in air freshener next to the chair seemed to have melted despite the fact that no fire had reached it. He scanned the room now, looking for more such air fresheners. Another was plugged into the far wall in the same room. That was strange, wasn't it? Two air fresheners in the same room. The inspector moved to the second air freshener. This one, unlike the one beside the recliner, was burned and distorted, but recognizable. The man gently tugged the device from the wall socket and held it up for the other three firemen to see.

"This is the primary source, men," the inspector said.

"An air freshener?" one of the firemen said incredulously.

"Yeah, but not a normal one. This one is very special. And I'll bet I find that the one over there by the chair is not just an air freshener either. I think we're looking at murder, gentlemen. Had it not been for that new sprinkler system we had the owners install, we might never have found this. Chalk this one up to the good guys."

"The dead guy is military," another of the firemen said. He had moved over to the body and noticed there were still identification tags around the dead man's neck. He didn't know anyone wore dog tags anymore.

"OK. I'll get on the horn and call the police and the NCIS. The guy's got to be from the base, and the navy is going to want to be in on this one."

"What about the body?" a fireman asked.

"We'll have to leave it until the police get here. Everyone is going to need to be in on this one. I've never seen anything like this," the fire inspector said, holding up the charred air freshener. "Someone went to a lot of trouble to kill this guy and then try to get rid of the evidence. And they didn't care who else they killed in the process. I want whoever is responsible for this. I want them badly."

"Regional Forensic?" a fireman asked.

"We'll have to see. Either there or the VA. The guy is military, and the VA Med Center has an agreement with the NAVSUPACT medical unit. But Shelby County is the only one set up to do a forensic autopsy, and that's what they're going to want to do with this guy. Notify the county to be expecting him as soon as the cops get finished."

Mexico City

John Ortiz clicked the shutter of the 500-mm lens camera, catching the comings and goings of several men who were obviously not employees of the moving company. Just exactly what the men were doing was not known to the DEA agent, but the faces were all too familiar.

The morning sun was beginning to beat down on Ortiz, who'd positioned himself atop a building just across and one hundred yards up the street from Mudanzas Mundial. It was not the best vantage point, but the telephoto lens made up for the disadvantages.

Already he'd shot two full rolls of film and was well into a third. Three rolls would be enough. He'd captured what he'd wanted. The men who'd entered Mudanzas less than an hour ago were now in the process of leaving. The erratic schedules of the departures were enough to convince Ortiz that something was going on in the building other than packing and crating household goods.

Branch Medical Clinic
NAVSUPACT

"I'm convinced Madsen had the X-rays. It's the only thing that makes sense," Captain Dean said into the telephone. His hands were sweating, and the phone was becoming slick in his grasp.

"Probabilities?" the voice on the other end of the phone line asked.

Dean swallowed hard before answering. "Ninety-eight percent sure," he responded. There was no immediate rejoinder to the figure. The perspiration flow increased, causing Dean increased discomfort.

"Not to worry. Contingencies have been planned for. We will continue on this end and deal with Dr. Madsen as planned."

"I can't be involved," Dean said into the phone.

The voice on the other end snickered. "Don't worry, *captain,*" the voice said. "You won't be implicated in this. I'm switching to voice-mail input, and you are to repeat your report so that it can be recorded. Don't forget to identify yourself so the computer will have the proper voice-recognition program loaded."

Captain Dean held the phone and waited for the proper program, then repeated the report. When he was finished, he hung up. He marveled at how deeply he had become involved in so short a time. Had he thought it through beforehand, he might have balked, but he had not. Well, there was no turning back now. He would have to follow through and hope that the man on the other end of the phone could deliver.

■ ■ ■

The technician watched the telemetry signals with waning interest. He'd seen the same readouts come across his console before. When he'd seen the first one, there had been a flicker of sympathy, maybe even empathy. But that had been a long time ago, and time and repetition did engender indifference, even when the object of interest was the death of another human being.

This one was . . . where? The tech checked the mapping computer—Memphis. One of a total of less than a hundred or so, if he remembered correctly. He would look that up later. Right now his task was to document the death of another subject as reported by the electronic instruments before him.

The signal had been relayed through the local cellular phone system using a subsystem and alternate computer program few knew about. The monitoring device transmitted the subject's pulse rate, a basic EKG scan, respiratory rate, and Chem 7 functions, in addition to the subject's GPS location. Not a lot of information, but enough.

This death, though, had been different, the tech noticed. He was just a reconnaissance tech, not a doctor or even a medical tech. But he'd been watching the signals long enough to know when something out of the ordinary had happened, and that's what had happened in Memphis.

There had been sudden respiratory failure preceded by an erratic heartbeat, and the subject had died within seconds of both. Pretty quick, he thought, even for a heart attack. He'd seen those come across his screen too; none had appeared like this one.

The tech clicked the computer mouse next to his console, bringing up the reporting form, and began to fill in the details of the death of the test subject. What exactly happened to the reports, the tech did not know or care. He was paid to make the reports and keep his mouth shut, and that was exactly what he intended to do with this latest death.

CHAPTER
SEVEN

Millington, Tennessee

The scene that greeted Kaci Callahan was one she'd seen at least a dozen times before. She had been at her desk in Building 238, at NAVSUPACT, when the call had come in. Kerry Hartford, the only other Naval Criminal Investigative Services agent available, had been over at BUPERS trying to run down a hacker who had entered the navy's personnel files night before last. That left Kaci as the lone NCIS agent to answer the call about the death in Millington.

There was still a knee-jerk reaction to women cops, but Kaci Callahan was one of the best NCIS agents in the United States. The idea of civilian law enforcement agents policing the military was one that had been around a long time, and nowhere did it work better than the Naval Criminal Investigative Service.

And none were better at it than the attractive redhead who now approached the car where Alan Freeman stood.

"Hi, Kaci," said Freeman, leaning against the car.

"What happened, Alan?" Kaci asked. Alan Freeman was one of two detectives on the Millington police force, and Kaci had worked with him before. She liked him, in a brotherly sort of way.

"Fire people say arson. Which makes it murder since there is one body in the apartment where the fire started."

"Military," Kaci sighed.

"Why else would we call you NCIS guys? Us poor folks from the city need all the help we can get from you high-powered government-type investigators."

Kaci turned to face Freeman, knowing what she would find. He was smiling; he always enjoyed joking with "government-types," as he called them, and Kaci knew she was one of his favorite targets. The good-natured banter made unpleasant tasks easier to cope with.

"So," the Millington detective began, "why is Naval Criminal Investigative Service sending its most decorated agent out on a homicide?" Freeman pushed off the car and walked over to Kaci. Both stared at the burned-out building.

"Luck of the draw," Kaci answered. "And the fact that Kerry's tied up with a computer problem over at BUPERS; Gene's in Georgia, down in Glynco at the Federal Law Enforcement Training Center, teaching at the Basic Agent Course for a week; and—"

"And 'the President' doesn't know enough to get in out of the rain," Freeman finished the sentence.

Kaci smiled. "It's not that, and you know it, Alan. John's a good agent. He just needs some more field experience. Besides, he's out of town." Both were referring to John Q. Adams—aka, "the President," because of his name. Someday Kaci would tell Alan Freeman that John

Quentin Adams really was a distant relative of the original John Quincy Adams, sixth president of the United States, but that could wait. Right now there was a dead man in the burned-out apartment, and Kaci wanted to get started on the investigation as soon as possible. "How much longer?" she asked.

Alan Freeman shook his head. "Not too much longer. The chief is going over the place right now. Bob Farrel is up there too. He said as soon as it's safe, he'd let us know."

Kaci nodded. Bob Farrel was a fire investigator for Shelby County, a short, round man whose demeanor and appearance sometimes projected the qualities of a slow-moving Santa Claus, which he most definitely was not. Farrel was one of the sharpest men Kaci had ever met, especially where fire was concerned. It would have been Farrel who had called the fire arson, even at this early stage; the death murder; and would somehow have discovered the body was that of military personnel.

"He's waving," Freeman said to Kaci. "Let's go. You know, if you were smart like Kerry, you'd have an inside job too."

Kaci swung and missed Freeman's right arm.

They started for the burned-out shell of a building. Up close, Kaci noticed, the damage was not what she'd expected. The Millington Fire Department must have been on the scene within minutes of the alarm. The fire department and the police department shared a building on Navy Road, a few blocks west of the apartment complex. The apartments were old, and despite being made of brick, susceptible to fire. There would be lots of evidence to sift through.

"Kaci, Alan," Bob Farrel greeted the two investigators as they approached. "We got a good one here, and I'll let the Detective Division and the navy battle over jurisdiction."

"No battle here, Bob," Kaci said. "It happened in Millington. There may be no connection to the military other than the fact that the victim is a service member. In that case, I'll gladly leave it to Alan."

"Buuut . . . ?" Freeman said, drawing out the single word question, implying there was always the unspoken "but" to contend with where the government was concerned.

"But, if there is compelling evidence that the nature of the crime, if there is a crime, proves to be inherently connected to the navy, then we'll just have to work together, won't we, Alan."

"We'll see what we've got and go from there. OK with you, Kaci?" he asked.

"Let's take a look," she agreed.

The three moved gingerly into the burned building. The stench of smoke mixed with water-saturated material was oppressive. Water dripped from the ceiling—the part that was left after the firemen had pulled it down—and the walls, pooling on the floor and making the carpet squishy beneath their feet.

"Over here," the fire investigator called.

Kaci and Freeman joined the fireman near the wall across from where a covered body lay in a burned recliner. The smell of charred flesh mingled with the smoke; the result was not pleasant.

Bob Farrel knelt down and pointed to the wall socket. "This is what started it."

"I thought this was a homicide," Freeman said. "If it started at a wall socket, how is that murder?"

"Here," Farrel pointed. "What's that look like?"

Both Freeman and Kaci leaned closer to the wall to examine what the fire investigator was indicating.

"Looks like one of those plug-in wall freshener thingamajigs," Freeman said.

"Not that you can tell too much about it in the condition it's in," Kaci added.

"You're both right. I left it in the wall until the photographer had pictures and you two got here." Bob Farrel reached down and pulled the air freshener from the blackened wall socket. "You've never seen one like this. This one was wired, including a small amount of a combustible substance."

"Wired?" Kaci and Freeman said simultaneously.

"Look," Farrel said, pulling the melted apparatus apart. "There's a small circuit board linked to a capsule of something or other. We'll find out what it is when we get it to the lab, but it could be anything from jelled gasoline to rubber cement. There's another one over next to the chair, but it's not the same. No combustible stuff in it."

The three moved over to the covered recliner, each unconsciously speaking more softly out of respect for the dead.

Farrel reached down and pulled the second air freshener from the wall socket. "This one has basically the same circuit board, a melted capsule, and another interesting item," he said as he separated the device, extracted what looked like another circuit board, and held it up.

"A microphone," Kaci said, immediately recognizing the tiny device.

"Very good," Farrel said. "Which raises the question as to why someone monitored the apartment, waited for this particular subject, and then started the fire."

"And one other thing . . .," Alan Freeman began.

"The empty capsule," Kaci finished. "What was in it?"

"Exactly. This is a strange case," Farrel went on. "So, who's going to take it on?"

Kaci and Freeman exchanged glances. "Both of us to begin with," Kaci said. "Alan will have overall coordination responsibility, and I'll act as a secondary investigator. My main interest is the military side of this thing, and since we're standing on civilian property, it's Alan's call. Chances are there's no military connection other than the victim having been in the military. Which brings up my next question. Who is he and what branch are we talking about?" Kaci asked.

"What about it, Bob?" Alan repeated.

"Army or Army Reserve. The guy still had his dog tags on."

"Identification tags," Kaci corrected.

"Whatever. Gives us a tentative ID until we can get the autopsy done."

"Shelby County?" Kaci asked, turning to Freeman.

"Yeah. Has to be. They're the only ones set up to do forensic."

"Tell them to check for an inhalant poisoning of some sort," Kaci said, thinking about the empty capsule in the air freshener.

"You got any ideas?" Freeman asked, making a note.

"Nothing other than the capsule. It seems to me that if the fire started on the other side of the room, that the smoke alarm would have awakened this guy . . . unless . . ."

"Unless he was already dead," the Millington detective completed the thought. "Which means something in the empty capsule might have killed him first, then the second one was set off to destroy the evidence."

"Which the fire didn't do very well because of the sprinklers and an efficient fire department," Kaci added.

"Not to mention the fact that evidence is difficult to destroy, even by fire," Bob Farrel added. "Most people think fire will destroy everything in its path, but they are only partially correct. There is always evidence, it just takes on a different form after a fire. In this case, if it's murder, the killer miscalculated drastically. We have a body with intact organs, even if identification will need to be made at Regional Forensic. Big mistake."

"Assuming there's something connected to the identity of . . .," Kaci checked the name on the ID tags she'd been handed by the fire inspector, "Sergeant Jerry Wallace that would have made destruction of the body imperative." Kaci turned to Freeman. "How long on the autopsy?"

"I'll get them on it ASAP. Murder takes priority over everything else. We should have preliminary results tomorrow sometime. Lab results will take a little longer, but we should have those by the end of the week, depending on what type of tests they run. Call it three days for most of the info. What do you want to do between now and then?" he asked Kaci.

"We'll assume the ID is confirmed. We'll work on that assumption unless Regional Forensic changes that. I'll get Wallace's medical records over to forensic. Looks like Jerry Wallace had roommates here. They will be easy to run down. If they are on NAVSUPACT, I'll take them. If they are outside, they're all yours. We'll start with that. What say?"

Freeman nodded. "We can get the names from the apartment manager and go from there." He turned back to the fire inspector. "Isolate this apartment when you certify it as safe to enter. Kaci and I will be back. After we get all our photographs, we'll transport the body over to Madison and get the Forensic Center on it."

"Somebody didn't like this guy," the fire inspector said, turning to view the corpse still sitting in the burned-out recliner.

"Maybe, maybe not," Kaci said. "Not every murder is based on feelings."

■ ■ ■

Nightmares, thought Jake Madsen, happened in the daylight too. What he saw before him was living proof.

The apartment building was surrounded by onlookers, each trying to get a closer look. Three fire trucks were still on the scene. Two of the fire companies were in the process of rolling their hoses. The third was wetting down the charred remains. Random tendrils of smoke still rose skyward.

Jake parked his Jeep Cherokee and got out. He pushed his way through the crowd, moving closer to the scene of destruction. He checked the small piece of paper in his hand that held the address he'd gotten from the corpsman on duty at the front desk of Branch Medical Center. It was the address of Jerry Wallace, and Jake's heart sank as he stared at the burned-out apartment before him.

Amazingly, no one tried to stop him from getting closer to the fire scene as he moved toward the apartment he now was certain had been Wallace's.

He stepped over fire hoses and dodged firemen as they went about their work. He finally located the number of the destroyed apartment; it was Jerry Wallace's! Jake felt the hair on the back of his neck stand on end.

"Careful, Commander," a voice called. Jake turned toward the speaker. His heart, which had just fallen into his stomach at the sight of the destroyed apartment, suddenly leaped back into his throat.

It was not possible! She was here! Then he recognized his error, and his heart fell again. Standing just to the side of the apartment, talking with another man, was a young woman who could have passed for Kathy's sister. Even now, his heart beat furiously at the sight of the dark red hair and sparkling blue eyes.

"You'll get those whites messed up pretty quickly around here," Kaci Callahan said. "Do you have some official business here . . . Doctor?" Kaci asked, noticing the medical insignia on Jake's shoulder boards.

That explained the access he'd been given, Jake realized. These people thought he was here in an official capacity. That meant the fire was in some way connected to the military . . . and to Jerry Wallace.

Jake walked over to the red-haired lady and the man to whom she was talking. "Jake Madsen," he introduced himself. Knowing that the woman before him was not Kathy did not lessen the effect she'd had on him only seconds earlier. The pain of his loss was now even more acute.

"Kaci Callahan. NCIS. And this is Alan Freeman with the Millington Police Department," she said, introducing the detective. "What can we do for you, Dr. Madsen?" Kaci asked, giving her full attention to Jake.

Again he felt the flutter in his chest as Kaci Callahan spoke to him.

The voice matched her appearance—a lot like Kathy's, but different, more assertive.

"I'm looking for Sergeant Jerry Wallace. He's one of my patients, and I was doing some follow-up." The lie came easily, but then it was not entirely a lie, was it?

"Anything in particular, Doctor?" the Millington detective asked curiously.

"Not much. I took some X-rays yesterday and just got them back. I'd had Jerry in the ward at Branch Medical Center at NAVSU-PACT, but we had a clerical error, and he was released this morning before I arrived. I tried to call, but didn't get an answer, so I thought I would drive over." *Two* lies in one sentence. He was getting good at this. *Remember,* he told himself, *lies mixed with truth are easier to recall.*

"That's sort of strange, isn't it, Dr. Madsen?" The question came from Kaci. Both investigators had now turned their attention to Jake. "I mean, not even general practitioners make house calls these days. I sure wouldn't expect it from a navy doc."

"Not so strange under the circumstances. I'm on two weeks active duty at BMC, and I'll be leaving soon. I didn't want to take the chance of missing the sergeant."

"Those X-rays must really be something to see, then. What's so special?" Kaci asked. Alan Freeman had backed off, taking a half step away from the small knot, effectively leaving the interrogation of the naval officer to the NCIS special agent.

Jake felt a twinge of concern. The questions were not difficult ones to answer, but he was not sure how much he should tell this . . . what? Policeman? Investigator? Navy official? All of the above? NCIS agents were civilians, but they had total jurisdiction in criminal matters involving the military personnel from Naval Support Activities.

"Nothing too esoteric about the film. I was headed home. I live in Memphis and work at the VA Med Center on Jefferson. I just thought

I'd stop by and talk to Jerry. I always take Navy Road heading back to Memphis. This was on the way."

Kaci Callahan looked at her watch. Jake understood the significance immediately. There were no flies on this lady, as his father used to say.

"I got off early today," Jake said timidly, hoping to avoid further explanation.

"I see," said Kaci, not pressing the point.

"The fire," Jake continued, trying to change the subject. "Sergeant Wallace's apartment?"

"Yeah," Kaci answered. "The sergeant is dead. We'll be removing the body in a moment and transporting it over to Madison Avenue."

"To the Regional Forensic Center," Jake concluded.

"We'll get the autopsy and go from there."

Jake felt as if a cold blast of air had just blown through his very soul. "Autopsy?"

"Standard procedure in homicides, Doctor. You should know that."

"But . . . how do you know it's murder?"

"We know, Dr. Madsen. What we don't know is why. Maybe the autopsy will shed some light on that. Unless, of course, you can tell us why you might think someone wanted to kill the sergeant."

Jake felt the NCIS agent's eyes on him, like he was a bug under an entomologist's microscope. There was something on the X-rays, but was what he'd seen on the films motive for murder? It didn't seem possible, but strange things had been happening in the past days. Certainly his dismissal by Captain Dean qualified as an unusual event, and that had been precipitated by his treatment of Jerry Wallace.

"I can get the X-rays with a simple administrative request, Dr. Madsen. You might as well tell me what was so important that it brought you here."

Jake looked into the blue eyes of Kaci Callahan and told his fourth lie. "The sergeant had a recurring case of pneumonia. I admitted him to the ward to check it out. That's all there was to it. You can get the X-rays, but that's all you'll find." In his mind, Jake knew the element of truth in his statement might have convinced the agent. But if it was possible to lie by *not* saying something, he'd just done that. He'd implied that Kaci Callahan could get the film from Branch Medical Clinic, which was not possible since he had the film in his Cherokee. He wanted to examine them more closely before deciding exactly what it was he was seeing. His intention, since he'd now been rather abruptly dismissed from active duty, was to talk to the chief of staff at the VA Med Center. Dr. Caroline Rhodes had probably seen this very thing before and could clear up the mystery in seconds. But until that time, he would hold on to the film himself.

"Thank you, Doctor," Kaci said, her blue eyes softening. "Let me have a phone number where I can reach you, just in case. You never know where one of the cases will lead."

"Sure, but you can call the VA anytime, and they can page me, if that's all right."

"Perfect," Kaci said, making a note.

"One question, if it's permitted," Jake said.

"Shoot."

"What about the condition of the body? Is it pretty much destroyed?" A thought had just occurred to Jake, but what he had in mind would only be possible if Jerry Wallace's body was sufficiently intact.

"Sprinklers saved the building, but not him. There is some damage, but it's going to be mostly exterior. Third-degree burns over 90 percent of the body, but that's about it. Why do you ask?" Kaci asked.

"No reason," Jake answered. "Just curious. Call me if I can help," Jake said, turning to leave.

"Dr. Madsen . . ." Kaci began.

"Jake. Just call me Jake," he said, turning back to face her.

"Jake," Kaci began again, "don't leave Memphis for the time being. I'll be getting back to you after the autopsy."

"Sure." Jake turned and walked toward his Jeep Cherokee, got in, and pulled out of the congested area.

Kaci watched as Jake Madsen pulled away from the destroyed apartment complex. There was something that did not quite add up, and she sensed it. That *something* involved Dr. Jake Madsen and the threads that connected him to a dead Sergeant Jerry Wallace, and she intended to find out what those threads were.

■ ■ ■

Across the street from the apartment complex, a man dialed a cell phone and waited for the answer at the other end of the line. When it came, he spoke briefly and to the point.

"He failed. I've talked to firemen who were in the apartment. The sergeant is dead and the body is burned, but there's enough there to autopsy. You might want a refund on this one," was all the man said before punching the "end" button on the cell phone and walking away from the scene.

■ ■ ■

The pager vibrated at his waist. The killer never activated the sound on his pager; he didn't want others glancing in his direction, not even casually. People's memories of certain events could be absolutely phenomenal, even to the sound of a pager going off.

He thumbed the button to display a message that made his blood run cold. The man turned away from the Northwest gate where he had been about to board a flight out of Memphis International Airport. He had an emergency meeting in exactly two hours. It would be unpleasant, he knew, but there were still ways to redeem the situation. There were always ways. Usually the remedies involved more deaths—gratis—but he would do what needed to be done to salvage his reputation. After all, reputation was really all anyone in his business possessed, wasn't it?

CHAPTER
EIGHT

Gorgas Army Hospital
Republic of Panama
June 14, 2000

The Panama Canal Treaty of 1977, negotiated by then President Jimmy Carter, provided for the complete turnover of the Panama Canal Zone—a zone five miles wide that extended from the Pacific Ocean to the Atlantic Ocean, covering the entire operational area of the Panama Canal—to the Republic of Panama by December 31, 1999. The turnover had required coordinated efforts between the Republic of Panama; the United States Navy, Army, Marine Corps, and Air Force; the Panama Canal Commission; the State Departments of both countries; the joint governments of Panama City, Colon, and Cristobal; the International Maritime

Commission; and a host of smaller, but vocal, entities in and around the Canal Zone.

The impact on the economy of Panama had been considered but not very carefully. With the canal no longer under the control of the United States, it made little sense to maintain the huge military presence in the area. Military bases had begun closing as early as the mid-1980s. The departure of the United States military, one of the largest employers in the country, afforded a mixed blessing. The canal came under Panamanian control, but the jobs associated with the military presence—jobs that employed mostly Panamanian nationals—were gone. And while the properties of the military bases and other Canal Zone areas did indeed offer lucrative opportunities in the redistribution of real estate, few Panamanians could afford to purchase the thousands of houses located on the closed bases or relocate their present businesses into the commercial facilities left behind by the departure of the United States. Consequently, the extensive holdings that had been part of the canal operation were now in the process of being reclaimed by the harsh Panamanian climate. Vegetation had grown to heights so spectacular that the buildings nestled among the green and growing sprouts could no longer be seen.

Gorgas Army Hospital, named for Colonel William C. Gorgas, the army doctor who had defeated yellow fever during the building of the canal, sat just below the summit of Ancon Hill, overlooking the Pacific entrance to the Panama Canal. Panama City's French Quarter, suffering from an advanced case of neglect, was visible from the hospital as well, and it reminded Doctor Oscar Ucar just how fortunate he had been in securing his own position for at least another two years. He had framed his letter of acceptance from the United States and cherished it, even if it had been printed and signed by a computer.

The hospital had been one of the last institutions to close, its sprawling grounds and stone buildings turned over to the Panamanian government less than a year ago. Ucar had been an internist working in Gorgas's internal medicine department. The job had been interesting, even stimulating at times, and had provided a higher standard of living for him and his family than might have been possible otherwise.

Ucar was tall, with flowing dark hair that he kept combed straight back. His dark eyes danced when he spoke, and he smiled easily. His patients, both military and civilian, liked the affable internist. And Ucar took care of his patients. He'd been educated in the Guadalajara, Mexico, School of Medicine and had done residencies at both Duke and Beth Israel.

The possibility of Oscar Ucar losing his job when the canal reverted to Panama had always been a concern, but one that the good doctor knew he had no control over. As it turned out, he had been the first doctor approached by the army colonel who had come to Panama to recruit doctors to stay on in the hospital after the turnover. What he would be doing had not been clear; but it was a job, it was medicine, and it paid three times what he could make at Panama's Punto Patilla Hospital. It was twenty times what he would have made if he'd had to practice within the *Seguro Social,* the Social Security system of Panama. Oscar Ucar had become accustomed to the finer things in life, and he had no intention of giving them up. The decision had been easy.

But now, as Ucar waited for the attendants to wheel the latest subjects into the autopsy room of the Gorgas morgue, he wondered just how much he was willing to endure for money.

The morgue was situated just across the winding street from the hospital's main complex. The road separating the hospital and the morgue split Ancon Hill in two, running from Fourth of July Avenue on the south to Fourth of July Avenue on the north. Fourth of July Avenue encircled Ancon Hill and had become famous—Ucar preferred the word *notorious*—during the student riots in the sixties. The riots had precipitated the talks of the Panama Canal turnover. Now those same demonstrators found themselves unemployed. Life did have its own ironies, Ucar thought as he watched the first of a dozen gurneys wheeled into the autopsy room.

Ucar, as well as every technician with whom he was working, wore blue Racal protective suits. The suits completely isolated the technicians and doctors from the outside environment, protecting the wearer from even the most deadly biological vermin in the world. Made of heavy-duty plastic and reinforced with Kevlar, the suits could withstand a lot of punishment, but even the durable Racal suits were no match for the Panamanian heat and humidity. The suits were periodically changed to ensure maximum protection for the wearers. Ucar was already sweating profusely. The ventilator on his back hummed gently, recirculating the air and providing a slight positive pressure in the event the suit was ripped. The idea was to keep what was on the outside of the suit on the outside, and what was inside, on the inside—and alive.

Ucar was not too worried about the possibility of contracting a deadly disease from the bodies now spread before him, but the corpses *had* come from South America, from somewhere near the border between Ecuador and Peru. While South America was not Africa with its vast array of viruses that fed on human tissue, it *was* still South America, and there were things down there that could kill just as effectively and just as grotesquely as Africa's Ebola and Lasa viruses. No one really knew what was in the jungles down there, so Ucar was taking no chances.

The technician on Ucar's right handed him a clipboard, and the doctor began speaking into the microphone hanging over the autopsy table. He recited the data from the clipboard verbatim; then, with that done, he began the autopsy. From the looks of it, he would be inside the Racal suit for hours. In the midsummer heat of Panama, the prospect was not inviting; but at least he could look forward to returning to his house that looked out on the Pacific Ocean over on Via Italia, in his upscale neighborhood. Whatever the drawbacks associated with his current position, lack of affluence was not one of them.

As the doctor cut into the first soldier, he wondered just exactly what happened to the autopsy reports, tissue samples, and blood samples he drew. It was only a fleeting thought, and Ucar returned to the business at hand.

American Embassy, Paseo de la Reforma
Mexico City

"Who is he?" DEA agent Albert Bell asked.

"I don't know. He's a new one," John Ortiz answered.

The two DEA agents were perusing the photographs Ortiz had shot yesterday from the rooftop overlooking Mudanzas Mundial.

"Let's run it by Josh upstairs. Spooks are supposed to know everybody down here," Ortiz said.

"Liaison officer," Bell corrected, and both men smiled at the euphemism they were now using for the CIA station chief.

"OK. We'll give this to Josh the Spook and let him run it for us. It will cost us, you know. Spooks don't give away information for free, not even to DEA agents."

"Shoot," Bell said, "this guy might even be on Josh's payroll. If that's the case, we can forget any information, but it's worth a try. In the meantime, I'll try my own sources and see what I can come up with."

"Agreed," Ortiz said. "What about Mudanzas? Did you find out anything on them?"

Bell opened the briefcase he'd carried into Ortiz's office. He extracted a file folder and opened it. "That tip we got was pretty much right on. Are you ready for this?"

"Shoot."

"Mudanzas Mundial, S.A. de C.V., is a wholly owned subsidiary of The World Transportation Systems Group. WTSG has holdings all over the world. Shipping, containers, rail yards, trucks, you name it. If it moves, they move it. Mudanzas is just one rung on a big corporate ladder."

"So you're saying they're legit? That's not what our informant implied."

Bell held up his hand. "One thing at a time. There's more. We're just at the tip of the proverbial iceberg. Mudanzas is owned by World Transportation, which is one of six holding companies held by International Group Holdings. There are more tentacles to this monster than a giant squid. IGH is a monster of magnificent proportions. They have holdings in the U.S., Mexico, Brazil, Venezuela, the U.K., Germany, Canada, a few African countries—these don't tend to be as profitable as others—Kuwait, Saudi Arabia, North Yemen, the Baltics, Iran, India, Pakistan, Indonesia, Japan, and the Republic of China," Bell recited from the list in his hand. "They pretty much have the world covered. Mudanzas, through World Transportations Systems, is part of their logistics operations. That's *their* description, not mine."

"There's nothing against the law in being big and making money," Ortiz pointed out.

"Nope. But let me bring it closer to home. Remember the fires that broke out up north a couple of years ago? Burned out half the desert in northern Mexico? The fires were so large the taint of smoke changed the weather systems as far north as Kansas and Oklahoma. Some of it even got into Illinois, Indiana, and Ohio."

Ortiz laughed out loud. "You're not going to blame Mudanzas with a conspiracy attack on the United States by changing the weather patterns are you?"

Bell kept talking. "There were some villages burned out up there when that happened, remember? Most of us thought it was unfortunate, but there wasn't much anyone could do about it. Heck, we had firefighters from the U.S. and Canada down here fighting the fires alongside the Mexican firefighters. It was like trying to put out a warehouse fire with a water pistol."

"Keep going," Ortiz said, leaning forward in his chair.

"Here's a list of the villages that were destroyed," Bell said, tossing the paper on the desk.

Ortiz picked it up and read the names; they meant nothing to him. "What's the point?"

"I'm getting there. Mudanzas is owned by World Transportation Systems, and WTS is held by International Group Holdings, which puts us pretty much at the top of the ladder. From there we start back down the ladder, only this time on a different rung."

"Go on."

"IGH has half a dozen other branches, all legit as far as we know. One of those branches off into petrochemicals."

"Sounds reasonable enough," Ortiz responded, getting irritated at his partner's obtuseness. "You just mentioned half the oil-producing countries in the world not five minutes ago."

"True. And from petrochemicals, it's a small hop to pharmaceuticals."

"Meaning?"

"Another branch of IGH snakes down until it gets to a company called Chemicos Norte Americano, S.A. de C.V. Chemicos manufactured under license from its parent company, North American Chemical Research, Inc., a U.S. corporation located in Little Rock, Arkansas."

"Little Rock?"

"Sounds strange on the front end, but Little Rock has the air facilities and Arkansas River ports, all within a few miles of each other."

"And World Transportation Systems has terminals in both places," Ortiz concluded.

"Exactly."

"And Chemicos?"

"Chemicos produces high-grade pharmaceuticals that are sold all over the globe, including all the countries I just named."

"There's no law against that," Ortiz pointed out.

"None. But it gives IGH access to virtually every major market in the world."

"Again, being successful is not against the law."

Bell ignored the remark and continued. "IGH has access to these countries, which means Chemicos Norte Americano has access to those markets, even if the path to those markets is convoluted."

"About as convoluted as this explanation," said Ortiz.

"Stay with me," Bell said. "IGH has world access, which means Chemicos has world access and the means to transport."

Ortiz looked at Albert Bell, beginning to understand what his partner was getting at.

"Here we have facilities capable of producing just about any chemical they want, they have a means of transporting that chemical over international borders, and they have access to every major market in the world. Those markets work both ways. Let me ask you a hypothetical question. Suppose you had the means to get raw materials out of producing countries, had the facilities to refine those products, and also had the transportation systems and established markets to receive the finished product. Don't you think you would entertain the idea of producing a product with a high resale value? One that you already knew there was a demand for?"

"That's insane!" Ortiz blurted out. "But feasible. You're saying Mudanzas is supplying illegal drugs all over the world?"

Bell quickly said, "I'm not saying illegal drugs, per se, but maybe questionable substances. It all fits, even down to what I'm about to tell you. You have this corporation producing questionable substances, dangerous even. Sometimes accidents happen. If something goes wrong, you also have the wherewithal to destroy a production facility, move the production to another site, and start all over again."

"What are you talking about? Industrial accident?"

"Chemicos Norte Americano owned a plant up north. One day it was there; the next day it was gone."

"Plants come and go."

"You don't understand what I'm saying. I mean it was *gone*. Disappeared."

"That doesn't happen."

"Not under normal circumstances, no. But we're talking about a monster corporation that thinks it can do anything it wants."

"So IGH closed a plant. That's not against the law."

"No, closing a plant is not against the law. Destroying a town might be, though."

"Now I know you've lost it," said Ortiz, starting to get up from his chair.

"There's a problem, the plant has an accident, a nearby village gets contaminated, and there are fires burning all around the area. You need to get rid of the plant and the village. Why not let the out-of-control fires take credit for the destruction? You're in the clear, the problem disappears, and you can start all over again in a different location, with no one the wiser."

"*If* there was an accident, and *if* you needed to get rid of a plant, and *if* you needed to get rid of a town, *then* it might make sense. But that's an awful lot of *ifs*."

"Not *if* you work in reverse order," Bell said in a low voice.

Ortiz stood up and walked to the window overlooking Paseo de la Reforma. Traffic was heavy, as usual, in midtown Mexico City. The smog had reappeared. What Bell was saying was crazy, but he was one of the best investigators the DEA had; so if Bell believed it, then there was something to it.

"Go on," Ortiz said.

"Chemicos Norte Americano filed a petition to open a new plant in the new industrial park in Queretaro. Why? They already had a plant in Tierra Quemada. That's the name of the place, by the way. The plant in Tierra Quemada was only a few kilometers from the village of Colinas Verde. The man I got most of my information from works with a man who had family in Colinas."

"Had. You've been reciting everything in the past tense," Ortiz said.

"The plant doesn't exist anymore. Neither does the village. Both are gone, and no one seems to know what happened to them. The area is restricted and guarded by the Mexican military. No one allowed in or out. Now there's a new plant. That plant produces chemicals too. From what I could learn, the same chemicals that had been produced in the Tierra Quemada plant. Why?"

"You got a lot of information in a short time."

"Credit NAFTA for that. I have a friend over at the Bolsa de Valores. With NAFTA in effect, any company dealing outside Mexico has to file papers, construction plans, end-user documents, and environmental impact statements. The Mexican government hasn't really decided how all the paperwork should be handled, so it goes through the Bolsa."

"So your friend at the Bolsa, the Mexican stock market, has access to the papers?"

"Exactly. Once there were a plant and a village. Now neither exists. There were fires raging in and around the area two years ago, just about the time both were wiped from the face of the earth. Convenient. Now there's a new plant in a new place, producing the same stuff, with a transportation system in place and international contacts to ship and sell all over the world."

"And the new Chemicos Norte Americano plant produces . . . what?"

"Chemicals. Fertilizers and insecticides."

"And you think there's something strange going on? Drugs, maybe?"

"I don't know. Possibly. Whatever went on up there, it's worth checking out. We can do that while you get Josh to run down the guy in the photograph. There may not be any connection at all, but I wouldn't bet my last paycheck against it."

"It's a long shot," Ortiz argued.

"So's the Mexican lottery, but that doesn't stop people from playing it."

"You want to go to Queretaro?"

"And Tierra Quemada. I want to see for myself what's going on."

"You just said the Mexican military is guarding Tierra Quemada. How do you plan to get in there?"

Bell smiled. "You can think of a way, I'm sure."

"Me?"

"Sure. I wouldn't think of going up there without you."

Ortiz grinned. "You don't like to drive."

"Exactly. According to the map, it's about a six- or seven-hour drive. If we have to, we can stay in the Days Inn at Matehuala. That's about halfway between here and the border, and only an hour and a half from Tierra Quemada."

Ortiz groaned. If there was one thing he did not like doing, it was staying in Mexico's versions of United States motels.

"When do you want to leave?" Ortiz asked.

"In the morning."

"I'll get the photo up to Josh and head for the house. I'll meet you back here first thing in the morning."

"Done," Bell agreed. "It'll be like a vacation."

This time John Ortiz groaned even louder, but he didn't say a word. There was no such thing as a vacation in the high desert of the Mexican plateau. And he had a bad feeling about the trip.

Tierra Quemada

It had been another day of survival, a difficult task in the bleak high desert of northern Mexico, but one the boy had become accustomed to.

He had not wandered far from his home in the last two years, preferring the land with which he was familiar.

The last years had been hard in both a physical and spiritual sense. At times, he had the feeling that God had abandoned him, just as all the others in his life had done. Perhaps, he thought in rare lucid moments, this was the punishment he was destined to endure for whatever unrevealed sin he might have in his life. But that went against the idea of the loving God he'd heard missionaries talk about. No, this was not God's punishment; this was man's greed, and he knew from whence had come the torture he was now experiencing.

The sun was setting, and the boy had to get back to the lean-to that provided a little protection during the cold desert night.

Nights were not pleasant. The boy huddled against the cold, sleeping only in short snatches, not wanting to surrender his entire being to the creatures and spirits of the desert night.

As the boy made his way back to his makeshift shelter, his thoughts returned to the day he had lost his life as he had known it, and he once again promised himself that he would deal with those who had caused it. He knew how that would happen, for he had made preparations. When revenge came, it would be sweet.

CHAPTER NINE

Memphis, Tennessee

Jake pulled his Cherokee into the driveway of his house on North Parkway. At first he just sat there, his hands and head resting on the steering wheel, his mind processing the events of the past few hours. He glanced at the X-rays still lying on the seat beside him. Captain Dean had wanted the film; so had the NCIS agent, Kaci Callahan. He had lied to both of them. The question in his mind now was, why? It had seemed as if some invisible force had pushed the falsehoods into his mind, but that didn't make a lot of sense, did it? Was he saying that the devil made him do it? Somehow, he didn't think so.

The afternoon sun was beginning to move behind the trees, but it was still bright enough for Jake's purpose. He pulled the X-rays from their protective envelope and held the first one up to the Jeep's window; it was the PA, the traditional chest X-ray. The abnormality was still there, bright and angular—man-made—defying identification. With just the PA, Jake might have dismissed the object. It appeared to be a normal heart pacemaker. Unusual for such a young soldier, but not unheard of. Pacemakers had been used not only to correct heart rhythm abnormalities but to treat transient anomalies as well. The tiny device was positioned correctly, just inside the left chest wall; and from all appearances, the wire that connected to the sinoatrial node—the electrical brain of the heart—was correctly positioned also.

Jake grabbed the lateral film, the one shot from the side. Again the object showed clearly, but there was a disturbing difference. What appeared to be the wire attached to the SA node in the PA film was misplaced in the lateral shot. The wire was offset toward the body's centerline too much, and it appeared to run just beneath the rib cage. Jake tried to recall basic anatomy. Surely, if this were a traditional pacemaker, the wire would have had to be placed closer to the node, not where it appeared to be in the second X-ray. If it was not there to regulate the heartbeat, then why was it there? The X-rays had been of considerable interest to Captain Dean. Was the device the reason Captain Dean wanted the film? What made the small object in Jerry Wallace's chest so important?

Jake pushed the X-rays back into the protective envelope. His first thought had been to drive to the VA Med Center, page Dr. Caroline Rhodes, and show the chief of staff the X-rays. She had more experience than he did, and perhaps she knew what the strange object was. That was still an option, but there were other options as well.

It was slightly embarrassing that he'd not thought of it earlier. His first stop would be Branch Medical Center and Jamie Parker. The corpsman from Indianapolis who had brought Jerry Wallace to see him yesterday morning would have some answers. That much was certain. Jamie had known about what he called the X-files. The young corpsman knew that such files were the exclusive domain of Captain Dean. Enlisted men always knew more about what was going on than the officers gave them credit for.

Jake checked the time. Branch Medical Center personnel would be off-duty in about an hour. He slid the X-ray envelope under the small Bible still resting on the seat beside him. For a moment, he felt the familiar pain of loss over Kathy's death. His hands went to the steering wheel again, and he dropped his head onto his hands. A heavy sob escaped from deep within his chest. He reached over and picked up the small book, holding it close to his chest. When he had the time, he told himself, he would go through the Bible page by page, reading what his wife had written in the margins. Words would be a poor substitute for the love and understanding she had provided in his life, but it was all he had now.

Jake carefully placed the Bible on the seat and backed out of the driveway. As he drove, he refined his plans. He would catch the young corpsman, Parker, as he came out of the medical center building, talk to him about the X-files and Captain Dean, then make the trip over to the VA Med Center, catch Dr. Rhodes, and show her the X-rays. Then, if there were still questions, he could drive to Madison Avenue and talk to the doctors at the Regional Forensic Center.

Jake wanted to be present at the autopsy. He wanted to see what came out of Jerry Wallace's chest. He was convinced that the object appearing on the X-rays was not a simple pacemaker. Perhaps Dr. Rhodes would dispel his doubt, but he still would be present for Jerry's autopsy. Jake felt he owed the young soldier that much.

■ ■ ■

Kaci Callahan found the recurring memory of Lieutenant Commander Jake Madsen disquieting, exciting, and . . . annoying. It was not that she disliked men. Quite the contrary. She had been popular in high school and college. But she had become interested in what most men considered a male-dominated profession, and most of the men she came in contact with were in the line of duty.

But there had been something about Jake Madsen, something in his eyes, a sadness that seemed to flow from deep within. Even as thoughts of the doctor filtered through her mind, one other detail rose to the surface: he had been wearing a wedding band.

Kaci was not sure why that bothered her. She had only met Jake a few hours ago, and the encounter had been brief. But as Kaci watched the crime-scene photographers finish their grisly task, it had been enough time for the image of Jake Madsen to be burned into her mind. What was it about the man? Certainly he was handsome; his physique suggested a love of competition and athletics. And he must be intelligent; he was a doctor.

Still, she was surprised at herself. This was not her normal reaction, especially to a man who might be part of an investigation. It was all very unsettling.

Kaci waited until all the photographs were taken and the firemen were rolling their hoses. Alan Freeman had released Wallace's body for transportation to the Regional Forensic Center office. Kaci got in her car and headed east on Navy Road, away from the apartment complex, and toward NAVSUPACT. She wanted to check in with her office, then she would walk across Essex Street to Branch Medical Center and request the medical file on the dead sergeant. The medical examiner would need the dental chart from the file to identify the body. She would personally carry the chart to the Forensic Center office.

Kaci had seen two autopsies in the line of duty—one during her training in Glyncoe, Georgia, and the other while she was working out of the Mayport Naval Station field office, in Mayport, Florida. Neither had been particularly pleasant. Both victims had died under questionable circumstances, but the bodies had been intact, not much more than clinical cadavers. The gruesome event had been the actual cutting into the human body. It had not been her favorite way to spend an evening, but bearable. In the case of Jerry Wallace, the body was anything but undamaged, and Kaci found herself wondering how she would react.

As she turned off Navy Road into the base, she realized that her hands were shaking slightly. She tightened her grip on the steering wheel, hoping the increased pressure would control the tremor. It didn't. She tried to force the image of Wallace's body from her mind. She had hidden her feelings from Alan Freeman while in the burned-out apartment, but now the full impact of the sight came crashing in on her. Even more repulsive had been the realization that one human being could heartlessly do such a thing to another. She did not know if Wallace had felt anything. Probably not, she concluded, but still, it was a horrible way to die, and if not for the victim, then certainly for those left behind.

Kaci pulled her car into the parking space, and in seconds she was climbing the stairs that lead to the second floor of the building where all the offices of the Naval Criminal Investigation Services were located. The small outer waiting room was empty, and the secretary, who was located behind a sheet of bulletproof glass, buzzed her through the door that led down the long corridor where her office was located. The door locked automatically behind her as she stepped through. Not only was the glass bulletproof, but the outer walls were lined with metal thick enough to repel even the largest caliber bullets. The NCIS did not take chances.

Her office was the third cubicle on the right, on the wall that faced away from the street. She sat down heavily, fatigue washing over her. After a few seconds, she reached for the phone and dialed the number for the Branch Medical Center's records office. When the phone was answered, Kaci identified herself and told the corpsman on duty that she would be over to retrieve the medical and dental files on Sergeant Jerry Wallace. There was a pause on the other end of the line, and Kaci wondered exactly what the problem was. Then the corpsman explained that the file she was requesting was a "special access" file, and that she would have to see the commanding officer of BMC to get the file. The NCIS agent was nonplussed by the explanation. She had dealt with restricted access files before. While it was true none of the previous files had been medical or dental files, they had still been restricted, and she had had no problem acquiring access to them. Kaci wondered briefly what could be so important in a medical file.

"Let me speak with the captain, sailor," Kaci said.

"I'm sorry, but the captain is out of the clinic at the moment," the answer came back.

"When will he return, sailor?" Kaci asked, her tone of voice carrying with it a slight sign of irritation.

"I'm not sure, ma'am," the corpsman answered.

"I'll be right over. Please inform your executive officer that I need to talk with him about the file, corpsman." Kaci hung up the phone and stared at the instrument. "Special file?" she repeated to herself. *Interesting,* she thought. *Very interesting, indeed.* She got up from her desk and headed for Branch Medical Clinic.

Howard Air Force Base
Republic of Panama

The C-130 sat on the tarmac of Howard Air Force Base. The base was situated on the west bank of the Panama Canal, sandwiched between the canal and the Pacific Ocean. Despite the restrictions imposed by the 1977 Panama Canal Treaty, the United States Air Force, with the permission of the Panamanian government, still operated transport aircraft from the field. Contingency plans, detailed in the treaty, called for the use of the air force base should U.S. troops be required to defend the Panama Canal against aggressors, both "foreign and domestic." Most Panamanians did not understand "domestic" to mean their own citizens, although that is exactly what the governments had in mind when that portion had been added to the treaty.

This particular Hercules—the C-130's nickname—was assigned to an air national guard unit from Fort Smith, Arkansas. The flight plan called for intermediate stops at Soto Cano Air Base in Honduras and Jacksonville Air Force Base in Jacksonville, Arkansas. The plane would cross into United States air space just west of New Orleans, refuel in Jacksonville, then continue on to Andrews Air Force Base just outside Washington, D.C. There, the plane would be met and the cargo transferred to a properly identified government agent. Then the C-130 would return to Fort Smith, all without the Herky Bird's crew ever touching the ground themselves.

The cargo was strange, at least as far as the enlisted loadmaster was concerned. It didn't make a lot of sense to use a huge cargo plane like the C-130 to transport something that could have fit into a small training aircraft. One thing was certain, this trip did not require the services of a trained loadmaster. It would have been better, thought the Air Force sergeant, to send a mail room clerk. The "package" was nothing more than a large ice chest, the kind that could be purchased at any base exchange. The chest had been delivered from Gorgas Army Hospital, placed near the forward bulkhead, and securely fastened. It was sealed with a lock to which the loadmaster was *not* given a key. That, thought the loadmaster, might have been the only concession to security, and he had to admit it was the first ice chest he'd ever seen with a security lock. But the chest was easier to transport than a couple of humvees or a company of airborne troops.

The loadmaster already knew the route and the time it would take to complete the assigned task. A computer had spit out the orders, along with the routing and time sequences. Sometimes, the loadmaster thought, computers just took it on themselves to do too much, but with luck, he thought, he would be back in Arkansas in time to catch his son's Little League ball game.

The Pink Zone
Mexico City

Located in *Zona Rosa*—literally, the Pink Zone—just off Paseo de la Reforma, Rafaelos was an Italian restaurant popular with tourists. The outdoor dining room offered the sights and sounds of a cosmopolitan city, as well as some of the best Italian cuisine in the city.

The sidewalk cafe also offered one other advantage, which gave John Ortiz and Joshua Gamez exactly what they needed for their meeting: the inability of interested parties to record the conversation. Traffic passing within a few feet of the sidewalk cafe effectively masked speech and rendered most recording equipment useless.

Ortiz sat across from Gamez, Mexico City's CIA station chief. Gamez had walked up Calle Londres from one end while Ortiz had come from the opposite. The DEA agent thought the precautions slightly theatrical, but the meeting had been called by Gamez, and the ground rules were his. Spooks would always be Spooks.

Ortiz thought the timing fortuitous. He and Bell were scheduled to head north toward Tierra Quemada and Queretero in a few hours. John had been packing for the trip when his phone rang. It had been Gamez, asking to meet, but not in the Embassy. *That* meant the station chief had something important to tell him. Contrary to popular belief, most of the employees within the city's largest embassy were Mexican nationals, not U.S. citizens, and the walls had ears.

"What's this about?" Ortiz asked after they had been seated and while he read through the menu. He saw no need to pass up a meal of the finest handmade Italian pasta, especially since the cost would be borne by his generous expense account.

Josh Gamez was reading the same menu. The position of the menus, both held high, precluded someone reading the two men's lips. Paranoia was a basic staple of CIA and DEA agents. Paranoia kept them alive.

"I've got an ID on the photo Al sent up," Gamez said noncommittedly.

"Interesting, I take it," Ortiz responded, the menu still held high.

"The name 'Zedillo' mean anything to you?" Gamez asked.

Ortiz felt his pulse quicken. He lowered his menu slightly, peering over the top edge at Gamez. The station chief had a smile on his face.

"Yeah," Gamez affirmed, knowing Ortiz had recognized not only the name but the significance. "Same family too. Not some distant cousin either. The guy in the photo is the president's brother."

Ortiz waited for the rest. He knew Gamez had a little of the theatrical in him, and besides, Ortiz didn't want to appear *too* interested. There was such a thing as intra-agency rivalry.

"His name's Abraham Solis Zedillo Hernandez. *Brigadier General Abraham Zedillo*," Gamez said slowly, dropping the man's second last name of Hernandez since most people from outside Mexico did not understand the need for the name in the first place.

Ortiz restrained his curiosity, saying nothing.

Gamez continued. "He's the president's youngest brother. Word is that the only reason he's a career military officer is because *that's* where he could do the least harm. It keeps him out of his brother's hair."

"That tells me *who* he is," Ortiz said, emphasizing the unspoken.

"But not the *what, where, when,* or *how?*" Gamez grinned.

"Why do I get the feeling that you're going to string this out as long as possible?" the DEA agent asked.

Gamez's grin widened. "It's been a long time since the CIA could give you DEA guys something absolutely original, and I'm enjoying myself."

"Spill it, Josh," Ortiz ordered, good naturedly.

"OK. General Zedillo is, as I just said, the brother of the president of Mexico. Sort of a Roger Clinton-Bill Clinton relationship. It turns out that President Zedillo needed a place to pigeonhole brother Abraham, and the Mexican military is really good about providing just such a place. The word on the street is that not even the president knows what goes on with that side of his family. Out of sight, out of mind. Unfortunately, brother Abraham is not the type to sit back and enjoy the largess of the gentleman army officer. The pay is not that great, and it's not very regular either. It's not unheard of in the military down here to provide one's self with a secondary income."

"Legal or otherwise," Ortiz added.

"Exactly. And since the latter usually offers greater benefits, that's the one Abraham chose."

"Drugs?"

"I'm getting to that," Gamez waved his index finger sideways at Ortiz, affecting the Latin gesture. "The other word is that Abraham was sent down to Chiapas to help quell the Zapatista uprising, and he came away from that experience with anything but the Mexican Medal of Honor."

"Contacts?"

"In a word, yes. But probably *not* the kind you're thinking of. I'm not sure this will fall within the jurisdiction of the CIA or the DEA. But about two years ago, while Zedillo was in command of a battalion down in Chiapas, something took place that never made the news, either here or in the States."

"Wait a minute. You just said a battalion. I thought Zedillo was a general."

"You catch on fast. He was a general, but it seems he wasn't competent to command even a battalion. Normally a colonel would have command responsibility at the battalion level, but the powers-that-be gave it to Zedillo. Sort of a slap on the wrist, as it turns out. Our boy Abraham was furious at the affront. And what better way to get even than to make a few million dollars out of it."

"There's only one way to make that kind of money that quickly," Ortiz argued.

"Maybe yes, maybe no. Zedillo found a very profitable avenue. Remember what happened two years ago down there?"

Ortiz thought for a moment. While he was thinking, the liveried waiter came, took both orders, and disappeared back into the restaurant proper. Ortiz picked up a breadstick and bit into it. Then suddenly, with a mouth full of bread, he said, "The massacre."

"You got it," Gamez confirmed. "Remember those stories that came out of the south? Rumors mostly. Never confirmed, except by some farmers."

Ortiz put the breadstick down; his pulse had accelerated again.

"Word was that someone down there had used chemical weapons on the Zapatistas. Killed hundreds, if I remember correctly. Even spread over into northern Guatemala and killed some of the Ketchi Indians. I don't remember anything being confirmed though," Ortiz added.

"Nothing ever was confirmed. As a matter of fact, it was hushed up about as well as anything can be down here. Heavy equipment moved in, buried the bodies, and disappeared. If it hadn't been for the Guatemalan government, I wouldn't even know this much. What I know comes out of our Zone One office," Gamez said, referring to one of Guatemala City's seventeen divisional zones. "The station chief in Guatemala City got wind of the Ketchi deaths and investigated on his own. An entire village of Ketchi was wiped out along the Usumacinta River. Whatever had been used on the Zapatistas drifted across the border. Chemicals have a way of not recognizing geographical boundaries, and the Mexicans could not cross the border to bury the evidence in Guatemala."

"Sloppy," Ortiz concluded.

"Very," Gamez agreed. "Anyway, the Guatemalan station chief discovered the Ketchi village. He was able to get some tests run on the q.t. Turns out that Zedillo used a type of sarin on the Zapatistas. Not the same stuff used in the Tokyo subway either. This stuff was supposedly ten times as deadly."

Ortiz felt his mouth drop open as Gamez narrated what could have only been the worst kind of nightmare. "Holy smokes, Josh! The man must be a nut case! You can't do that sort of thing these days! And anyway, where did he get the stuff?"

"You can do it if you've got the right backing, and the source is part of the story you will want to know."

"Yes?" Ortiz asked, sweat now beginning to form on his brow despite the cool, Mexico City temperature.

"The sixty-four-thousand-dollar question, or questions. It happened. What I've just told you is classified so highly, you couldn't get the information if you were the President of the United States or the devil himself. And this conversation doesn't go any further either. Whatever you do, you need to understand I'm not involved."

Ortiz started to say something, but the waiter arrived with the food, and he waited until the man had served the meal before continuing.

"I don't understand, Josh. You're telling me this, and in the same voice you're telling me I can't use it."

Josh Gamez held up one finger for emphasis. "No. That's not true, John. I'm saying that if this conversation ever comes up, I don't know a thing about it. I will, if necessary, testify in a court of law, under oath, that this conversation never took place, and that I consider you to be the worst kind of heretic."

"But . . ."

"But," Gamez continued, "what you do with the information is your problem."

Ortiz shook his head. "I don't think I see the connection, then. DEA isn't concerned with chemical warfare, no matter how obscene it is."

"Maybe not," Gamez said. "But DEA *is* concerned with a certain company in a certain northern state here in Mexico. That company is associated with a moving company named Mudanzas Mundial, the same company our friend Abraham Zedillo is seen entering in the photograph Al Bell sent me. A company that used to exist in one location but now exists in another will also be of interest. And, in addition to that, the DEA, if they are not already interested in a certain Mexican village that no longer exists, will be interested in that village before too much longer."

"Colinas Verde," Ortiz whispered, his blood suddenly chilled by the prospects.

"Eat your pasta, John," CIA station chief Gamez said.

John Ortiz looked down at his spinach fettuccini; he was no longer hungry.

■ ■ ■

The C-130 belonging to the Arkansas Air National Guard had been gone only ten minutes when a second Hercules transport landed at Howard Air Force Base in the Republic of Panama.

This time the cargo was much different. Seven coffins, all a neutral gray in color and lined up in the back of a five-ton truck, waited for the second aircraft. The grisly cargo was transferred to the C-130 with little fanfare and no conversation. The loadmaster secured the coffins, notified the aircraft commander that the load was secure, and strapped himself into his jumpseat at the base of the stairs leading to the flight deck. The C-130 taxied onto the runway and accelerated toward the end of the paved strip that ended at the Pacific Ocean. When the wheels of the aircraft lifted off the tarmac, the plane had been on the ground exactly seventeen minutes.

CHAPTER
TEN

Memphis, Tennessee

The meeting had not gone well. The man had met his contact at a well-known barbecue restaurant on Poplar Avenue. As good as the world-famous barbecue had been, the meal had lost its savor during the conversation. Now the man had a short list of three names, complete with addresses, photographs, and orders that could easily cost the man his life. But that was his job, and his reputation demanded that he complete the contract.

The assassin—that's how the man thought of himself, rather than *murderer* or *killer,* for the term conveyed a certain specialization of which the man was proud—drove carefully, entering the outer limits of

NAVSUPACT's geographical boundary. It was an "open" naval facility, meaning that there were no Marine Corps guards manning the gates leading into the base, a fact for which he was most grateful. Most of the fences had been removed, and the base was open to anyone who cared to "come aboard," to use the navy term. That did not mean, the assassin knew, that he had *carte blanc* to do whatever he chose. There was still the security force to deal with.

The assassin slowed his rented car to match the posted speed limit signs. It would not do to get a speeding ticket.

The man turned left onto Oriskany Street. His circuitous route would allow him to drive past the security headquarters for a quick analysis of the security force. He expected most of the white Ford Taurus patrol cars to be parked in front of Building 237 at this time of day. It was shift change, and most of NAVSUPACT was in the process of securing the buildings for the day. A perfect time for his reconnoiter; his car would be just one among all the rest. Maybe, with luck, he would pick up one of his targets and commence his assignment this very night.

He came up to the Shields Building on his right and slowed to five miles under the posted speed limit. Several white Ford Taurus patrol units were parked there, but none directly in front of the building. Since the bombing at the Murrah Federal Building in Oklahoma City, all parking areas within fifty feet of any NAVSUPACT building had been restricted. He counted five of the white Tauruses—probably, the man thought, the entire contingent of security units. Perfect.

He turned onto Singleton Avenue and then a few seconds later onto Essex Street and into the parking lot of BMC. The lot was half full, allowing him to pull his rented car into a space between two other cars and turn off the engine.

The assassin again checked the three names on the list, then glanced at the photos. An added bonus was that one of the intended victims was a quite attractive young lady.

The man scanned the parking area; one of the listed automobiles was parked in the staff parking area. He checked his watch. This time of day, according to the information before him, there should have been two of the three cars in this parking lot. The third, belonging to the attractive one, would be parked at another building. But he could get to the lady later. One target was better than none.

He calculated that he could afford to wait thirty minutes, or until half the cars in the parking area were gone. After that, a man sitting alone in a car would become too noticeable. He would leave if that happened, and intercept two of his intended targets at their home addresses. But for now, he would wait. He had learned patience, courtesy of the United States military establishment.

■ ■ ■

Kaci Callahan paused as traffic eased at the corner of Singleton Avenue and Essex Street on NAVSUPACT, then she stepped across the street and headed for the entrance of Branch Medical Center. She noticed that the parking lot was almost half full, but patients and staff were beginning to filter out of the building. She had to dodge a couple of corpsmen exiting as she entered the building.

She found her mind wandering. As she approached the appointment desk, she realized what had her distracted: Lieutenant Commander Jake Madsen. Or at least the eyes that she thought were the saddest eyes she had ever seen. She had seen the man for how long? A few minutes at most, and at the tragic scene of a murder, no less. Was that the connection?

"Yes, ma'am," the corpsman behind the desk said.

Kaci looked up, not realizing she had reached the appointment desk. She shook her head slightly to dislodge the thoughts of Jake Madsen and turned her attention to her current task.

"Your Exec, sailor," Kaci said, showing the corpsman her NCIS identification. She noticed the reaction the ID caused in the man. It was not every day that most sailors had to deal with the Naval Criminal Investigative Service. It was, Kaci knew, a little intimidating, something akin to learning that the FBI was questioning one's grandmother.

The corpsman picked up the phone on the desk behind him and spoke for a moment. "The commander is in his office," the sailor said. "Just down the passageway, first office on the right," the corpsman pointed.

"Thank you," Kaci said, heading down the corridor, not waiting for an escort.

She knocked on the door and heard the "enter" command through the solid wood door.

Commander Russell Nettleton rose from behind his desk as Kaci entered. "Russell Nettleton," he said, holding out his hand. "Please, have a seat."

Kaci shook the man's hand, noticing that he was not much taller than she was, with thinning hair and watery eyes. She guessed him to be fifty, give or take ten years. Old for a career naval officer. She surmised that Commander Russell Nettleton was one of the career military doctors who had been shuttled into a position where he could do the least amount of damage in the time he had left before retirement was forced on him.

"What can Branch Med do for you today?" Nettleton asked, taking his seat behind the desk and trying to assume an air of authority.

"I'm investigating the death of a NAVSUPACT soldier, Commander. I just came from his apartment, which was burned out. I need to get the man's medical and dental files over to the Shelby County Regional Forensic Center for identification purposes." Kaci produced a form she had already filled out requesting the file. The form made the request official, and moved it from merely casual to required.

Commander Nettleton took the form and read it slowly. Too slowly, Kaci noticed, as if he were trying to think of a way to refuse the official

NCIS request. There was no way he could, but Nettleton would have to learn that for himself.

"This seems to be in order, Miss Callahan. I will consult with Captain Dean, and we will transfer the file as soon as possible, if that will be all right."

"That won't be all right, Commander," Kaci responded firmly. "I want the file now. I will carry it over to Regional Forensic myself," Kaci said with authority. "This case is a priority. It's a murder case, Commander." She saw the commander blanch at the statement. *What is going on here?* Kaci wondered.

"Uh, I'm not sure I can accede to your request, Miss Callahan. Captain Dean—"

"Captain Dean has no option but to *accede* to this order, Commander," Kaci shot back, hoping that Nettleton had picked up on the sarcasm in her voice. She had a dead soldier in the Shelby County morgue, and now this navy commander wanted to play games. She was in no mood to tolerate any nonsense from him or his commanding officer. "Captain Dean is not here at the moment, which means you are acting in his capacity. I have presented you with an official request for information, so my advice, Commander, would be to honor the request as quickly as possible."

"Perhaps, Miss Callahan, we should wait for Captain Dean to return—"

Kaci cut him off again. "You can wait, Commander. I can't. I want the file on Sergeant Jerry Wallace right now, if you please. I will wait right here while you get it."

"Miss Callahan," Nettleton began, "I don't think you understand what you're requesting. Wait for Captain Dean to return, and I'm sure he can explain the problems associated with this particular file."

Kaci Callahan rose from her chair, placed her hands on the desk in front of her, and leaned over to stare into the watery eyes of the commander. "I *understand* the fact that I have a dead soldier, and that

BMC is trying its best to hamper my investigation. Now you get the file, Commander, or I will walk back across the street, fill out the proper papers, and cite you with obstruction of justice in a criminal investigation. The choice is yours, Commander."

Nettleton was sweating. Although the air conditioner was humming in the background, the air had become heavy, almost stagnant. The office was oppressive.

"If this is for identification purposes only, then perhaps I can release enough information to verify the soldier's ID. Would that be sufficient?"

Kaci sat back down. Something strange *was* happening here. Already she had more questions than she had answers and *that* was disturbing. Still, her first responsibility was to verify the person who was on a refrigerated slab over at Madison Avenue.

"I'll accept the information as long as I am sure that the information is sufficient for forensic purposes."

"Fine," Nettleton said, rising from his desk. "I'll get that for you right now." He hurriedly left the office.

Kaci had no illusions now. The very fact that the man had *escaped* the office when all he had to do was push the small intercom button on his telephone was proof enough. Commander Nettleton had another agenda concerning the information she had requested. She would keep that in mind.

It took almost fifteen minutes for him to return to the office. He carried a medical file folder and handed it to Kaci. She accepted it, not bothering to examine the contents since she was certain the information that would confirm the identity of Jerry Wallace was contained within the folder. What concerned her now was what information was *not* included in the file. She would address that at a later date.

"Thank you, Commander," Kaci said. "If I need any additional information, I will let you know."

"I'm certain you will," Nettleton responded, a hint of resignation in his voice.

■ ■ ■

Cars were beginning to stream out of the Branch Medical Center parking lot as Jake pulled his Jeep Cherokee into an open space.

As he switched off his ignition, he realized a weak point of his plan to intercept Jamie Parker in the BMC parking lot: he did not know what type of car the young corpsman drove. It was possible that Jamie had already left, in which case, Jake realized, his plans would have to be reordered. Already there were no more than a dozen or so cars left in the parking area. Jake looked around, trying to decide what type of car a young corpsman might drive, but it was useless. He glanced at the small Bible on the seat beside him. He reached for it just as the front door of the Med Center opened; it was Jamie Parker. Jake's mood changed instantly.

He got out of his Cherokee and walked toward the young corpsman, intercepting him before he reached his car.

"I need to talk to you, Jamie," Jake said.

The corpsman's face changed. BMC was a small command, and the military grapevine was extremely efficient. He'd already heard about the altercation between Captain Dean and Dr. Madsen. What's more, Jamie had been reprimanded by Dean for allowing Jake to treat Jerry Wallace in the first place.

"What about, Doc?" Jamie asked.

"Jerry Wallace, and his X-file."

"Look, Doc—"

Jake held his hand up and stopped the protest he knew was coming. "Just a few minutes, Jamie. It could be important."

"Doc, I can't talk about that. Jerry—"

". . . is dead," Jake stopped the corpsman in midsentence. He could tell by the astonished look on the young man's face that he had not heard about the fire at Jerry Wallace's apartment. For Jake, it was further confirmation that something was not right.

"I . . . I hadn't heard that," Jamie replied, his voice faltering.

"Then will you talk with me?"

"OK, Doc, but not here. Not even here on base."

"You name the time and place."

Jamie Parker thought for a moment. "Overton Park. The golf course. You know it?"

Jake was not a golfer, but he knew exactly where Jamie was indicating. Overton Park Zoo was no more than a few blocks from his house, and the nine-hole executive-style golf course was located in the same complex as the zoo.

"I know it," Jake said.

"There's a bench between the second and third holes, down the path in the forest. I'll meet you there at"—Jamie checked his watch—"six-thirty."

That was more than an hour and a half, but Jake knew it was the best he could do. Something had spooked the young corpsman. "Six-thirty," he agreed. He noticed Jamie looking around the parking lot, as if he were being watched. Jake found the gesture disturbing. He waited as the corpsman got in his car and started to leave. Jamie suddenly stopped and spoke through the rolled-down window.

"And, Doc," Jamie began.

"Yeah, Jamie?"

"Change clothes. That white uniform looks like a bull's-eye from a hundred yards away."

As the corpsman pulled out of the parking area, Jake wondered why the request bothered him. The uniform was only a bull's-eye if someone were aiming at it.

As he headed for his Cherokee, he saw Kaci Callahan exit Branch Medical Center. She saw him and stopped. Jake walked over to her.

"Working on the Jerry Wallace case?" Jake asked, wondering at himself for asking the question, but relieved when she answered.

"I just got his medical and dental records. Regional Forensic will need at least the dental records to identify the body."

Jake was unable to hide his surprise.

"You're shocked," Kaci said. "I can tell."

"I didn't expect you to get the records so easily," Jake responded.

"You expected me to have problems with the records?" Kaci asked innocently.

Jake hesitated. It didn't follow that Wallace's files should have been surrendered so easily if the file was restricted. An "X-file," in Jamie Parker's words.

"Just so you'll know," Kaci continued, "I only got enough information from the files to identify the body. I don't know what Nettleton extracted from the file, but I have the feeling it was a lot. What do you know about the restricted status on Wallace's medical file?"

"Nothing," Jake said. "I only learned about the files yesterday morning. I'm not allowed to see the files either."

"We need to talk," Kaci said simply.

"When's the autopsy?" Jake asked.

"Tonight. Alan Freeman asked that it be done ASAP. I'm carrying these files to Regional Forensic myself."

"I'll meet you there tonight," Jake said.

"Eight o'clock," Kaci said.

Jake automatically did the time calculations and knew he could make the meeting with Jamie Parker at Overton Park Golf Course and still make the 8:00 P.M. date with Kaci Callahan. Jake was chagrined that he thought of the meeting with Kaci as a *date*. He felt vaguely disloyal to Kathy's memory.

"Eight o'clock," Jake agreed.

"I'll see you there," Kaci concluded, leaving Jake standing in the middle of the parking lot.

■ ■ ■

It had been an auspicious chain of events, no matter how the assassin viewed what had just occurred in the last half hour. Not only had he identified the three subjects of his current employer's interest, but he had pinpointed two locations, one quite out-of-the-way, where at least two of the three subjects would be together at one time. This information enabled him to develop a basic plan where he could complete the entire assignment by midnight tonight and be out of Memphis before the bodies were even discovered. His luck had taken a propitious turn.

CHAPTER ELEVEN

Overton Park
Memphis, Tennessee

The sun was just beginning to settle in the western sky as Jake neared the small clubhouse that served the Overton Park Golf Course.

As he moved up the walk toward the first tee, he saw a father with his two young sons about to tee off. For a moment he was surprised that they were starting this late in the day, but then he remembered the sun would not actually set until well after 8:00 P.M. Jake suddenly felt a deep sense of loss at the sight of the father and his sons. Fatherhood was something he would never experience.

The thought of his wife brought a lump to his throat. The love they had shared had been something special, almost magical.

The whack of a golf ball being struck brought Jake back to reality. He watched the father and his sons walk off the first tee and trot down the first fairway. Jake reversed direction and headed for the clubhouse. He needed a map of the golf course to find the path through the forest Jamie Parker had told him about.

Jake pushed open the door to the clubhouse. It was dark inside, even with the lights burning. Dingy was an appropriate description, Jake thought. Not at all what he expected at a golf course. A thin pall of cigarette smoke drifted above the bar that stood against the far wall. Odd tables and chairs were scattered about the room to his right. A television attached high on the opposite wall was broadcasting a re-run of the 1977 Masters on the Golf Channel. One man stood behind the bar, smoking and watching the TV.

Jake approached the bar, not exactly certain what he was seeking.

"Yeah," the man said, not taking his eyes off the television screen.

Jake noticed a small, wooden stand that contained a bundle of cards. He pulled one from the stand; it was a score card with the layout of the golf course printed on the reverse side. "Found what I'm looking for," Jake answered, worried that the man might question his right to be there. The man only grunted.

Jake quickly left the clubhouse, examining the score card as he stepped out the door and into the summer evening heat. He looked to his left, toward where the father and two sons were walking down the fairway. The score card showed the path from the second green to the third tee. It cut through the Overton Park forest, just as Jamie had said.

The entrance to the pathway reminded him of a green tunnel. He could not see the end, only the entrance. The sun had dropped lower in the sky, grazing the tops of the trees to his left, leaving the shadows deep and purple along the pathway. The air was moist and heavy. Jake checked his watch; it was 6:15, fifteen minutes before he was due to meet Jamie.

Jake entered the shadowed pathway leading through the urban forest. He had changed into a sport shirt, khaki slacks, and a pair of well-worn cross-trainers. Perspiration ran down his back, and he could feel a cool ring beginning to form just at the waistband of his slacks. The shadows grew longer, the light fading quickly within the leaf-formed corridor. Jake was uncomfortable, and he increased his pace. The quicker he could get to the other end, the better he would like it.

The path turned at a right angle toward the third tee. A single bench sat at the edge of the forest. Jamie Parker sat on the bench.

Jake felt a sense of relief wash over him. Jamie rose from the bench as Jake approached. The young corpsman had changed from his white uniform into a pair of denim jeans, a denim short-sleeved shirt, and running shoes. His eyes continually darted from right to left, as if searching for some unseen danger.

Jake found himself on alert too. He felt his pulse quicken but shrugged off the feelings.

"OK, Jamie," Jake began as he neared the corpsman, trying to ignore the unsettled feeling, "what's the story?"

"Good to see you, too, Doc," Parker shot back.

"Don't give me that," Jake continued as he approached the bench and the corpsman. They both sat down. "You got me involved with this when you wanted me to treat Sergeant Wallace yesterday. You *owe* me an explanation."

The corpsman shook his head. "I know, Doc. I appreciate your willingness to help. Don't think I don't. But what I know really isn't that much. Besides, you said Jerry was dead."

"He is. At least we're pretty sure he is."

"What do you mean?"

"It was an apartment fire. The body was not a pretty sight. It's going to take dental records to identify the body, but it's a good guess right now that it is Jerry. I'm sorry, Jamie," Jake finished, surprised at the corpsman's expression of genuine concern.

"That explains the NCIS agent, then," Jamie said, almost to himself.

"Her name is Kaci Callahan," Jake supplied.

"She got some of the file, but not all of it. Word is in the clinic that Commander Nettleton released only enough information for identification purposes."

"That's pretty much the story. I met her just after I talked to you at the clinic earlier this afternoon."

"Captain Dean reamed me out pretty good about getting you to treat Jerry," Jamie said. "I guess he dumped you for the same reason."

"Yeah, you're probably right. He wasn't happy with either of us, and I need to know why. His reaction wasn't logical. What's going on with Jerry Wallace that makes his medical file so restricted?"

Jamie nervously looked around now, as if someone else might hear what he was about to say.

"Come on, Jamie. Maybe I can help."

The young corpsman shook his head. "You're not in a position to help either of us, Doc. You don't know what you're asking."

"So enlighten me."

Jamie cleared his throat.

"Start with what you know about Jerry and his file," Jake suggested, hoping to break the deadlock.

Jamie cleared his throat again. "Jerry was being studied," he said bluntly.

"Studied? In what way?"

Jamie shook his head again. "I'm not sure," the corpsman hesitated, looking down at his hands. "That's one of the things the captain keeps pretty much secret."

"Tell me about Captain Dean, then," Jake suggested, trying to find a better starting point.

"The captain keeps the records," Jamie began. "There's a secure filing cabinet in his office. It stays locked most of the time. There are a few others who have access to the filing cabinet. Commander Nettleton, the exec, the senior chief, and the administrative petty officer can get into the cabinet. That's how I got Jerry's file for you yesterday. The chief keeps his key inside his locker in the dressing room. I sort of 'borrowed' it."

"And those are the only people with access to the files?"

"As far as I know."

"How many files?"

"Only five. I've never seen any of the others. Only Jerry's."

A noise filtered down the pathway leading from the second green. Both Jake and Jamie stopped at the sound; they stared into the deep shadows, seeking the source of the sound. Muted footsteps filtered from within the overgrowth.

Three figures emerged from the dimness: the father with his two sons. They were talking and joking as they made their way toward the third tee. Jake saw Jamie visibly relax as the three moved past the bench. When the three golfers reached the distant third tee, Jake returned to his questioning.

"So Jerry's is the only file you've seen?"

"That's it, Doc. I'm not even sure who the other files belong to. Like I told you this morning, Jerry is . . . was a friend."

"Then let's talk about Jerry. What do you know about him? About his condition?"

Jamie shifted on the bench, turning his back to the tee where the father and sons had just teed off. "Pretty much the same as you saw, Doc. Usually exhibits some type of respiratory distress. Normal temp, pulse rate, and blood pressure. The works. The only abnormality seemed to be the respiratory problem. There are blood tests, but I've never seen the results. You're the first one I know of who has taken X-rays and not immediately had them inserted in the file. Still got the film, sir?" Jamie smiled.

Jake smiled back. He could tell by the way Jamie had asked the question that he really did not want an answer.

"That's what I thought," Jamie went on.

"An 'X-file'," Jake inserted. "Why the letter X? Just so it will sound like a popular television show?"

This time Jamie took his time before answering. "There's a reason for that, but I'm not sure how accurate my information is. It's all hearsay, sir."

"I'll accept speculation, Jamie. I need to know what's going on."

Jamie opened his mouth to speak just as another sound escaped from the deepening shadows of the surrounding forest. This time neither Jake nor Jamie paid much attention to the sound until the wooden bench next to Jamie Parker's left shoulder shattered into a thousand splinters! A bullet had exploded into the wood, missing the corpsman by less than a inch!

Central Mexico

"We're not going to make Matehuala by nightfall," John Ortiz told Al Bell as the two moved north from Mexico City on Highway 57.

"We'll drive till we get there," Bell responded.

"You ever drive this road at night?" Ortiz asked.

"Bunch of times. Even before the government finished all the cuotas," Bell answered, referring to Mexico's four-lane toll roads that resembled the interstates in the United States. "Even drove the libres more times than I care to remember. Driving those public roads was exciting. You never knew when you would run up on a donkey or horse in the middle of the road. Mostly people saw them too late. Eighteen-wheelers would pass down the middle of the two-lane road and expect you to get off on the shoulder. Passing three wide on a two-lane road can get pretty interesting. Worked pretty well too," Bell continued. "Shoot, you get the timing down, you could drive from Mexico City to the border in less than ten hours. Driving these four-lane cuotas is better than driving the freeway system in the States. The transports won't pay the high tariff, so we pretty much get the four-lane to ourselves."

"You're the expert on this trip, Al," Ortiz said. "Just get us there in one piece."

Bell chuckled at the remark, knowing all the time that the statement contained more truth than fiction. The road from Mexico to the Texas border *was* dangerous.

"What about the meeting with Gamez?" Bell asked.

Ortiz looked out onto the high desert just outside his window. "That's an interesting twist. We may just have time for me to tell you what Gamez told me before we get to the motel."

Bell stole a glimpse at his partner, then concentrated on his driving.

As a brown landscape shot by outside the car for the next hours, John Ortiz told Al Bell what the CIA station chief in Mexico City had relayed to him.

When he was finished, neither man spoke. Bell broke the silence. "Are we in over our heads?"

John Ortiz didn't answer for a moment, then when he did, it was in a low whisper. "I don't know, Al. I pray not."

Memphis, Tennessee

Kaci Callahan muttered under her breath. She'd been stuck in a traffic jam for more than an hour. The line of traffic behind her was out of sight. From the looks of the billowing column of black smoke, Kaci knew that even if the disaster she could not see were cleaned up in five minutes, it would be an hour before the traffic would move. She was going to be late for Jerry Wallace's autopsy.

Kaci pulled the Wallace medical file out of her briefcase and opened it. It was a bare-bones file with nothing more than personal history, generic data, and the single-sheet dental record used by every U.S. military organization. For a moment, she thought about her argument that NCIS cars should have been equipped with fax machines as well as the radio that now hung useless beneath the dashboard. With a fax, she would have been able to send the dental chart to the Regional Forensic Center.

Kaci began reading the file. Much of the dental jargon was like reading shorthand: it held no meaning for her. There were a pair of small X-rays attached to a cardboard holder, along with a full set of dental X-rays. She extracted the X-rays and gazed at them using the setting sun streaming in her righthand window as backlighting. The small X-rays reminded her about the X-rays Jake Madsen had mentioned, and she wondered about those. As she replaced the small X-rays, she noted a small comment scribbled in pencil just beneath where the two small films had been attached. It read, "No X-ray exposure without prior consent". There was no notation as to where such authorization should come from. The obscure note bothered Kaci. It also reminded her of Jake Madsen.

Lieutenant Commander Jake Madsen. She had had every intention of having Kerry Hartford access the doctor's personnel file from the BUPERS computer. She had never, in all her years with NCIS, done such a thing, but the temptation had been almost too strong to ignore.

There was something about the doctor that she could not explain. The memory of the small gold ring on Madsen's left hand haunted her. It was crazy, she knew. He was a married man. Yet never, not even when she was dating in high school and college, had she met a man who had had such a profound effect on her. What was it about the man that made him stick in her memory?

Kaci checked the clock on her dashboard: 6:30. If the fire department could clear the wreckage, she could still make part of the autopsy, at least in time to identify the body. And if she made the autopsy, then she would see Jake Madsen. That thought buoyed her spirits. Kaci decided that if the simple *thought* of Jake Madsen could elicit such a feeling of euphoria, then she wanted to know more.

CHAPTER TWELVE

Memphis, Tennessee

He had missed. At the last second the excited shout of a young boy scream-ing somewhere on the golf course had disrupted his aim, and the bullet speed-ing from the silenced muzzle of the Glock 10-mm automatic had smashed into the wooden bench just to the right of where he had been aiming. His second shot had found its target, but it had not been a killing shot. The corpsman was on the ground, but he was moving, assisted by the doctor.

The assassin rolled to his left and stood up, using a thick oak tree to cover his movement. He started for the bench. Since neither of the men he sought would be armed, he could take them easily enough, but he would have to do it quickly.

Province of Kosovo
Near the Macedonian Border

Colonel Frank Melhart sat in the commander's seat of the Bradley Fighting Vehicle, keenly aware that by doing so he was totally back in his element. Melhart considered himself a warrior, and warriors were born to fight, to command, *to battle.* As chief of staff for Special Operations Command, Central Command, he had been sent TDY to Kosovo—part of the former Yugoslavia and still one of the hottest flashpoints in the world—as an observer with the specific assignment of observing the movements and tactics of the new Independent Kosovo Police Force. It was not an easy assignment and one that he wished would end sooner than the month that was scheduled.

The Bradley was attached to a unit of a peacekeeping force that had been inserted into Kosovo earlier in the year. This NATO force, consisting mainly of British SAS forces, was halted on a mountain road above a deserted village that sat in the valley below. From where Melhart sat in the north, he overlooked what appeared to be paradise.

The valley was green. A small river twisted across the valley floor, beginning in the upper left corner—the northeast—and meandering toward the upper right—the northwest. The village was located in a small bend, straddling the river. At the point where the river entered the village, the view of the water was obscured by the buildings until it exited the village on the near side and continued to the northwest, finally cutting a passage through the mountain ridge at that point.

From a distance the town appeared idyllic. The sun reflected off the whitewashed walls of the houses and stores below, the brightness almost blinding, even from a distance. Dark roofs offered a counterpoint to the brilliant walls and the dusty streets. Somehow, the village had escaped the carnage the Serbian police force had heaped on most villages in the area. Melhart could almost feel the coolness he knew could be found in the thick walls of the structures below. There was only one thing missing, as far as Frank Melhart could tell: there was no evidence that a single living soul occupied the village.

"Is that the correct village, Major Higgenbothem?" Melhart asked the SAS major standing next to him on the outside of the Bradley.

The major referred to the map he carried, checking the Global Positioning System readout in the Bradley against the latitude and longitude he'd recorded in his notebook. "That's it, Colonel. Seems we may have a problem."

Colonel Melhart thought ruefully that Major Henry Higgenbothem had just demonstrated the British knack for understatement. The village below should have been occupied by the nearly one thousand residents.

"The reports are true?" Major Higgenbothem asked quietly, the concern in his voice mirrored in his eyes.

"I don't know, Major," Melhart answered slowly. "The only way to find out will be to go in. I have to admit, I'm afraid of what we're going to find in the village."

"The Serbs?"

"I don't know, Henry," Melhart said. "We should wait until we get into the village."

"The sooner the better," the British major urged.

"Let's move out, then," Frank Melhart suggested, knowing he had no power to order the major into the village.

The abbreviated motorized column moved down the dry road, snaking around the mountain and heading for the abandoned village. It took the column less than fifteen minutes to reach the outskirts, where Major Higgenbothem halted the advance.

"What do you think?" Higgenbothem asked Melhart.

The colonel hopped down from the Bradley on which he'd been riding and walked fifty yards forward of the halted vehicles. There was no evidence of movement of any kind. Melhart stood for a long minute, scanning the village. Something was not right. Worse than that, something was *very wrong!* You could *guess* when something was not right, but the feeling of something being wrong was a feeling that set off warning bells and snatched at your gut.

The first confirmation that Colonel Melhart was right was the air-burst explosion less than a hundred yards from the armored column. A second air-burst exploded fifty yards closer at an altitude of less than five hundred feet.

Already the British SAS troops were scrambling to button-up the Bradleys; there was only one reason for the airburst of less than lethal magnitude, and every man in the column knew what that was.

Colonel Melhart watched the explosions with a cool detachment he would not have thought possible. He knew as well as the SAS troops what the airburst meant, and he also knew he had been caught out in the open and the odds of his survival were somewhere in the neighborhood of one in a million.

The first effects of the chemical caused Melhart's body to jerk spasmodically; his breath was expunged in a massive muscle spasm that wracked his body with more pain than he could ever remember experiencing. The muscle spasms lasted mercifully less than thirty seconds; Colonel Melhart was dead before the last commander's hatch was closed on the Bradley Fighting Vehicles behind him.

The engines of the Bradleys were running. To a man, the drivers hoped they could at the very least move the vehicles out of the chemical's range while the rest of the troops ripped at the gas masks carried in pouches mounted near each man's station. Normally it required less than two seconds to don the gas mask. Training exercises had ensured the speed necessary to save a trooper's life in a normal chemical attack. Unfortunately, "normal" did not apply to the chemical that had just been released by the airburst explosions.

The Bradleys would be discovered three hours later, their motors still idling, when another patrol rolled into the deserted village looking for the NATO peacekeeping force that had failed to respond to extensive efforts to contact them. The bodies were removed from the BFVs and moved to a makeshift morgue where each man was unceremoniously put in a black body bag, loaded onto an Air Force C-140, and airlifted to Andrews Air Force Base after an intermediate stop at Ramstein Air Base, Germany.

The C-140 was met, the bodies transferred to a refrigerated truck, and the truck driven off the air force base—its destination, a sprawling single-story building on the outskirts of Alexandria, Virginia. The facility was funded through multiple riders to appropriation bills that were all innocuous enough to ensure that not a single congressman would show any interest in the relatively small amounts represented by the riders.

An announcement would be made in two weeks, detailing the deaths of the men on the SAS patrol. NATO would publish a list of the men who died, but not before every family member of the dead men had been notified. Only one name was that of a United States soldier: Colonel Frank Melhart. The rest of the bodies were shipped back to England for burial, after first verifying that the bodies could be safely handled without protective gear.

The death of the SOC Central Command chief of staff would send shockwaves throughout the United States military community. The death of Colonel Frank Melhart and the unquenchable curiosity of a Reserve Navy doctor and an NCIS agent in Memphis, Tennessee, would begin the demise of a most hideous organization. Yet before that happened, more people would die.

Overton Park Golf Course
Memphis, Tennessee

The second bullet ripped through Jamie Parker's left shoulder. Jake Madsen pulled the wounded corpsman down and away from the bench where they had been talking. The first bullet had taken Jake by complete surprise. There was only a muffled pop that Jake now knew had been the sound of the silencer. Before the muted sound or the splintered bench had registered in his mind, a second pop had driven the next 10-mm slug into Jamie's shoulder. The blood had spurted out, bright and red, washing over the corpsman's shirt and staining his jeans. Jake knew immediately that the young sailor's brachial artery had been severed. He would have to act fast to save the young man's life, but there was a problem. The killer was still stalking them in the Overton Park forest.

Jake could distinguish movement now. He had taken refuge behind a large oak tree growing next to the bench. He peered out from behind the tree, searching the shadows for the source of the gunfire.

The sun had fallen to just above the horizon. The tree line was masking the sun's rays, lengthening the shadows and darkening the forest floor. With darkness would come the hope of salvation, but Jake realized that he and Jamie might not make it to nightfall.

A third bullet slammed into the tree just to the right of Jake's head. Inside of four seconds, five more bullets snaked out of the darkness, seeking targets other than the oak and pine trees of the forest. Jake swung around, shifting position, pulling Jamie with him. More bullets found the trees, thumping into the soft wood; some sped deeper into the forest. Jake could hear the tree limbs snapping as the bullets shattered the green stems and the noise echoed back from the darkness.

A shuffling sound came from his left. Jake shifted his and Jamie's position yet again, reacting now to every sound. More bullets raced out of the darkness, smashing into tree trunks to Jake's right. He'd moved too quickly, reacting to a sound that had not been that of the shooter. He had exposed himself and Jamie!

The corpsman was moaning, the initial shock produced by the bullet's impact wearing off. Blood soaked his clothes along his left side. *Two pints!* Jake thought. Jamie had lost two pints at least, and he could do nothing.

He pulled Jamie prone, positioning him as far behind the tree as possible. Bullets pierced the growing darkness. Jake realized he would not have a chance to save Jamie's life if he could not stop the man with the silenced gun. But he had to stem the blood flow.

Jake ripped at the denim of Jamie's shirt, quickly tearing the shirt into makeshift bandages. He folded some of the fabric into layers, forming emergency pressure dressings. Then he ripped the remaining material into strips. These he would use to secure the folded bandage to the wound. Jake pressed the folded material into the exposed wound; Jamie groaned. Carefully, but as rapidly as he could, Jake secured the folded bandage using the fabric strips. It was only a stop-gap measure, but it would have to do. Jake knew he needed time to work his way around behind the shooter and hopefully lead him away from Jamie. With luck, he might be able to lead the man away then work his way back to Jamie.

Jake could hear the traffic on Poplar Avenue. Car headlights were beginning to wink on. Jake could just make them out from the depth of the forest.

More bullets whizzed by Jake's head. The first one had been close. The second and third had followed the same path as the first, but Jake had scrambled further behind the tree.

He checked Jamie's pulse; it was rapid and thready. There was no way to tell how much blood the corpsman had lost at this point.

Jake checked the bandage he'd applied. It seemed to be doing the job. The blood flow had been reduced. There was still some seepage, but the corpsman's condition was stabilizing.

It was dark now. There would be no more golfers coming down the wooded path. Darkness, Jake knew, was his only ally, and he would have to use it if they were to survive.

"Don't move, Jamie," Jake whispered to the semi-conscious corpsman. "I'll be back. Just *don't move.* Do you understand me?"

There was no response other than a low moan from the sailor's lips.

"Jamie!" Jake whispered urgently. "Do you hear me?" He shook the young man. "Do you understand?"

Jamie opened his eyes. "Got it, Doc," he said through clenched teeth. "Just don't forget where you left me."

Jake smiled in spite of the circumstances. Jamie still had a sense of humor. It was a good sign, Jake knew. A sign of determination. Jake patted Jamie's shoulder. "I'll be back," he promised.

Jake looked up. The tree canopies had melted into each other in the darkness.

Jake moved now, his night vision coming slowly. Night movements had never been part of his military training, but he knew the physiology of night vision. He protected his eyes from the dim light that filtered through the forest from Poplar Avenue. Jake turned his back to the street. He kept his head low, his attention riveted deeper into the forest, his eye movement continuous to more easily pick up any movement from the depth of the woods.

The shooting had ceased. There were no more pops. No more bullets whizzed through the trees. Jake gave thanks for that until he realized that the very fact that nothing was happening meant that *something* even more lethal was occurring: the killer was working his way toward Jake!

Fear gripped him. Sweat poured from his body, soaking his clothing. A clammy feeling overtook him despite the summer heat. He needed to move, but which direction? The darkness was now so profound that Jake could not make out anything more than six feet away. A shuffling sound came from his left. Was it the killer? An animal? What? There was no way of knowing. Any movement might be seen by the man with the gun. That was probably what the killer was waiting for, Jake realized. But the killer would have to be strategically positioned to be able to catch any movement in the thick growth of the forest. Jake had a chance.

The young doctor had never felt so alone. Suddenly his thoughts went to the small Bible that lay on the seat of his Jeep, and to the passage Kathy had marked: *I can do all things through Christ, who strengthens me.* It was the first time in his life that he understood the Scripture. Jake felt a sense of peace infuse him.

He moved now, confident in his direction, knowing that shots would not come from the darkness. Death would not find him this night, he was confident. But he also knew he had to claim the Bible promise for a young sailor who lay wounded on the dark forest floor, and the only way to claim that promise was for him to carry it to Jamie.

There was movement in the distance. Jake picked it up, knowing that the source of the movement was the killer, the man with the gun. He moved toward the movement, keeping trees between himself and the source of the sound. He was certain that Jamie was somewhere off to his right, out of the possible line of fire. His strategy was working.

The forest was eerily quiet. Even the traffic sounds from Poplar Avenue seemed muted in the depths of the forest. Somewhere to Jake's right lay North Parkway and his own home. East Parkway was the connecting artery. He would try to squeeze the killer between the two traffic arteries, keeping the corner formed by the two streets on his right. The strategy would provide him with a frame of reference he hoped the killer would miss.

Jake moved now with confidence. He stumbled once, dragging a fallen tree limb behind him with his foot. He reached down and picked up the limb. It was smooth; the bark had been worn away. The limb was about four feet long and weighed almost five pounds.

God had provided a weapon.

Jake smiled at the thought, wondering if Kathy was watching over the ramparts of heaven, seeing his foolishness.

A sliver of light glinted off something in the distance, attracting Jake's attention. He moved in that direction, his footsteps light against the moist earth of the forest. He stopped periodically, listening, tuning in to the surrounding sounds of the forest, filtering the noises. There was one that did not belong, an unnatural man-made sound in a natural world, and Jake moved in that direction.

Already they were far away from where he'd left Jamie Parker. The club Jake had picked up felt good in his hands. His confidence was building.

Suddenly a bullet pounded into the tree next to his head! The killer had found him first! The bullet had come out of the dark, but from which direction? Jake dropped to the ground, rolling to his right. Small branches and sticks jabbed at him as he rolled on the forest floor. He felt tree roots rip at his clothing. Jake held onto the club.

There were footsteps now. Running, rushing, the sound of tree limbs whipped against a body rushing through the forest. A dark spectre appeared just above Jake! The killer had found him!

Jake leaped to his knees, the club held like a baseball bat. The dark mass bearing down on him came like a jungle cat rushing to the kill. Jake prepared himself, the club poised.

Suddenly the rushing form changed directions, rushing at right angles to the path he'd just been on. The man had not seen him, Jake realized. It made no difference, the man was still going to pass close by. Jake prepared himself.

The man rushed by. Jake could see the deadly pistol, the silencer protruding from the muzzle. Jake struck, the club rotating from behind him, from the hip level. The contact shook Jake to the core. It was like hitting a brick wall with a baseball bat. Something cracked; Jake was not sure if it was the club or the man's leg.

The killer screamed, the sound penetrating the night. Jake dropped the club and sprinted for the far side of the forest, seeking the place where he'd left Jamie. Bullets thumped into the trees around him, off-target, the killer's aim disrupted by the pain.

Jake sprinted through the forest despite the danger. He ignored the limbs that whipped at his clothing and face. He could see the traffic now, flowing down Poplar Avenue. Jake used the traffic as a compass, angling off the headlights, racing for Jamie.

Almost without warning, Jake found the wounded hospital corpsman. A small groan alerted him, and he slowed his flight through the trees. Miraculously, Jake realized he could see the forest floor. Jamie lay against the oak tree where Jake had left him. The young sailor had pulled himself up against the tree; his back rested against the large tree trunk. The movement had probably saved his life. The shoulder wound was now elevated, preventing, in conjunction with Jake's stopgap pressure bandage, further blood loss.

Jake knelt beside Jamie; he took a quick pulse rate. The rate was still rapid and thready, but it had not degenerated. Jake could see that Jamie's eyes were open. He had to get himself and Jamie out of the forest, and then he had to get Jamie to the Med, Memphis's only level-one trauma unit.

I can do all things through Christ who strengthens me. Jake felt the Bible verse race through his mind like an electrical charge. Was it true? He was about to find out.

Jake reached down and grasped the sailor's arm, lifting and standing at the same time. He hefted the young sailor onto his shoulder; Jamie moaned.

Jake felt energized. Whether it was the circumstance that demanded survival or the single-line Bible verse, Jake could not tell. It didn't matter. He had Jamie Parker on his shoulder and was racing effortlessly toward his Jeep Cherokee. The car came into view parked in the street beside the Overton Park Golf Course. In seconds, Jake had the corpsman in the rear seat of the Cherokee, and he was behind the wheel. He wheeled out of the park area, heading for the traffic flow on Poplar Avenue. He turned west and headed for Memphis's multihospital complex.

In ten minutes Jake pulled into the emergency entrance of the Med. Trauma nurses and doctors were on the scene in seconds. Jamie was gently removed from the rear seat of Jake's Cherokee and strapped to a gurney.

Jake followed the gurney. Suddenly Jamie's eyes flickered open; he focused on Jake and whispered, "Janus. It's Janus." The young corpsman then lapsed into unconsciousness.

Jake stopped in his tracks. What had Jamie meant? The young doctor's blood seemed to chill within his body. The single word had seemed to answer every question from Jamie Parker's point of view. The answer had been simple.

The answer had been Janus. But what was Janus?

CHAPTER THIRTEEN

The Regional Forensic Center
1060 Madison Avenue
Memphis, Tennessee

No one called it the morgue. The police, both county and city, called it simply, "the Forensic Center." There were other names, but those were used only between the policemen themselves, and never where family members could hear.

Darla Adams stood in the area reserved for body identification as an ambulance pulled into one of the two parking places reserved for the unloading of bodies. She watched the two-man team unload the contents. It was strange, she thought, and somewhat disturbing that she thought of the dead person within the ambulance as "the contents." But it came with the territory. When she'd first come to the Regional Forensic Center, she wondered if she would be able to do the job. Death seemed to hover over the building like a virulent cloud. But she had been amazed at the short time required to become completely detached. Death was a river that carried its victims, as well as the families of those victims, on a painful journey that seemed to have no end. More than once she had wondered if there really was a God, and if there was, did he know what went on in this building?

Darla was one of four autopsy technicians working at Memphis's Regional Forensic Center. The body being off-loaded at the moment would be assigned to her. She would collect all the data, do the actual cutting, and submit all the information to a staff doctor for examination and evaluation. If there was something strange or disturbing, the doctor would examine the body personally. Such exams were rare.

The ambulance crew wheeled the body into the center and onto the large scale just inside. The first task performed on any corpse entering the center was the weighing. The scale next to the viewing area was large enough to accept the gurney on which the body rested. The weight of the gurney would later be factored out.

The preliminary information on the victim, Darla had been told, was that he was a soldier from Naval Support Activity, Mid-South, and he had died in an apartment fire near the military base in neighboring Millington. That meant in addition to the 200-cc bottle of blood she normally took from the body, she would be drawing a smaller vial of blood from the victim as well. The smaller vial was a standard vacuum tube used for routine blood tests with one exception: the vial contained a small amount of sodium fluoride. Called a "NAF tube," it would be sent to the lab to determine the level of carbon monoxide contained in the blood. From this it could be determined if the soldier died from smoke inhalation. There would be, of course, a certain level of carbon monoxide in the blood of any burn victim, but the levels necessary to produce death were pretty much standardized, and the information was vital in the autopsy report process.

"OK, guys, through there," Darla pointed. The ambulance crew wheeled the gurney off the scale and headed for the large door of the huge cooler that housed other bodies on similar gurneys. There were no individual file-like cabinets at the Regional Forensic Center. None of its occupants had ever complained about the lack of privacy.

With the gurney in the cooler, Darla dismissed the ambulance crew and went to the desk situated just outside. There was a note that an NCIS agent would be in shortly to observe the autopsy. That was fine with Darla. That meant she had a few minutes to herself, and a cup of coffee would be nice. Midweek wasn't as busy as the weekend, and Darla liked the night shift anyway. It gave her additional time to study for exams. She was in her first year at the University of Tennessee Medical School, just up the street, and the relative inactivity of the weekday Forensic Center provided her with not only the finances she needed to pursue her lifelong dream of becoming a doctor but also the time to assimilate the massive quantities of information the UT professors seemed to regard as absolutely critical to that pursuit.

She would draw the blood and other fluids and wait for the NCIS agent to show up. With luck, she would get in a few decent hours of study.

And what, she wondered, was an NCIS agent?

Congressional Oversight Subcommittee Room
U.S. Capitol
Washington, D.C.

Freshman Congressman J. Fredrick Bryant, from the Second Congressional District of Iowa, flipped through the thick report that lay before him. He and the other six members of the oversight subcommittee were working late. However, the other six members seemed to know exactly what they were doing, and Freddy Bryant was determined not to demonstrate the feeling of total ignorance he felt. Freddy had, since he'd been elected, followed the sage advice of his farmer-father: better to keep your mouth shut and let people wonder if you are stupid than to open it and remove all doubt. So far, it had worked.

The report was not thick, Freddy thought, it was gargantuan. If he read the entire thing, he would be reading for the next month. Better to listen and learn what the others on the subcommittee thought were the salient points.

The subcommittee chairman cleared his throat, and Freddy closed the report. This meeting was closed, meaning that the public and the media were not allowed in the room. It still seemed ludicrous to Freddy to call a meeting *closed* when there were aides and pages filtering in and out of the room, but he was getting used to it.

"Gentlemen, this meeting will come to order," the Republican congressman from Oklahoma said, nodding at the same time to the secretary who would record every word of the "closed" meeting. Freddy wondered what would happen during the year. It was an election year, and every senator and representative up for reelection was busy posturing for the media and their constituents. As one of three Democrats on this Oversight Subcommittee, he wondered what was so important that it required a meeting in the middle of a reelection campaign. After all, this subcommittee had met only once in the previous eighteen months, and that for nothing more than orientation. It was not one of the more important committees on the Hill, with a singular function of reporting to the larger and more important Oversight Committee on the production of chemical weapons in first-world countries. Freddy had been under the impression that President Richard Nixon's executive order on November 25, 1969, had effectively stopped production of such weapons. He was shocked to learn that the Executive Order had applied only to biological weapons. Chemical weapons were still legal and apparently a high priority. There was little chance, in Freddy's estimation, that that would change. The Honorable J. Fredrick Bryant from the Second Congressional District of Iowa would be shocked by what he would learn in the next three hours.

It would also cost him his life.

■ ■ ■

Kaci Callahan could see the traffic beginning to move. The billowing smoke from the accident had ceased almost an hour ago. The police were now trying to get traffic moving once again. She checked her watch. It was almost nine o'clock, one hour past the scheduled autopsy time. Kaci glanced at the medical and dental file next to her on the seat. With luck, she thought, the autopsy would not begin without it. It would make more sense to do everything at once.

The automobiles in front of her started to move, brake lights blinking on and off. The flashes became farther and farther apart; traffic was moving.

Minutes later, Kaci saw the Madison Avenue exit. The Regional Forensic Center was housed in the former Memphis Eye, Ear, Nose, and Throat Hospital. The name was still etched into the stone facade. A yellow sign indicated it was now the Forensic Center. Further down Madison, Kaci could see the hulking shadow of Baptist Memorial Hospital. Just north of Baptist was the Med, and over on Jefferson, its new addition barely visible, was the Veterans Affairs Medical Center. The VA Med Center reminded her that she was supposed to have met Jake Madsen at the Forensic Center, and she wondered if he had already come and gone. She found herself hoping he was inside, waiting on her, and then she dismissed the thought as juvenile. Just as quickly, the thought was back, and Kaci smiled at the idea of seeing the young doctor again, even as she tried to dismiss it, reminding herself of his wedding band.

She parked her car and got out. The Jeep Cherokee Jake Madsen had been driving earlier in the day was not there, and she felt her spirits fall.

The lights were on in the building, and Kaci walked to the double glass doors where yellow light leaked out into the parking lot. A sign attached to the brick next to the doors indicated that the medical examiner's office should be accessed through the door to the north. She ignored the sign, pushed open the glass doors, and entered a small waiting room containing a door set in the wall to the left along with a square viewing window. She was in the identification area. A sign informed anyone entering that only unidentified bodies could be viewed at the facility, and only then for identification purposes. Kaci shook off the feeling of doom that seemed to ooze from the walls of the Forensic Center. Jake Madsen was nowhere to be seen.

■ ■ ■

Ambulances had been rolling into the Med for the past two hours in a seemingly unending stream. Jake Madsen had found himself entwined in the human tragedy that played itself out in the streets outside the hospital and the trauma rooms within. A tanker had overturned on the freeway, spilling its entire cargo of high-grade gasoline onto the pavement and igniting an inferno. The more seriously injured had been transported to the Med. Others, less seriously injured, had been transported to Baptist Memorial, Methodist, some children to LeBonheur over on Jefferson, and some even to Baptist East and Methodist North.

Jake had just stepped out of the emergency room, where he had left a wounded Jamie Parker, when the ambulances had begun rolling in. Now as he gathered himself, he was amazed that he had forgotten all about the young corpsman's bullet wound. The past two hours had been nothing but a blur of activity. When the doctors at the Med had learned he was a VA doctor, they had enlisted Jake's aid to treat the less seriously injured victims pouring in from the freeway accident. Jake's service had freed the trauma teams to do what they did best: save lives.

Now, as Jake stood outside the Med, he remembered not only the young corpsman but the words Jamie had spoken before disappearing into a treatment room. Jake felt a chill each time he muttered the words under his breath: *Janus. Janus?* What was it? Was Janus the reason Jamie Parker had been shot? Was that the reason someone had tried to kill both of them? Or should the question be, *who* is Janus? Somehow the last question disturbed him. It didn't make sense, but Jake was realizing that few things in the world made sense anymore—especially since Kathy had died.

She had been the one who had made sense out of the world. She believed in the existence of God, in good and evil. It all made sense to her. But Jake was a scientist. Faith was not part of his experience. He had even pretended to ignore her when she talked about the existence of God, the importance of faith, and the eternal consequences of salvation. Now he wondered if there was more to what Kathy believed than he thought.

A siren jerked Jake back to the present. He watched as yet another emergency vehicle off-loaded another accident victim. He wondered if this one was burned. Like Jerry Wallace.

Jerry Wallace! The autopsy!

Jake checked the time. It was just after 9 P.M. He was late for the autopsy at the Regional Forensic Center, and he had probably missed seeing the NCIS agent Kaci Callahan again. That thought suddenly consumed him.

Jake scrambled to his Jeep Cherokee and headed for the Forensic Center. It was only a few blocks away, and Jake could feel his pulse begin to race at the very thought of seeing the NCIS agent again. The excitement left him with a sour feeling. Was this disloyalty to Kathy? She would always be there, he knew. He would have to learn to deal with that.

The Forensic Center came into view, and Jake turned into the parking lot. There were six cars. Jake wondered if one was Kaci's, but then he noticed the white license plate with the words U.S. Government stamped into the metal. It was an NCIS car.

Just as Jake switched off the ignition, the lights went out in the Forensic Center. *Power failure,* Jake thought. But when he scanned the surrounding buildings, the lights still burned in all of them. Whatever had happened, it had happened only to the RFC building. As Jake got out of his car and started for the door of the center, a cold chill settled over him. Why were the lights out in the center and nowhere else? Something was not right.

■ ■ ■

Darla Adams had risen when the red-haired woman had entered the viewing area. It had to be the NCIS agent, even though she did not know exactly what a NCIS agent was. Darla had just stepped through the door that separated the viewing area from the body identification area when the building went dark. There was a backup system; battery powered emergency lights were supposed to illuminate the primary hallways and areas when such a failure took place. A generator situated in the basement provided emergency electricity until MLGW (Memphis Light, Gas and Water) could restore power, but it appeared as if the generator was not doing its job. Curious, Darla thought, but not too worrisome. MLGW was pretty good about getting things up and running again. The electricity would probably come on in a few minutes.

Darla had stopped in the doorway. The sudden loss of light had rendered her temporarily blind; her eyes had not adjusted.

"This happen often?" the red-haired lady asked from out of the darkness.

Darla started to laugh when something or someone brushed past her. Who was that?

"What was . . . ?" Darla began.

"What happened?" Kaci asked from the blackness.

"Something . . . someone just rushed past me," Darla answered, her voice quivering, her fear instantaneous.

"What about emergency lights?" Kaci asked, moving toward the technician in the dark.

Her voice still betraying her fear, Darla said, "They should have already come on. I . . . I don't understand it. And the basement generator should have come on too. This place has to have refrigeration."

"Yeah, I can imagine," Kaci responded, finding Darla Adams in the dark. "Where was whoever pushed past you heading?"

"I'm not sure. It happened so fast. I . . . I'm just not sure. Back down the hallway, I think. Maybe toward the basement."

"Any reason for someone to break in here? Drugs? Needles? Any of that stuff?"

Darla thought for a moment. "Sure. Needles I mean, but not sterile ones. We don't need them. And there aren't any drugs. Not the kind someone would want to steal. Nothing to get high on."

As the women stood in the darkened building, the front door of the center opened. Both women turned toward the door. A figure was framed in the dim outside light.

■ ■ ■

"What's going on in here?" Jake Madsen asked in the dark.

"Who is it?" Darla Adams asked of the dark figure.

"Dr. Madsen from the VA. I'm supposed to meet someone here."

"I'm here too, Jake," Kaci Callahan answered. "There's someone else in here too," she added quickly.

Jake moved toward the voices of the two women. His eyes were becoming accustomed to the darkness. Kaci and the technician took on a blurred form in the low light; they were huddled together just inside the door leading to the identification room.

"Someone else?" Jake asked, nearing the two women. "You mean someone who should not be here?"

"Exactly," Kaci said, stepping away from Darla. "Someone headed for the basement, maybe."

"And you think we should go after this someone?"

"I'm going after whoever it is," she said defiantly. "You can stay here if you want."

Jake reached out and grasped Kaci Callahan's arm gently. The touch was almost electrifying, and he wondered if she felt it too.

"If you're going down there, I'm going too," Jake told Kaci.

"You stay here," Kaci told the autopsy tech, then turned back to Jake. "Come on, then. Let's find out what's going on here."

With Kaci leading the way down the darkened hallway, the two made their way through the maze of hallways that was the Regional Forensic Center. The building was square, four stories, and laid out in what, under normal circumstances, would have been a logical floor-plan. But the darkness changed all that.

Kaci and Jake felt their way through the building. The old building creaked, and dark shadows crawled across the floors where dim light from the outside penetrated the interior gloom.

"Not my idea of fun," Jake whispered as they made their way deeper into the building.

"Quiet!" Kaci ordered. She was leading, her hands on the walls to avoid running into unexpected obstacles.

"Stairs," Jake said.

"OK," Kaci agreed.

The two moved down the stairway slowly, negotiating the single switch-back and ending at a closed door. A creak echoed from the other side of the door; it was not the creak of an old building settling in on itself; the noise was that of someone moving in the distance.

Kaci Callahan's hand shot out, stopping Jake in his tracks. Both had heard the noise.

Kaci reached for the doorknob, and twisted it slowly. Suddenly a scream echoed through the building, magnified down the closed stairwell!

Jake jerked his head toward the sound from above. The autopsy tech was being attacked!

Kaci and Jake both ran, realizing it had been a ruse to isolate the technician. Whatever was sought, was sought upstairs from the huge cooler.

Jake was leading now. He took the stairs three at a time despite the darkness. Kaci was behind him, taking the same stairs two at a time, but easily keeping pace. Footsteps reverberated off the concrete walls of the stairwell. Jake burst through the door at the head of the stairs, turned left, and raced down the darkened hallway.

Another scream ripped through the building. Jake renewed his efforts; Kaci matched him step for step. The two turned toward where they had left the technician. The only sound now was the pounding of their footfalls on the tile floor. Just before they reached the identification area, the lights flared on.

Jake slid to a halt. Kaci almost ran into him from behind. Both were blinded by the sudden return of illumination.

Darla Adams ran to meet them. Her eyes were wide, her face ashen under the artificial light, fear evident.

"What happened?" Jake asked, grasping the autopsy tech by the shoulders. Kaci was at his side.

The tech pointed behind her. "The . . . the cooler. They were in the cooler," she stammered.

Jake realized he'd been right. The target had been the cooler all the time! Jake raced for the huge door leading into the gurney-lined interior.

"Jerry Wallace! Where is Wallace?" Jake demanded.

"Who?" the autopsy tech asked, confusion now compounding her fear.

"The burn victim from Millington," Kaci explained as she entered the cooler.

"He was just brought in," Darla Adams explained. "Over there," she said, pointing to a gurney next to the far wall.

Jake could see that the sheet covering Jerry Wallace had been removed. Now, as he looked around the interior, Jake felt his skin begin to crawl. There were five more gurneys in the chilled room, each with a body on it. Three were uncovered. Someone had been searching for a specific body, ripping the sheets from the bodies as they went.

The last gurney, the one Darla Adams had said was that of Jerry Wallace, was also uncovered, but with a difference. Wallace's destroyed body was totally revealed, and fluid leaked onto the cooler floor from an unseen source. Jake approached slowly, reverently. There had been enough sacrilege this night; the young sergeant deserved better.

"What is it?" Kaci asked, seeing Jake approach the body.

"Give me a minute," he answered, holding his hand up for Kaci to remain where she was. He moved next to the gurney, and his eyes went to the young soldier's chest. An incision, quick and abrupt, the edges jagged and raw, had been made just under the left armpit. The skin had been retracted in haste, an instrument inserted, and something removed. Jake knew exactly what had happened. Someone had unceremoniously removed the device from Jerry Wallace's chest, the device that showed on the X-rays he'd had taken. The X-rays that were now his only proof of something foreign having been inserted in the soldier's body. The X-rays that lay on the seat of his Jeep Cherokee.

"We need to talk," Jake said over his shoulder to Kaci. "Quickly." Jake headed for the parking lot.

■ ■ ■

"Well, it's not broken," the young emergency room doctor told the man seated before him. "But it's sure going to be sore for a while. I'll give you something for the pain."

"Thanks, Doc," the dark man answered, a slight Spanish accent tainting the otherwise perfect reply.

"How did you say this happened?" the young doctor asked again while writing out the prescription for the pain medication, then turning to a medical record and writing some more.

"Tripped out my back door, just like I told the nurse," the man replied. The reply was not curt, but there was no further explanation.

"Pretty bad trip. You should be more careful. You'd better stay off that leg for a while."

"Yes, Doc, I'll be more careful next time. Much more careful."

The emergency room doctor handed the man the prescription. "You can take care of the charges at the desk."

"Thanks, Doctor," the man said, getting up and heading for the cashier's window.

The young doctor watched for a moment, marveling all the while at the amount of pain the human body could absorb. The man's legs looked as if they had been struck by a baseball bat. The right leg had been bruised and bloodied; the left had not been much better, but at least the skin had not been broken on the left one. It had taken twelve stitches to close the laceration on the right leg. The pain medicine would be needed in an hour or so when the lidocaine wore off.

It was not unusual to see Hispanics in the emergency rooms these days, the doctor mused. Memphis was said to have at least eighty-five thousand Hispanics within the city limits. But there had been something about this one, something the young doctor could not put his finger on. Maybe it had been the stoicism with which the man had endured the pain and the minor surgery. Perhaps it had been the questions concerning emergency room procedures, especially where gunshot wounds were concerned. The questions had been innocuous enough, at least at first. But they had grown more specific, more detailed, and the doctor realized now that he'd been led along in the questioning much like a small child in a kindergarten class. It had been an impressive display of applied psychology, he realized. And *that,* he now recognized, was the difference: the intelligence lurking behind the dark eyes. Not an everyday, run-of-the-mill, type of intelligence but a cunning that disguised itself behind the simple face of a not-so-simple man. The doctor scribbled the last note on the chart, looking at the name and realizing that there must be a few thousand "Juan Ramirezes" in Memphis and the surrounding vicinity. *Sort of the Spanish version of "John Smith,"* the young doctor thought before tossing the file on top of a growing stack and pulling the next from an even larger stack.

■ ■ ■

The man calling himself Juan Ramirez crumpled the prescription for the pain killer and tossed it on the ground outside the hospital emergency room. The young doctor had told him that most gunshot victims were taken to the Med, just down the street. That would be his next stop.

Juan Ramirez—the assassin—began walking, the pain in his legs reminding him that he not only had a date with a young sailor in whom he had put a bullet but also a young doctor who had almost crippled him with a *palo.* Juan wished he could find the same stick and beat the doctor to death with it, but he would be satisfied with putting a bullet in the man's brain.

CHAPTER
FOURTEEN

The Veterans Affairs Medical Center
1030 Jefferson Avenue
Memphis, Tennessee

The pounding filtered down from the floors above. Demolition was, at best, a messy business, and, at worst, absolutely arcane.

Dr. Caroline Rhodes swiped at the dust that seemed to have a special affinity for the top of her office desk. As chief of staff for the VA Medical Center, Rhodes worked within a dichotomy that threatened to drive her crazy. *Crazy,* she was aware, was not a psychiatric word; it was her word, and it fit her state of mind perfectly.

The administrative duties of a chief of staff were as varied as the services offered by the Veterans Affairs Med Center. There were three associate chiefs of staff: one for ambulatory care, one for research and development, and one for education, plus the Learning Resources Service, all within her sphere of influence. Administration for the various areas took time, time she would have preferred to spend on patient care, for Caroline Rhodes had been a physician long before she had been an administrator. Thus the dichotomy.

Her specialty was internal medicine, which fell within the Ambulatory Care Unit, her first love, if you didn't count her husband, Alex.

Alex Rhodes was a reproductive endocrinologist with a burgeoning practice in upscale Germantown, east of Memphis. The only argument in their thirty-plus-year marriage was the one in which he insisted that she quit work at the VA and stay home. She refused; he acquiesced.

Caroline Rhodes had a quality that seemed to be lacking in recently trained physicians: compassion. It amused her that some medical schools had begun teaching a course on the subject. She already knew what those academics did not know and might never learn: compassion was not something that could be taught. You either had it or you didn't.

That was why she had entered medicine in the first place, and it was what kept her in it. It had been compassion and the joy of patient care that had brought her to the VA.

The chief of staff shuffled through a sheaf of papers on her desk. Noise pounded above; dust settled on her desk.

"Naomi, find out how long that blasted noise is going to continue, please," Caroline called to her secretary sitting in the outer office.

"The director said about an hour. He told the contractor to limit the noise as best he could, but you know the contractor," Naomi Collins answered her boss.

"Yeah," muttered Caroline, "I know."

The VA Med Center was in the last throes of what those working there affectionately called "the seismic addition syndrome." A new hospital addition had been built on the west parking lot to conform to earthquake parameters. Memphis *did* sit on the New Madrid fault, and the VA could not wait to see if the expected earthquake would collapse the older building on the heads of its occupants. The older building rose above Jefferson Avenue, less than two miles east of the Mississippi River and the base of the fault line. A great earthquake in the 1800s had changed the course of that great river, causing it to flow backward. With the new "earthquake resistant" addition finished (nothing, after all, was "earthquake proof") and the bed patients moved, a contractor had been called in to demolish all but six floors of the original structure that now housed the administrative offices. Cost estimates and building costs being what they were, partially demolishing and renovating was considerably cheaper than building new administrative offices. So Caroline, as chief of staff, along with all other administrative types, including the VA director, maintained their offices in the older building while the contractor removed the top floors above their heads. It was an innovative and controversial action, but except for the noise and dust, it seemed to be working.

Caroline Rhodes muttered under her breath and turned back to her administrative duties. The sooner she could get it out of the way, the sooner she could get back to what she really loved: practicing medicine. As she signed her name to the latest organizational chart to be issued by the office of the director, her beeper vibrated on the pocket of her white lab coat.

She reached down and depressed the button; the screen displayed a short message and nothing more. It read: "Your office. One hour. Jake."

Caroline Rhodes smiled in spite of herself. Jake Madsen was one of her favorites; but in the year since his wife had died, he had become increasingly moody and temperamental. The cryptic message was just another indication of Jake's growing lack of patience. Not only that, but she had already heard about Jake's summary dismissal from Branch

Medical Clinic out at NAVSUPACT the day before. The Memphis medical community was tight-knit, especially the U.S. government part of
it. It had not taken long for word to reach her from NAVSUPACT.
Caroline Rhodes wondered if the message had something to do with
the incident. Maybe Jake wanted to come back to work. If that was the
case, she had just the place for him. He was not due back until next
week, when his two-week tour of duty would have ended, but she
could always use extra doctors. She would put him on the first floor
working out of the "floater tray" in the walk-in clinic.

Some of the walk-ins needed nothing but consolation, but those
who needed to see a doctor got to see the "floater." And that, Caroline
decided, would be the perfect place for Jake Madsen.

Tierra Quemada, Mexico

"How much longer?" John Ortiz asked.

"Not much," Al Bell answered, his eyes glued to the road ahead.

The two DEA agents had made Matehuala during the night and
had checked into the Days Inn. It had been a fitful night, and both
were tired.

Bell had found the road leading to Tierra Quemada and the village
of Colinas Verde. The information that had come from Mexico City's
CIA station chief played through each man's mind like a never-ending
tape.

The automobile's tires threw up clouds of thick dust in the car's
wake. The temperature was in the low fifties in the early morning
desert. Both men could feel the effects of the dry climate. An ice cooler
rested on the floorboard of the rear seat, full of bottled water and
hastily made sandwiches.

Despite the preparations made for their physical well-being, Ortiz
held the single most important item vital to the two men's survival:
a Magellan, a hand-held Global Positioning System Receiver, purchased at the Mexico City Wal-Mart with personal funds. The GPS

was electronically linked to twelve GPS satellites orbiting the earth and could identify, within feet, the position of the two men. More importantly, it could guide the men back to the programmed starting point of Matehuala and the Days Inn.

John Ortiz checked the battery charge on the small instrument, then turned it off and stored it safely away for the time being. One never knew about Mexico's high desert. Caution was never over-played.

"The map says a few more kilometers," Ortiz told Bell, a map now replacing the GPS.

"If the factory is gone, how will we know when we reach the site?" Bell asked his partner.

"Gamez said the Mexican army was still guarding the place. Better to pull up short and do some recon work."

"Pick a spot to leave the car," Bell suggested.

Ortiz went to the map, chose a mountain within a few kilometers of their objective, and directed Bell. A few "klicks" should be enough. The Mexican army was not known for being overly security conscious.

In minutes, the DEA agents were out of the car and working their way around the base of the mountain, toward the extinct village of Colinas Verde.

■ ■ ■

They were strangers; he had never seen them. There were two of them, *acting* like the strangers they were, creeping over the low out-croppings of rock and sand. He knew where they were going; he just didn't know why, and that intrigued the boy.

The others he knew. They had been here for a long time. They were the ones who had killed the village, had buried it in the desert sands, and to this day prevented any intrusion into what the boy con-sidered sacred ground. Sacred because it was now a burial ground, the resting place of his family and friends. And it would one day be his own grave, for he had so chosen. The time was drawing near; preparations had been made, plans finalized.

The plan had been the difficult part, for there had been nothing left with which to work—until the Mexican army moved in and set up a security perimeter. The army had thus provided the necessary equipment and supplies for the boy to fulfill his ultimate goal. He had stolen what he'd needed. Those things were stored away in the shallow cave that was now his home. It had taken a long time.

Todo lo puedo en Cristo que me fortelece, the boy thought to himself, mouthing the sacred words. And it had certainly proved to be true. He would never have believed possible the things he had accomplished in the past . . . what? Weeks? Months? Years, perhaps? It didn't really matter. The time was near.

■ ■ ■

The land was barren as a moonscape. Ortiz and Bell inched their way up the short rise. Bell pulled out a pair of binoculars and eased them up just past the crest of the rock behind which he and Ortiz had crawled. What greeted him was astounding to the DEA agent.

"Oh man," Bell exclaimed beneath his breath. "Look at this," he said to Ortiz. "This is incredible."

Ortiz eased up the rock beside his partner and uncased his own binoculars. His right foot slipped on the rock, and his knee hit the hard surface with enough force to tear his pants. Ortiz cursed quietly.

Bell looked at his partner and grinned. "Careful. You don't want to make any noise here. Trust me."

Ortiz moved up the rock, being careful not to slip again. He pushed his binoculars over the rock and focused them. What he saw was exactly as Bell had described it: incredible. He realized another thing about what he saw below him. The road the two agents had taken into the valley was a secondary road. The main road wound down the valley, and that road was heavily guarded by what looked to be at least a battalion of Mexican army. Had they taken that road, they would have already been in military custody, and *that* could have had tragic consequences. Due process was not a concept understood by the Mexican government. It could not be expected from the Mexican military.

Below where the two DEA agents lay with their binoculars focused on what used to be the village of Colinas Verde was sufficient evidence that something out of the ordinary had occurred in this high desert valley.

It was not the same orderly, geometric display of tents and vehicles that might be seen from the U.S. military under similar circumstances, but there was no doubt at least a battalion of Mexican army soldiers patrolled what looked to be nothing more than a barren spot in the high desert.

Ortiz felt a nudge in his ribs and swung his binoculars toward a spot Al Bell indicated. He tried to understand what it was he was seeing, but for some reason the scene did not register with him.

"What am I looking at?" Ortiz asked Bell.

"The spot just beyond the encampment. Two, maybe three klicks," Bell answered.

Ortiz adjusted his field of vision, scanning the area. There was nothing there. Not the nothing that so often defined the high desert, but *nothing at all!* Ortiz felt a sudden moment of terror sweep over him. The desert floor seemed as barren as the moonscapes he'd seen during the Apollo moon landings. There was . . . what? Nothing. *Nothing!*

The area was at least a few kilometers square. The size of a small village, perhaps, Ortiz thought. A village? The village the CIA man had told him about back in Mexico City?

Colinas Verde.

The terror passed over him again. This time the fear was different, more intense. Ortiz shivered.

"What do you think?" Bell broke the short silence this time.

"I think there used to be a village down there. It's the right size. Gamez said something about the village of Colinas Verde. According to the map and the GPS, it should be right out there. But it's not, and the Mexican army is."

"*That* is an understatement. I've never seen the Mexican army operate, but it looks like they mean to keep everyone out of that place."

Vehicles were now moving below where Bell and Ortiz lay. All the activity centered around a larger tent, strategically placed near the center of the camp. Smaller tents—platoon-sized tents—surrounded the larger tent. Another tent, even larger than the command tent, was the scene of secondary activity.

"The mess tent," Ortiz said, indicating the larger tent. "The command tent is the smaller of the two. Something is happening."

"Change of patrols, maybe," Bell suggested.

"Maybe. We need to get closer, check out that barren area beyond the camp."

Bell balked at the suggestion. "Think about that for a moment, John. Look again. There's nothing out there at all. Let me emphasize that: *nothing*. No animals scurrying about. No vegetation of any kind. No soldiers. No tents. No vehicles. Nothing. What does that tell you?"

Ortiz nodded while continuing to observe the area. The patrols had formed up below, and vehicles were beginning to move out, using a semi-defined road that led from the camp to the barren area that used to be a living, breathing village.

"You may be right. You are *probably* right. But I want some samples of that barren dirt."

Bell reacted to his partner's statement as violently as he could under the circumstances. He lowered his own binoculars, turned to Ortiz, and grabbed him by the shoulder.

"This is not DEA jurisdiction. If anything, it's Mexican army jurisdiction. Even if there is a connection, that connection would be through the CIA, not the DEA. Maybe even the NSA, which I doubt. But whatever the connection, it is *not* DEA."

"I'm going down there," Ortiz said, ignoring Bell's argument. "You stay here. If something happens, get the information to Gamez back in the city. I have a feeling he'll know what to do."

"You're nuts," Bell responded, almost coming up from his hiding place. "You go down there and get caught, you know what will happen. The Mexican government will put you in a jail cell somewhere, and maybe think about a trial in a couple of years. You know how the system operates."

Activity in the camp increased. More vehicles were moving out now, tracking along the worn road leading to what used to be Colinas Verde. Other vehicles, mostly well-worn military Jeeps, were raising dust trails coming *from* Colinas Verde. There was no doubt a patrol change was in progress.

For John Ortiz, the patrol change offered the perfect opportunity to infiltrate the area.

"Look, I'm going to just wander into camp, make my way to that village area, get some samples, and get out. You wait, give me four hours, then get back to the city and Gamez."

Bell was about to answer when both men heard the unmistakable sound of a round being chambered into an AK-47. Bell and Ortiz turned to see a five-man patrol, all armed with the Russian version of the automatic weapon, standing with their rifles pointed at the two DEA agents. The man who had chambered the round pointed his rifle at John Ortiz and began to squeeze the trigger ever so gently.

Ortiz cursed in Spanish beneath his breath, knowing he and Al Bell were about to die in the high desert of Mexico.

■ ■ ■

It was coming apart, the man knew. But his job was not to evaluate the situation, only to relay the incoming information, making

certain that the information got to its destination unhindered and accurately. For that simple task he was paid well over one hundred thousand dollars a year, provided with the home where he now lived in
Alexandria, Virginia, and counted among the government employees
whose names would never see the light of day in any directory.

Over the years, the information he handled had been sporadic at
best. There had been times when no information had been transferred
for months at a time, but when the information flowed, it flowed with
an urgency that the man admired. What became of the data he so
faithfully reproduced and transmitted he did not know, nor did he care
to know. He had been carefully chosen for just that quality: his morbid lack of curiosity. So he had relayed the information as instructed
for more years now than he cared to count, never once violating the
security agreement he had signed in those early days. The pay was too
good, the perks prodigious. And there *was* that one other incentive: he
knew should he ever compromise the organization for which he
worked, he would be eliminated from the face of the earth as easily as
he swatted at the mosquito that buzzed around his head. The combination of perks and persuasion was formidable.

The man went back to his computer terminal. Information was
coming in now from more than half a dozen points around the globe.
There was even some rudimentary data being transmitted from
Mexico. Nothing earth-shaking, but interesting.

Combined with the other information that traversed the dedicated
satellite links, the man knew his first assessment of the situation was
correct. Things *were* coming apart. It would be evident as soon as all
the information was collated and transmitted. What was done with it
after he finished was not his concern. He planned on fishing today.

■ ■ ■

The boy watched with increased interest. The army patrol had
captured the strangers. He'd seen that before too. Strangers who

inadvertently wandered into the secured area were taken to the large tent in the center of the camp. A vehicle would appear, the prisoners taken away into the night desert, never to be seen again. That's what would happen to the two with the binoculars. It was a shame; the boy had begun to think the two men were different. He could have used them in his plan, but they would be dead by nightfall.

The boy slithered away from his own vantage point, careful not to move too quickly or make any noise. The time was coming quickly now, and he would do nothing to jeopardize that time.

Retribution would be a beautiful thing, especially since it had been so long in coming.

CHAPTER
FIFTEEN

VA Med Center, Memphis
Office of the Chief of Staff

The noise pounded in Jake's brain. He was not sure if it came from the construction crews or his own mind.

It had been a long night, from the shooting of Jamie Parker to the strange happenings at the Regional Forensic Center on Madison. At the bidding of Kaci Callahan, he had reported what he knew of the shooting, and he had listened as Kaci methodically recounted the events at the Forensic Center. By the time they were finished, it had been well after midnight.

Kaci had agreed to meet him at the VA Med Center in the morning. He had only briefly mentioned the X-rays he had with him. It had been somewhat of a confession on Jake's part. Kaci had graciously not mentioned the fact that she had asked about the film at the murder scene. Jake had been grateful for that. He already felt responsible for what had happened to the young navy corpsman. The Med would be his next stop after talking with Dr. Caroline Rhodes. He wanted to check on Jamie, but his first objective was to find out what the strange device was that had been planted in Jerry Wallace's chest, and why it had been so important that someone stole it from his corpse last night.

Jake took the elevator to the second floor, turned down the hall, and headed for the chief of staff's office. He wondered how long it would be before Kaci showed up.

As Jake turned the corner heading for Dr. Rhodes's office he heard the elevator door slide open behind him. He turned to see Kaci Callahan step out.

The physical similarities between Kaci and Kathy were extraordinary. Even their names seemed to have a certain symmetry: Kaci and Kathy, Kathy and Kaci.

Jake waited as Kaci caught up with him. He watched every movement as she approached, and he realized it had been the sight of Kaci, her nearness, her understanding, that had triggered the intense pain and longing he'd felt for Kathy last night. Kaci reminded him of how much he'd lost.

And in that understanding, Jake felt a renewed sense of pain and loss, but this time he also felt a new emotion, one he thought had died over a year ago: excitement. He was truly glad to see Kaci.

"Good morning, Commander," Kaci said, stopping at the corner of the corridor where Jake stood.

"I thought we settled that last night," Jake responded, turning as he said it and heading for Dr. Rhodes's office.

Kaci fell into step with Jake. "I thought about it. You're still a navy lieutenant commander, and I'm still an NCIS agent. There's an official relationship to be maintained. It's probably best we do that."

Jake felt disappointment sweep over him at Kaci's statement. Last night they had broken through the official barrier, but now Kaci was reinstating it, maintaining an official distance. Jake wondered why.

"If that's the way you want it, Miss Callahan," Jake replied more curtly than he intended. He turned into the second office on the right and entered the outer office of Dr. Caroline Rhodes, chief of staff of the Veterans Affairs Medical Center.

Kaci followed him into the office, wondering if she'd just done something to offend Jake.

Caroline Rhodes was in the next office. She saw Jake walk in. "In here, Jake," she called.

Jake walked past Naomi Collins's desk. "Morning, Naomi," he said to the secretary. He didn't wait for a response. Kaci was two steps behind.

"What's the story, Jake?" Caroline asked. "I got your page and that cryptic message. Since when does a mere doctor order around the chief of staff?"

Jake grinned. He loved Caroline Rhodes. She was a mother figure who always seemed to know the right thing to say and just how to say it.

"I thought that was why you were here," Jake said, walking over to her and giving her a big hug. "To protect and serve."

Caroline returned the hug with gusto. "You have me confused with the police," she answered. "I'm here to try and keep young doctors in line. You are making it difficult. What's the story about being dismissed from Branch Medical Center out at NAVSUPACT yesterday?"

Jake stopped for a moment. There was never anything that Caroline Rhodes did not know, just like his mother. He could never get away with anything.

"And who is this?" she continued, indicating Kaci.

"Dr. Caroline Rhodes, VA Chief of Staff, meet Kaci Callahan, NCIS agent from NAVSUPACT."

"So," she said, moving to shake hands with Kaci, "the navy has assigned you your own Naval Criminal Investigative Services agent to watch over you. Kaci, how are you?"

Kaci took the hand, noticing the strength and sincerity the grip conveyed. She suspected Dr. Rhodes was a good doctor. "Nice to meet you, Doctor."

Caroline stood back after the introductions, her smile now evaporated. "Tell me about it," she ordered.

All three sat down as Jake began the explanations, beginning with the examination of Sergeant Jerry Wallace and ending with the incident at the Regional Forensic Center and the resultant police reports.

"That's about it," Jake concluded.

"*That* is enough," Rhodes responded. "What about it, Miss Callahan? Is that pretty much the story?"

Kaci nodded her affirmation. "Pretty much. My perspective might be a little different since it's an official investigation for me, but Jake's got the facts down the way it happened."

Jake noted with satisfaction that Kaci had already dropped the "official" navy title of commander, and reverted to "Jake."

"And these X-rays you're talking about. You've got those with you?" Caroline turned to Jake.

"Here in the envelope."

"That's what I thought. And you want me to look at them and tell you what there is about them that would precipitate such a chain of events? Is that it?"

"You were the only one I could think of under the circumstances. Whatever's on the film, it got me kicked out of the clinic at NAVSU-PACT, got a young corpsman shot, and a soldier murdered."

"That's a pretty far leap, considering the evidence," Caroline said.

"I'd have to agree," Kaci chimed in. "We don't know that one has anything to do with the other. I prefer to reserve judgment until we have a legitimate link between what might be isolated events."

"You two can think what you want. I'm just a simple doctor, and I can jump to conclusions if I want to, and right now, that's exactly what I want to do," Jake responded, pulling the X-rays from the folder. "It's not that often I get shot at. It makes me jumpy. Here, take a look at these and tell me what you think." Jake handed the two X-rays to Dr. Rhodes.

The VA chief rose from her chair and jammed them both into a viewing box mounted on the wall just behind her desk.

"Do you know what that is?" Jake asked.

The VA doctor hesitated, moving to get a better view of the illuminated film.

"What did you think, Jake?" Rhodes asked, her voice controlled, moving over to make room for Jake at the viewing box.

"My first thought was the obvious. It looked like a normal pacemaker. I was curious, of course."

"Curious?" she asked.

"It appeared to be a normal pacemaker, just like I said. But what was it doing in a soldier? And if this soldier needed it, why was he still on active duty? Then I noticed the anomalies, and my curiosity really took off."

"You're talking about what looks like a misplaced wire, and the fact that the device is slightly offset in relation to where a real pacemaker might be positioned," Caroline said, looking back at the X-ray.

Jake peered at her for just a second. He had the feeling she was admitting to knowing what the strange device was. The revelation was disturbing.

"If it was a pacemaker, then the wire is in the wrong position in relation to the chest wall and the heart, and the entire device is offset too much. It's not a pacemaker, is it, Caroline?"

Dr. Rhodes flicked off the viewing box and returned to her chair. Jake did the same, joining Kaci in front of the desk. He glanced at Kaci. She had said nothing during the brief exchange, but he knew her curiosity was about to overwhelm her. It was one of the things that made for a good investigator, and Jake suspected the lady was one of the best NCIS agents in the organization. It was as curious to Jake that he was equally dividing his thoughts between the strange device in Jerry Wallace's chest and the young lady seated at his side. It had been a long time since his curiosity had been so stimulated, and now there were two subjects of interest for him. He smiled inwardly.

I can do all things through Christ who strengthens me. Did that include this? Jake wondered, remembering his wife's handwritten message in the Bible. Did that mean he could be equally interested in another woman, and at the same time, the mysterious device in the chest of a dead soldier? Or rather, Jake reminded himself, the device that *used to be in the chest of a dead soldier.*

"Jake, I want you to take these films to Dr. Matthew Ellis. You know him?"

Jake nodded. "Researcher over in SCIU. Working on nerve regeneration, I think."

"SCIU?" Kaci asked.

"Spinal Cord Injury Unit," Jake replied.

"Take the film to him before we go any further," Caroline suggested. "Then, if you have any more questions, we'll talk about them."

Jake sat forward on the edge of his chair. Now his imagination was working overtime. This was not like Caroline Rhodes. She was one of the "good guys." A straight shooter who normally answered questions directly. If she was skirting this issue, it had to be indicative of the seriousness she felt this information deserved. Jake wanted to ask more questions, but he could see the concern in the chief of staff's eyes. They were almost pleading, and Jake knew he would do what she asked without further inquisition.

"He'll tell me what this is?" Jake stated finally.

"He'll explain what he can, and he'll do it better than I can. What I know about this comes from an administrative point of view. Matt

Ellis is the expert. Go see Matt. Take Miss Callahan with you. I'll call him right now and set it up. By the time you get over there, he'll be ready for you."

Jake rose from his chair. Kaci followed suit. "You'll be around when we're finished?" Jake asked.

"I'll be in the hospital all day long if you need me." Caroline picked up the phone and pushed four numbers. "I'll get Matt right now. You take off."

Jake obeyed, and Kaci followed him from the office.

"What was that all about?" Kaci asked as they emerged into the corridor outside the office.

"Let's get over to SCIU. The quicker we find out, the quicker we may know what is going on here. And after that, I want to check on Jamie Parker at the Med."

The two moved down the hospital corridor, heading for the Spinal Cord Injury Unit, Dr. Matthew Ellis, and some answers.

Neither noticed the man who watched them from beneath the navy blue cap with the insignia of a currently operating missile cruiser displayed on it. The man waited until they were well down the corridor before following at a normal pace. He did not want to be noticed, not now. Even his limp would not attract attention. This was, after all, a hospital.

Branch Medical Center, NAVSUPACT

Captain William Dean sat in his office at Branch Medical Center and wondered what had gone wrong. That the situation with the reserve doctor, Lieutenant Commander Jacob Madsen, had gone so wrong so quickly was beyond belief. But the computer-generated report was sitting right there on his desk, and that meant something had occurred to initiate a status report concerning BMC, his own involvement, and the precipitous dismissal of Jake Madsen from BMC the day before.

Dean had reported the dismissal and the X-rays that he had discovered were taken on one of the study subjects. There was a rumor that the soldier who had died in an apartment fire yesterday had been the same Jerry Wallace. Dean was in the process of verifying the information at this very moment, but it was only an informal inquiry. Official inquiries were risky, generating status reports during the process, and such reports were like a highway leading back to him. Perhaps a quick call to Pensacola would suffice. Yes, that would be his first line of defense. That he was even thinking in terms of defense bothered him. That meant he anticipated being held responsible for the problems that would most surely arise from the incidents of the last few days.

Maybe he still had time to head it off. The captain picked up the phone and dialed.

Tierra Quemada, Mexico

No one was more surprised to see the two DEA agents being ushered into the command tent than General Abraham Solis Zedillo.

Zedillo looked up from the desk where he was reviewing contact reports for the secure area that had once been the village of Colinas Verde. The reports were completely negative, as they had been for the last few months. The inhabitants of Tierra Quemada had learned to avoid the area of the dead village, making his job easier.

But the two men who were being escorted at gunpoint into the command tent meant that the contact reports were wrong.

Zedillo knew the men. At least, he thought he recognized one of them. The face was familiar, and that was disturbing. The last place he needed to meet someone he actually knew was in the high desert of Tierra Quemada. The area was supposed to be secure. The patrolled perimeter extended more than three kilometers from the former village limit and circumscribed the extended border for almost forty kilometers. There should not have been a living soul within viewing distance of what had once been a vibrant village.

But here stood two men, attesting to the fact that security had been compromised.

Zedillo came out of his folding camp chair and walked toward the two men. The one on the right was the familiar face. Where had he seen the face before? He looked Latin, but there was something about the eyes, about the lack of subservient demeanor before a superior that bothered the general. These men were not Mexican citizens who had wandered into the secure perimeter and had been captured in the process. They were something else. But what? Who?

"What have we here?" Zedillo asked the guards in Spanish, his gaze fixed on the man he thought he knew. There was a flicker of recognition in the man's eyes; he understood Spanish. Maybe he *was* Mexican. In his experience, few citizens of the U.S. understood Spanish, or even cared to learn it.

"We found them observing the village, *Señor* General," the senior guard replied. "They had these," the man continued, handing Zedillo the two sets of binoculars.

Zedillo felt his blood run cold within his veins. The binoculars were a type issued to U.S. military troops and other official agents, such as the FBI, CIA, and DEA.

That was it! The man was a DEA agent stationed in Mexico City. He worked out of the American Embassy on Paseo de la Reforma, but he could not remember the man's name. The other man was not familiar to him.

"Well, gentlemen, what have you to say for yourselves?" Zedillo asked in Spanish.

Neither man responded. Zedillo grinned.

"It is not like you do not understand my language, gentlemen," Zedillo pressed. "Is it not a requirement for DEA agents to understand the language in which they work? Surely you know this."

The flicker in the two men's eyes told Zedillo that he had guessed correctly. The question now was why? Why the DEA? Did they not know of Colinas Verde? Had the reports of the village not filtered through even the cumbersome government bureaucracies of the United States? Were not the U.S. and Mexico allies in this venture? And if so, did it make sense that the DEA would be interested in Colinas Verde, and by extension, in the new chemical plant now located in the new industrial park just outside of Queretero?

He needed answers, and he needed them quickly. There would not be time to send lengthy inquiries to his control officers in the Pentagon. He needed answers now, and that meant getting them from the two men before him. It would not be pretty, but it had to be done.

"Take them to the hut," Zedillo ordered. "I will be along in a moment. And do not let them out of your sight. Find a dozen more men, armed. Be sure your weapons are loaded. You have permission to use them should either of these men try to escape."

Zedillo watched as the men left the command tent, then he went to his desk, opened the notebook computer that lay there, and connected to the secure satellite link that would relay all he knew at this point to those same control officers at the Pentagon. He would not wait for a response. He had his own work to do, and the captured men *were* on *his* sovereign soil. He would deal with them in his own way.

The Pentagon
Office of Weapons Development

The Zedillo report was received from the secure satellite downlink, transferred to the coded office, and there, stored in computer memory under the master code name, Janus.

The office was small, less than one hundred square feet, with two large desks jammed into the space along with three filing cabinets and the single computer console that rested on one of the desks. There were no nameplates on the desk nor on the door of the tiny office. No single person was assigned to the office. It was a secondary assignment, and the office was manned only under certain, very restricted circumstances. Lately, the office had been manned more often than usual, but today it remained empty. The only action was the low-priority message being received from the high desert in north central Mexico.

Such reports were relayed to the control computer on a regular basis, most coming from a man in Alexandria, Virginia. Some came into the master computer from direct downlinks. All were collated, recoded, and stored in the computer's memory, awaiting the time when in-depth analysis could be done.

CHAPTER
SIXTEEN

"It's a PSM," Dr. Matthew Ellis said unemotionally.

Ellis had a head of dark hair generously sprinkled with strands of gray that were more yellow than gray. The hair sat atop a square face that appeared mildly intelligent but boring. He wore a rumpled sport shirt and wrinkled slacks under a crisp lab coat that was open. Ellis looked more like a disgruntled golfer than a world-class researcher. The appearance disguised a brilliant, analytical mind.

"PSM?" Jake asked.

"Personal status monitor," Ellis replied.

"Can you be less cryptic, Doctor?" Kaci said. "I've got a murder case on my hands. I need information. Last night at the Regional Forensic Center, this PSM, as you call it, was ripped from the chest of a murder victim. I want to know what it is, how it got there, and what's so important about it."

Jake sat back in his chair, watching with amazement and not a little respect as the NCIS personality of Kaci Callahan began to dominate the conversation. He had been right; she *was* good. And assertive. And competent. And all those things that make for a good agent.

It had taken them a good five minutes to walk the distance from Caroline Rhodes's office to the Spinal Cord Injury Unit. Jake had checked in with the unit's chief and had been directed to the lab of Dr. Ellis by the chief's office clerk.

Ellis had been waiting in his office. Caroline had already interceded, directing the research doctor to answer any questions put to him by either Dr. Madsen or the NCIS agent accompanying him.

Ellis cleared his throat. "Miss . . ."

"Callahan," Kaci repeated.

"Miss Callahan. I appreciate your predicament. I'm just not sure how much I can tell you."

"Then let me clarify my position, Doctor. I'm a Naval Criminal Investigative Service general crimes agent. I have the body of a U.S. Army soldier stationed at Naval Support Activities, Mid-South, in a cooler at the Regional Forensic Center less than two blocks from here. Last night someone conspired to rip from the chest of that dead soldier a device you just called a personal status monitor. Now, I may only be a Southern girl, but I wasn't born yesterday. It doesn't take a rocket scientist to know that the death of that man and the incidents of last night are related, now does it, *Doctor?*"

Jake smiled inwardly. He was glad *he* was not being questioned by Kaci Callahan.

Dr. Matthew Ellis balked. "You don't quite understand, Miss Callahan. It's not just a matter of explaining what a PSM is and what it does. It's a matter of national security."

Kaci exploded. "Oh please, Doctor. Don't start throwing the buga-boo of national security into this. What in the world does national security have to do with that soldier in the morgue?"

"The very action of your asking that question throws even more doubt into this situation," Ellis continued. "It's not my idea, you under-stand. I don't care about the program anymore. It was a way to get additional government funding at a time when funding was difficult to come by. Most people think the government wastes a lot of money, and it does, but trying to get some of that same money for independ-ent medical research is just a series of hoops to be jumped through. I had to work the system. I was involved but only on the research end. I needed the money to begin the nerve tissue studies. But that was a long time ago. I've been out of the program for quite a while."

"Program? What program, Dr. Ellis?" Jake asked, moving forward to the edge of his chair.

Ellis shifted in his own chair, the doubt obvious in his expression. "I'm not sure I can tell you that," he replied.

"Try, Doctor," Kaci said, her voice more gentle than it had been only seconds earlier. "I've got one dead boy, and the possibility of oth-ers. I need to know everything you can tell me about what you know."

Jake glanced in Kaci's direction. He wasn't sure where the state-ment about "others" came from, but the thought chilled him. Then he remembered that Jamie Parker had been shot, and he had almost been shot. There *was* the possibility of other deaths, if the two incidents were connected.

"Someone shot a naval hospital corpsman last night, and tried to kill me," Jake said. "Tell us what you know, Dr. Ellis."

The shock on Matthew Ellis's face was real; the doubt remained, but he began, and the first words out of his mouth chilled the very marrow of Jake Madsen.

"I was involved just after Vietnam. The program was simply called Janus."

Jake and Kaci exchanged quick, fearful glances. Last night at Regional Forensic, Jake had told Kaci about what Jamie Parker had said to him before being wheeled into the ER at the Med. Janus had surfaced again. They waited for Ellis to continue.

"I don't know all the details. Quite the contrary. I was contracted to do follow-up studies on soldiers returning from Vietnam. Personal status monitors hadn't even been invented in those days. We had to wait until the navy came up with the Global Positioning System before those came along."

"What kind of studies?" Kaci asked.

"Medical. The effects of chemicals used in Vietnam."

"You mean like the Agent Orange thing?" Jake added.

"That, and others. My studies with Agent Orange are one of the things that brought me to the VA. But that's an entirely different story. My studies in the late seventies had more to do with the effects of other chemicals."

"Other chemicals?" Jake queried.

"Chemicals that weren't supposed to be used over there. Chemicals that weren't supposed to be used anywhere anymore."

"You're talking about chemical warfare?" Kaci asked.

"Exactly. It was used by both sides. How much or how little, I couldn't tell you. My job was research."

Jake felt his blood chill even further as questions began to form in his mind. "Research on whom, Dr. Ellis?" he asked.

"Military personnel."

"Our military personnel?" Kaci asked in shock.

"Exactly. I studied the effects certain chemicals had on our returning military people."

Both Jake and Kaci sat quietly for a long moment. Then Jake asked, "Earlier you mentioned the name, 'Janus.' Do you know anything other than the name?"

"Janus was the program. I don't know anything about it other than the name and what my part in it was," Ellis explained.

"First things first, then," Kaci interrupted. "The PSM. Explain that. That's my most immediate concern. A soldier might have died because there was one of those devices in his chest."

"Have you read the papers lately?" Ellis asked, ignoring the NCIS agent's question.

Kaci's puzzled look forced him to continue.

"Italy is probably the best example I can think of at the moment."

"Italy?" Kaci repeated in a stunned voice, wondering if the researcher had lost his mind.

An amused look crossed the researcher's face. "You really don't read that much, do you? Well, it seems the Italian industrialists and the old money altruists are more or less under siege in that country. Oh, it's not the only place, but it is the most obvious."

Her impatience showing, Kaci said, "Your point being?"

"My point being that the monied bourgeoisie of that country are probably the number one consumers of the PSM."

"How so?"

"They are having them implanted so they can be found in case they are kidnapped by their Italian Mafia. Makes it easier for the police to find them and might even prevent a kidnapping or two. Of course, that has yet to be proven, but the theory is valid."

Kaci and Jake sat speechless once again, the truth beginning to dawn.

Jake continued. "What you are saying is that this personal status monitor is some sort of homing device for a human being. One that can't be dumped into the trash at a whim."

Ellis smiled. "Now you're catching on. And don't forget, our own country is using them for things as mundane as pets. It's not so far-fetched."

"And part of this Janus thing is the PSM that was in Jerry Wallace?" Kaci asked.

Ellis held up his hand. "I can't go that far. I don't know that the Wallace kid *was* part of Janus. I do know that what I'm looking at on this X-ray is most definitely one of the PSMs that was being used in the program. That would lend credence to the conclusion that Wallace was in the program, but you will have to confirm that from other sources."

"I understand your reluctance, Dr. Ellis," Kaci continued. "Let me ask you this, then, off the record."

"Those are the words I've been waiting to hear," Ellis said. "Continue."

"To the best of your knowledge, the device you see on this X-ray is what you call a PSM. You know that such devices are, or were, being used by a program within the U.S. government known as Janus, and you think at this point that the reason Jerry Wallace might have been killed was to protect the program?"

"As you said earlier, that might be a leap."

"Off the record, Doctor. I'll never implicate you in this," Kaci affirmed.

"Then, yes, I think your young soldier was killed to protect Janus."

"Who is Janus?" Jake Madsen asked.

Ellis chuckled mirthlessly.

"What's so funny?"

"Janus is not a 'who,' it's a 'what.' And if you have any designs on exposing it, you can forget it. It's been going on longer than both of you have been alive, and it will continue to thrive. Forget about it."

"What about the PSM, Doctor," Kaci pressed. "Surely the industrialists you talked about in Italy aren't having the large devices planted in their own chests."

"You are right about that, Agent Callahan. The ones used in Italy are nothing more than small computer chips, implanted in various locations. Not like the one we see here at all."

Kaci breathed deeply, almost afraid to continue. "Why the difference?"

"The one on this X-ray is more than just a simple homing device, like the Italian models. This one is a true monitoring device. The one on the X-ray is linked to the Global Positioning System's satellites. It's equipped with highly sophisticated monitoring systems that relay data on almost every body system back to a central point. I assume the information is collated, distributed, and studied at that point, but that really is only speculation on my part. That's the reason it's larger and designed to resemble a pacemaker, just in case a curious doctor should shoot a film of one by accident. As it seems has occurred," Ellis said, glancing at Jake.

"What about when you were involved in the study? How did you transfer your findings?"

"The same way we do today, although I admit it is much quicker now."

"Computer?" Kaci suggested.

"Computer," Ellis confirmed. "All the information is uplinked to a satellite and then downlinked to some unknown location. Unknown, that is, to me, and probably any other researcher who might be involved with Janus today."

Jake could hold his tongue no longer. There were too many loose ends, too many questions that did not connect directly to Jerry Wallace and Kaci's investigation that he wanted answered.

"You say Janus is not a person. What is it? What is it studying?" Jake asked.

Ellis laughed now, loud and audaciously, almost defiantly. "Janus? What is it? Why Dr. Madsen, it's *Janus*. It's a system, an inhuman series of links that no one man has control over."

"A system?" Jake repeated, bewildered.

Ellis laughed louder, the sound reverberating from the walls of the small laboratory. "Yes, Madsen, a system. An impersonal, inhuman system, sired from the minds of madmen years ago and perpetuated to this day by a prosaic proletariat."

"Sounds like a rather harsh indictment, Dr. Ellis," argued Jake.

"Perhaps, but accurate nonetheless. Systems like Janus depend on it, thrive on it. The prosaic, I mean. The uncaring public."

"Of which you are one," said Kaci.

"Of which I am one of the worst," Ellis agreed, meeting Kaci's glare. "I know what's going on, and yet I persist in ignoring it on the grounds of my own meager prosperity. Strange, isn't it, that mankind can so easily ignore the one thing that makes life on this earth bearable. Other people, I mean. We have the infinite capacity to overlook anything that might pull us out of our own comfort zone, even if that 'something' is killing people."

"Janus, Doctor. Tell us about Janus," Kaci said quietly.

The research doctor looked down, his eyes searching the floor before him. He retrieved a small scrap of paper from his desk and wrote for a moment. "This will tell you more," he said, handing the scrap of paper to Kaci. With that, he began, "Janus is—"

The researcher's words were cut short by three evenly spaced spits that came from the doorway of the lab. Three small circles of red magically appeared on the white lab coat Ellis was wearing, just over the doctor's heart. A look of surprise spread over Matthew Ellis's face just before he slumped to the floor, dead.

Kaci and Jake sat stunned. Kaci was the first to realize what had happened; she moved with a fluid grace and speed that Jake would later remember as phenomenal.

A man stood in the lab's doorway, fumbling with a small pistol, a silencer protruding menacingly from the short barrel.

"Move!" Kaci ordered as she dove for the cover of the desk, pushing Jake as she went.

Jake dove in the opposite direction, seeking the protection of the desk too. But even as he scrambled to put the desk between himself and the killer, he knew it was useless. Neither he nor Kaci had a weapon, and it was only a short distance from the doorway to the desk. He was about to die, and his thoughts were strangely divided between his wife, Kathy, the athletic and intelligent Kaci Callahan, and the killer in the doorway.

■ ■ ■

"Chief," Security Officer Jack Harrison called out from his seat in the VA hospital's security camera monitoring room. "We got a shooter. Laboratory section over at SCIU." Harrison's voice was even, the statement factual, but there was no mistaking the anxiety.

The security monitoring room was located in the basement of the original section of the hospital, just around the corner from the small warren of security offices where Chief of Security Carl Gilliland normally would have been sitting at his desk tending to the countless tasks demanded by his position. But today Gilliland was in the monitoring room, a cup of coffee in his hand, discussing the upcoming training seminar to be held by his training officer on the proper use of the newly installed camera surveillance system that linked almost a hundred strategically placed cameras to the basement room.

"Wh . . . What?" Gilliland sputtered.

"Yeah, Chief. A shooter over in SCIU. Dr. Ellis's lab. Looks bad." Harrison typed on the keyboard before him, bringing up the images on the screens of the larger monitors. "There was no indication that the guy was carrying. Looked like a normal patient. Even had a limp. Couldn't pick him out until right now. He just shot Dr. Ellis."

Carl Gilliland almost choked on the sip of coffee he'd just taken. "Who's closest?" he asked, moving over Harrison's left shoulder.

"Ferguson," Harrison answered quickly after checking his status board.

"Get him over there, but tell him what's happened, and tell him to stay clear. Get the MPD on the horn, and get them here right now. Tell them to use the east entrance to SCIU for the primary response team. And tell Ferguson I'm on the way. Call the alert."

Jack Harrison scrambled to obey his chief's orders, and in seconds, the entire on-duty security force of the Veterans Affairs Medical Center was moving toward the Spinal Column Injury Unit, along with the men in the force's two marked cars that had been patrolling the parking lots and surrounding streets. Harrison was not sure what the security force could do. None of them carried weapons. They would have to wait for the Memphis Police Department.

■ ■ ■

Kaci scanned the office for anything she could use for a weapon, anything she might use to stave off the next attack from the man standing in the doorway. She found nothing. She glanced over to where Jake had taken cover. They were both covered by the bulk of the desk, but that would do little good if the killer chose to come around the desk, which he most surely would. In the other direction lay Dr. Ellis, blood splotches already enlarged against the white lab coat.

The shooter had not yet advanced from the doorway. Kaci could hear him fumbling with the automatic pistol. The pistol had jammed. It might be her only chance.

She could hear the man retracting the slide mechanism, working it, trying unsuccessfully to eject the jammed brass from the chamber.

Kaci moved with catlike precision, swinging around the end of the desk where she'd taken cover, the end opposite from where Jake crouched.

Jake saw the lithe movement as Kaci charged from around the desk. His first thought was that the NCIS agent had lost her mind, and then the logic of the attack registered with him. The noise he had been hearing was that of a jammed pistol, and Kaci was taking advantage of what might be their only opening to charge the shooter, to save their lives.

Jake scrambled from where he'd taken cover. He was two steps behind Kaci. The agent had found something to use as a weapon, but Jake could not make it out.

He could hear sirens wailing in the distance. Someone, probably the security force, had called the Memphis Police Department. He knew the internal security force would be racing for this section of SCIU, but if the killer in the doorway got the jammed brass ejected from the pistol, it would do little good.

Kaci was within ten feet of the doorway when the spent brass flew from the chamber and the pistol slide glided forward, forcing a live shell into the chamber.

The killer smiled as he raised the weapon, the ugly muzzle coming up even with Kaci's head.

A shot rang out through the laboratory, loud and obscene.

Jake froze. He expected to see Kaci thrown to the floor by the force of the blast, but she was still on her feet. She, too, had stopped. The man in the doorway had lowered his pistol.

The shot! It had not been the silenced spit he'd expected from the small automatic carried by the killer. The sound had been the report of a large-caliber handgun, a 357 Magnum or larger. Jake's ears still rang from the sound. Had the MPD already arrived?

Kaci stood in the middle of the lab, her attack cut short by the pistol's report. She was amazed to see the killer slump forward and fall to his knees.

Jake and Kaci reached the assassin at the same time. Kaci pulled the silenced automatic from the man's hand, shoving it out of reach. The gesture was not necessary. The man's eyes were rolled back in his head.

Jake felt for a pulse; Kaci raced into the hospital corridor, searching for the shooter.

Jake found a faint pulse at the base of the man's neck; Kaci found an empty corridor.

"Let's get this man to emergency, quick. We may be able to do something."

The man's eyes opened briefly, and Jake knew the race to the emergency room would be futile. The man was dying. The bullet had punctured the right ventricle of the heart; the man would be dead in a matter of seconds.

"Why?" Jake asked quietly, looking into the man's face.

The whisper that escaped was the most frightening word Jake had ever heard.

"Janus," the assassin said just before the last of his life's blood was pumped from his damaged heart.

Jake looked up to see Kaci returning from the hospital corridor. "Who?" was all the question he could form.

Kaci shrugged. "Do you believe in guardian angels? There was no one in the hallway. I went both directions. Whoever did this escaped. What about him?" Kaci asked, pointing at the dead assassin.

"He only said one word."

"Janus," Kaci said in a low voice.

"Yeah," Jake confirmed. "Janus."

Kaci pulled out the piece of paper on which Dr. Ellis had written, and read it.

"What's it say?" Jake asked.

"It's a Web address. Internet. It must be the address where all of the research info he was talking about is sent."

Jake waited. He could see Kaci had more to say.

"The main part of the address is Janus."

"But that's not all, is it?"

"No. The end is 'dot, gov'."

"Gov?"

"That means it's a government project," Kaci explained.

"You're telling me that our own government is trying to kill us?" Jake asked incredulously.

"So it would seem," Kaci replied.

The two were still staring at each other when the uniformed men of the Memphis Police Department and the security force of the VA hospital arrived in the laboratory.

CHAPTER
SEVENTEEN

Fairfax County, Virginia

For a man in his mid-seventies, Peter St. Clair was remarkably well preserved. A shock of white hair framed a well-tanned face. Bright blue eyes crowned a thin nose and mouth, lending an air of animation to his appearance. The effect reminded many people of the actor/dancer Fred Astaire. The resemblance amused St. Clair, who preferred to remain in the background whenever he performed his own brand of magic, which for the last few years had been accomplished informally through clandestine offices of the State Department.

The road leading to St. Clair's Fairfax County home was narrow and winding—a lane really—lined with evergreens that formed a protective line and added to the mystery of the house. The house itself was less than an hour from Washington, D.C., but a whole world removed from the hustle and bustle of America's seat of government.

The old brick structure was three stories tall, the facade a perfect example of post-war stoicism, the war of reference being the Civil War. Ivy-covered walls accented the brick, giving the building the feeling of permanence and solidity, both attributes that had been ascribed to St. Clair himself on many occasions.

Peter St. Clair moved in circles of influence and power. He had served U.S. presidents going back to Dwight David Eisenhower. Republicans and Democrats alike sought his counsel, knowing that there were few enough Peter St. Clairs in a world that could have used more of his patrician manners coupled with his pragmatic thinking.

St. Clair's first official State Department appointment had come under the Kennedy administration. It had not been his last, and through a series of increasingly important appointments, Peter St. Clair had taken on the unofficial title of "the Ambassador."

Now, in retirement and semireclusion, St. Clair continued to affect the world from his Fairfax County home, not because he wanted to, but because it was expected of him, and St. Clair had never refused to take up the gauntlet in the cause of democracy nor shrink from the duty to which he believed he had been called.

One of those duties had long been a proverbial thorn in his side, but it had been one he had utterly believed in at the beginning. Now, after more years than he cared to acknowledge, he wasn't so sure.

St. Clair reviewed the information on his oversized computer screen. He had never liked the idea of electronic communications, resisting until it was impossible to do so any longer. But though it was necessary, he did not like the instantaneous communication style.

For St. Clair, communication had always been an art form—the art of expression and communion. True communication required an exchange of ideas, and ideas were most readily exchanged when one could look into the other person's eyes, observe the demeanor, note the reactions. Really astute communication was not the exchange of words, it was the interweaving of two souls bound by mutually accepted canons. For St. Clair, diplomacy was the nearest thing to a religion he had ever known.

In a word, communication was understanding, and to Peter St. Clair's way of thinking, understanding was lost in the electronic age of digital transmissions.

Nevertheless, he had surrendered to the electronic age, and an oversized computer screen had been his window to the world outside Fairfax County for the past five years. What he had learned via the electronic highways and byways was that progress and change had taken on totally different meanings from what he remembered.

So had organization, for organization was what he most often saw represented on his computer screen. And even as the electronic age allowed for more and varied aspects of an organization to develop and mature, it also allowed for parts of the same organization to alter and atrophy, all without the slightest knowledge of the supposed master.

When such alterations occurred, and no control was in place, the results could be disastrous. Proof was not difficult to find.

St. Clair slowly typed in a command, his aging fingers showing the first signs of arthritis. The computer performed the search while the old ambassador reached for the glass of cabernet sauvignon that sat next to the lamp on a separate table. He drained the glass, savoring the gentle bouquet of the red wine. By the time his eyes had returned to the computer screen, the sought-after file was displayed.

Yes, he thought. *I was right. The program is coming apart, just like I warned years ago. No one would listen then, and there is no reason to think they will listen now. But I have to try.*

Peter St. Clair jabbed at the mouse with his right hand, wanting to remove the vile evidence from his computer screen. He could no longer tolerate the information. Not that it was not vital; it was. It was the way in which such information was obtained that was abhorrent to him.

As the computer shut down, he reached for the phone, intent on voicing his opinion once again. But as his finger hovered above the buttons, he realized that there was no one for him to call to express his dismay. *That,* he realized, was where the problem lay. *There was no one.* No human being had more than a minor understanding of the procedures that had so long ago been instituted in the heat of necessity. He would have to think about his plan of attack. Suddenly the old man understood something that shook him to his very core. *He* understood more about the problem than the ones tasked with the responsibility of executing it. That meant *he* was responsible for bringing it to light. He, Peter St. Clair, the elder statesman, had the responsibility of exposing Janus. If he could live long enough to do it. If he could not do it, there *was* no one else.

■ ■ ■

Captain Dean waited on the tarmac of Millington Municipal Airport as the C20G made its approach into the tiny airport north of Memphis.

In his briefcase he carried a single set of orders requiring his presence at Naval Hospital Pensacola by 0400 hours. The only other items in the briefcase were five medical folders, four of which included dental charts and all X-rays. The fifth contained the medical file, but the dental charts were missing. The fifth file was on Sergeant Jerry Wallace, whose body lay in the Regional Forensic Center's cooler.

The five files represented the entire contingent of what Dean knew as the "X-files." The name seemed ridiculous and overly dramatic, but he understood the designation better than most, for Dean understood Janus. Janus, the Roman god of two faces. *J* was the tenth letter in the alphabet. The letter *X* was also the Roman numeral ten. J equals ten. Ten equals *X*. *J* equals *X*. The X-files—the five files he now carried.

The sleek Gulfstream landed and taxied to where Dean waited. The stairs descended, and Dean boarded.

There was no doubt why he was being summoned to Pensacola again so soon after having just been there, and that realization made the order disturbing.

He had informed his control about the X-rays taken of Jerry Wallace. He had expressed his concern but had had to admit to not having seen the films. He could not verify that the films revealed the presence of the personal status monitor implanted in Wallace's chest, but he had admitted there was a good chance of that happening. The presence of the device would most certainly raise questions, even though the electronic tracker and monitor had been designed to resemble a normal pacemaker. The presence of a pacemaker in a soldier's chest would most assuredly raise questions.

Dean had also admitted to dismissing Lieutenant Commander Jacob Madsen from Branch Medical Clinic. That might have something to do with the summons to appear in Pensacola. Under the circumstances, his control had not liked the idea of the young doctor being out of contact with BMC. It would have been better, the contact had said, to have left Madsen where he was so his activities could have been monitored. Dean had reluctantly agreed, but the deed had been done.

And now Dean was on the Gulfstream, headed south to meet with his contact concerning the remaining test subjects. Dean had a feeling deep in his soul that something was not right.

■ ■ ■

"What do you think, gentlemen?" General Abraham Zedillo asked.

John Ortiz and Al Bell scanned the interior of building. From the outside, the structure had appeared to be no more than an additional command structure nestled among the other tents of the encampment. The white structure, complete with air conditioning and florescent lights, consisted of an aluminum outer frame that was capable of being erected in a matter of minutes.

"Impressive," Ortiz ventured the first comment.

"Yeah," Bell added. "Looks like we were right."

Zedillo laughed. "Please, let us continue the tour. I am sure you will find most of what I am about to tell you very interesting. Especially since it will be the last thing you see and hear on this earth."

Accompanying the two agents and Zedillo were six Mexican army soldiers, all armed with M-16s and commanded by a tough-looking sergeant. Their orders had been made perfectly clear to the two agents: shoot to kill both DEA agents if *either* attempted to escape. The orders had been issued in Spanish, but they had been clear.

The structure in which the DEA agents found themselves was a complete chemical and medical laboratory. Bell was amazed despite the predicament in which he found himself. Ortiz, on the other hand, was not as impressed as his partner.

The laboratory was cool, quite cool. Ortiz could hear the low-frequency hum of rushing air channeled through large ducts. The lab's air conditioner was probably the only air conditioner within a couple hundred miles. Ortiz wondered why.

Two white-coated lab technicians sat on high stools across the room. The room itself was probably no larger than two hundred square feet—much smaller than the exterior dimensions suggested. The two techs paid no attention to the intruders nor the rifles carried by the guards. They had seen it all before.

"Chemical testing," Ortiz said to no one.

"Very good, Mr. Ortiz. That is exactly what is going on here. I am impressed with your knowledge."

"Don't be," said Ortiz quickly. "I'm not impressed with the Mexican army being involved in the drug trade."

Zedillo laughed loudly. "Drug trade? Is that what you think? Now

I am not so impressed with your knowledge. This has nothing to do with drug trade."

Ortiz glanced at Bell. His partner was still mesmerized by the operation.

"What exactly does it have to do with, then?" Ortiz asked.

"Actually," Zedillo said quietly, almost as if he did not want the guards to hear, "it has to do with your own country and military. You can understand my reticence in discussing this here. Most of my men do not understand English, but it would be better to discuss this in a more secure location."

Ortiz turned to face Zedillo. "*Our* military and *our* country? You will excuse me, General, if I find that hard to believe."

Zedillo sighed. "I see you are determined to discuss this. Very well, perhaps it is time for my troops to hear the truth as well."

"Excuse my skepticism, but I find it hard to believe that you know anything about truth, General."

Zedillo's smile left him. "You are insolent, but that will change. And truth is something I doubt your own country can lay claim to. You think this is all the result of some Mexican error?" the general said with a sweep of his hand. "How wrong you are. This used to be a thriving village."

"Colinas Verde," Ortiz said.

"You know of it, then. That is good, because you should know it was your government who was responsible for its destruction and the death of the entire population."

"I find that hard to believe," Bell finally said.

"Perhaps, but it is the truth. It was equipment from your army that came in and buried this village once it was dead. It was your army engineers who sealed this area. It was your government who caused this disaster."

"All I see are Mexican soldiers," Ortiz challenged.

Again, Zedillo smiled and shrugged. "We are doing our part. That is all. And that part is almost finished. It is just bad luck that the two of you turned up here now. A month later, and there would have been nothing here to find."

"And what exactly used to be here?" Ortiz asked.

"*That* is a very good question. Not only was the village of Colinas Verde here, but there was a branch of Chemicos Norte Americano, S.A. de C.V., located here. That company, in case you do not know, is a wholly owned subsidiary of North American Chemical Research, Inc. If you know anything, you know what type of research and production NACR is involved in."

Ortiz and Bell looked at each other, the truth beginning to flicker in the backs of each of their minds. They *were* familiar with NACR. The entire web of corporate entanglements raced through Ortiz's mind. Mudanzas Mundial represented transportation. North American Chemical Research and Chemicos Norte were suppliers, of a kind. Whatever was going on here was not local, not national, but international. The real question was, what *was* going on here?

"I can see by your faces you *are* familiar with this company. It is to the United States' great dishonor that your government must manufacture such weapons on the sovereign soil of another country."

"And to your eternal damnation that you have profited from it," Ortiz interjected.

Zedillo smiled again, raising his hands above his head in a sign of surrender. "I see you understand more than I am giving you credit for. It is true. There is always opportunity in conflict. It is just a matter of discovering what that opportunity is."

"And, if I am correct, you are saying that the United States was contracting to produce some sort of weapon here, and something happened. Colinas Verde was wiped out, along with the chemical plant, which I assume has been relocated. Our military helped to cover it up, and your military is monitoring the situation, via this remote lab, until you can determine that this land is safe to leave to the snakes, roadrunners, and Gila monsters. Is that about it?"

"Quite astute. And exactly on target. I am sure my contact would not mind my enlightening you on what happened here, but to tell the truth, gentlemen, I do not have the time, nor the inclination. I am tiring of this little game, and so you will excuse me." Zedillo turned to leave the laboratory.

"And what is to be done with us?" Ortiz asked, knowing the answer already, but wanting to hear it from the mouth of the general.

"Why, gentlemen, you will become the last people to die in Colinas Verde. It will be appropriate that the last to be buried on this land are citizens of the United States, don't you think? Apropos, if you ask me."

"And all your information will be relayed via the SATCOM link to wherever it is you relay the information," Ortiz interjected. He had noticed the small satellite dish as they approached the lab. He had seen the same equipment in England during a tour of duty over there. The equipment was what the Brits called a MANSAT SATCOM terminal. The dish was no larger than a common direct satellite television dish in the U.S.

"You are observant. And yes, the last of the information pertaining to this area will be relayed to a master computer via our SATCOM link. What happens to it after that, I do not care."

"Except that you get paid for the last installment," Ortiz said.

"Quite," Zedillo answered. "And now, excuse me, gentlemen."

The last words that General Abraham Zedillo said before leaving the laboratory sent chills through both Ortiz and Bell.

"*Matanlos,*" Zedillo ordered in Spanish.

With that one word, the DEA agents' deaths had been ordered as coolly as if Zedillo had been ordering breakfast.

■ ■ ■

The first explosion seemed distant. The boy raced toward the next fabricated igniter, touched a wooden match to the fuse, and sprinted for the next. The series of explosions were designed to attract the attention of the Mexican soldiers, force them to investigate, and allow the boy to begin the next series of explosions that would prove more deadly.

His planning had been meticulous. It had taken the boy almost two years to formulate the plan and scrounge the needed materials. But he had done it, always remembering why he was still alive and in the desert. It had been ordained for him to avenge the death of his village. And now the time had come.

Todo lo puedo en Cristo que me fortelece, the boy recited as he sprinted for the next igniter—the words serving as a mantra of death.

CHAPTER EIGHTEEN

Veteran's Affairs Medical Center

"Run the tape again," Carl Gilliland ordered.

Jack Harrison punched the rewind button on the tape equipment, and the images on the monitors reversed themselves.

Chief Gilliland, Jake, Kaci, two uniformed policemen of the Memphis PD, a detective sergeant, and FBI agent Frank Conners all crowded around Jack Harrison as the VA security officer manipulated the tape machines in the basement monitoring room of the VA Med Center. The group had been reviewing the tapes recorded earlier, trying to identify who might have shot and killed the assassin who had killed Dr. Ellis and had nearly done the same to Jake and Kaci. It had been a bizarre set of circumstances.

It didn't make a lot of sense at this point. An assassin had killed Ellis just before the doctor had revealed all he knew about an organization known only as Janus. Then, as if by magic, Ellis's killer had himself been murdered in the corridors of the VA Med Center. It had been a fortuitous act, since the killer was about to kill both Jake and Kaci. But even Kaci, with her fast thinking and quick reactions, had not been able to catch a glimpse of the second shooter. The Memphis police had seen no one; neither had the VA Med Center security officers. It seemed as if the killer's killer had simply vanished into thin air. The tapes held the key to the disappearance of the second killer.

"There," Gilliland pointed at the largest monitor screen in the room. "The guy wearing the baseball cap. What about him?"

Harrison manipulated the controls, focusing on the man Gilliland had indicated. The others in the room crowded around the monitor. The image grew as Harrison enlarged it, the man in the baseball cap coming into focus.

The man wore a long-sleeved shirt despite the summer heat, tattered jeans, old running shoes, and a baseball cap pulled down over his eyes. The eyes themselves were covered by wraparound sunglasses. All in all, an effective disguise.

The cameras followed the man down one corridor, through a large double door, and into the next corridor. A screen display showed the time in the bottom right corner.

"Timing's right," Kaci Callahan muttered to no one.

Harrison let the tape run.

"There," Jake said, pointing to the screen.

Another man had appeared coming from the opposite direction of the first man. The second man was similarly attired, the only difference being the degree to which the clothes he wore were tattered. He, too, wore a baseball cap, this one, the tape showed, was from an aircraft carrier. The first man's cap had been from a guided missile cruiser, but both caps were the military-operations type worn by navy personnel when they were aboard ship. Such caps were almost standard equipment for vets frequenting the VA Med Center.

"There's a third one," the MPD detective said, touching the monitor screen. "Same getup, different cap. Sunglasses, the whole nine yards."

The three men moved in sequence, advancing and covering each other while moving toward the Spinal Cord Injury Unit.

Carl Gilliland moved closer to the screen. He was angry. He did not like disturbances in his hospital, and murder, especially a double murder, was the worst kind of disturbance.

"It's a hit team," Kaci said in a low voice.

"Yeah," the MPD detective sergeant agreed. There was grudging admiration in his voice.

"And we can't identify any of them," Gilliland said, almost to himself.

"Look at them," Kaci continued. "They know the cameras are there, and they never look at them. They keep the bills of their caps down and the sunglasses in place. And their clothes are too generic to give us any help."

The group watched as the three men advanced on SCIU. The lead man, the original man wearing the cap from the guided missile cruiser, pulled out an automatic pistol. He kept his body between the cameras and the weapon—even the identification of certain pistols could lead to identification of their users.

Two of the men stopped at opposite ends of the corridor while the first moved closer to the door that everyone in the room now knew was the door to Dr. Ellis's laboratory. The man stayed out of direct sight line of Ellis's killer.

The tapes were running without sound; no one cringed when the man raised the automatic pistol and the weapon bucked once in the man's hand. Already the two cover men were making their way back down the corridors they had previously used. The shooter replaced his pistol slowly as he walked. He turned the first corner and ducked into a restroom. There was no camera in the restroom. Another link to Janus had been removed.

"Advance it," Gilliland ordered.

Harrison thumbed the video tape player's controls, and the tape advanced to see the man exit the restroom. He fell into step with another patient, and the two walked out together.

"Simple and effective," Kaci said. "And I doubt enhancing these tapes will give us any clues as to who the men were."

"Probably not," Gilliland agreed. "Still, let's get them to the lab. Harrison, copy the tapes and send the originals to the FBI lab. Unless you want to take them with you, Frank," Gilliland said, addressing the FBI agent.

"I'll take them. I'm going back to the office, and I want to show the tapes to Russ." Russell Prentice was the special agent for the Memphis Field Office. The VA was a Federal installation, and thus the involvement of the FBI.

"You'll be taking over the investigation?" Gilliland asked.

Conners shrugged. "That's up to Russ. We'll probably coordinate information from here and the MPD and see what develops."

When the clean-up tasks were over, Kaci, Jake, and Gilliland were standing alone in the basement corridor of the VA Med Center.

"What now?" Gilliland asked.

Kaci answered. "We're going to head up to the second floor and finish our conversation with Dr. Rhodes."

"Then we're heading over to the Med to see how a certain hospital corpsman is doing. I'd almost forgotten about Jamie Parker in all this."

"I don't see how you could forget about Jamie. We were almost killed by the same guy who shot him," Kaci said.

Jake reacted as if he *had* been shot. The thought had not occurred to him. His admiration for Kaci was growing with every second that passed. She had certainly been willing to put her life on the line for him back in the lab. He could still see glimpses of Kathy in Kaci, but the similarities, other than their appearances, were becoming fewer and fewer, and that was not all bad.

"Better give Dr. Rhodes a call before you head in that direction. I think I have her listed as being out of the building." Gilliland went to a computer keyboard and typed for a moment. "Yep. She's gone."

"You keep track of all the doctors on that thing?" Jake asked.

"Just the important ones. Just for your information, you're not on it," the security chief said with a large grin.

Jake pretended to ignore the good-natured ribbing.

"That's strange about Dr. Rhodes," he remarked. "She said she was going to be in the hospital all day. But that's OK. We'll head for the Med. Right?"

"Right," Kaci answered.

The Med was only a few blocks away, and in less than five minutes Jake and Kaci were walking in the door. Jake realized he did not know where to find Jamie since he had left the hospital last night while the young corpsman was still in the emergency room. By now Jamie would be in a room. Jake approached the information desk and asked for the number.

"The name again?" the clerk asked.

"Parker. Jamie Parker. He was brought in last night with a gunshot wound to the shoulder," Jake explained calmly.

"I'm sorry, sir. I don't have him listed on the room registry. Perhaps you should talk to the ER personnel. They could have transferred him somewhere else."

"Thanks," Jake said and headed for the emergency room. As he walked, he said, "I haven't thanked you for saving my life in the lab."

Kaci kept pace with Jake as they walked down the hallway. "Wasn't me, if you remember correctly. It was some guy in a baseball cap whom we can't identify."

"But you would have. That's what counts."

Kaci laughed.

Jake liked the way she laughed. It was a husky laugh, an honest laugh, not one of those forced chuckles that seemed to stop at the mouth. This laugh was genuine, almost sexy, Jake realized.

They came to a corner and turned. The ER was just down the hall and through a pair of automatic doors.

A half dozen patients were waiting to see doctors. Jake went to the nurse's window.

"Excuse me, I'm trying to locate Jamie Parker." Jake quickly explained who he was and the circumstances, and waited until the nurse searched her computer.

"Would you wait here a moment?" the nurse said, as she left the terminal and headed back into the maze that was the ER proper. She was back in minutes, a white-clad resident in tow.

"Dr. Madsen. I'm Dr. Warner. You're looking for the young sailor who came in last night."

"Jamie Parker," Jake said, glancing in Kaci's direction. Her eyes met his; concern was reflected in the look.

"Jamie died last night, Dr. Madsen," the resident said.

Jake felt as if he had been kicked in the chest. The room began to spin. Jake caught himself.

"We don't know what happened," the young doctor continued. "Everything seemed to go well down here. We transferred him to ICU, just as a precaution. He shouldn't have been there more than a few hours. Somehow, he died there."

"When will the autopsy be ready?" Jake asked, thinking that he was becoming involved in too many autopsies.

"Well . . . that's the problem, Dr. Madsen. We won't be doing an autopsy."

"What are you talking about?" Kaci jumped in. "There has to be an autopsy. The kid was shot."

"I understand. But that's out of our hands. The Department of the

Navy requested the body be flown to Pensacola for autopsy. It left here this morning."

Jake and Kaci stood, their surprise total. People who knew about Janus were disappearing before their very eyes. Who was left? Captain William Dean, Commanding Officer of Branch Medical Clinic at Naval Support Activities, and Dr. Caroline Rhodes, who was out of the hospital at the moment. A coincidence? Jake was beginning to wonder.

With Dr. Rhodes unavailable, it made sense to try and speak with Captain Dean. Kaci pulled out her cellular phone and prompted Jake for the number of BMC. She asked for Captain Dean. Jake could sense her frustration beginning to build. Suddenly she closed her phone's cover so forcefully she almost broke it.

"What's the problem?" Jake asked as the two stood back from the nurses window in the Med's ER.

"Dean's gone. The desk corpsman said he was headed for Pensacola."

"Along with the body of Jamie Parker," Jake added.

"Exactly. I've got a bad feeling about this, but I can't pin it down."

"We still have the body of Jerry Wallace over at the Forensic Center. Maybe we better head over there and see what we can find out," Jake suggested.

"Might as well. That looks like the only lead we have left."

"Other than the piece of paper Ellis gave you."

"You're right. How could I forget that?" Kaci pulled the paper out and read it again. "It's a Web address, but I have to admit to not being the best on a computer."

"Then that makes two of us. My wife used to do those things," Jake said, surprised that he could mention Kathy without a sense of guilt washing over him.

Kaci noticed the statement. "I noticed your ring at the fire. Tell me about your wife."

Jake hesitated. The statement about Kathy having been the computer whiz of the family was true, but it had been an offhand statement. Jake was not sure he could share anything more intimate about her with Kaci. But in a few minutes, he was deep into the story about how they met, what their life had been like, and how much he had loved her. It was strange, sharing such information with a total stranger, but then Jake realized he no longer thought of Kaci as a stranger.

"And she died," Kaci said evenly.

"Yeah," Jake said, choking on the word.

The two were outside the Med now, headed for Jake's Cherokee. They walked slowly. It was warm, and traffic had thinned out.

"And you think you did something to kill her," Kaci said gently as they crossed the street on a red light.

Jake didn't answer until they were across the street. "I used to think that. I'm a doctor, and she died. It was a viral infection, and it went to her brain. It was horrible."

"And what could you have done about it?"

Again Jake was slow in answering. "Nothing. Viruses aren't like bacteria. You can't kill them with antibiotics. There's no treatment. That's what makes viruses like Ebola and Lassa so deadly. There's just nothing you can do."

"And that frustrated you," Kaci said intuitively as they neared the Cherokee. "You still think there was something you should have done. Could have done."

"In my mind, I know there was nothing I could have done. In my heart, it's a different story."

"I envy her," Kaci said as Jake opened the Jeep's door for her.

"How so?" Jake asked, pausing with his hand on the door.

"She had someone who loved her very much, in a way a lot of people will never know. And you loved in a way most of us will never experience. She must have been very special."

"She was," Jake replied, his voice full of emotion. "Come on. Let's get over to Forensics."

Neither said a word during the short ride from the Med to the Regional Forensic Center on Madison. Jake pulled into the parking lot and shut off the engine. He and Kaci headed for the door that led into the waiting room. As they walked, Jake thought about the short conversation he'd just had with Kaci. Was there another woman in the world besides Kathy whom he could feel so deeply about? And if there were, could that woman be Kaci Callahan?

I can do all things through Christ who strengthens me. Surely the verse did not include *this.* Kathy could not have meant for him to see the verse in this context. But then, as Jake thought about it, that was just the kind of person Kathy had been. He felt his throat constrict at the thought. He would have to think about it further. Kathy was still his love, and he was not ready to give her up. Not yet, anyway.

Jake pushed open the door and held it for Kaci. *At least,* he thought, *she's not so liberated as to be upset by my holding the door for her.* Maybe that was a start.

"Just the people I was waiting to see," Darla Adams called from the room next to the scales.

"What's up?" Jake asked.

"Got some interesting news about your burn victim," Darla said.

"How interesting?" Kaci asked.

"Interesting enough that you can file murder charges if you catch whoever did it."

"Then it was murder."

"No doubt. Not a trace of smoke or burned tissue in the mouth, nostrils, esophagus, or trachea. Not that that really mattered. The tissue samples and blood told us all we needed to know."

"Which was?" Kaci said.

"He died of cyanide poisoning."

"Cyanide?" Jake almost shouted.

"Breathed it in. In its gaseous form, it's almost instantaneous in producing death. There's no doubt about it."

"I didn't smell anything at the fire scene," Kaci said, her tone questioning.

Darla smiled. "I'm not surprised. That stuff about smelling almonds and such is overplayed in the movies."

"You mean, that's not how it is?" Jake asked, now curious. He had to admit he was less than well-informed on forensic matters.

"Yes and no," the technician said. "When you smell cyanide, it does smell like almonds, but chances are you are not going to smell it."

"How so?" Kaci asked.

"The ability to smell residual cyanide is an inherited trait. You can either smell it or you can't, and there's nothing you can do about it. And the chances of you having the particular gene that allows you to smell it is pretty remote. No, I'm not surprised you didn't smell it."

"Is the report written up?" Kaci asked.

"Not yet. And it'll have to be signed by the doctor when she gets back. She had to go to Jackson to testify in a trial. I don't expect her back until sometime tomorrow."

"When the report is signed, can you fax a copy to my office over at Naval Support Activities?"

"Sure, no problem," Darla replied.

"Let's go," Kaci said to Jake, turning on her heels and heading for the door.

"Where to?" Jake asked, following after the NCIS agent.

"NAVSUPACT. I want to talk to Kerry Hartford."

"And who is Kerry Hartford?" Jake asked, trying to keep up with the fast-walking agent.

"Another NCIS agent, only he's a very special one."

"I thought you were a special one," Jake said, surprising himself.

Kaci turned and looked at Jake, shook her head, and said, "Open the door, boy, and I'll tell you about Kerry."

Jake did as he was ordered, then walked around and got in the Cherokee. Kaci talked as he drove.

"Kerry's a computer jock. He's been over at BUPERS working on a hack job."

"What kind of job?"

"Someone tried to hack into the computers at the Bureau. Who knows why. Maybe they wanted to promote themselves, but whatever it was, Kerry's been over there working on that problem."

"It never occurred to me that BUPERS would have such a problem," Jake said, weaving through the midtown traffic.

"Where there's a computer, there's a hacker. And where's there's a hacker, there's Kerry. If it's navy, that is."

"He's good, huh?"

"The best I've ever seen, and I've seen a few."

"And you're going to give him that Web address and turn him loose. Is that it?"

Kaci laughed. Again it was an attractive laugh. "You're pretty smart for a mere doctor. That's exactly what I'm going to do."

"Hoping for what?" Jake asked as he headed north on Danny Thomas Boulevard toward NAVSUPACT.

"I don't know. Whatever he can find, I'll take. I have a feeling we may not see Captain Dean again. I'm running out of people to question."

"Yeah," Jake said, thinking about Jamie Parker. "I know what you mean."

Kaci pulled out her cell phone again and dialed a number from memory. "Kerry," she said when it was answered. "I'm on my way back to the office. Can you get away for a few minutes? Good. I'll see you at the office in half an hour. I've got a murderer I want you to run down for me," and she disconnected before Kerry Hartford could respond.

"A murderer?"

Kaci looked out the windshield at the passing landscape. "Somebody's killing people, and I'm going to find out who," was all she said.

■ ■ ■

The Gulfstream C20G banked hard to the south, pinning Captain Dean against the curved side of the sleek jet and making him wonder what was happening on the flight deck. He glanced out his window to see nothing but water below. *The pilot must have made the turn over the Gulf of Mexico, heading in for Pensacola Naval Air Station's main runway,* Dean thought.

But the white jet leveled out, and when Dean searched for land on either side of the airplane, all he saw was the Gulf. Something was not right.

He felt his ears pop gently. That was a clue that the aircraft had begun its descent, but a descent to where? He peered out the small windows again, first on one side, then the other. Still nothing but water. His ears continued to alert him to the aircraft's descent. What was going on?

Dean's attention was drawn to the forward section of the cabin. The copilot was working his way toward the rear, where Dean was seated. When he arrived, Dean looked up with what he hoped was a disgusted look on his face. He would berate this Lieutenant Junior Grade (JG) for inefficiency and insubordination just because he felt the need to exert some authority.

Dean looked up, shocked at what he saw. The copilot held an automatic pistol in his right hand. Dean started to open his mouth but was cut short by the motion of the pistol.

"Not a word, Captain," the copilot said. "Get up."

Dean was frozen to the seat.

"Up," the man repeated.

Dean began to rise but was stopped by the buckled seat belt. He unbuckled the belt and stood as far as he could in the small jet.

"Move forward, Captain," the man ordered.

Dean moved, feeling as he did so, the slowing of the aircraft. What was going on?

"Lieutenant—" Dean began.

The copilot jammed the muzzle of the automatic pistol into the base of Dean's neck. "Shut up, Captain, and walk."

Dean swallowed hard; he began to sweat despite the jet's air-conditioning system. The two men reached the limit of the forward bulkhead. The Gulfstream bucked in some low-level turbulence. Dean reached for a handhold, sweat pouring from him now.

"Open the door," the copilot ordered, punctuating his order with a wave of the pistol.

Dean blanched. This could not be happening!

"The door, Captain," the order was repeated.

Dean was frozen.

"Fine. I'll open it for you. After all, you are a captain, and I'm only a JG." The man opened the door, and a wave of warm, moist air swept into the cabin. The airplane had not been pressurized!

"Stand in the door, Captain."

Dean could not move. The copilot jammed the pistol into Dean's left kidney. Dean grunted, forced to move by the sheer force of the blow and the excruciating pain.

He turned to plead his case, but the next thing he knew he was free-falling through space. In less time than he would have thought, the world went dark as Captain William Dean slammed into the surface of the Gulf of Mexico from an altitude of less than four hundred feet. Coastal radar would not have seen the body falling; the aircraft was too close to the water.

The copilot closed the door and moved back onto the flight deck.

"Everything go all right?" the pilot asked.

"The package has been delivered. Just like FedEx."

"I use UPS," the pilot joked back.

The Gulfstream flew a northerly route, heading for Ronald Reagan International Airport. The Gulfstream's long-range fuel tanks meant there would be no stopping to refuel. The pilot set the automatic pilot, turned the plane over to the copilot, and went aft.

"Wake me in two hours," the pilot said as he squeezed between the two flight deck seats.

"Affirmative," the copilot said. "Should I transmit the message?"

"Sure. Someone might want to know we just made the world safer for democracy."

The copilot punched some buttons on the control panel, waited to make sure the frequency was correct, then pushed "transmit." The coded message was received just outside Washington, D.C., in a computer room where no one stood watch.

CHAPTER NINETEEN

Tierra Quemada, Mexico

As in Dante's version of hell, pandemonium reigned.

A series of explosions rocked the Mexican army camp just outside Colinas Verde. The primary explosions had been distant—the timing spaced almost two minutes apart. Those explosions had reached the camp as low-frequency rumbles rather than the sharp report of explosions. But they had moved increasingly closer, marching across the landscape like an invisible assault force. General Abraham Zedillo had had no alternative but to send out several squads of soldiers to investigate.

John Ortiz and Al Bell had moved with equal resolve. Zedillo had left them to the guards, and both men had moved with the first explosion.

Ortiz threw himself into the nearest guard, bowling the man over and knocking the weapon from the surprised man's hands. The surprise was complete. The guard rolled into the guard nearest him, throwing the man to the ground in a domino effect. The man's gun clattered to the ground.

Bell moved in response to his partner's actions, duplicating the maneuver. Bell's guard, however, had time to react, and succeeded in holding on to his M-16.

Already, John Ortiz had an M-16 in his hands. The remaining guards had been unsure of themselves, all except the sergeant. The tough-looking sergeant had moved almost as quickly as the two DEA agents. He had grabbed an M-16 from the nearest soldier and released the safety. The muzzle of the rifle had been leveled at Bell when three 5.52-mm bullets spit from the weapon.

Bell scrambled for the weapon the second guard had dropped when Ortiz attacked. Bell depressed his own trigger just as the sergeant's M-16 erupted. The first bullet hit the sergeant in the throat, penetrated, and kept going through the wall of the lab. Bell felt a burning in his right calf. The sergeant had been thrown backward by the impact of the first bullet, causing the last two bullets to miss Bell.

Ortiz had his M-16 aimed at the rest of the guards. The expressions on their faces told him that none had ever experienced an exchange of gunfire.

More explosions rocked the camp. This time they were closer. Rumbles reached the interior of the lab like low, rolling thunder. The sound of men running could be heard even over the lab's air-conditioning.

"Al. You OK?" Ortiz called out.

"Took one in the calf. Hurts bad, but I'll be all right."

"What about the sergeant?"

"Dead," Bell answered.

"All right, let's get these guys somewhere secure, then I want to run that computer and see what we can find out."

"We don't have time for that, John," Bell argued as several more explosions rocked the camp. "And where are those explosions coming from?"

"Heaven," Ortiz said grimly.

■ ■ ■

It was working even better than he'd hoped for. Every explosion created even more confusion. Soldiers who had never been under fire were racing about the camp in wholesale disarray. A few officers and senior non-coms were trying to organize the rabble, forming them into squads, and following the earlier squads that had been sent to investigate the explosions.

But the squads were investigating what had already occurred, not realizing that the explosions were coming nearer and nearer the military complex itself. The troops were being sucked into a trap that neither they nor their leaders recognized.

The boy was well ahead of the squads sent to quell the explosions. Already he was lighting a fuse that would blow a group of vehicles to the high heavens. As the boy ran from fuse to fuse, he chanted the mantra: *Todo lo puedo en Cristo que me fortelece.*

The boy didn't know the meaning of the verse. He remembered only the words themselves from a sermon by the Padre. For him the words meant revenge.

He lit yet another fuse and sprinted for the next in the series. Even before he reached the next fuse, the two-and-a-half-ton military truck was blown into the air, its own fuel tank rupturing and adding to the strength of the explosion.

Soon, the boy knew, his revenge would be complete.

■ ■ ■

Ortiz typed furiously on the computer's keyboard.

"Come on, John," Bell urged. "Those explosions are getting closer. They're liable to blow us to kingdom come if we don't get out of here."

"Patience, Al," Ortiz said. "In case you haven't noticed, those explosions are coming in a circular pattern, moving toward the center. We have some time. And besides, whoever is setting them saved our lives. We owe him something."

"And what would that be?" Bell asked, his hand reaching for his damaged right calf. He had wrapped a makeshift bandage around it. The bleeding had stopped, but the pain was getting worse. The aspirin back in the car would help, but only a little.

"Maybe I can backtrack on this computer and find out where this information is going."

"You know better than that. Can't be done."

"Don't say 'can't.' I'm doing it." Ortiz watched the computer screen as information ebbed and flowed across the screen. There was something strange about the presentation of the information displayed. Not the information itself; that seemed normal. But the format in which the information was showing up on the screen seemed alien.

Then it hit him, and John Ortiz almost jumped for joy. Instead, he grabbed the mouse, moved the cursor to one of the strange formats, and clicked on it. He had been right. The strange format had a purpose behind it. It was a form of Uniform Resource Locator, a URL, a link to underlying information on the computer's Web or Internet.

Instantly, new information appeared. Ortiz sat mesmerized, soaking in the information, knowing what he was going to do next.

He took a piece of paper, wrote down the pertinent information, and shut down the computer. "OK, let's get out of here."

"Where to?" Bell asked.

"The border. McAllen or Laredo, whichever is easiest and quickest. I need to get to an airport, and you need to get to a hospital."

"Given a choice, I'll take McAllen," Bell said, following Ortiz. "But this time you get to drive."

"Gladly. Let's get to the car before whoever is blowing this place to pieces blows up our car."

Bell and Ortiz left the lab, running for where they had left their car. Ortiz lagged behind, letting Bell move at his own pace, protecting his partner.

By now the military camp was complete chaos. The explosions were centering on the main facilities of the camp. Tents, vehicles, and equipment were being blown into the air as if some giant were tossing toys about. Soldiers scrambled to avoid the explosions.

Ortiz and Bell were just two more people trying to escape the carnage. In minutes, without anyone trying to stop them, the two DEA agents were back at their car, and Ortiz was starting the engine. He jammed the accelerator to the floor and headed the car away from the latest explosion, this one throwing the hard shell of what had once been the laboratory high into the air.

"How long?" Ortiz asked Bell.

"Three, four hours to McAllen. No more. Let me see the info you wrote down."

Ortiz fished the paper from his pocket and handed it to Bell. Bell read it. "This where you're going?"

"Yeah. What do you think?"

"I think it'll be nicer than the Mexican desert, but you better watch yourself. I won't be there to do it for you."

"I'll remember that. I'll get you to a hospital, and then I'll get a flight."

Bell nodded and leaned back against the seat. His leg was beginning to throb. He'd be more than happy to let Ortiz handle this gig from now on.

■ ■ ■

The plan had worked perfectly. Of the many explosives the boy had stolen from the army and planted, only two had failed to go off. The last, by far the largest, had blown the command center into tiny pieces. The boy had watched the man he knew to be the leader of the army frantically trying to organize the gaggle of soldiers. It had been useless. The boy had lit the final fuse and had run. When the final explosion rang in his ears, he knew his revenge was complete. He had turned just in time to see the man the rest of the men called the General explode before his very eyes. This general had been the same man he'd seen two years earlier, burying his village, killing those he'd loved, destroying his life. Now the general had been repaid for his transgressions.

■ ■ ■

Peter St. Clair did not notice the "hit" noted on his computer screen when he powered up his system. He was searching for more information on Janus, and he knew where to go to get it.

The "hit" had come from outside his own system, and it indicated that someone, somewhere in the world, had logged into his system via the Internet. St. Clair continued to search for the information he sought, unaware that his computer was communicating with an outside system.

The information exchange initiated by the external system was completed, the information transferred, and the connection terminated, all before Peter St. Clair knew his own computer had betrayed him.

During the same time, the Ambassador had found the information he was seeking, noted the name and phone number of the man to whom he wished to speak, and shut down his computer. He did not notice that a small red light still glowed on the console of his CPU.

CHAPTER TWENTY

Kerry Hartford was tired. He'd been working nonstop at the computer terminal in his office next to Kaci Callahan's for the last two hours. The idea of hacking into someone else's computer system had appealed to him. After all, he was usually the one trying to expose the perpetrator, and it was a strangely exhilarating feeling to be the one on the "wrong side" of the law.

The Web address Kaci had given him had seemed straightforward enough, and he had entered it as it had been written. It had only taken a few moments for his Web browser to discover multiple links to other Web sites, and he was busy examining those sites for any clues that might lead him in some other direction. Of course, it was difficult finding clues when you weren't really sure what form those clues would take.

"Any luck?" Kaci asked, sticking her head around the door.

Kerry didn't look up from the computer screen. "Lots of luck. All bad. These seem to be pretty traditional Web sites. The information is strange, but that's not too unusual. You get strange info on a lot of sites."

"Nothing on Janus, though?" Kaci pressed.

"Nothing yet, but I've got a feeling I'm getting close to something."

"In that case, I'll leave you alone and let you get back to whatever it is you do with that keyboard and that screen."

"Yeah," Kerry said absentmindedly, "you do that." Then he input some more data and waited for the computer to respond. There was something very strange going on, but he just couldn't put his finger on it.

Kaci walked back into her office. Jake sat in one of the two chairs facing her desk. Kaci took the chair behind the desk.

"Anything?" Jake asked.

"Nothing concrete, but Kerry's getting close. I can feel it."

"I hope so. This is the craziest thing I've ever been involved in," Jake said. "I mean, there are four dead, two missing, and heaven knows what else. Things don't add up." An additional phone call to the VA Med Center had not produced Dr. Rhodes, and it was not like the chief of staff to be away from the hospital for an extended period of time. Kaci had already made a note to call back.

"On the contrary. Things always add up, it's just up to us to find the right formula."

Jake sat forward in his chair. He had warmed to Kaci Callahan, finding her not only attractive but also intelligent and intuitive. It had been a long time since he'd felt that way about any woman except Kathy. Even now, the memory of his wife tied his stomach in knots, and a part of him wondered if his feelings for Kaci could be construed as unfaithfulness?

Jake's thoughts shot to Kathy's small Bible. The marked passages came to mind at the strangest times, but the one that kept haunting him was the one where Kathy had claimed the passage for him. *I can do all things through Christ who strengthens me.* The fact that Kathy had chosen the verse meant even more. In a strange way he did feel strengthened; even the pain of remembering was not as severe as it had once been.

He could not deny his attraction to Kaci. Even now, as she sat behind her desk, Jake felt a kind of magnetism, a pull. And it was not just the NCIS agent's looks, he told himself; it was everything that made up what he now knew was a very complete and confident personality. He was interested in Kaci Callahan, and that bothered him.

"How about something to eat?" Kaci said.

Jake pulled himself back to the present. He was hungry, he realized. "What did you have in mind?"

"Memphis barbecue."

"When you say that," Jake said, liking the idea, "you have to be more specific. Dry or messy?"

Kaci laughed, her mirth echoing down the hallways of Building 238.

"You're right; there is a very distinct difference. Lets go to Corky's on Poplar. I feel like getting messy."

Jake smiled. The laugh had confirmed it: he cared about this red-haired, affable lady.

"Let's go," Jake said, sliding his chair back toward the wall.

"Let me tell Kerry where we'll be," Kaci suggested. She stepped from the office and was back in minutes. "Kerry says he thinks he's on to something, but it could be hours before he breaks through. He'll buzz us on my cell phone. Let's go."

"We'll take my Jeep," Jake said.

"Your chariot will do just fine," Kaci joked, lightening their mood.

They walked out of NCIS headquarters, got into Jake's Cherokee, and headed for Memphis.

Neither noticed the neutral-colored Ford Taurus that had pulled out behind them and now followed a quarter of a mile back.

Traffic was light, and in less than thirty minutes, Jake and Kaci were seated in a back booth at Corky's, one of Memphis's best barbecue restaurants. They both ordered a barbecue pork platter and were soon up to their elbows in barbecue sauce.

Suddenly Jake burst out laughing. Kaci had the red sauce all over her face. She grinned broadly, then joined Jake's laughter.

"Don't say it," Kaci said. "I know I make a mess when I eat this stuff, but I can't help myself. It's the best barbecue in the world."

Jake stopped laughing and caught his breath. "I couldn't agree with you more. If it ain't pig, it ain't barbecue."

They both laughed again and finished the meal. After a third glass of iced tea, they were ready to head back to Naval Support Activities.

"This is on me," Kaci said, picking up the check that lay between them.

Jake thought about protesting, but then thought better of it. He only raised his hands in submission. It would do no good to argue with the NCIS agent, no matter what the subject.

It took almost an hour to get back to NAVSUPACT. Jake had followed an internal route within the freeway system that surrounded the city. He had turned onto Austin Peay Highway and headed north. Now he was heading for the east entrance to the navy base. The land around him was flat farming land, mostly planted in soybeans. The green seemed to leap from the fields in a brilliant display of color.

Jake let the Cherokee have its head.

"Better watch your speed. The base cops will give you a ticket, and there's no reprieve from those guys," Kaci said.

Jake looked at his speedometer; he was doing almost seventy-five miles per hour in a fifty-five zone. He pushed on the brake. The sharp protest of squealing tires jerked their attention to the car behind them. Jake had reacted too quickly; he had not seen the trailing car.

It was a cream-colored Ford Taurus, and it had apparently been following them too closely. When Jake applied his brakes, the Taurus had barely reacted in time to avoid slamming into the rear of Jake's Cherokee.

Jake watched the Taurus fishtail behind. A sense of guilt flowed over him. It had been his inattention that had caused the incident. But what had the Taurus been doing following so closely? The driver of the Ford would have to shoulder part of the responsibility.

The Taurus straightened as Jake watched in the rearview mirror. He could see two men in the car. He breathed a sigh of relief that no accident had occurred, and went back to driving.

The Taurus shot by the Cherokee in the left lane. The roadway was divided, and the Taurus had plenty of room.

"Wow! I must have made them angry," Jake muttered.

"Look out!" Kaci yelled.

The Taurus had slammed on its brakes in front of Jake. Jake barely had time to react, jamming his foot down on his own brake pedal. The Cherokee swerved, fishtailing like the Taurus had, the tires smoking and screaming under the abuse. The high center of gravity of the Cherokee threatened to topple the vehicle onto its side.

The Taurus had stopped ahead. Jake was able to stop the Cherokee on the shoulder of the highway. Now he was angry.

"Those guys are crazy," Jake fumed.

"Maybe. But let's get out of here. I don't have any desire to become roadkill for a couple of redneck crazies," Kaci said.

The two men had gotten out of the car and were walking toward the Cherokee.

"Maybe I should try to reason with them," Jake suggested, putting his hand on the Jeep's door handle.

"Duck!" Kaci screamed, her left hand shooting out, forcing Jake down behind the steering wheel just before the windshield of the Jeep exploded inward from a hail of bullets.

"Back up! Back up, now!" Kaci screamed.

The Jeep was still running, so Jake threw the transmission into reverse and jammed his foot against the accelerator. The Cherokee leapt backwards, throwing gravel as it went, careening into the plowed fields.

Jake could feel the Cherokee bouncing over the planted mounds of the soybean field. Both he and Kaci still had their heads down, using the dashboard as protection against the bullets that pounded into the Jeep's body. The steering wheel jerked like a live snake in his hand. He pressed harder on the accelerator. The Jeep responded, leaping over the planted rows. The soybean plants whipped by in a green blur.

The bullets ceased; Jake and Kaci raised their heads. The Jeep was still accelerating backwards. Jake slowed. Every loose item in the vehicle was flying through the air. They could see the two men walking into the edge of the field. One man worked the slide of some type of automatic weapon. The other was shoving shotgun shells into what Kaci knew was a pump-action 12-gauge shotgun. From the noise the weapon had made, it was apparent that the wooden plug that limited the number shells that could be used had been removed. These men were killers. Men of Janus.

"Keep going," Kaci ordered. Jake obeyed. Kaci looked behind the Jeep. The car was heading for the far edge of the field where the land gradually sloped down to a drainage ditch.

"Head for the ditch over there," Kaci said, pointing so Jake would know where she was talking about.

Despite the power steering, Jake struggled with the steering wheel as the vehicle bounced over the rows. More than once the combination of speed and irregular surface threatened to toss the Jeep onto its side.

Jake made the ditch. The gentle slope of the terrain made it impossible for them to see the two shooters. Sirens wailed in the distance. They were on the outskirts of NAVSUPACT. The sirens would be the base security force racing in the directions of the shots.

Jake braked the Jeep to a halt, spun the wheel, and headed parallel to the ditch. The path would put them well out of range of the two men—if they still pursued them—and onto the pavement, headed away from the killers.

The Jeep's tires found the pavement. Kaci swiveled in her seat, searching for the Taurus. It was nowhere in sight.

"They're gone," she told Jake.

Jake checked the mirror. He could just make out the blue lights of the base security force heading in their direction. He pulled the Cherokee to the side of the road.

"I hope you know these guys," Jake said to Kaci. "The security men, I'm talking about. I have a feeling we already know who those other two guys were, and they weren't just irate motorists, either."

"I think you're right about that. No casual motorist is going to be carrying an ArmaLite rifle and a 12-gauge shotgun with the plug removed."

"I'll agree about the ArmaLite, but don't be too sure about the shotgun. There are plenty of those running around this part of the country."

Kaci started to say something but was interrupted by the arrival of two white Ford Tauruses, the standard patrol car of the NAVSUPACT Security Division.

Four NAVSUPACT security officers walked toward them. Kaci got out of the Cherokee.

"Kaci. What the heck is going on?" one of the men asked. "We could hear shots all the way back to the base."

"I don't know, Harry. Some guys in a cream-colored Taurus tried to blow Dr. Madsen's Cherokee into the next county." Kaci recounted the story of the near collision and her conclusion that the incident was not merely an outburst of an angry driver.

"Did you get a license number?" the officer asked.

"Nothing. It all happened too quickly. We barely got away from the two lunatics," Kaci told the man.

"We'll put out the info on the wire. We might get lucky, but there have to be a few hundred cars like that."

"Yeah, I know. Do what you can, guys," Kaci said just as her cell phone rang. She answered the phone, listened for a few minutes, then terminated the connection without saying another word.

"What was that?" Jake asked. He had been silent while the security officers had been talking with Kaci, but the strange reaction of Kaci on the phone had his curiosity up.

"That was Kerry. He's got something, but he wants us to see it firsthand. Sounds like he might have stumbled onto something with that Web address."

"I'm sure you're right about that. Whatever that Web address leads to is probably already responsible for four deaths, and I have a feeling it almost killed us just now."

"Let's go see what Kerry's got," she said. She turned to the security men. "I'll help finish your report back at the base," she said.

The officers headed back. Jake and Kaci followed in Jake's mangled Cherokee. Despite the damage done by the shotgun and automatic rifle, the Jeep still ran.

"Rugged. Just like the commercials say," Jake said over the wind noise coming through the shattered windshield.

This time, Kaci did not laugh.

■ ■ ■

While Al Bell rested comfortably in a private hospital room in McAllen, Texas, John Ortiz boarded a flight that would route him from the Texas border town, through Nashville, Tennessee, and on to Washington, D.C. His eventual destination was written in a small notebook he carried. He would rent a car and drive the hour or so it would take to reach the address. He was becoming more and more interested in the man whose name was written in his book. This same man was probably responsible for the near death of his partner, and maybe even the death of the desert village in the highlands of Mexico.

Ortiz checked his watch. It would be dark by the time he arrived in Washington. He would spend the night in a motel near the airport, and drive out into the Virginia countryside in the morning. After all, the man he sought would still be there in the morning, and he needed the time to think.

■ ■ ■

"What are you talking about, Kerry?" Kaci asked NCIS agent Kerry Hartford.

Jake and Kaci sat in Hartford's office while the computer expert fed information to the laser printer next to his computer. Hartford pulled the sheets out as they finished printing, manually collating the information and handing it to Kaci Callahan.

"It means you and the young doctor here are into something deeper than you realize. It took me some time to realize what I was working with, but once I recognized the format, it was easy."

"I still don't understand what you're talking about, Kerry," Kaci repeated.

Hartford sighed and started over. "The Web address your Dr. Ellis provided was only the proverbial tip of the iceberg. Once I understood what was going on, there were multiple links embedded in the test formats of all the other Web sites I found."

It was Jake who spoke first. "You might as well be talking Greek," Jake responded. "What kind of links?"

The computer expert turned to Jake. "Hypertext links, those little things on the Internet you can click on to get to another site. Usually they are words in text that are different colors, and you put your cursor on those, click the mouse, and presto, you are somewhere else."

"And you're saying there were several of those at the Web site Dr. Ellis gave us before he was killed," Kaci went on.

"Exactly. Except the links I found weren't like the nice little colored key words you normally find. These were embedded in the text. Hidden."

Jake and Kaci looked at each other, neither completely sure of what Kerry Hartford was trying to say.

"They were not there to be found by the casual browser," Kerry went on. "And there was a reason for that."

"Go on," Kaci ordered.

"The Web site was a medical site. It contained all sorts of information. Nothing really esoteric, but not the kind of stuff you would normally find, or even want to find, while browsing the Web. Lots of medical jargon, test results depicted on graphs, conclusions that wouldn't mean a thing to a layman. That sort of stuff."

"But you said nothing very esoteric," Jake interjected.

"Not really," the agent continued. "I couldn't understand what it was talking about, but I could make out that it really wasn't very interesting stuff. Then I went back and read some of the text. It didn't make sense. Not in the sense that the syntax of sentences and words were formed in a logical sequence. I wasn't really aware of what was going on until I searched several of the sites. Words were out of sequence, like the person composing the text was not American."

"Words were reversed," Kaci offered.

"Exactly. As if a romance language speaker was writing in English. Adjectives were reversed. There was no possessive case to speak of. Antecedents were in the wrong location. That kind of thing."

"You're talking about what would be normal in Spanish, for example, but not in English," Jake jumped in. "Like saying 'the owner of the car' instead of 'the car's owner.' Or like 'the car green' instead of 'the green car'."

"Now you're getting it," Hartford acknowledged. "That's the way some of these Web sites read, only they were in English, which was kind of strange, especially since the jargon was medical. So I started going over the words, the odd ones anyway, one by one, and bingo, there were the links."

Kaci slipped forward in her chair. "So there were links in words that didn't indicate that they were links. They were hidden."

Hartford nodded excitedly. "That's what it looks like to me. And the Web pages the links connected to were as strange as the method used to get there. Those pages were written in real medical jargon, this time in syntax I recognized. And the subject was not very nice."

"But that's not what made you call me, is it?" Kaci asked intuitively.

Hartford smiled. "No. This is what made me call you," he said, handing a computer printed sheet of letter-size paper to Kaci.

Kaci took the paper and read it quickly, then looked up. "Is this the truth?" she asked.

Hartford shrugged his shoulders. "That I can't tell you. That's something you'll have to determine for yourself. I can tell you this much: there is a connection there, at least through the Internet, and the steps that were taken to hide it leads me to believe there has to be something to it."

Jake watched the two NCIS agents discussing the paper that Kaci held. He knew enough not to interfere, but his curiosity was getting the better of him. Just as he was about to ask Kaci about the paper, she turned to him.

"Are you up for a trip?" she asked.

"What . . . ?"

"I'll tell you on the way. We need to catch a plane tonight," she said.

"I don't know . . .," Jake began.

"I do," Kaci cut him off. "You're technically still on active duty, and I'm actively investigating a murder. You'll come with me, under my authority. Now let's get moving."

"One more thing before you leave," Hartford said. "Take this with you." He handed Kaci a computer disk. "I collect computer viruses. It's a hobby. That's one of the more lethal. Use it if you have to. Insert it in any computer online, and click on download. It also works in DOS. Press 'control,' 'shift,' 'escape,' if you can't use the mouse. I don't know what's going on, but whatever it is, it's controlled by computers somewhere, and that disk will crash any system connected to it. It just might come in handy."

Jake watched openmouthed as Kaci accepted the disk, rose, and walked out of the office without another word. His gaze fell to Kerry Hartford, who only shrugged again and motioned with his head. Jake got up and followed Kaci out of the office. He knew he was in over his head. He just hoped the attractive NCIS agent he was following was not.

CHAPTER TWENTY-ONE

The newspaper headline reflected the failed peace accords in the Balkans, particularly in Kosovo. Peacekeepers had been dispatched to the region in mid-1999 and had met with limited success since that time. Had it not been for the headlines announcing the death of a squad of soldiers, mostly U.S. soldiers, in the area, the bold type beneath the newspaper's fold would have garnered more interest. It read, "Congressman J. Fredrick Bryant Killed in Hit and Run." The police had a lead on the color of car, but that was about it. The report went on to tell how Bryant had come to Congress from the Second District in Iowa, and how he was a member on the Congressional Oversight Committee for Strategic Weapons Development. There was nothing in the story about what exactly the committee did. It was what was *not* in the story that had cost freshman congressman Freddy Bryant his life.

■ ■ ■

Jake and Kaci had changed planes in Cincinnati. Thunderstorms had been rolling in on the airport when they arrived, and the takeoff of their connecting flight into Washington, D.C., had been delayed. They had arrived in Washington one hour later than scheduled.

The full front page of the *Washington Post* was displayed at a newsstand as Jake and Kaci walked by. Jake watched as Kaci stopped dead in her tracks. She extracted the paper she'd received from Kerry Hartford and reread the material. Congressman J. Fredrick Bryant, who the *Post* was reporting as having been killed, was listed among other names on the printout.

Kaci bought a paper and read the entire story as Jake waited.

He remained silent as she read. He had already learned when to speak and when not to. Kaci had her own way of getting things done, and Jake was becoming attuned to it.

Kaci handed the newspaper to Jake. "Read this," she said, indicating the story on the front page.

Jake did as she directed and then looked up. "OK. What about it?"

She handed him the paper she'd received from Kerry Hartford. Jake scanned the information. It was the first time he'd seen the paper, and from the contents, he was not sure he wanted to know any more. But one thing stood out. The name of J. Fredrick Bryant was displayed on the document as well as on the front page of the *Post*. People were dying all around them, and it was only now beginning to make sense.

"Is this right?" Jake asked, handing the paper back to Kaci.

"I don't know. I thought it might be some sort of hoax. Now I don't know. That's one of the reasons I brought you along. With your medical training, you could be of some use. But this information seems to confirm my greatest fears."

"That fear being that what Kerry found out is really true, and it is happening right now," Jake added.

"Right. If the information on that paper is right, we have multiple murders on our hands, and it seems those murders have been committed at the highest level of government."

Jake shook his head. "Not just at the highest level, but with consent of those governing. That's not only an atrocity, it's a sin against all that is sacred," Jake said, surprised at his choice of words. Those were words Kathy would have used. Never before had he referred to something as sacred. Jake suddenly became aware of something in his back pocket. He reached in and extracted the small Bible, not remembering when or why he had put it there. He didn't need to flip the book open to know what the most important verse was for him. He knew the passage in Philippians by heart, and it surprised him that he no longer questioned its promise. The promise not only Kathy had claimed for him, but a promise made to him by a living God in whose existence he now believed. The realization surprised him, and he smiled to himself.

An inner peace infused him. What was the word Kathy had used? Conversion? The word applied, he realized. He could *feel* it. He *had* changed. Not outwardly, but certainly drastically. Jake smiled.

"Let's get out of here," Kaci said.

"The address on the paper?" Jake asked.

"That's the only one we have at this point," Kaci answered, striding toward the car rental agency located in the airport.

It only took a few minutes to rent the car and pack away the two small suitcases each had brought. In less than thirty minutes Jake and Kaci were on the Washington Beltway, heading west toward Virginia.

■ ■ ■

A morning surge at the car rental counters had caused John Ortiz a delay he'd not counted on. Upon his arrival the previous evening, he'd checked into the hotel nearest the airport and then called Al Bell's hospital room in McAllen, Texas. He'd talked to Al for only a few minutes, verifying that his partner was all right and that the best medical attention possible was being provided. After assuring Ortiz of the care,

Bell had insisted that Ortiz hang up the phone and get on with the job at hand.

The job at hand was proving to be a bit of a dilemma. Although Ortiz was a DEA agent, a government employee, he was currently far outside his jurisdiction. It probably would have been prudent, Ortiz thought as he made his way outside to where his rental car was parked, to have remained in Mexico and directed this portion of the operation from there. But that would have required written reports, formal requests, and the like, all of which took time—time John Ortiz did not have. And there was something personal about this part. He owed his partner his personal attention.

Ortiz found his car, tossed his luggage into the trunk, and opened the small book he carried in his pocket. He scanned the list of names, chose one, noted the address, and headed out of the parking area. Although he had crossed the border from Mexico to the United States with his weapon, he'd left it behind with Bell since he could not have boarded the plane with it. It was easier to obtain another one locally than to fight with the airlines over his own weapon.

Ortiz checked the address one last time, turned as he exited the airport, and headed for downtown Washington, D.C. The side trip to obtain a weapon would cost him a couple of hours, but he would be in the Virginia countryside before sunset, giving him plenty of time to check things out in the daylight.

■ ■ ■

There were three of them now. The third had joined the other two upon their arrival at Baltimore's Baltimore-Washington International Airport. Baltimore had been the destination of choice, knowing that the NCIS agent and the navy doctor had taken a flight into Ronald Reagan National Airport in Washington, D.C. Not that they were too worried about being recognized. That was not the problem. After all, they were certain the doctor and the agent had not seen their faces when the two had launched the failed ambush on them just outside Naval Support Activities, Mid-South, a few hours earlier. To the killers, it seemed as if the doctor and NCIS agent had a guardian angel looking out for them.

The two had taken a Northwest flight out of Memphis into Baltimore. They had used the in-flight phone to alert the third man of their arrival, using a preprogrammed channel to activate the third man's pager/beeper. The men wore identical beepers that were connected to an international network by orbiting satellites and controlled by a central computer in a basement in Washington, D.C. Orders coming to them via the beepers were irrevocable, and the three men had never had occasion to question the orders received via the small electronic devices.

Before long, the three were traveling southwest along Interstate 95, heading for the Virginia farm country outside Washington, D.C.

■ ■ ■

Peter St. Clair wondered what had happened to his computer. It seemed to have a mind of its own lately. He had important business to execute, and his terminal was not cooperating.

Already today, multiple E-mail messages had been returned to him via his electronic system. Always before, such messages had found their way to the addressee, but not this time. It was as if the person to whom he was writing no longer existed, and that did not make any sense at all.

St. Clair double-checked the addresses of the returned E-mails. They seemed to be correct. Of course, he had made such mistakes before. It was easy to overlook a period here or there, thus throwing off an entire address. But that did not seem to be the problem this time. The mail simply had not been delivered to the right people and had been returned via the electronic net.

Frustrating was what it was, St. Clair thought. Frustrating and counterproductive. It was just what he had been complaining about all this time. Electronic communication, despite its overwhelming popularity, was really not communication at all.

The Ambassador forgot about the returned E-mail for a while. He typed a few commands, waited, then clicked on a recognized Uniform Resource Locator. The information came up instantly. As he scrolled down, his heart leapt into his throat. It was worse than he'd thought. Janus was out of control, and there seemed to be nothing anyone could do to stop it. The returned E-mails had been his first attempt to stem the tide of blood that seemed to be pouring from the Janus system, but that avenue had been unsuccessful. He would have to find another way.

But it would be dark in a few hours, and if he wanted to get in his daily walk, he would have to hurry. Maybe the walk would clear his head. He needed that. There was too much stuff rumbling through his brain right now. He needed to think.

■ ■ ■

"Impressive," Jake said absentmindedly.

"Very," Kaci agreed, looking at the house through the windshield of their rented car.

"Right address?"

Kaci checked the address as Jake drove the rented compact along the wooded lane.

"Right address. It's hard to believe all that has happened was started in that house," Kaci said.

"Stranger things have happened," Jake said. "What I can't believe is what's on that sheet of paper. I know that's only a thumbnail sketch of what's been happening, but it's almost beyond belief."

"Maybe we'll get some answers from the master of the house," Kaci said.

"Maybe," Jake said. Then he realized what Kaci was saying. "Wait a minute. Are you suggesting that we just drive up to the front door and ring the door bell?"

Kaci looked at Jake, enjoying his discomfort. "That's exactly what I'm suggesting. You know of a better way to go about it?"

"No, but—"

"There's no *but* to it. Pull up to the front door, but keep the motor running."

"You're joking."

"Absolutely. You can come in with me."

"Oh, man, how did I get into this?" Jake moaned.

"You tried to help a soldier who had been exploited, and it got out of hand. Now let's see what we can do to put an end to the killing."

Jake turned the car around at the first opportunity and headed back for the house. He pulled into the stone-pillared driveway, noting that the name on the pillars was the same one Kaci had been given by Kerry Hartford: St. Clair.

Well, Mr. St. Clair, Jake thought, *get ready for Kaci Callahan. You may have met your match.*

CHAPTER TWENTY-TWO

Fairfax County, Virginia

Jake drove slowly up the white-graveled lane that led to the St. Clair mansion. The name Peter St. Clair was as well-known as any in the free world. Jake's stomach churned as he and Kaci approached the house. It didn't make any sense at all. How could one of the world's premier statesmen be involved in something as diabolical as Janus? And what was Jake Madsen doing here?

Jake felt Kaci's eyes on him as he guided the rental car up the lane.

"You're thinking the same thing I am," Kaci said.

"Oh really? Kathy used to do that to me. She knew what I was thinking before I did," Jake replied. "So, what am I thinking?"

"That something's not right with all this. How could a man with St. Clair's reputation be involved in Janus? Is that about it?"

Jake smiled as he halted the car in front of the wide portico, the tires crunching gently on the loose gravel. The sun was beginning to set in the west, and the shadows were lengthening. Large trees lined the lane. Despite the heat and humidity of the Virginia countryside, the shadows felt good.

"That's exactly what I was thinking. I can't believe a man who has spent his entire adult life working for the good of mankind can be mixed up in Janus."

"Don't forget. We don't know the whole story behind Janus. We only know what Kerry found on the Web, and someone had to put that information there. There's no guarantee that what we know is true, or for that matter, even exists at all."

Jake opened his door. Kaci did the same. "You don't believe that any more than I do," he said over the roof of the car. "People have died because of Janus. We know that much."

"People have died, and we think it's because of Janus, but we have no real proof, no connection."

"Now you're getting technical on me," Jake said, coming around the car.

Kaci followed Jake up the marble steps of Peter St. Clair's home. "I have to be technical. I'm a cop, no matter what else you think I am."

"Yeah, you are. You just don't remind me of any cop I've ever known."

Kaci stopped on the top step and looked at Jake. Jake turned. "Are you flirting with me, Dr. Madsen?"

"I'm trying, Miss Callahan, but I'm not very good at it. It's been a long time."

Kaci smiled warmly. "Keep it up. You'll get the hang of it sooner or later. Now, let's see if Ambassador Peter St. Clair can shed any light on this Janus thing."

Jake rang the doorbell.

"There's no one home," a voice said from behind them.

Jake and Kaci turned to face Peter St. Clair. His alarming good looks, deep blue eyes, and snow-white hair had the same effect on them as it had had on countless friends and enemies of the United States over the years: they were completely at ease.

Kaci stepped forward and offered her hand. St. Clair took it, a combination of greeting that allowed her hand to remain in his for an extended period of time.

"And you are?" St. Clair asked.

"Naval Criminal Investigative Service out of Naval Support Activities, Mid-South, in Memphis, Tennessee, Ambassador St. Clair," Kaci said. "This is Dr. Jake Madsen, currently on active duty with NAV-SUPACT also."

"Yes," St. Clair said slowly. "I've been expecting you."

Kaci met Jake's gaze with a look of disbelief. What was going on?

■ ■ ■

There were now three cars of three men each, all converging on the same point in the Virginia countryside. They knew the name of the owner of the house where they were bound, but even the name of Peter St. Clair did not deter them from carrying out the orders they had received.

One car, the car carrying the original three men from the Baltimore-Washington International Airport, was an hour away. Two more cars, both coming from the Anacostia Naval Station in Washington, D.C., were fifteen minutes behind the first car. Identical pager/beepers were attached to each man's belt, all linked to the same communications system. Orders flowed in on the small devices simultaneously, and each man read and acknowledged the orders, never questioning them.

In two hours, at the most, the nine men would kill those they had been ordered to kill, and if one of those men was the old ambassador,

Peter St. Clair, that was a moot point. The fact that there might be others with the old man was also irrelevant. They would do what they had been ordered to do.

■ ■ ■

John Ortiz cursed the map in his lap. The light was beginning to fade as the sun set, and he had to pull over to study the map and locate his destination. He silently chastised himself for ever becoming involved with General Abraham Zedillo and the strange organization he now knew as Janus. At least, that's what the computer readout he printed off of the Mexican military's computer said the name was. Ortiz thought he remembered hearing the name somewhere before, but he was not certain. In any case, it made little difference. He had a name and address, and all he had to do was find the house, somewhere in this hot and humid Virginia horse country.

According to the map, he was no more than an hour from the location he sought. The sun was setting quickly now, and Ortiz knew he could not afford to lose any more time.

■ ■ ■

"Please, sit down. Can I get you something to drink?" St. Clair asked both Jake and Kaci. "I've just come back from my evening walk, and I'm going to have a light drink, just to help me relax. You both look like you could use something too."

"Nothing for me, Ambassador," Kaci replied.

"Nor for me," Jake said.

"Ambassador St. Clair, I want to thank you for seeing us," Kaci began, "but I'm a little perplexed—"

"About my statement outside?" St. Clair interjected, concluding the statement the NCIS agent had begun.

"It was rather strange, you have to admit," Kaci continued.

Jake Madsen sat, listening.

Peter St. Clair went to an antique sideboard and poured himself an inch of golden liquid in the bottom of a large tumbler. He sipped slowly as he turned back to Kaci and Jake.

"Not so strange," the old ambassador replied after a second sip. "Oh, I didn't know it would be you two specifically, but I knew someone would come. They had to."

"Again, a cryptic remark with little meaning for us," Kaci pressed.

"Perhaps. But let me explain." St. Clair downed the last of the drink and placed the glass on the sideboard. "When I say, 'I knew you would come,' I'm sure we're talking about the same thing."

"Janus," Jake said quietly.

"You see, we are on the same playing field," St. Clair responded with a wry smile. "Yes. Janus. I knew someone would come for me. It was inevitable."

"I don't think I understand, Ambassador," Kaci said.

"You had to come. I will admit that it never occurred to me that it would be an NCIS agent as lovely as you, nor a Navy doctor, but it does make sense."

Kaci and Jake met each other's gaze, both with questioning looks in their eyes.

St. Clair laughed lightly. "I'm too old to worry about what comes next." Then the ambassador's mood changed. The smile was gone and a deep sadness seemed to overwhelm him. "Just do what you have come to do and be done with it. I have been unable to stop you; now it will be up to someone else. But let me assure you of one thing: Someone else will stop you! Sanity will someday be restored, and your kind will be eliminated."

Kaci and Jake stared in confusion. St. Clair had changed before their very eyes, transformed from the hearty, able ambassador to an old man, slumped before them in an attitude of complete defeat. Neither understood what was happening.

"What are you waiting for?"

"Ambassador," Jake began, rising from his place. "I think you may have a misconception of why we are here."

"You are here to kill me, are you not?"

Kaci gasped. "Not at all, Ambassador," she said. "We are here to learn what we can about Janus, and maybe stop *it.* I'm here investigating the murder of a soldier from NAVSUPACT, and possibly the deaths of others. Janus is the only thing that links all the deaths, and we got your name and address by hacking into your computer."

"My computer?" Peter St. Clair exclaimed.

"Your computer," Jake said.

"That's not possible."

"It's not only possible, but it was done," Kaci continued. "I've got a very good computer man who's an NCIS agent back in Memphis, and he's the one who did it."

St. Clair waved his hands in the air as if trying to dispel a smoke cloud. "You don't understand. There's no connection from my computer to any other. It's not a server-type computer, and if it's not a server, it can't be hacked into."

"You're online, aren't you?" Kaci asked.

"Of course. But that connection is terminated each time I turn off my computer."

"I understand what you're saying. I also know that we hacked into your system here, and got your name and location as being the head of Janus," Kaci said.

St. Clair fell into his chair. "That's just not possible. I expected someone to come, of course. But the people who would come would be here to kill me, to keep me from telling the world what I know about Janus. Obviously, you are not those people, which means someone else is probably on their way here right now to kill me. And to kill you too, if you're still here when they arrive."

Kaci felt outrage well up inside her. It was obvious that St. Clair knew about Janus, and that was information she wanted badly, but it was also apparent that something else was going on. Something deadly.

"Why don't you start from the beginning. What exactly is Janus?"

Peter St. Clair sighed, leaning back in the deep wing back chair. "The beginning," he said. "That was a long time ago."

■ ■ ■

John Ortiz had found the right road. Unfortunately, he had overshot his intended turn and was still thirty minutes away from the house of Peter St. Clair. The DEA agent wheeled the car around and headed back in the direction from which he had just come, cursing and fuming at the country roads. It was bad enough to have to travel backroads while working in Mexico, but this was the United States, and he'd expected better.

Ortiz tossed the map into the seat beside him and concentrated on his driving. He would not miss the turn-off this time.

■ ■ ■

The first car turned onto the access road that led to the mansion of former ambassador Peter St. Clair.

"We wait for the other two cars," the man in charge said to the other two men with him. "We don't want to blow this one."

Neither of the other two men spoke. The driver pulled off the road, parking in the fading light of late afternoon. The other two cars could be no more than ten minutes away. They would wait. Then they would kill Peter St. Clair as ordered.

CHAPTER TWENTY-THREE

"It began in 1914," St. Clair said in a soft voice, as if afraid that voicing the events of the past somehow would give them new life.

"World War I," Jake said in a low voice, matching the statement of the old ambassador.

"World War I," the old man repeated. "Janus was born in those days. Days of conflict. Days of revenge. Days of hate."

"I don't understand," Kaci said.

The light within the room was beginning to fade, and St. Clair flipped on a lamp. The soft light filled the room with a golden glow. It was somehow appropriate.

"There's never been a war like it," Peter St. Clair continued. "Not even the next war, which pitted the same forces against each other once again.

The Second World War was a direct result of the need for revenge that came out of the first war. The Treaty of Versailles was revenge, pure and simple, on the allies' part, and Germany would later revolt against what they saw as the injustice of the treaty. Janus was born in the cauldron of revulsion and redress from World War I, and further propagated in World War II and the wars to follow."

Jake and Kaci said nothing. The outside light faded further.

"It started in Germany. In the factories, the laboratories, the manufacturing facilities."

"We're talking about chemical warfare here," Jake interjected.

"We're talking about killing people at the wholesale level. About an atrocity so huge, it's hard to believe. And we're talking about human experimentation. And you are right. Chemical warfare was born in those dark days. It was a way, the German high command thought, for breaking out of the horrid trench warfare that had bogged down their army in France. The Germans used combinations of chlorine, mustard gas, phosgene, and others. Our soldiers had never seen anything like it. The effects were devastating. The first to feel the effects was a battalion of Canadian troops. Most died. Those that did not were either blinded or rendered invalids for the rest of their lives. The lucky ones died."

"What has that got to do with Janus?" Kaci asked.

"Janus was born out of those battles. If the Germans were developing chemicals to use on the battlefield, then it was incumbent on the allies to do the same thing. To do that, it was necessary to conduct research—research that could not be done under the existing laws of a civilized society."

"We're talking about our own processes now," Jake said.

"Yes. Our manufacturers. Our chemical plants. Our hospitals, laboratories, developmental systems. The entire spectrum necessary to combat the horrors of chemical warfare, for it was thought the best way to force the Germans to limit their use of chemicals was to use our own."

"But the Germans had a head start. They had the research, the experience, and the processes for manufacturing chemicals."

The old man sighed heavily. The telling of the horror was almost more than he could stand. It had been a long time since he'd had to face the reality of Janus. Yet he could feel the relief that came with the purging of the information.

"Exactly," Peter St. Clair said evenly, controlling his emotions. "We had the ability to produce, but what were we to produce? What effects did we want to achieve? What studies had to be conducted to achieve our goals? And then it came to the men whose vision it was to produce such abominations. The greatest and best study subjects were our own men who had been exposed to the Germans' chemicals and had survived."

"A form of guinea pigs," Jake said sadly, his voice cracking.

"May God forgive them . . .," Kaci whispered.

The old man nodded. "The exposed men were shipped back here and put through a systematic investigation and examination of the effects of chemicals on their bodies. But too few had actually survived in those early days. More were needed for study. The military was learning, albeit slowly, methods for combating the Germans' chemicals. But that did not slow the growing interest in developing our own chemicals. Quite the contrary. It only served to intensify the effort, for if we could successfully combat the use of chemicals, could not the Germans do the same thing? Would it not be necessary to develop even more potent and viable chemicals? Chemicals against which there was no defense?"

"That's a nightmare in the making," Kaci whispered.

"That it was, Ms. Callahan," St. Clair agreed. "But that was the frame of mind in those days, and the studies went forward."

"But how?" Jake asked. "You just said that there were too few study subjects for that purpose."

"Janus," Kaci said, beginning to understand.

"Janus," St. Clair nodded. "Janus was born in those dark days. More study subjects were needed, and where better to get them than from our own men. After all, those soldiers exposed to certain chemicals would most certainly survive, be shipped back to the States, and here could be studied, further advancing our own chemical program."

"But I thought the Germans stopped using chemicals later on. Besides, the advent of gas masks and protective suits mitigated the effects of the chemicals," Jake argued.

"You are correct. The Germans stopped using chemicals. But the interest in weapons-grade chemicals did not wane just because the Germans found the weapon too difficult to control. We continued studying the effects of chemical weapons on the human body. If we could not depend on the Germans to provide us with test subjects via their aggression, then it became imperative that we supply our own subjects."

Jake and Kaci gasped, the sound of horror filling the lighted room, the dawn of reality beginning to break. Neither could speak.

"It's true," the old man continued, tears now filling his eyes despite his best efforts to blink them back. "We used chemical weapons on our own troops. Oh, nothing that would kill, not outright. There was still some warped sense of honor in those days, and murdering our own troops crossed the line of even commercial development. But chemicals were used, knowing that the subjects would be shipped back to the States, placed in hospitals, and studied quietly for the effects. Where possible, commercial concerns footed the medical bills, conducted the studies, and reaped the rewards, all without exposure. It was a deception worthy of a master."

"Janus, in other words," Jake said.

"The Roman god of gateways and doors. The god with two faces. The two faces of deception and mayhem," the Ambassador said.

"But that was more than sixty years ago," Kaci interrupted. "I'm concerned about a murder that happened recently. I want to know what happened to Sergeant Jerry Wallace. Why he had some sort of homing device implanted in his chest, and why someone saw fit to rip it from his dead body."

"That," St. Clair began, "takes us to World War II, the Korean Police Action, Vietnam, Granada, Panama, Desert Storm, Kosovo, and on. Once begun, a program like Janus can quickly become an embarrassment for politicians. Don't get me wrong. Most political figures know nothing about Janus. It's a program funded through various riders attached to large spending bills that pass through a complacent Congress with virtually no oversight at all."

"Congressman J. Fredrick Bryant," Kaci said in a small voice.

St. Clair turned to face Kaci. "You are a very perceptive young lady. Bryant was a member of a single oversight committee tasked with funding certain covert military operations. Black operations, and of those, Janus was the blackest. He was present at a meeting of that committee for the first time since his arrival on Capitol Hill. Someone had made an error in judgment by appointing him to the oversight committee, but the damage was done, the effects realized too late. Bryant had the temerity to ask about Janus. Janus was included in a bill they were voting on to the tune of two million dollars. Not much money in the great scheme of things, but enough for the young congressman to take notice."

"And for his interest, he was killed," Jake added.

"It would seem so," St. Clair said. "Just as many have been killed in the past."

"What about Veterans Affairs? We have had our share of Agent Orange and Gulf Syndrome patients. What about that? Is that part of Janus?"

"No," the old man shook his head. "Those problems are legitimate concerns, and the VA is dealing with them in a legitimate manner. None of those are part of Janus. The problem is that some test subjects end up in the VA system, or some other system, military or civilian, and are discovered. Discovery presents a problem."

The light had faded completely outside the window. A gray darkness had overtaken the countryside. The air was still; the leaves on the trees motionless. The world had come to a standstill outside the St. Clair mansion. The yellow light from the study where Kaci, Jake, and the old man sat spilled out onto the marble portico. Birds grew silent as night fell.

"The problem we had with Jerry Wallace," Jake said, "was the type of discovery you're talking about."

"So it would seem," the old man nodded. "Your Sergeant Wallace was discovered. When that happened, he had to be removed from the equation."

"You say that too easily," Kaci said.

"I suspect you're right about that, young lady. It comes from my own form of complacency. I got to a point where I thought my advanced age was reason enough to withdraw from the battle. I was wrong."

Jake stood up and stretched. He had not realized how long he'd been sitting. He was stiff; his joints cracked.

"You're telling us, then, that Janus is an organization whose single function is to study the effects of chemical weapons. But what comes after that?" Jake asked.

"I'll answer that," a fourth voice intoned from the doorway of the study.

Jake, Kaci, and St. Clair turned in unison. The man who stood there clutched a Glock automatic pistol in his right hand, the pistol held lightly, as if the man knew what to do with it. It was aimed midpoint between the three, ready to move in any direction.

"By the way, you left the front door unlocked. Very sloppy. I locked it," John Ortiz said, then continued. "To answer your question, what happens after that is that a chemical is produced, probably in another country, shipped out for further testing, then provided to the highest bidder. Isn't that the short version, Mr. St. Clair?"

"You seem to know the answers, Mr. . . . .," the old man responded.

"Ortiz. DEA agent from Mexico, where one of your chemical producers let the production process get out of hand and destroyed a village, and everyone in it."

"I'm afraid you may have the wrong idea, here, Mr. Ortiz," Peter St. Clair said wearily. "I'm the least of your worries where Janus is involved. You should more rightly be worried about those tasked with the enforcement and maintenance of the Janus secret."

"And who would that be?" Ortiz asked, stepping into the room.

"That's what I don't know," St. Clair answered. "It's what I've been trying to discover for several years. I keep running into roadblocks. Now it seems there is another obstacle in my path."

"Are you referring to me?" Ortiz asked.

"You, and these two here," St. Clair said, pointing to Kaci and Jake. "Something is happening, and I'm not sure what it is. How did you all find me?" the old man asked.

Kaci held up the printout she'd received from Kerry Hartford. Ortiz displayed a similar printout he'd taken from the printer in the Mexican army camp in Tierra Quemada.

St. Clair examined the printout from Kaci. "Interesting. There's just enough detail here to whet the appetite, but not enough to expose really pertinent information. And as strange as it seems, the information points to me as being a principal within the Janus structure."

"Which you are disavowing, I suppose," Ortiz said, stepping into the room.

"It is ludicrous, especially since I have been the driving force in trying to *expose* Janus."

Jake, Kaci, and Ortiz all looked at each other, questions forming.

"It's true. I became involved in Janus years ago. I was a fool in those days, believing what I was told and not investigating further. After all, I was part of the government whose task it was to keep the world safe, and Janus appeared to be a way in which to serve that purpose. When I discovered the truth about Janus, I began trying to stop it. I've had little success."

It was John Ortiz's time to question the old ambassador. Not having been present for most the explanation, Ortiz asked, "What exactly did you discover about Janus?"

St. Clair turned to Ortiz. "Janus has a single purpose—"

"The development of chemical weapons for the United States," Kaci interjected.

"The development of chemical weapons, period," St. Clair corrected. "It started out as a project of the allies in World War I and moved to the United States but quickly progressed past those stages. It now seems to have a mind of its own. Janus is its own driving force. It is now not only funded in the U.S., but by all NATO countries and many former Warsaw Pact countries as well." The old man went to the desk in the room. He extracted a large, computer-generated report printed on large green-and-white sheets. "Here are some statistics you've never seen, nor even imagined. Each of you has been touched in some way by Janus, but these documents contain more truth than even you may be able to absorb."

John Ortiz moved further into the room. "Let me get this straight. You're telling me that the chemical devastation that my partner and I found in Mexico is part of this Janus thing?"

"You got your computer printout from where?" St. Clair asked Ortiz.

"From a Mexican army computer near the site of what used to be a village in the Sierra Madre highlands. The Mexican army was keeping people out. The village had been buried a couple of years ago."

"And you just walked into the camp and printed this out?" St. Clair said, referring to the paper Ortiz held.

Ortiz smiled, remembering the recent events. "Not exactly. I'm not sure why, but that camp started blowing itself apart. I suspect second-party sabotage, but that's something I'll look into when I get back.

Anyway, in the confusion caused by the explosions, Al and I were able to get the printout. It led here."

"Al?" Kaci Callahan asked.

"Al Bell is my partner in Mexico. He took a bullet in the confusion. I left him in good hands in a McAllen, Texas, hospital. I'm here alone."

"All that does not bode well, Mr. Ortiz," St. Clair said.

"Meaning?"

"Meaning," Kaci continued, "that if we have the printout, it's almost a dead certainty that others have the same readout. And if we're here, chances are there are others here too."

"Others," Jake said, turning from the window where he stood.

"The protection division of Janus, or whatever they call themselves," St. Clair said. "It would seem Janus has four of us where it wants us, and there can only be one reason for that."

"Janus got us here to kill us," Kaci said.

"I'm afraid you're right, Ms. Callahan," the old ambassador said.

"But who is Janus?" Jake asked, his anger beginning to build. He was not sure what he was angry about, but the emotion was seething just below the surface. He and the rest of the people in this room had been manipulated, moved like pawns on a chessboard.

Peter St. Clair seemed to wilt with the asking of the question, as if the weight of the world had suddenly been shifted to his narrow shoulders.

"Janus is . . . Janus," St. Clair said disgustedly.

Jake advanced on the old man. "That's no answer. That's an evasion."

"Yes," St. Clair said, sitting behind his desk. "That is exactly what it is, but the answer is also the truth."

"You're talking in riddles," Jake said.

Kaci Callahan recognized the exhaustion on the old statesman's face. Her voice was gentle now, quiet and soothing in the confines of the warm room. She knelt beside St. Clair, her hand going to his arm in a calming gesture.

"Janus is what?" Kaci asked softly.

St. Clair's hand went to Kaci's, relishing the touch of the young lady.

Ortiz holstered his Glock and moved closer to where St. Clair was sitting.

Jake Madsen had watched the quiet exchange between Kaci and St. Clair. He recalled similar incidences between himself and Kathy. That had been Kathy's way too. The way of persuasion, of gently cajoling, of *understanding.* Tears crept into his eyes as he remembered. His hand went to his pocket where the small Bible still rested. The verse in Philippians sprang to his mind, and he recognized the timeless truth contained in the words, a truth that could not exist without the presence of a supreme God.

Jake moved closer to hear the old man's response. His anger had faded, replaced by an understanding that seemed to transcend all other emotions. For Jake, it was a new experience, and he mouthed a silent prayer of thanks to the God he'd discovered in a simple one-line passage in his wife's small Bible.

Jake knelt beside Kaci and St. Clair. His hand joined Kaci's and the old man's. It was a strange bond, but a bond nonetheless.

"What about Janus?" Jake asked kindly, his hand squeezing Kaci's, and in the process, the old man's.

Peter St. Clair looked down at both Kaci and Jake, relief mirrored in his eyes. He would finally be able to unburden himself of the singular horror he'd born for so long.

Ortiz moved closer, swept up in the emotion as well.

Peter St. Clair opened his mouth to speak.

Suddenly the window just to the right of where he sat exploded inward, throwing shards of glass over the four people assembled there, covering the desk with sharp fragments.

Kaci pulled at the old man, forcing him to the floor behind the desk.

John Ortiz pulled his pistol, but held his fire.

"What . . . who . . . ?" Jake asked, as he joined the others behind the desk.

"Janus," the old ambassador said in a low voice. "Janus has come for us."

■ ■ ■

There were nine of them now. The cars had been left beside the lane, far enough from the main road to prevent detection, but close enough for a quick escape after the job was finished.

The leader knew the goal. He was not in complete agreement with the objective, but it was not his place to question the orders of his superiors, whoever those superiors might be. The orders had been transmitted—via the secure satellite link—directly to his beeper/pager and activated by the correct code word. The entire contingent of agents with him had been alerted in the same manner.

All was in order; the four people in the St. Clair mansion had to die.

The lead agent maneuvered his men around the house. He'd used simple binoculars to examine the room where the four subjects were currently located and had seen at least one of them with a weapon. That meant that caution was the order of the day. There would be no open attack with guns blazing. Better to secret his men close, get them inside, and kill with a minimum of noise.

But something had gone wrong. What, he was not sure, but movement within the house had caused one of the men on the left flank to open fire. Already the windows of the room where the four subjects were located had been blown from their frames. It was a mistake. One man had a gun, and there might be more. He needed to know. He could not afford to lose a man in this operation, and failure was not an option.

Failure was never an option where the safety of Janus was concerned.

The agent smiled crookedly at that thought. *Where Janus was concerned.* A strange statement, he thought, since he actually had no idea who or what Janus actually was. He and his group were tasked with protection, and protection is what they provided. The fact that he had never been told what it was he was protecting did not bother him. He was paid well, had all the benefits of any other government employee, and for the most part, was asked for little in return.

Tonight was the exception. Such nights occurred about twice a year on average, and the man had to admit a vague curiosity concerning what he was doing in the forested countryside of Virginia about to kill four people. On closer examination, however, he had to admit he didn't really care.

He would do his job. He would kill for Janus.

CHAPTER TWENTY-FOUR

"Janus has come!" the old man shouted, his voice echoing eerily through the mansion. St. Clair tried to rise from where Kaci held him to the floor. All reason seemed to have deserted him, and Kaci struggled with the flailing old man.

Jake joined Kaci, easily pinning St. Clair to the floor. John Ortiz moved toward the shattered window to scan the exterior of the house. It was dark. The light from the single lamp hindered his efforts to distinguish movement in the darkness. He gestured with his pistol. Jake understood.

He moved toward the lamp, leaving Kaci to handle the ambassador on her own. St. Clair did not move. All the fight was gone from him.

Jake reached the desk and jerked at the cord of the lamp, pulling it from the desk onto the floor. The bulb shattered, plunging the room into darkness.

"That will slow them down for a while," Ortiz said, scrambling from the window back to where the other three now lay on the floor.

"Who . . . ?" Jake asked.

"Janus," the old man choked, this time with effort, as if all the air had gone out of a balloon.

"But how?" Kaci asked. "And why now?"

The voice that came out of Peter St. Clair was now a voice of age and agony, of reason and logic.

"The computer readout I showed you. It's all there. You thought you knew what was going on, but you only know part of the story. The rest of the story is in that readout."

"Your computer?" Kaci asked.

St. Clair looked at the NCIS agent, not understanding the question. Even in the darkness, confusion showed on his face.

Jake looked at Kaci, wondering what she was asking too.

"Yes, . . . my computer," St. Clair answered, confusion reflected in the words.

"Where is it?" Kaci asked.

Again confusion splayed across the old ambassador's face. He motioned. "The next room."

Ortiz held up his hand. "Wait. Don't move just yet. I don't know how many there are. Where's the phone?"

"On the desk," Jake said, pointing.

"It won't work," Kaci said matter-of-factly.

The three men looked at her questioningly.

"We can call the cops," Ortiz said. "There are people out there with automatic weapons who want to kill one or all of us. If this old man is right, the four of us have a life expectancy of about sixty seconds if we don't get some help."

"The phones won't work," Kaci repeated. She turned to St. Clair. "Your computer is connected to your phone lines for E-mail, Internet, and Web access. Right?"

"Of course," St. Clair answered, nodding.

"Who installed the system for you?"

Again confusion showed on St. Clair's face. Light from the moon and stars was beginning to light the landscape. With their eyes adjusting to the darkness, features and expressions were now recognizable.

"I . . . I don't understand."

"Who connected your system, and for what purpose?" Kaci repeated impatiently.

"I . . . I think they were technicians from the State Department," St. Clair answered.

A fusillade of automatic weapon fire filled the room again. The walls were riddled. The desk was pounded with rifle fire.

"They've got listening devices," Ortiz yelled. "Move, quietly. We've got to get out of this room."

Jake and Kaci pulled St. Clair across the floor. Ortiz led the way, heading for the back of the house and the room where St. Clair had indicated his computer system was located.

All four were now on their knees, scrambling for the protection of additional walls and distance. They made the next room. Jake and Kaci helped St. Clair get comfortable against an interior wall.

The old mansion was well constructed. The outer walls were formed of quarried stone and would withstand anything short of an artillery shell. Metal bars protected the windows. Security doors were in place on the entrances. The interior doors were equally formidable. The real danger lay in penetration of the house by the killers outside. It would be almost impossible for them to get a clear, killing shot from the outside. They would have to get into the house.

"What's this about the phones?" Ortiz repeated once the group was settled in.

"They won't work," Kaci reiterated. "At least, that's my guess." She turned to St. Clair again. "You said technicians from the State

Department installed your computer system. Are you certain they were from State?"

Peter St. Clair thought for a minute. "No. I just assumed that was the case. State wanted me to have the system, to monitor world events and such from here. I assumed Foggy Bottom was responsible. What are you saying?" the old man queried, his curiosity building.

"You also monitored Janus from your computer, didn't you?" Kaci asked.

"Of course," St. Clair answered. "That was part of the deal."

"Janus installed the computer," Kaci said.

Jake and Ortiz looked at the NCIS agent when she said that. Jake understood immediately.

"Janus was monitoring Ambassador St. Clair," Jake said, uncertainty reflected in the statement.

"I think so," Kaci said in Jake's direction. "And since the computer is tied to the phone lines for access reasons, I suspect Janus has control not only of the computer, but the phone lines as well."

"Better the devil you know," John Ortiz said.

"It makes sense," Jake agreed. "As long as the Ambassador was doing nothing more than monitoring systems, then better to let him live in peace. We're the wild cards in the deck."

"And Ambassador St. Clair was right. Janus brought us here. We're all involved in some way, and now we're all in one place at one time."

Ortiz picked up a phone he'd noticed when they'd moved into the computer room. "Dead," he said to the other three, holding the instrument up for all to see.

Kaci pulled her cell phone out and punched the activation button. "Dead too," she said. "Janus is covering all the bases."

■ ■ ■

It wasn't as easy as he'd thought, the man had discovered. The house was more than a house; it was a fortress. The exterior resembled a castle, with about as much stone on the walls as one might find in one of the old English models. And it was not just the cheap, veneer-type rock, either. The home had been built when fieldstone and quarried rock were the order of the day for the landed gentry. Nothing short of an atomic bomb would damage the house.

And that was not all. Sometime during the past thirty or so years, some enterprising metal works had talked the owner of the house into installing iron window bars and security doors. The man could see the escape knobs located to the left of each of the window bar sets, for use in case of fire, but those could only be activated from the interior of the house, not from the outside. As far as he could tell, the house was about as secure as a proverbial Fort Knox.

The man pulled a radio from his belt. "What have you got on the back?" he asked the invisible person on the other end of the transmitter.

"Secure," the answer came back.

Secure? the man wondered. *What* was secure? The attack plan or the house, or both? He cursed at the cryptic answer and thumbed the radio again.

"The house? What about the house?"

"Locked up tight. We've got iron bars on the windows and the doors. Upstairs and downstairs. Someone is paranoid. Doorknobs can only be opened from the inside. We've already tried them," the disembodied voice answered. "And you can forget breeching the walls or the roof. The roof looks like quarried slate."

That was what he'd wanted to know in the first place, the man thought. He would need more firepower.

"Where are they?" he asked the man next to him.

The man removed a miniature set of headphones and said, "They've moved to an interior room. They're talking in low voices, like they know we've got ears out here. Somebody in there knows his business. And, oh yeah, they tried the phone."

"As least something is going right. Get a unit up here with a set of Jaws," the man ordered.

"Done," the man to his right said, talking into a separate radio.

"We'll wait. With no phone, there's no problem with the police; the security system is tied to the computer, so it's down; and we're too far out in the country for the shots to be heard. We have time," the man said, settling into his spot near the front door of the St. Clair mansion. "Hold your positions," the man radioed to the remainder of the assault team. "An hour. Maybe less." The man cursed once again, bemoaning the fact that he'd not loaded in a set of Jaws of Life. The jaws were the kind used by most fire departments to extract victims from mangled automobile wrecks. Now he would use them to extract four enemies of Janus.

■ ■ ■

"What about weapons?" the DEA agent asked.

Kaci turned to St. Clair. "Ambassador. Do you have any weapons in the house? Guns?"

"In the den, through there," St. Clair pointed. "There's a gun safe built into the west wall. The keys are above the door on the right."

Kaci glanced at Jake. "Let's go," he said.

"Keep low," Kaci ordered as the two moved from the computer room toward the den.

"I can see I'm going to have to rethink this relationship," Jake said as they moved through the house.

"What relationship?" Kaci asked.

They were in a hallway. It was dark. Kaci stopped, and Jake followed suit.

"Let our eyes adjust to the dark," she said.

"Good. Gives me a chance to tell you something," Jake began.

"Don't start, Jake Madsen. I've seen scenes like this in movies, and they never made sense. We're fighting for our lives here. So just don't start."

Jake chuckled. "You're frightened."

"You're right. We could get killed here," Kaci responded, trying unsuccessfully to sound angry.

"No," Jake laughed gently, "you're scared I might say something romantic. Something stupid."

"Something romantic in this situation would be something stupid."

"Not necessarily. It might be one of the sanest things I could do. You feel it too," Jake said. It was a statement, not a question.

Kaci reached out in the dark, taking Jake's hand and squeezing it gently.

Jake responded. It was enough, at least for now.

Kaci said, "Let's find that gun safe."

The two moved in unison, carefully and quietly. John Ortiz was right, Kaci knew. Whoever was outside had listening devices, probably installed when the computer system had been set up. She suspected that the devices were hampered by the massive construction of the mansion, but she was going to be careful, nonetheless.

"In there," Jake said, approaching a room just off the corridor.

"Right."

Jake and Kaci moved into the room. The moon was high now, and it cast a brilliant white light over the countryside. Part of the light spilled into the den. Kaci knew the men who waited outside would not like that.

The den was masculine in decor and aroma. The familiar smells of leather and pipe tobacco dominated. From what she could see, the walls were decorated with sporting photographs and antique golf memorabilia. Old sets of golf clubs were mounted on stained boards and hung on the wall in places of honor. Kaci made a mental note to ask about the clubs—if she got out alive.

"Over here," Jake said in a whisper. The gun safe was built into an interior wall to allow for the safe's depth. Jake reached above it, found the key, and fumbled it into the slot. He pulled open the safe. The door was heavy, but swung open without so much as a squeak.

The interior of the safe was as dark as midnight. Jake and Kaci looked at each other. Kaci snapped her fingers, pushed Jake away from the door, stepped in, and pulled the door shut behind her.

Jake stood on the outside of the safe, knowing what the NCIS agent was doing.

Kaci made certain the door was shut, then fumbled along the wall near the door. She found the light switch and flipped in on. What greeted her inside the gun safe would have gladdened the heart of a Marine Corps company commander.

Peter St. Clair was obviously, or had once been, a shooting enthusiast. One wall was lined with shotguns of all types. Double barrels, single-shots, and automatics by every manufacturer of worth were lovingly nestled in padded racks. Kaci marveled at the collection. One of the shotguns caught her eye. She went to it and picked it up. It was one of Browning's original designs for a lever-action, 10-gauge shotgun. She had never seen one before. She replaced the gun and surveyed the rest of the weapons in the safe.

On the wall opposite the shotgun collection were rifles, and on the end wall was St. Clair's collection of pistols, from older British Wheatherby models to the latest polymer automatics.

Below the weapon collection, metal, fireproof cabinets housed ammunition.

Kaci pulled three Remington automatic rifles from the wall, chose three automatic pistols, and corresponding ammunition. Then she pulled two automatic shotguns from their rest. She quickly unscrewed the caps where the wooden plugs would be found, slipped the plugs out, and replaced the caps. She piled the ammunition near the door and stacked the rifles and shotguns next to the wall. Next she forced the pistols into her waistband, then surveyed what she had. Satisfied, she flipped off the light and waited for what seemed to be an eternity.

There is no such thing as night vision in absolute darkness, and absolute darkness was what Kaci faced in the gun safe. When she pushed the door open, she was pleased to find she could see; the short wait had been worth it.

Jake met her.

"Take these," Kaci whispered, handing the rifles to Jake. "They're all the same caliber, so we don't have to fumble for different ammunition. The plugs have been removed from the shotguns, so we can use five shells in each gun."

"Holy smokes," Jake exclaimed under his breath. "The old man must have an arsenal in there."

"That pretty much describes it. Let's get this stuff back to the computer room. I need to ask the Ambassador some more questions."

■ ■ ■

"I lost two of them," the man with the listening device said.

The man cursed again. "What about the other two?"

"The old man and another male voice," the listener said.

"And you don't know where the other two went?"

"That house is not the best for listening. And we don't have microphones on all the windows yet. We're working on it."

"Get it done. I want to know where every warm body is so we can get this over with when the Jaws get here. Understood?"

"Yes, sir," the man answered, wondering if his boss knew just how difficult it would be to penetrate a house built like a medieval castle.

CHAPTER TWENTY-FIVE

"Holy smokes," John Ortiz exclaimed, then caught himself. He whispered, "Where did these come from?"

"The safe," Kaci answered. "A pistol, a rifle, and a shotgun for the men. I'll take a pistol and a rifle. Load 'em up," she ordered, dumping a box of shotgun shells on the floor, along with .30-caliber rifle ammunition and 9-mm pistol ammo. "The rifles are all the same, as are the pistols and the shotguns. You can't confuse the ammo."

"Lady's pretty sharp," Ortiz said, directing his statement to Jake.

"Yeah," Jake answered in a whisper. "I'm beginning to figure that out."

"Both of you shut up. The walls have ears, remember?" Kaci snapped. "Ambassador St. Clair," Kaci turned her attention to the old man slumped against the wall. "Let's get back to your computer. We know the phone system is controlled by it, which probably means the security system is too."

"I never thought of that, but you're probably right," St. Clair agreed.

"And we can assume Janus installed this system, which means it's set up to function under the guidance of someone else."

"A Web master," Ortiz suggested.

"Or someone like that," Kaci nodded.

"Which means the messages we found, this address, Ambassador St. Clair's name, is all a ruse," Jake added.

"It's beginning to seem that way," Kaci said. "Right now my investigation is a thorn in the side of Janus."

"As is mine," Ortiz said.

"Exactly. And apparently what the Ambassador was doing is also contrary to what Janus wants at this moment, so we've all been brought here for extermination."

"And the pest control company is outside the house right now," Jake joked sardonically. "The question is how?"

"The computer," Kaci said, moving to the desk where the oversized monitor was located. She slid along the floor, keeping low. There was only a single window in the room, and it appeared to be located on an interior courtyard of some sort. The chances of the killers being in the courtyard were remote, but Kaci was taking no chances.

Jake watched as Kaci moved to the computer, then he moved over too. "What do you think?"

Kaci pointed to a tiny red light still glowing. "Take a look. The system is up and running."

A protest came from St. Clair. "That's not possible. I turn the system off when I finish with it."

"It's not only possible," Kaci said, "but I would say the presence of those armed men out there is proof positive. What were you going to tell us about Janus before this started?" Kaci addressed St. Clair.

The old man cleared his throat. Moonlight illuminated the room from the single window. Ortiz had moved to a vantage point from where he could cover any movement outside the window. He listened from his post.

"Your friends are right. You are a very special person. And you are right too. I was going to tell you about Janus. You know about the beginning, the war. Or, to be more specific, the wars. Plural. For the wars were the testing grounds, the proving grounds for Janus."

"But we know what Janus is. It's a chemical weapons development program," Kaci said. "You've told us that much."

"True," the old man agreed, "but there is much more. And what I have to tell you, what I have learned in the last few weeks and days is the most frightening part of all."

Ortiz listened intently from where he stood watch at the window. Jake and Kaci looked at each other in the dim light of the filtered moon.

"Janus is not human," Peter St. Clair said in a low, agonizing breath. "God in heaven, Janus is not human!"

Jake and Kaci met each other's gaze. What was this old man saying? *Not human.* What was not human? Janus was real. Janus was the team outside the house trying at this moment to kill everyone inside the house. Janus had killed Jerry Wallace. Janus had killed Jamie Parker and spirited his body out of Memphis. Janus implanted homing devices in the chests of young soldiers and experimented on them. Whatever Janus was, it was real.

"That's insane," Kaci finally said.

"Yes. Insanity is part of it," St. Clair agreed, his voice growing weaker as he spoke. "I should have realized it earlier. That tiny glowing light confirms it for me," the old man said, indicating the light on the computer's CPU. "I *have* been monitored. Janus has been keeping tabs on me, not vice versa. And now I know that."

"What are you talking about, Ambassador?" Kaci asked.

The elder statesman smiled weakly. "Have you ever seen the movie *WarGames?*" he asked.

"Sure. On video. It was before our time," Jake told the old man.

St. Clair smiled again. "It was before anyone's time. The concept that is. Remember, it's about a computer that controls its own programs. In the case of the movie, the computer was playing a war game between the United States and Russia. Only the game was real, and control of our nuclear missiles was vested in the computer program. The computer was about to launch a nuclear strike that would have ended the world."

"Are you saying, Ambassador, that Janus is acting like this wargames computer?" Jake asked.

"With one exception. Today, we really do have computers that learn. Oh, I'm not talking about programmed artificial intelligence. I'm talking about *learning. Real learning.* The assimilation of ideas and concepts to form a basis for action."

"With all due respect, sir," John Ortiz said from the window, "that's not possible."

St. Clair turned to the DEA agent. "You think not. You're here, aren't you?"

"That could have been accomplished by humans," Ortiz argued.

"But it wasn't," St. Clair shot back, life returning to his voice. "We now have computers designing computers. Codes and languages that only other computers understand. That in itself is frightening. But the scenario goes further. Computers have interacted with one another."

"Some are designed to do just that," Ortiz continued his argument.

"That is true. But recently, in studies, such computers have begun to exhibit traits that are not normal."

"How so?" Kaci asked.

"Computers—robots, to be specific—designed to perform specific functions and to interact with each other within the parameters of the program have exhibited behavior that was not programmed into the system."

"You're saying those computers have *learned?*" Jake asked, astonished.

"You tell me. The computers took on a 'passive' and an 'aggressive' personality. There was no rhyme or reason, except to say that the 'passive' robot surrendered its own will to that of its 'aggressive' counterpart."

"How did the programmers explain the actions?" asked Kaci.

"That's just it. They didn't. They didn't program the computers; another computer did. The programmers pulled the program, studied the language, and concluded that they had no idea what the language meant. The programming computer had devised its own language and had programmed the robots with the language. And the robots learned."

"And you think that is what's going on with Janus?" Jake asked. "Because if that's it, we can just pull the plug, so to speak."

"You don't know much about computers, do you?" Kaci stated.

"Enough to know that they work on electricity, and you can cut electricity."

"If you can identify the sources," St. Clair interjected. "Turn off my machine," the old man ordered.

Jake reached over and flipped the switch on the CPU. The light went out. A sound from within the machine told him that it was winding down.

"There you go," Jake said.

"And it's off?"

"You don't see any lights do you?"

"What about the clock?"

"What about it?"

"If you start the computer back up, will it have the correct time?"

"Sure."

"How?"

Jake saw what St. Clair was getting at. Janus must be working on the same fundamental principle as a computer's clock. The more he thought about it, the more parallels he could draw to the human body. Even the human body could be stopped, but it required some doing. It would require equal diligence to stop Janus. But the idea that Janus was a computer program and nothing more required a tremendous leap of faith. And if you couldn't pull the plug, then what could you do?

"So what do we do?" Kaci asked.

"I don't know," St. Clair said simply. "But we have to do something. Look at the printout I was about to show you."

Jake worked his way over to the desk that held the huge printout and began going through it. "This is unbelievable," he muttered.

"Let me see," Kaci said.

Jake worked back to Kaci, handing her the portion of the printout he'd already scanned. Her reaction was the same. "This is monstrous," she said, looking up at Jake, then turning to St. Clair. "How can anyone do this?"

"*Anyone* did not do that," St. Clair reiterated. "That's part of what put me on to it in the first place. Everything that's taken place as reflected by those reports is too logical, too linear."

"Too linear?" Kaci said, looking at the old man. "What does that mean?"

"Don't you see it? What you have before you is action/reaction. Almost in the form of a linear equation. One thing leads to another. One action is followed by another action, which is followed by another."

"Go on," Jake urged.

St. Clair continued. "Everything has a certain symmetry to it, a plan, but not an imaginative plan. It's like there's some master playbook somewhere, with all possible options listed with corresponding actions. A equals B; B equals C; A equals C. No imagination."

"Like a computer," Kaci said. "A very, very good computer, but a computer, nonetheless."

"An extremely good computer. One that's been programmed to perform certain functions, funded by our complacency, and turned loose on the world."

"Funded by our complacency. What's that mean?" Ortiz asked.

"Just what I said," St. Clair said to the agent. "We fund most of what gets funded by our complacency. We elect our officials in the same manner. We do our jobs, raise our families, and generally exist within our own small universe of apathy."

"That's pretty cynical, especially for a world-class statesman," Jake told the old ambassador.

"That's what makes me a good statesmen. I recognize the realities."

"How so?" Kaci asked. "Are we still talking about Janus?"

"Absolutely. Most of us are pretty apathetic. We don't really care what goes on around us as long as it doesn't affect us. Well, that's self-interest, pure and simple. So you can easily equate apathy and self-interest. As long as the economy is booming, let the leaders do what they want. After all, it doesn't affect me. As long as I can do what I want, when I want, with as little inconvenience as possible, then I don't care how or why I am able to do that. As long as what Janus is doing does not affect us personally, so what? Let it go. The problem with that line of thinking is expressed in a single line by John Donne. I don't remember it exactly, but the idea is that one man's death diminishes me, for I am a part of mankind. We're all a part of mankind, and don't think for a moment that what goes on around us does not affect us."

"You ought to be a preacher," Ortiz said from the shadows.

Jake and Kaci smiled.

"Maybe I should have been," St. Clair said with a hint of sadness. "It would have been easier. At least there's uncompromised truth within the pages of the Bible. That's not true in any other document."

"So you're saying that not only is Janus possible, there's a very real possibility that it exists, and in the form you suggest?" Kaci asked.

"I'd guarantee it. Whatever is happening here, it's the result of some computer program run wild."

"A computer with its own security force?" Ortiz asked.

"The security was set up long ago. I doubt they even know who issues their orders. Apathy, don't forget, infects the human race like a virus."

"The virus!" Kaci exclaimed. "The virus!"

"What are you talking about?" Peter St. Clair asked.

"The one Kerry Hartford gave you," said Jake, remembering the disk.

"Exactly. Maybe we can bring down Janus," Kaci said excitedly.

"Virus? Hartford? What are you talking about?" St. Clair continued, confused.

Before Kaci could rummage through her purse and find the disk she'd been given by Hartford, a window on the far side of the house blew in. The four could hear glass raining down in the room, and then they heard the sound of a gasoline engine being started. The engine sounded like a chain-saw engine, only with a deeper, throatier roar. Almost unheard over the roar of the engine was the next sound that sent chills through the four hostages.

Running footsteps in the house!

The killers were in!

CHAPTER TWENTY-SIX

The four moved in unison.

The killers were in the house, searching for them.

Kaci directed the defense, her instincts taking over, her orders flawless. She whispered commands that were immediately accepted by the other three.

"There," she pointed to a cabinet close to the wall where John Ortiz stood.

The DEA agent understood, racing for the protection of the heavy wood and the darkness of the corner.

"Stay with the Ambassador," Kaci whispered urgently to Jake. "And get behind the computer desk, out of sight. If they have listening equipment, they probably have NVGs too."

"NVGs?" Jake said rhetorically. He was navy, but he was navy medicine, not combat. He had no idea what Kaci was talking about.

"Night Vision Glasses. In the dark, they can see us, but we can't see them," Kaci explained.

"Great," Jake responded sarcastically.

"Check the weapons. If what Ambassador St. Clair said is correct, these guys are in here to kill us."

"Oh, it's correct all right," said St. Clair. "We're about to be killed on orders of a computer."

"Somehow, that makes it sound obscene," Jake said.

"I'm going to set up an ambush. Stay here," Kaci said before moving off in the darkness, hugging the walls for what protection they could offer.

"Behind the desk, Mr. Ambassador," Jake said, guiding St. Clair to the protection of the furniture piece.

I can do all things through Christ who strengthens me. The words repeated in Jake's head.

■ ■ ■

Kaci worked her way along the darkened corridor. She'd started out in what she thought was a flanking movement within the confines of the mansion. Her intention was simple: she would outflank the intruders and shoot them before they could shoot her. As she moved silently along the hallway, she found herself thinking about Jake.

She had not been able to get the young doctor out of her mind since they'd met. At first, she'd considered it a mild annoyance, but now she was beginning to ask herself if she loved this Jake Madsen. If that were the case, she had picked a strange place and time to admit it, she told herself.

There was noise to her right. She'd moved along the corridor, entering one of the mansion's many rooms and exiting into yet another corridor. She stopped. If the killers had NVGs, they could have her in their sights this very minute. The thought sent a chill up her spine. For a quick moment, she felt as if someone were watching her. She moved.

A bullet thumped into the door facing near her left shoulder. A killer had had her in his sights, and she had moved at just the right moment!

Kaci scrambled for the next room. She was taking a chance, she knew. There could be killers already in the room. But the room was situated away from where the shot had originated, and away from where the killers had entered the house. She needed time, and flight was the only way to provide it. The room was the answer.

Shots rang through a distant part of the house. Kaci forced the thoughts of Jake from her mind. The first shots were answered by the roaring boom of a 12-gauge shotgun. Chances were the killers were not carrying shotguns, so that meant that either the DEA agent, John Ortiz, or Jake had loosed a barrage from their Remington shotguns.

Screams filled the dark corridors.

■ ■ ■

"The window," the man shouted. "Get back to the window."

The sound of running feet accompanied the order, the sound of footfalls softened by expensive carpets and area rugs.

"Get Siemens," the man ordered. "Get him to the window, now!"

More running. Whispered orders were issued. Whispered responses followed. Action resulted. Men moved in the darkness, seeking shelter and ultimate escape. They had wandered into a hornet's nest, and the hornets had stung.

"Who else?" the man asked as the killers made their way to the broached window.

"I don't know," one of the killers answered as he scrambled out of the opening. "I think Quintera went down," he said as he climbed out the window.

The man forced himself to think, to slow down, to evaluate. Where had the weapons come from? Who were these people? And for the first time in his career he asked, *Why am I doing this?*

Who were these people? he wondered. He might need to know. It could affect the outcome of the current assignment. He would contact Janus and get an answer.

The last man crossed the broken window ledge. Already two had been carried out. Two out of nine. Seven left. How many were still inside? His listening devices had identified four, but could there be more? He needed to know.

The man followed the last man out the window, reached for the beeper attached to his belt, and punched in a coded message. The answer came back, cryptic and chilling: continue. That was not the answer he'd expected. He punched in the coded inquiry again, and again the answer returned, this time slower than the first, but still the same: continue.

He needed help. Backup. Four against seven were not odds he relished, especially when the four inside had and knew how to use weapons. Shotguns at close range had a way of evening the odds.

■ ■ ■

Jake felt his heart jump into his throat at the first shots. Bullets impacted near John Ortiz, but Jake saw the shooter, and loosed a close-in barrage of 12-gauge shotgun fire. The man had screamed and gone down, and Jake felt a moment of pride. Then reality set in. He was a doctor, and he saved lives. He did not take them.

"You OK, John?" Jake called to the DEA agent.

"Thanks. That guy almost got me."

"They're not wearing those night goggle things," Jake said.

"Puts us on more even footing," Ortiz answered, knowing his statement was overly optimistic. They were outnumbered by skillfully trained assassins. Only pure luck—and a little oversight on the leader's part—had enabled their team to take the first casualty.

"Stay alert," Ortiz said from the shadows. "They're in here."

Jake didn't answer. He knew the agent was right. Numerous gunshots had echoed from the old walls like shots in a cave. It was impossible to tell where they had come from. Jake's thoughts went to Kaci. Where was she?

Whatever else Janus wanted, it wanted them dead. If Peter St. Clair was right, there was a good chance that more men were on their way into the Virginia countryside right now. Soon, there would be a small army outside the mansion with only one intention—extermination.

Jake wondered how the men outside received their orders, but he dismissed the thought. This was the age of electronic communication and satellites. Everything else being equal, communication was the least of the killer's worries.

Then Jake remembered the rest of the story. What was it St. Clair had said? Janus was not human. Janus was a machine, and machines had weak points, vulnerabilities, just like humans.

Just like humans.

Just like humans, Jake exulted.

Humans were, for the most part, a hearty breed. It took a lot to bring a human being to his or her knees, and even then, the human body was adaptable, changeable. *That* was about the only part Charles Darwin had gotten right. The human body had the ability to adapt. It was that ability that allowed human beings to generate antibodies against certain diseases. But a computer could not do that. A computer had no protection against disease.

And Kerry Hartford had provided a disease.

Jake scanned the room quickly. It was getting dark now. The moon had reached its apogee and was quickly receding, taking its reflective light with it. He did not dare turn on the lights. That would invite disaster.

Jake found Kaci's purse and dumped the contents on the carpet. At first he had difficulty distinguishing between the individual items in the darkness. But his eyes quickly picked up the reflection of the one item he sought. The CD! The virus!

It looked like any other CD. Jake picked it up and crawled from where he and St. Clair were concealed. He flipped the switch of the CPU and listened as the hard drive and other components powered up.

In a few minutes St. Clair's theory would either be proved or disproved. If proved, there was a good chance they would all survive. If disproved, they would all soon be dead. Jake suddenly felt an unfamiliar sensation: recognition of his own mortality.

The computer booted up. The monitor blinked on. Jake had not taken that into account, and his eyes had trouble adjusting to the bright appliance. Too late, he realized his mistake.

Just as his vision adjusted, the large monitor exploded in front of him! Jake dove for cover. The noise was deafening. Smoke issued from the destroyed monitor, along with electrical crackling and sparking.

"Down," Ortiz shouted. "That came from the hallway."

Someone had been left behind when the rest of the hit team had escaped through the window. Jake had not considered that, and he had almost paid for that oversight with his life. He'd been silhouetted against the monitor, and the killer had missed. How, Jake did not know, but missed he had.

I can do all things . . .

A second shot rang out. The report was different, shorter. It was the sound of a pistol.

A thump echoed through the mansion—the sound of a body hitting the floor.

Jake's pulse accelerated; his head hurt. Had the body been Kaci?

Then from the shadows came her voice. "He's down. How's everyone else?"

"OK in here," Jake answered.

"OK here," Ortiz responded.

"Great," Kaci said. "That was one I've been tracking. Sorry I let him get that shot off. I lost him around the corner. The rest are outside. I think they must be waiting for backup. Our only chance will be to get out of here, and do it fast."

Just as Kaci finished speaking, the sound of cars driving up in the gravel drive outside could be heard through the open window.

"Too late," Ortiz said in a low voice.

"I think you may be right," Kaci agreed. "How's the Ambassador?"

"I'm fine. Can't say I like what these thugs are doing to my house, but then I don't suppose I have a lot of say in the matter."

Kaci laughed at the old man. Even in the midst of a siege, he had a sense of humor.

"Here they come," Jake said as he jacked a shell into the shotgun. He checked the rifle, then leaned against the computer desk and checked the pistol. He decided to use the shotgun. The Remington was a better close-in weapon.

"I'm going back to the interior. I can do more damage from there," Kaci said, and she was gone like a ghost.

"What a woman," John Ortiz said in admiration.

Jake felt a surge of pride in the statement, further proving to himself that he loved Kaci Callahan.

"The computer," Peter St. Clair said to Jake.

"It's destroyed," Jake reminded the old man.

Shots again rang out through the house. Not the syncopated, deliberate firing that it had been, but indiscriminate firing, multiple bursts that meant the killers were coming into the house with renewed firepower. Three-shot bursts followed one another in close rapidity. The killers were advancing in two-by-two cover positions, one man covering the other while the first burst into the room and sprayed it with fire. Then the second man followed, firing his own weapon. The rooms and everything in them were being systematically destroyed. It would not be long before the killers made it to the computer room, Jake knew. While he and John Ortiz might get some of them, sheer numbers would finally win out—and it appeared that the killers had the numbers.

They were now heavily outmanned and outgunned.

Janus had found them, and death seemed close behind.

"The computer," St. Clair repeated, this time in a demanding tone.

"Gone," Jake said, wondering what the old man thought a bullet actually did to a computer's insides.

"No. Only the monitor. The CPU's still up and running," St. Clair hissed urgently.

Jake started at the words. The old man was right. *He was right!*

The computer *was* still operating. The assassin's bullet had found the monitor, but it had not touched the rest of the system. The virus disk might still work using the keyboard commands. There would be no way to monitor the progress, but there was a chance.

Jake retrieved the disk, checking to be sure which side was the correct side. He could only insert it in the drive and hope for the best.

The sound of shooting moved methodically closer. The sound was now filling the room where they waited. Jake wondered where Kaci was. He had heard nothing that might indicate they had killed her. There was still hope. And Jake knew that Kaci was not the kind to offer herself as a sacrifice, either. She would go down fighting, taking some of the killers with her, no doubt. Since there had been no indication of a gunfight, Jake felt that wherever she was, she was still safe and untouched. His spirits were buoyed by the thought. There was still hope.

A blast from the DEA agent's shotgun suddenly lit the darkness; the report was deafening. The killers had reached the computer room! Jake grabbed the virus disk.

I can do . . . the words came . . .

Getting to the disk drive of the computer CPU meant exposing himself. Fortunately, the killers had retreated for the moment, driven back by the blast from Ortiz's shotgun.

. . . *all things* . . . the words continued . . .

Jake inched his way around the computer desk, moving toward the still-functioning CPU and its CD drive.

. . . *through Christ* . . . please, Lord, Jake prayed . . .

The red light blinked in front of him. The old man was right. The computer was still operating, still functioning, still *communicating with Janus.*

. . . *who strengthens me.* The ultimate promise.

Jake punched the small button that opened the CD drive, placed the virus-laden CD in the tray, and gently closed the drawer—all the while feeling a calm he would not have believed possible.

The small light next to the CD drive lit up. There was a sudden lull in the shooting, and Jake could hear the CD spin up. He pressed "control," "shift," and then "escape," the correct sequence of keyboard commands. The computer began extracting information from the disk, transferring it to Janus.

A shot slammed into the desk near Jake's head, and he scrambled to reach the protection of the desk. Two more bullets found the wall behind the desk.

The sound of Kaci's 9-mm pistol echoed through the house, a sharp counterpoint to the automatic weapons used by the assault team members.

"One down!" a male voice yelled from the darkness.

A second shot rang out. Again Kaci's 9-mm.

"I'm hit!" a voice screamed.

Jake knew the killers were feeling the wrath of one very determined NCIS agent.

Then the bullets began coming in waves. Muzzle flashes lit the room. The effect was eerie, and Jake found himself mesmerized by the ghastly display. He forgot about the computer and the CD. Had some of the bullets found the CPU? Surely they had. If so, had it stopped the transfer of the virus? There was no way to know.

The wall behind where he and St. Clair were sheltered began to burst apart. Large chunks of plaster and wood showered down on them. Jake could distinguish the resonance of John Ortiz's shotgun as it resounded in answer to the strident sound of the automatic weapons. And then the shotgun went silent.

The sound of automatic weapons being reloaded reverberated through the house. Empty magazines were discarded, high-velocity rounds were jacked into waiting firing chambers.

Jake could no longer hear. The concentrated sound of the weapons being discharged in such close quarters had temporarily deafened him. He glanced over to where St. Clair crouched against the wall. The old man raised his head. He was alive.

"Madsen," John Ortiz shouted.

Jake heard his name called as if through a haze. "Here," he responded.

"What's happening?" the DEA agent asked.

"They're leaving," the answer came from Kaci Callahan who had made her way back to the computer room. "They're just leaving," she repeated.

"What's going on?" Jake asked, rising from behind the desk.

Peter St. Clair rose from where he had been hiding. "The computer," he said. "It has to be. Check it out."

Jake moved to the front of the desk. Bullet holes riddled its surface. Splinters of wood protruded from the desk at odd angles, all the result of bullet impacts. The desk was destroyed.

Amazingly, the computer had not been hit; the small red light glowed in the darkness.

"They're pulling out," John Ortiz said from the doorway. He'd gone to the window to check on the assault team. The would-be killers had disappeared into the night.

"I've got an old monitor in the closet over there," St. Clair said, indicating a closet against the far wall. Ortiz went to the closet, found the monitor, and placed it next to the destroyed one on the desk. In seconds, St. Clair had the replacement monitor up and running. The message on the screen startled each of them. It read: Terminate Assault.

Jake and Kaci looked at each other. The message had apparently been transmitted to the assault team. That's why they had called off the attack.

"The virus," St. Clair said. "It worked."

"Remind me to kiss Kerry Hartford when I get back to Memphis," Kaci exclaimed.

"Only if you get to him first," Jake responded.

John Ortiz went to the keyboard and tapped in a command. Nothing happened. "It's locked up tighter than my father's garage," Ortiz said.

Jake looked at the DEA agent. "What's in your father's garage?"

"A 1959 Corvette. Fully restored."

"And that, my friends," Peter St. Clair interjected, "is tight."

"So this terminal was hooked to Janus, and when the virus on the CD crashed the Janus system," Kaci summed up, "the system automatically recalled its security personnel."

"Looks that way. Of course, we have no way of tracing the system or the computer. It could be in a million different places," St. Clair reminded the group. "But I think it's safe to say that whatever that virus was, it was pretty potent."

"Deadly might be a better word. It sure saved us," Jake said.

"There's still a lot here I don't understand, Ambassador," Kaci commented.

"I'm sure there is. Let's check out the house and make sure our friends have departed, then we can try to answer some of your questions," St. Clair said.

Jake took Kaci's hand, stopping her momentarily. "And I'll take my kiss before you get to that Hartford guy back in Memphis," he said with a glow in his eye.

Kaci reached up and gently kissed Jake on the forehead. He frowned.

"Patience, my dear. Patience," she grinned and then was gone.

■ ■ ■

The man peeked at his beeper again. He had never received such a message before, but he knew better than to disobey. All the other men in the assault team had received the same message simultaneously, and each had obeyed instantaneously.

The team had abandoned the killing ground and had made it back to the cars, along with the wounded. From what he could tell, they had done no damage to the targets, but they themselves sustained considerable damage. Was that the reason for the recall? Had they gone after the wrong targets? What was the reason?

The man entered a code that would send a direct inquiry to Janus. He waited, and when he felt the beeper vibrate against his side, he looked at the readout. What he read shocked him. SYSTEM FAILURE was all that showed on the screen. The man tried to resend his inquiry, but the screen stubbornly refused to erase the System Failure message. Something had locked up. He would find out what it was, and someone would pay for this night's work, he promised himself.

EPILOGUE

The four sat in what remained of Peter St. Clair's den. The assailants had mangled the walls, windows, and furniture with indiscriminate shooting. The chairs were still serviceable, but only barely. St. Clair held the computer printout he'd earlier shown the other three.

"It's all here," St. Clair explained. "I first became aware of certain atrocities a little more than two years ago."

Kaci and Jake scanned the printout while Ortiz listened.

"Here's an attack on a U.S. Army patrol in Saudi Arabia," Kaci said, her finger on a line on the printout. Jake looked over Kaci's shoulder at the information.

"That's the attack Jerry Wallace told me about," Jake said in an awed voice.

"Jerry Wallace?" St. Clair repeated.

"The murder I'm investigating," Kaci added. "Jake saw him during sick call one morning, and everything started from there."

"Just like I said," the old ambassador continued. "Somewhere along the line, some of the test subjects got out of hand for one reason or another, and Janus had to act."

Jake felt his anger building. "You're saying that Jerry Wallace was nothing more than a test subject for Janus, and because he came to see me during sick call, he was killed?"

"Precisely. And it was not the first time something like that happened."

"But it will be the last, you can count on that," Jake promised.

"Perhaps. Nevertheless, that attack in Saudi Arabia started me wondering. I had been tracking the Janus activity, and even though I had personal doubts, there had never been any real evidence. The activity could be accounted for in a more-or-less logical manner."

"Until Saudi Arabia," John Ortiz said.

"Until Saudi," St. Clair confirmed. "I began checking different areas of unrest and cross-checking them with Janus activity. Some corresponded, but not all. Some even made sense, in a morbid sort of way. You'll find Sadaam Hussein's chemical attack on the Kurds listed on that printout. I'm still not totally convinced that was not a Janus scenario. The problem was that there were no survivors to study, and no evidence was ever transported to study facilities."

"It sounds so ghastly," Kaci said in a whisper.

"*Ghastly* is not a strong enough term," St. Clair said. "In fact, I doubt that there is a word in the English language strong enough to describe the work of Janus."

John Ortiz moved in closer, joining the group. "And you want us to believe that this was all the work of a *computer?*"

St. Clair smiled. "I understand your skepticism. But you pay your bills every month, don't you? Where does that bill come from? How many people pay whatever is listed on their charge card bills without ever inspecting what it is they are being charged?"

"That's not the same thing," Ortiz argued.

"It's *exactly* the same thing. We live in a society that just doesn't care anymore. If a piece of paper is spit out by some high-speed printer somewhere telling us we owe a certain amount of money, we believe that piece of paper. Janus did not start out as a completely automated system. Men initiated Janus. But slowly, over time, as computers and programs became more and more sophisticated, those men left the day-to-day operations to the computer—until finally, one day, there were no more men."

"What about those men who just tried to kill us?" the DEA agent asked. "*They* seemed alive enough!"

"Service men. Collection agents. Hired killers. They all work the same way. Have you had your refrigerator worked on lately?"

Ortiz shook his head, wondering where the old man was going with this line of questioning.

"All service technicians ever see is a readout on a small computer screen they carry in their service van. Where did the order come from? Chances are, someone called a computer using a touchtone phone, left the information, and that information was relayed to the technician without ever having passed through human hands. Who knows, someday your refrigerator will simply make the call for you. It will be connected to the Internet and the World Wide Web, and when its computer tells it that something is wrong, it will call in its own malfunction. You may only learn about it when someone shows up to repair it. Or, it may be built with redundant systems, like a space shuttle, and it will be repaired over the Web instantly. You'll get the bill from another computer, and you'll pay that, too, without ever wondering what it was all about. So you see, the idea behind Janus is *not* a lot of hogwash, excuse the expression. It's happening."

The group sat silently for a moment, the three outsiders trying to

EPILOGUE

absorb what Peter St. Clair had just told them, trying to imagine a world that not even George Orwell could have envisioned.

"The rest of the information on that printout is equally gruesome," St. Clair continued.

"Attacks ranging from the Balkans to South America to Asia," Kaci read.

"One of those attacks, the one in Kosovo, is the one that really got me going on this. Janus killed a friend of mine in that one," St. Clair said in a low voice, the pain of loss evident.

"The British peacekeepers?" Kaci asked, consulting the readout.

"There was an American colonel with them. Frank Melhart was the son of an ex-classmate at Princeton. Colonel Melhart was the reason the patrol was ambushed," the old man said in a broken tenor.

"I don't understand," Jake said gently.

"The patrol was composed entirely of British SAS troops, with the exception of Frank Melhart. The best I can deduce, when Frank's name came up on the assignment board to go out as an advisor, Janus targeted the patrol. That pattern had been appearing more and more frequently."

"What pattern?" Kaci asked.

"A pattern that ensured only a limited number of Americans would be caught in the attacks, but one that also would ensure that at least one would be shipped back to the States for evaluation."

"Less American exposure, less political turmoil," Kaci said.

"That had to be the plan."

Ortiz exploded. "You're talking about a computer, for heaven's sake! As if this Janus had the ability to reason, to think for itself."

"It does. Or it did," St. Clair responded. "Whatever you think, the attacks were taking place. One on the border between Ecuador and Peru cost the lives of several men. Those bodies were shipped through Panama, actually autopsied there, and the tissue samples shipped to the States. To a laboratory not too far from here. I've tried talking to them but have had no luck. The bodies were transported to Andrews Air Force Base, and that's the last place I could track them to. I suspect the lab will be closed in short order now."

"It's almost too incredible to believe," Jake Madsen finally said. "Jerry Wallace had a monitor implanted in his chest, and he was being monitored by a computer."

"Or by people who *thought* the computer, Janus, was being directed by others. But the task of directing the work of Janus had long been abdicated to a program. A very sophisticated program, to be sure, but a program, nonetheless."

"Where do we go from here?" Kaci asked. "I can't write a report saying that a computer killed Sergeant Jerry Wallace. I'd be laughed out of NCIS."

"And I can't report that the destruction of a Mexican village, a chemical company, and a battalion of Mexican army troops in the Mexican desert, not to mention one partner in the hospital in McAllen, Texas, was all due to the whims of a machine gone berserk," John Ortiz fumed.

"Not a machine gone berserk," Jake interjected. "A society whose members' own self-interest outweighs that of the society of which they are a part. People, probably nice people, who just don't want to be bothered by events that don't or can't affect them."

"That's the futility in all this," St. Clair joined in. "There's no real answer, no resolution. To echo a famous quote, 'We have met the enemy, and they are us.'"

"It's chilling," Kaci said.

"Let's get this place cleaned up," Jake offered.

"Try the phones," Kaci suggested.

John Ortiz picked up the phone nearest him and listened, then held it up in the air. "One dial tone, made to order," he said. "Who do I call?"

"After you call the police," St. Clair said, "call a cleaning service. I'm not about to tackle this job."

The laughter eased the tension in the room.

EPILOGUE

"Messy or dry?" Jake asked Kaci as they walked from Building 238 on NAVSUPACT.

"I think I'm in the mood for dry today," Kaci answered.

"Good," Jake said. "That means we get to hold hands after we eat. That messy Memphis barbecue is great, but it puts a dent in the love life," he joked.

Kaci laughed. "What about the hospital?"

"I was on early. Worked the 'floater tray,' and Caroline gave me the rest of the day off."

"Bless her heart. I still can't believe she was only at her husband's clinic when everything happened that day. I was sure she'd been caught up in the Janus thing."

"I know. I'm glad she wasn't," Jake said, reaching for the handle of his new Jeep Cherokee. "I don't think I told you this. When she responded to her beeper message about her husband being injured in a car accident, and left the hospital to see about him—turned out to be false message."

"A beeper message?"

Jake stopped short of helping Kaci into the Jeep as their eyes met. *A beeper message.* And they both knew Janus *had* been at work.

Neither said another word until they reached the Rendezvous Restaurant.

"Best dry barbecue ribs in Memphis," Jake said, helping Kaci from the Jeep.

"When does your fellowship begin?" Kaci asked, not wanting to broach the subject of Janus again, even indirectly.

"Next week. I start on the computer models and then work from there. It's a great opportunity, and Caroline and the VA are behind me 100 percent. We're targeting a certain type of arthritis. If we find a cure, it will be a great breakthrough for folks almost totally disabled by the disease. The work that's already gone on in the VA is going to be of tremendous help."

"I didn't even know the VA did that kind of stuff until you told me about it."

Jake held open the door of the restaurant as Kaci entered. "Yeah. Most people don't know how much the VA actually does. Maybe I can help change that too."

"Smells great in here," Kaci said.

"Looks great too," Jake said, his gaze locked on Kaci.

Kaci swung at him, missing on purpose, then laughed.

"I hope you don't do that at the wedding," Jake said, pulling a chair out for Kaci. "Might cause a scene."

"Just wait and see," Kaci smiled. "Now sit down."

"I know I'm making a mistake. I'm already doing what you tell me to do without question."

Kaci reached over and took Jake's hand. "Just keep doing that. You never know where it will get you."

Jake squeezed the hand that had saved his life six months earlier, knowing he loved Kaci Callahan with all his heart—a heart that also knew Kathy would understand.

Data Processing Center
Pine Bluff Arsenal
Pine Bluff, Arkansas

"Hey, Lieutenant," Specialist Albert Wiley called across the computer center. "I got a bug."

First Lieutenant Scott Clowney sauntered over to the terminal where Wiley sat. "What's the problem, Wiley?" Clowney asked.

"You got me, Lieutenant," Wiley answered. "You're the officer in charge, sir. You tell me. I can't get the computer to accept data."

"OK, Wiley, get up. Let me have your seat."

"Yes, sir, Lieutenant, sir," Wiley responded condescendingly, knowing the jab would go right over Clowney's head. He was right.

Clowney took the seat at the terminal and typed for a few minutes. "Locked up," the lieutenant announced after two minutes.

"Very good, Lieutenant. But I already knew that."

"OK. Let's re-boot and start over."

"Come on, Lieutenant. That means I lose everything. Ain't there a way to save the stuff I've already done?"

But it was too late. Clowney had already set the re-boot procedure in motion. The screen blinked off; then after a few seconds, it popped back on.

"What the heck is that?" Wiley asked, peering over Lieutenant Clowney's shoulder.

"Get the Procedures Manual," Clowney ordered.

Albert Wiley went to a metal bookshelf, pulled a thick, loose-leaf binder from the shelf, and returned. He plopped it down in front of Clowney and watched as the young officer paged through the thick book.

"Here it is," the lieutenant said finally.

"What, sir?"

"The procedure for this message."

Wiley looked over Clowney's shoulder again. "That's not the same message, sir," Wiley pointed out.

"Close enough for government work, soldier," the officer said as he keyed in the commands. In seconds the screen was back up, displaying the data the specialist had been working on earlier.

"Hallelujah. You did it, Lieutenant. I'll have to get you a cup of coffee for that," Wiley said, impressed.

"Forget the coffee. It's end of watch. That's the reason I wanted to get this out of the way. Our reliefs are already here. Let's get out of here."

Albert Wiley watched Lieutenant Clowney walk from the room, thinking for the first time since the young officer had arrived at the

Pine Bluff Arsenal that maybe he was all right. In any case, it was end of watch, and Wiley knew his girlfriend was waiting for him outside. The specialist had more important things to do.

Al Wiley took over the driving as his girlfriend, Pamela Masterson, slid over, but not too far.

"What was the holdup?" she asked. "You were ten minutes late."

"Nothing much. Had a message on my computer. Lieutenant Clowney fixed it."

"What did the message say?"

"Not much. Typical computer stuff. The message said, 'System Re-boot Required/Remote'."

"What's that mean?" Pamela asked.

"I think it means we had to re-boot a system's program in another area. I'm not sure. We re-booted and it worked, so what do I care."

"That was it?"

"Yeah. Except for the system name that appeared along with the message."

"What was the system name?" Pamela asked, snuggling next to Wiley as the specialist drove from the U.S. Army Chemical Weapons Storage Facility in Pine Bluff, Arkansas.

"Janus."

■ ■ ■

If you enjoyed this book
contact John F. Bayer @

P. O. Box 640552
El Paso, Texas 79904

JohnFBayer@aol.com

Breakthrough Language Series

FRENCH

Stephanie Rybak

The Language Centre, Brighton Polytechnic

General editor Brian Hill

Head of the Language Centre, Brighton Polytechnic

Series advisers

Janet Jenkins International Extension College, Cambridge
Duncan Sidwell Principal Modern Languages Adviser, Leicestershire, LEA
Al Wolff Producer, BBC School Radio

Pan Books London, Sydney and Auckland

Acknowledgements

Our very warm thanks to Olive Rybak for her extensive help with the preparation of the course.

Our thanks also to
Danielle Drinkwater for researching *Did you know?*
Annie Métral for checking the manuscript.
Our French friends – regrettably too numerous to name – for helping with the recordings in France.
The Polytechnic of Central London for the studio recordings.

We are grateful to the following for permission to reproduce copyright material
The Librairie PLON for the recipe from Michel Oliver's *La pâtisserie est un jeu d'enfants*.
Les Éditions Gallimard for Jacques Prévert's poem *Déjeuner du matin* from *Paroles* and for the timetable on p. 123.
The SNCF for the brochure on TEN sleeping carriages.
The Syndicat d'Initiative of La Roche-sur-Yon for their tourist brochure.
The French Government Tourist Office for the photographs on pages 97, 121, 205 and 211.
Olivier Stapleton for the photographs on pages 47 and 122.
Wendy Kay and Mary Glasgow Publications Ltd for the photographs on page 18.
Paride Bruzzone for the photographs on pages 53, 93, 97, 102, 104, 111, 145 and 199.

Tape production: Gerald Ramshaw, Claire Woolford
Acting: Pierre Valmer, Carolle Rousseau, Yves Aubert
Book Design: Gillian Riley
Illustrations: Rowan Barnes-Murphy

First published by Pan Books Ltd 1982
This edition published by Macmillan Education Ltd 1988
Reprinted 1989,1990 (three times)

Published by
MACMILLAN EDUCATION LTD
Houndmills, Basingstoke, Hampshire RG21 2XS
and London
Companies and representatives
throughout the world

Printed in Great Britain by
Billing and Sons Ltd
Worcester

ISBN 0-333-48190-9

Contents

How to use this course

Following this course will help you understand, speak and read most of the French you are likely to need on holiday or on business trips. The course is based on recordings made in France of ordinary French people in everyday situations. Step by step you will learn first to understand what they are saying and then to speak in similar situations yourself.

Before producing the course we talked to hundreds of people about why and how they learn languages. We know how important it is for learning to be enjoyable – and for it to be usable as soon as possible. Again and again people told us that there was not much point in knowing all the grammar if you were unable to ask for a cup of coffee! In this course you will learn to ask for a coffee in the very first unit – and the only explanations of grammar will be ones that actually help you understand and use the language.

General hints to help you use the course

- Have confidence in us! Real language is complex and you will find certain things in every unit which are not explained in detail. Don't worry about this. We will build up your knowledge slowly, selecting only what is most important to know at each stage.
- Try to study regularly, but in short periods. 20–30 minutes each day is usually better than 3½ hours once a week.
- To help you learn to speak, say the words and phrases out loud whenever possible.
- If you don't understand something, leave it for a while. Learning a language is a bit like doing a jigsaw or a crossword: there are many ways to tackle it and it all falls into place eventually.
- Don't be afraid to write in the book and add your own notes.
- Do revise frequently. (There are revision sections after every three units.) It helps to get somebody to test you – and they don't need to know French.
- If you can possibly learn with somebody else you will be able to help each other and practise the language together.
- Learning French may take more time than you thought. Just be patient and above all don't get angry with yourself.

Suggested study pattern

Each unit of the course consists of approximately fourteen pages in the book and ten minutes of tape. The first page of each unit will tell you what you are going to learn and suggest what we think is the best method for going about it. As you progress with the course you may find that you evolve a method of study which suits you better – that's fine, but we suggest you keep to our pattern at least for the first two or three units or you may find you are not taking full advantage of all the possibilities offered by the material.

The book contains step-by-step instructions for working through the course: when to use the book on its own, when to use the tape on its own, when to use them both together, and how to use them. On the tape our presenter Pierre will guide you through the various sections. Here is an outline of the study pattern proposed.

Dialogues Listen to the dialogues, first without stopping the tape, and get a feel for the task ahead. Then go over each one bit by bit in conjunction with the vocabulary and the notes. You should get into the habit of using the PAUSE/ STOP and REWIND buttons on your cassette recorder to give yourself time to think, and to go over the dialogues a number of times. Don't leave a dialogue until you are confident that you have at least understood it. (Symbols used in the notes are explained on p. 6.)

Key words and phrases	Study this list of the most important words and phrases from the dialogues. If possible, try to learn them by heart. They will be practised in the rest of the unit.
Practise what you have learnt	This section contains a selection of exercises which focus your attention on the most important language in the unit. To do them you will need to work closely with the book and often use your tape recorder – sometimes you are asked to write an exercise and then check the answers on tape: other times you are asked to listen first and then fill in answers in the book. Again, use your PAUSE/ STOP and REWIND buttons to give yourself time to think and to answer questions. Pauses have been left to help you to do this.
Grammar	At this stage in a unit things should begin to fall into place and you are ready for the grammar section. If you really don't like grammar, you will still learn a lot without studying this part, but most people quite enjoy finding out how the language they are using actually works and how it is put together. In each unit we have selected just one or two important grammar points.
Read and understand and *Did you know?*	In these sections you will be encouraged to read the kind of signs, menus, brochures, and so on you may come across in France and you will be given some practical background information on French customs and culture.
Your turn to speak	Finally, back to the tape for some practice in speaking the main words and phrases which you have already heard and had explained. The book only gives you an outline of the exercises, so you are just listening to the tape and responding. Usually you will be asked to take part in a conversation where you hear a question or statement in French, followed by a suggestion in English as to how you might reply. You then give your reply in French and listen to see if you were right. You will probably have to go over these spoken exercises a few times before you get them absolutely correct.
Answers	The answers to all the exercises (except those given on tape) can be found on the last page of each unit.

If you haven't learned languages using a tape before, just spend five minutes on Unit 1 getting used to the mechanics: practise pausing the tape, and see how long the rewind button needs to be pressed to recap on different length phrases and sections.

Don't be shy – take every opportunity you can to speak French to French people and to listen to real French. Try listening to French broadcasts on the radio or tuning in to the excellent BBC radio and television broadcasts for learners.

Bon courage!

At the back of the book

At the back of the book is a reference section which contains:

Symbols and abbreviations

If your cassette recorder has a counter, set it to zero at the start of each unit and then fill in these boxes the number showing at the beginning of each dialogue. This will help you find the right place on the tape quickly when you want to wind back.

◆ This indicates a key word or phrase in the dialogues.

m.	masculine	pl.	plural
f.	feminine	lit.	literally
sing.	singular		

1 Talking about yourself

What you will learn

- exchanging greetings
- observing basic courtesies
- using numbers 1–10
- understanding and answering simple questions about yourself
- the documentation you need for France
- some useful addresses for the tourist

Before you begin

Before you start, read the introduction to the course on p. 4. This gives some useful advice on studying alone, and all the details of the specific study pattern recommended for the course.

Look at the *Study guide* below. It has been designed to help you make the most effective use of the unit, so that you will go on from understanding the gist of the recorded dialogues to understanding them in detail and finally to being able to produce a number of key words, phrases and sentences yourself.

We shall be trying to develop your ability to *follow the gist* of spoken French right from the start. So begin by listening to the first group of dialogues on the tape without using your book, and without worrying about the details of what is being said. This will prepare you for hearing French in France without panicking because you can't understand every word.

Study guide

	Dialogues 1, 2: listen straight through, without the book
	Dialogues 1, 2: listen, read and study one by one
	Dialogues 3, 4: listen straight through, without the book
	Dialogues 3, 4: listen, read and study one by one
	Dialogue 5: listen straight through, without the book
	Dialogue 5: listen, read and study
	Dialogues 6, 7: listen straight through, without the book
	Dialogues 6, 7: listen, read and study one by one
	Study the *Key words and phrases*
	Do the exercises in *Practise what you have learnt*
	Study the *Grammar* section
	Do the exercise in *Read and understand*
	Read *Did you know?*
	Do the tape exercises in *Your turn to speak*
	Finally, listen to all the dialogues again straight through

Dialogues

If you have a cassette recorder with a counter, put it to zero and note the counter reading for each dialogue in the rectangle. This will help you find the dialogues more quickly when you want to listen to them a second time.

1 *Saying hello*

Robert	Bonjour, Madame. Bonjour, Monsieur.
Stephanie	Bonjour, Monsieur.
Henri	Bonjour, Madame.
Jean-Claude	Bonjour, Madame.
Stephanie	Bonjour, Monsieur.
Michel	Bonjour, Madame.
Anne	Bonjour, Monsieur.
Michèle	Bonjour, Mademoiselle.
Nicole	Bonjour, Madame.
Nicole	Bonjour, Messieurs-dames.

2 *And when the evening comes. . .*

Michel	Bonsoir, Monsieur.
Christian	Bonsoir, Monsieur.
Stephanie	Bonsoir, Monsieur.
Luc	Bonsoir, Madame.
Bernadette	Bonne nuit.
Barbara	Bonne nuit.

3 *Thank you and good-bye*

Robert	Bon. Merci. Merci, Madame. Au revoir, Madame.
Réceptionniste	Au revoir, Monsieur.
Robert	Au revoir, Monsieur. Merci.
Julie	Merci.
Réceptionniste	Bonnes vacances.
Julie	Merci. Au revoir, Madame.

♦ **merci** thank you
♦ **au revoir** good-bye
une réceptionniste a receptionist

The most important expressions are marked with a ♦; these are the ones you should try to remember. They will be listed again on p. 14.

1 ♦ **bonjour** good morning, good afternoon and hello.

♦ **Madame** literally means Madam, but see below.

♦ **Monsieur** literally means Sir. We no longer call people Sir or Madam in ordinary conversation in English but it is a matter of politeness to use **Monsieur** or **Madame** in French. They also mean Mr and Mrs and in writing are often abbreviated to **M** and **Mme**.

♦ **Mademoiselle** literally means Miss. It is used in the same way as **Monsieur** and **Madame** but for an unmarried woman – or one who looks too young to be married. Written abbreviation: **Mlle**.

♦ **Messieurs-dames** ladies and gentlemen. If you go into a small shop where there are other customers waiting, it is normal to say **Bonjour, Messieurs-dames** (or even just **Messieurs-dames**).

2 ♦ **bonsoir** good evening. Used for both hello and good-bye after about 5 p.m.

bonne nuit good night.

3 ♦ **bon** literally means good. It is used here, and often, to wind up a conversation – we would say 'right' or 'OK'.

♦ **bonnes vacances** (have a) good holiday. **Vacances** is always used in the plural, (with an 's' on the end).

4 *Please*

Paul   S'il vous plaît, Monsieur?
Jacques   Un café et une bière, s'il vous plaît.

Réceptionniste   Votre nom, s'il vous plaît?
Nicole   Durand.
Réceptionniste   Et votre prénom?
Nicole   Nicole.
Réceptionniste   Et votre adresse, s'il vous plaît?
Nicole   Six (6), avenue Général-de-Gaulle.

♦ **et** and
votre your
un nom a surname
une adresse an address
un prénom a forename
une avenue an avenue

5 *Learning to count*

Nadine   Un crayon, deux crayons, trois crayons, quatre crayons, cinq, six. Tu comptes avec moi?
Pierre-Yves   Nnnn.
Nadine   Un, deux . . . tu dis? Deux, trois, quatre, cinq, six, sept . . .
Pierre-Yves   Maman!
Nadine   Huit.
Pierre-Yves   C'est quoi?
Nadine   Neuf.
Pierre-Yves   Maman!
Nadine   Dix!
Pierre-Yves   Non!
Nadine   Tu comptes avec moi?
Pierre-Yves   Non! C'est quoi?
Nadine   C'est un micro.

un crayon a/one pencil
Maman Mummy
♦ **non** no

4 ◆ **s'il vous plaît** please. Used here as a polite way of attracting someone's attention.

◆ **un café et une bière, s'il vous plaît** a coffee and a beer, please. If you ask for **un café** you will be given a *black* coffee. You will learn how to ask for coffee with milk in Unit 3. **Un** and **une** both mean 'a', or 'an' or 'one' (see *Grammar*, p. 17). There is very little difference between a café and a bar in France, so a mixed order of coffee and beer is not unusual in either. You will learn how to order drinks and snacks in Unit 3.

5 ◆ **un, deux, trois, quatre, cinq, six, sept, huit, neuf, dix** 1, 2, 3, 4, 5, 6, 7, 8, 9, 10.

tu comptes avec moi? are you going to count with me? (lit. you count with me?) Putting a questioning tone into your voice is enough to turn a sentence into a question in French. There are two words for 'you' in French: **tu** is only used to people you know well (see p. 17 for further explanation).

tu dis? are you going to say it? (lit. you say?)

◆ **c'est quoi?** what's that? (lit. it is what?). The little boy has spotted the microphone!

c'est un micro it's a mike (microphone). **C'est** is a very useful phrase meaning 'it is' or 'that is' e.g. also **c'est un crayon** (that's a pencil).

6 *Are you English?*

Henri	Vous êtes anglaise?
Stephanie	Oui – et vous?
Henri	Je suis français. Vous êtes en vacances?
Stephanie	Oui.
Henri	Vous êtes de Londres?
Stephanie	Ah non – de Brighton. Et vous?
Henri	Moi, j'habite Paris.

♦ **oui** yes

7 *Getting to know you*

Jean-Claude	Bonjour, Madame.
Stephanie	Bonjour, Monsieur.
Jean-Claude	C'est . . . euh . . . Madame ou Mademoiselle?
Stephanie	Mademoiselle.
Jean-Claude	Ah bon . . . vous êtes anglaise ou américaine?
Stephanie	Anglaise – et vous?
Jean-Claude	Je suis français. Et . . . vous habitez Londres?
Stephanie	Ah non – Brighton.
Jean-Claude	Ah bon, Brighton. Moi, j'habite Paris. Vous êtes touriste?
Stephanie	Je suis en vacances, oui.
Jean-Claude	En vacances? Ah bon. Et vous êtes avec un groupe ou vous êtes toute seule?
Stephanie	Toute seule.
Jean-Claude	Toute seule?

　euh er
♦ **ou** or
　américaine American (lady)
　un/une touriste a tourist
♦ **en vacances** on holiday
♦ **avec** with
　un groupe a group

6

♦ **vous êtes anglaise?** are you English? If Henri had been speaking to a man he would have said **vous êtes anglais?** (See *Grammar* p. 17, for an explanation.) Most French people use **anglais** (English) to mean British.

♦ **et vous?** and you? A useful way of returning a question. **Vous** is the normal word for 'you' whether you are talking to one or more persons.

♦ **je suis français** I'm French. A woman would say **je suis française**. (See p. 17) 'I'm English' would be
je suis anglais (if you are a man)   **je suis anglaise** (if you are a woman).

vous êtes en vacances? are you on holiday?

♦ **vous êtes de Londres?** are you from London? If you were talking to a French person you might want to say **vous êtes de Paris?** (are you from Paris?).

♦ **moi, j'habite Paris** *I* live in Paris (lit. me, I live in Paris). The **moi** is used here for emphasis. Note also:
j'habite Londres I live in London   **j'habite Newcastle** I live in Newcastle

7

c'est Madame ou Mademoiselle? is it Mrs or Miss? He could quite politely call her either, but he wants to know whether she is married.

vous habitez Londres? do you live in London?

♦ **ah bon** oh yes. Used to acknowledge what someone has said.

♦ **vous êtes avec un groupe?** are you with a group? You might want to answer: **non, je suis avec ma famille** (no, I'm with my family).

toute seule on your own (lit. all alone). A man alone would be **tout seul** (see *Grammar* p. 17.)

Key words and phrases

Here are the most important words and phrases which you have met in the dialogues. You should make sure you know them before you go on to the rest of the unit as you will need them for the exercises which follow. Practise saying them aloud.

bonjour	good morning, good afternoon, hello
bonsoir	good evening
Monsieur	Sir, Mr
Madame	Madam, Mrs
Mademoiselle	Miss
Messieurs-dames	ladies and gentlemen
oui	yes
non	no
bon	good, right, OK
merci	thank you
au revoir	good-bye
s'il vous plaît	please
un café et une bière	a coffee and a beer
un	one
deux	two
trois	three
quatre	four
cinq	five
six	six
sept	seven
huit	eight
neuf	nine
dix	ten
c'est quoi?	what's that?
vous êtes français?	are you French? (*to a man*)
française?	(*to a woman*)
et vous?	and you?
je suis anglais	I'm English (*for a man*)
anglaise	(*for a woman*)
vous êtes de Paris?	are you from Paris?
j'habite Londres	I live in London
je suis en vacances	I'm on holiday
avec un groupe	with a group
avec ma famille	with my family
ah bon	oh yes, oh really?
bonnes vacances!	have a good holiday!

Practise what you have learnt

This part of the unit is designed to help you cope more confidently with the language you have met in the dialogues. You will need both the book and the cassette to do the exercises but all the necessary instructions are *in the book*. You will have more opportunity to speak at the end of the unit.

1 Listen to the conversation on the tape as many times as you like and fill in the woman's particulars on the form below. (You'll find them jumbled up beside the form.) You can check your answers on p. 20.

anglaise   Paris
avenue   Smith
7 (sept)   de
Gaulle
Barbara

| Nom (M/Mme/Mlle) .... |
| .... |
| Prénom .... |
| Adresse .... |
| .... |
| .... |
| .... |
| Nationalité .... |

une nationalité a nationality

2 How would you say hello in each of the situations below? Remember that it is polite to add **Monsieur, Madame, Mademoiselle** or **Messieurs-dames**. Write your answers in the spaces, then check them on p. 20. You won't need your tape recorder.

1. ....

2. ....

3. ....

4. ....

5. ....

6. ....

3 Choose the right words and phrases from the list below to put in the gaps in the conversation. Write them in first and then check them on p. 20. You won't need your tape recorder.

êtes   s'il vous plaît   bonjour, Madame   au revoir   en   merci, Madame   je   suis   vous   bonnes

Waitress	Bonjour, Monsieur.
Customer	....
	Une bière, ...
Waitress	Oui, Monsieur.
	(*Brings it*) Votre bière, Monsieur.
Customer	....
	Vous êtes de Paris?
Waitress	Non, je ....de Rouen.
Customer	Vous ....française?
Waitress	Oui – et ....?
Customer	Moi, ... suis anglais.
Waitress	Ah bon? Vous êtes ....vacances?
Customer	Oui.
Waitress	.... vacances, Monsieur!
Customer	Merci, Madame ....!

4 Now a chance to practise the numbers 1–10 – vitally important to know in all sorts of situations, from saying how many cream cakes you want, to how many people you want rooms for at a hotel. See if you can write in the answers (in words, not figures) to the sums below.

a. deux + deux = ...
b. quatre + un = ...
c. cinq + trois = ...
d. neuf + un = ...
e. huit − cinq = ...

f. dix − trois = ...
g. six − quatre = ...
h. deux × quatre = ...
i. trois × trois = ...
j. dix ÷ deux = ...

Now cover up the sums above. Play the next bit of the tape and try to write down the numbers you hear. This time write them in figures, not words. They should be the same as the answers to the sums above. You can check your answers on p. 20. Numbers given on the tape:

a. ....
b. ....
c. ....
d. ....
e. ....

f. ....
g. ....
h. ....
i. ....
j. ....

★★ Remember to look back at the *Study guide* on p. 7 to check your progress.

Grammar

Grammar can seem off-putting or even frightening, so the *Grammar* section in each unit will be kept as short and simple as possible. Its aim is to give the basics of the language so that you will have firm ground to build on. It will show you how the language works, but shouldn't inhibit you or make you afraid to open your mouth in case you make a mistake. MAKING MISTAKES DOES NOT MATTER AS LONG AS YOU MAKE YOURSELF UNDERSTOOD, but having an idea of the basics of grammar helps you to put words together. If you are not sure of grammatical terms like 'nouns', 'articles' and so on, there is a glossary on p. 221. Normally you won't need your tape recorder when you study this section.

Gender

All French nouns belong to one of two groups (called *genders*): masculine or feminine. Sometimes it is a matter of common sense: **un Français** (a Frenchman) is obviously masculine, and **une Française** (a Frenchwoman) is obviously feminine. However, the gender of most nouns is not obvious: we can see nothing masculine about 'pencil' (**un crayon**) or feminine about 'beer' (**une bière**). You can tell the gender of most French nouns if they have the words for 'a' or 'the' in front of them. Get into the habit of noticing genders – but don't worry about getting them wrong because people will still understand you. You might like to note that feminine nouns and adjectives often end with an '-e'.

Un and une

The word for 'a' or 'an' in French is **un** in front of a masculine noun and **une** in front of a feminine noun. (**Un** and **une** also mean 'one', i.e. 'number one'.) You have met **un** and **une** in the phrase: **un café et une bière, s'il vous plaît.**

Other examples are: **un nom** (a name), **un groupe** (a group), **une adresse** (an address), and **une nuit** (a night).

Adjectives

(descriptive words: big, blue, old, French, English)
You will have noticed in dialogues 6 and 7 that when stating his nationality a man says **je suis anglais** or **je suis français** but a woman says **je suis anglaise** or **je suis française**. This is because an adjective describing something masculine has a masculine form and one describing something feminine has a feminine form. So you say **un café français** (a French coffee) but **une bière française** (a French beer). (All but the most common adjectives come *after* the noun in French.) You had another example in dialogue 7 when Stephanie says she is **toute seule** (all alone). A man would have described himself as **tout seul**.

In the vocabulary lists after the dialogues the gender of adjectives will be indicated by (**m.**) or (**f.**).

Être to be

The verb 'to be' is as irregular in French as it is in English – and just as important. Here is the present tense. It is also recorded on your cassette after the dialogues, so practise saying it until you know it.

je suis	I am	**nous sommes**	we are
tu es	you are	**vous êtes**	you are
il/elle est	he/she is	**ils/elles sont**	they are

Note that:

1 The normal word for 'you', singular or plural, is **vous**. However, there is a more intimate form, **tu**, used to one person who is a close friend or member of your family. Young people tend to use **tu** much more freely among themselves than older people. As a general rule, you are advised to call people **vous** unless invited to use **tu**.

2 **Ils** is the normal word for 'they'. You only use **elles** if all of 'them' are feminine, e.g. if you are talking about a group of women. In fact, if you have 100 women and one man you still use **ils**.

Read and understand

This is a French identity card (**une carte d'identité**). Can you answer the questions about its owner? (Answers p. 20)

Hte Savoie Haute Savoie department of France (see p. 159)
porte des lunettes wears glasses

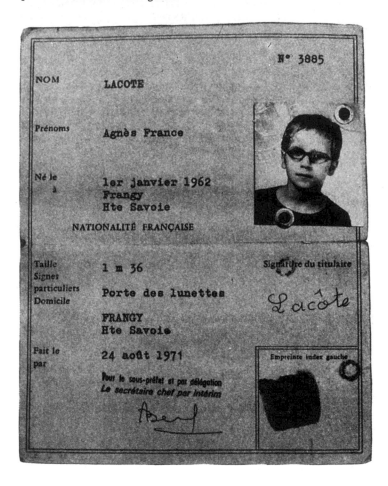

1 What is her surname?

....

2 What are her first names?

....

3 In what town does she live?

....

4 What is her nationality?

....

5 In which year was she born?

....

Did you know?

Courtesy

It is easy to appear rude because you don't know the customs in a foreign country, so courtesy phrases (**merci, s'il vous plaît** etc.) are very important. In French for example it is polite to use **Monsieur, Madame** or **Mademoiselle** when you are speaking to someone, particularly with short phrases like **oui, non, bonjour** or **merci**, which sound abrupt on their own. The French go on calling each other **Monsieur, Madame** or **Mademoiselle** long after the supposedly more reserved Briton has gone onto first-name terms. The French also shake hands with friends and acquaintances every time they meet or say good-bye. Kissing (on both cheeks) is reserved for family and close friends.

Identity cards

From the age of eighteen, everyone in France has an identity card – **une carte d'identité**. It is carried everywhere and contains an official photograph as well as a signature. As a tourist you are generally advised to carry your passport with you at all times. If you are driving you *must* have your driving licence as well as your passport in the car with you, and be ready to produce them if a policeman asks you for **vos papiers** (your papers). The 'green card' is no longer compulsory, but the AA and RAC strongly recommend it as without it your insurance cover is limited to third party liability.

Travel to and from French-speaking Europe

In addition to the AA and RAC and travel agents, the following are good sources of information and brochures:

France
The French Government Tourist Office
178 Piccadilly
London W1V 0AL
Tel. 01 493 6911

French Railways
179 Piccadilly
London W1V 0AL
Tel. 01 493 9731

Belgium
The Belgian National Tourist Office
66 Haymarket
London SW1Y 4RB
Tel. 01 499 5379

Switzerland
The Swiss National Tourist Office
Swiss Centre
1 New Coventry Street
London W1V 3HG
Tel. 01 734 1921

Your turn to speak

The exercises for this section are on your cassette. They will give you practice at saying aloud some of the most important language that you have learnt in this unit. Pierre will tell you what to do. You will probably need to go over the exercises a few times until you are familiar with the method used.

1 In the first exercise you are asked to imagine that you are in a bar or café and want to order beer and coffee. Pierre will prompt you on the tape. Remember to be polite!

2 This time you will play the part of an Englishman in France. A young Frenchwoman comes up to you and starts talking. Pierre will prompt you when you have to reply. Remember **et vous?** is a useful way of turning a question round and asking 'what about you?'.

And finally Before you go on to Unit 2, wind back and listen to all the dialogues again straight through. Also look back at the section *How to use this course* (p. 4) and the *Study guide* (p. 7) and make sure you have sorted out how each unit works. You will find you will cope more smoothly with the next unit.

Answers

Practise what you have learnt p. 15 Exercise 1 Mme/Smith/Barbara/7 avenue Général-de-Gaulle/Paris/anglaise.

p. 15 Exercise 2 (1) Bonjour, Madame (2) Bonjour, Monsieur (3) Bonsoir Mademoiselle (4) Bonjour, Messieurs-dames (5) Bonsoir, Monsieur (6) Bonsoir, Messieurs-dames.

p. 16 Exercise 3 Bonjour, Madame/s'il vous plaît/Merci, Madame/suis/êtes/vous/je/en/bonnes/au revoir.

p. 16 Exercise 4 (a) quatre 4 (b) cinq 5 (c) huit 8 (d) dix 10 (e) trois 3 (f) sept 7 (g) deux 2 (h) huit 8 (i) neuf 9 (j) cinq 5.

Read and understand p. 18 (1) Lacôte (2) Agnès France (3) Frangy (4) French (5) 1962.

2 Yourself and others

What you will learn

- understanding and answering questions about your job
- understanding and answering questions about your family
- asking similar questions of others
- saying things are not so
- using numbers up to 20
- something about the geography of France
- something about other French-speaking countries

Before you begin

The study guide set out below is very similar to the one in Unit 1.
Remember that the first stage of listening to the dialogues straight through
is important even if you do not understand much of what is being said. A
great deal of success in language learning depends on being able to pick out
the words you know from a torrent of words you don't, and then making
some intelligent guesses. You can also get an idea of the *pattern* of the
language from the first listen-through. For instance, in dialogue 2 in this
unit you will hear snippets of conversation with people saying what their
jobs are. No-one expects you to understand words like 'accountant' or 'civil
servant,' on your first listen-through, but you should notice that most of the
people speaking use **je suis** to say what they do for a living, just as we use
'I am' in English.

Study guide

Dialogues 1, 2: listen straight through without the book
Dialogues 1, 2: listen, read and study one by one
Dialogues 3, 4: listen straight through without the book
Dialogues 3, 4: listen, read and study one by one
Dialogues 5–7: listen straight through without the book
Dialogues 5–7: listen, read and study one by one
Study the *Key words and phrases*
Do the exercises in *Practise what you have learnt*
Study the *Grammar* section and do the exercises
Do the exercise in *Read and understand*
Read *Did you know?*
Do the tape exercise in *Your turn to speak*
Finally listen to all the dialogues again straight through

Dialogues

Remember to use the box to fill in the number from your counter when you start playing the tape.

☐ **1** *Do you work?*

Anna Vous travaillez?
Henri Ah oui, je travaille.
Anna A Paris?
Henri Oui. Et vous?
Anna Oui, moi aussi je travaille – à Paris également.

☐ **2** *Saying what your job is*

Henri Je suis commerçant.
Fabienne Je suis secrétaire.
Claude Je suis comptable.
Georges Je suis homme d'affaires.
Brigitte Je suis dans l'enseignement – je suis professeur de gymnastique.
Lisette Je suis employée dans un établissement d'enseignement – je suis fonctionnaire.
Claude Euh . . . j'ai un emploi de bureau . . . c'est bien, ça?

un commerçant a shopkeeper, tradesman
un/une secrétaire a secretary
un/une comptable an accountant, book-keeper
un homme d'affaires a businessman
un professeur a teacher
de of
(la) gymnastique gymnastics
un/une fonctionnaire an administrator, a civil servant

Other vocabulary given by the presenter on the tape:
un facteur a postman (man or woman)
un plombier a plumber
un/une dentiste a dentist
un médecin a doctor (man or woman)
un coiffeur a hairdresser (man)
une coiffeuse (woman)
un/une réceptionniste a receptionist
un ingénieur an engineer (man or woman)
en retraite retired

☐ **3** *A wedding anniversary*

Stephanie Vous êtes mariée?
Denise Oui, nous sommes mariés depuis trente-six ans demain.
Stephanie Félicitations! Et vous avez des enfants?
Denise Six enfants.
Stephanie Des garçons ou des filles?
Denise Quatre filles et deux garçons.

marié (masculine)
mariée (feminine)　} married
mariés (plural)
un an a year
♦ **félicitations!** congratulations!
un enfant a child
un garçon a boy
une fille a girl, a daughter

1   **vous travaillez?** literally, 'you work?' but with a question in the voice it becomes 'do you work?'

♦   **je travaille** I work. With **je** the verb ends in **-e** instead of **-ez**. (See *Grammar*, p. 31.)

♦   **moi aussi** I too or me too.

     à Paris in Paris. **A** can also mean 'at' or 'to'. Note that you don't have to put accents on capital letters in French, except **É**.

2 ♦   **je suis homme d'affaires** I am (a) businessman. For some professions there is only one word in French e.g. **ingénieur**, **professeur**, while others use two words according to whether you are a man or a woman e.g. **coiffeur** (m.), **coiffeuse** (f.).

     je suis dans l'enseignement I am in teaching.

     employée employed. The word also means a female employee. **Employé** (without a final **-e**) means employed, for a man, *and* a male employee.

     un établissement d'enseignement a teaching establishment. The French like long words! In this case she means a school – the simpler word for a school is **une école**.

     j'ai un emploi de bureau I have an office job: **un emploi** = a job, **un bureau** = an office. (See p. 31 for the verb **avoir**, to have.)

     c'est bien, ça? is that OK? (Literally, it's good, that?). Claude is shy in front of the microphone! **Bien** also means 'well' or 'good'.

3 ♦   **vous êtes mariée?** are you married? If this had been addressed to a man it would have been written **vous êtes marié?**

     nous sommes mariés depuis trente-six ans demain we've been married 36 years tomorrow (lit. we are married since 36 years). **Mariés** has an s because it refers to more than one person. When you make a statement in which past actions are still continuing you use this construction, e.g. also
je suis marié depuis un an   I've been married for one year
je suis marié depuis deux ans   I've been married for two years
. . . and I'm still married!

     vous avez des enfants do you have any children? **Des** means 'any' *or* 'some'. (For **avoir**, to have, see p. 31.)

     des garçons ou des filles? boys or girls? French nouns are almost always preceded by **des** (some), **les** (the) or some other 'article' (see *Grammar*, pp. 31 and 45.)

4 *Family questions*

Michel   Vous êtes marié?

Christian   Oui – et vous?

Michel   Non, je ne suis pas marié – je suis célibataire. Et vous, avez-vous des enfants?

Christian   Ah oui, j'ai trois filles: Claire, Isabelle et Céline.

Michel   Avez-vous des frères et soeurs?

Christian   Ah oui, j'ai . . . trois frères et deux soeurs.

Michel   Et votre père vit toujours?

Christian   Ah oui, oui – et ma mère aussi.

♦ **célibataire** single
un frère a brother
une soeur a sister
un père a father
ma my
une mère a mother
aussi also, too, as well.

5 *A first encounter*

Henri   Vous habitez chez vos parents?

Guylaine   Oui.

Henri   Et vous travaillez?

Guylaine   Oui, je travaille.

Henri   Où ça?

Guylaine   A Paris.

Henri   Quel travail?

Guylaine   Je suis secrétaire.

Henri   Vous avez un patron?

Guylaine   J'ai plusieurs patrons.

Henri   Ils sont gentils?

Guylaine   Dans l'ensemble, oui.

Henri   Et moi, je suis gentil?

Guylaine   Je ne sais pas: je ne vous connais pas.

vos parents your parents
quel? what? which?
un travail a job
un patron a boss
plusieurs several
moi me

4   **je ne suis pas marié** I'm not married. See *Grammar*, p. 31 for an explanation of the negative **ne . . . pas**. There are more examples in the dialogues which follow.

♦ **j'ai trois filles** I have three daughters, e.g. also **j'ai trois frères** (I have three brothers.)

    avez-vous des enfants? do you have any children? This is the same as **vous avez des enfants?** spoken with a questioning tone.

    et votre père vit toujours? and is your father still alive? (lit. and your father lives still?)

5   **vous habitez chez vos parents?** do you live with your parents? This question is like the English 'do you come here often?'!

    chez means 'to/at the home of', e.g. **chez moi, chez nous, chez Michel.**

    où ça? where's that?

    gentils nice, kind. The word ends in **-s** because it is plural, describing her boss*es*.

    dans l'ensemble on the whole.

♦ **je ne sais pas** I don't know, i.e. I don't know *a fact*.

♦ **je ne (vous) connais pas** I don't know (you), i.e. I don't know *a person*. It helps to think of **connaître** as meaning 'to be acquainted with' – like the Scottish 'do ye *ken* John Peel?'

6 *Saying no!*

Henri Vous voulez sortir ce soir?
Guylaine Je ne peux pas ce soir.
Henri Vous n'êtes pas sûre?
Guylaine Si, si, je suis sûre!
Henri Vous parlez anglais?
Guylaine Très mal.
Henri Ça n'a pas d'importance. Vous n'apprenez pas l'anglais?
Guylaine Je recommence à apprendre l'anglais.

très very
mal badly
vous apprenez you learn
je recommence à I am starting again to
(**je commence** I am starting)
apprendre to learn

7 *Numbers 1–20*

Yves Un, deux, trois, quatre, cinq, six, sept, huit, neuf, dix, onze, douze, treize, quatorze, quinze, seize, dix-sept, dix-huit, dix-neuf, vingt.

onze 11
douze 12
treize 13
quartorze 14
quinze 15
seize 16
dix-sept 17
dix-huit 18
dix-neuf 19
vingt 20

6 ♦ **vous voulez sortir ce soir?** do you want to go out this evening? The one word **sortir** means 'to go out'. Note also **demain soir** (tomorrow evening).

♦ **je ne peux pas** I can't. **Je peux** (I can), or any other verb, is made negative by putting **ne** and **pas** either side of the verb (see *Grammar*, p. 31).

vous n'êtes pas sûre? you're not sure? Before a vowel **ne** shortens to **n'**. See also **vous n'apprenez pas?** (aren't you learning?).

si, si, je suis sûre yes, yes I'm sure. **Si** is used for 'yes' when you are contradicting e.g. **vous n'êtes pas sûre? Si, si** (Yes, I am). If a man had been speaking his answer would have sounded exactly the same but 'sure' would have been spelt **sûr**.

♦ **vous parlez anglais?** do you speak English?

ça n'a pas d'importance that doesn't matter (lit. that has no importance.)

7 ♦ NUMBERS ARE IMPORTANT! You can't get very far without being able to use and understand them. Practise the numbers 1–20, saying them after Yves, and then counting on your own.

Try this game: write the numerals all over a blank page, then without looking, stab a pen or pencil at the page. Say the number nearest to where your pen falls.

Key words and phrases

Here are the most important words and phrases that you have met in this unit. Be sure you know them, and practise saying them aloud.

je travaille	I work
je suis (homme d'affaires)	I am (a businessman)
moi aussi	me too, or I too
vous êtes marié?	are you married?
mariée?	
non, je suis célibataire	no, I'm single
vous avez (des enfants)?	do you have (any children)?
j'ai (une fille)	I have (one daughter)
félicitations!	congratulations!
vous parlez anglais?	do you speak English?
français?	French?
vous voulez sortir (ce soir/demain soir)?	do you want to go out (this evening/ tomorrow evening)?
je ne peux pas	I can't
je ne sais pas	I don't know (*a fact*)
je ne connais pas (Jean)	I don't know (John i.e. *a person*)

onze 11
douze 12
treize 13
quatorze 14
quinze 15
seize 16
dix-sept 17
dix-huit 18
dix-neuf 19
vingt 20

Practise what you have learnt

Practice is vital if you are to remember the language you have met in the dialogues. For this section you will again be using both your book and your cassette. If you use the PAUSE or STOP button on your tape recorder you can repeat phrases after the speakers to improve your fluency and accent.

1 On the tape you will hear some numbers between 1 and 20. Write them down in figures. You can check your answers on p. 34.

a...................... b...................... c...................... d......................

e...................... f...................... g......................

2 Select the correct job from the box below and under each of the drawings write in how that person would say what his/her job was. The first one has been done for you. Answers on p. 34.

a *je suis professeur de gymnastique*

b. ....

c. ....

d. ....

e. ....

f. ....

g. ....

h. ....

i. ....

facteur *médecin*
en retraite *comptable* *professeur de gymnastique* *dentiste*
secrétaire *plombier* *réceptionniste*

3 Listen as many times as you like to the conversation on the tape and then tick the correct answers below. (You can check your answers on p. 34.)

a. He is
- [ ] English
- [ ] French
- [ ] American

b. He says he speaks French
- [ ] very well
- [ ] quite well
- [ ] very badly

c. He lives
- [ ] in England
- [ ] in France
- [ ] in America

d. She lives
- [ ] in London
- [ ] in Paris
- [ ] in Madrid

e. She is
- [ ] a nurse
- [ ] a teacher
- [ ] a secretary

f. He is
- [ ] an accountant
- [ ] a civil servant
- [ ] a teacher

4 See if you can fill in the family tree below from the information given. (Answers on p. 34.) You won't need your tape recorder.

Vocabulary: **le mari** the husband
mais but

1 Robert est le mari de Denise.
2 Ils ont trois filles.
3 Michèle est mariée mais elle n'a pas d'enfants.
4 Pierre est le mari de Michèle.
5 Claude est le mari de Brigitte; ils ont une fille, Monique.
6 Philippe est le mari d'Odette; ils ont deux garçons, Bertrand et Jean-Luc.

Denise = ROBERT

BRIGITTE = CLAUDE   MICHÈLE = PIERRE   ODETTE = PHILIPPE

MONIQUE

BERTRAND   JEAN-LUC

Grammar

Parler

The verb **parler** (to speak) follows the same pattern as hundreds of other verbs with infinitives ending in **-er**. Note that French makes no distinction between *I speak* and *I am speaking*. Here is the present tense of **parler**.

je parle I speak
I am speaking

nous parlons we speak
we are speaking

tu parles you speak
you are speaking

vous parlez you speak
you are speaking

il/elle parle he/she speaks
he/she is speaking

ils/elles parlent they speak
they are speaking

Other verbs following this pattern include **donner** (to give), **pousser** (to push), **tirer** (to pull).

Avoir

Apart from **être** the most common irregular verb is **avoir** (to have).

j'ai I have
tu as you have
il/elle a he/she/it has

nous avons we have
vous avez you have
ils/elles ont they have

You can hear both these verbs pronounced on your cassette, after the dialogues.

Des

Des is used in French with nouns in the plural, and would be translated in English by *some* or *any* e.g.
j'ai des soeurs I have (some) sisters
vous avez des enfants? do you have any children?
Notice that French nouns add an **-s** in the plural, but this is *not* pronounced.

The negative

In French, *not* is expressed by putting **ne** before the verb and **pas** after it. e.g.
je ne suis pas français I'm not French
je ne parle pas français I don't speak French
When the verb begins with a vowel or an *h* which is not pronounced, (*h* is usually silent in French) the **ne** is abbreviated to **n'**. e.g.
elle n'est pas française she isn't French
je n'habite pas Paris I don't live in Paris

Exercise 1   Put the following sentences into the negative: (Answers p. 34).
e.g. **je parle français   je ne parle pas français**

a. Je sais ..... *JE NE SAIS PAS*
b. Nous sommes mariés ..... *NOUS NE SOMMES PAS MARIÉS*
c. Je suis célibataire ..... *JE NE SUIS PAS CÉLIBATAIRE*
d. Vous habitez chez vos parents ..... *VOUS N'HABITEZ PAS CHEZ VOS PARENTS*
e. Vous travaillez bien ..... *VOUS NE TRAVAILLEZ PAS BIEN*
f. Vous avez dix francs ..... *VOUS N'AVEZ PAS DIX FRANCS*
g. Je connais Henri ..... *JE NE CONNAIS PAS HENRI*
h. Je suis fonctionnaire ..... *JE NE SUIS PAS FONCTIONNAIRE*

Exercise 2 The verbs in the list belong in the conversation below. See if you can fill the gaps correctly. (Answers p. 34).

j'habite   j'ai   je recommence
je travaille   vous parlez   vous êtes
je suis   vous habitez   vous avez

Man	VOUS ÊTES ....mariée?
Woman	Non – et vous?
Man	Moi, JE SUIS ....marié.
Woman	VOUS AVEZ ....des enfants?
Man	Oui, J'AI ....trois enfants: une fille et deux garçons.
Woman	VOUS HABITEZ ....Versailles?
Man	Non, Paris. Et vous?
Woman	J'HABITE ....chez mes parents à Versailles et JE TRAVAILLE ....à Paris.
Man	VOUS PARLEZ ....anglais?
Woman	Très mal. JE RECOMMENCE à apprendre l'anglais.

Read and understand

In dialogue 2 you heard the voices of Claude and Lisette Dampierre and their daughter Fabienne. Read this passage which gives you more information about them and answer, in English, the questions below. (Answers p. 34.)

Monsieur Dampierre est français. Il habite Versailles, au 15, avenue Pompidou, et il travaille à Paris, dans un bureau. Il est comptable. Madame Dampierre travaille dans un établissement d'enseignement; elle est fonctionnaire. Ils ont deux enfants: une fille et un garçon. La fille, Fabienne, est secrétaire à Paris et elle parle très bien anglais. Le garçon, Daniel, travaille dans une école.

a. What is Monsieur Dampierre's nationality? ....

b. What is his address?

....

c. Where is his office? ....

d. What does he do? ....

e. Where does Madame Dampierre work?

....

f. What does she do? ....

g. How many children do they have? ....

h. What does Fabienne do?

....

i. Where does their son work?

....

j. Which of them speaks English well?

....

Did you know?

France is twice the size of Great Britain but has a slightly smaller
population and, though 65% of its people live in towns, it is still in the
main a rural country. For administrative purposes it is divided into twenty-
two **régions** (see map) and also into ninety-five **départements** (the nearest
equivalent to the English county), classified in alphabetical order and
numbered 1 to 95 (e.g. 01 Ain, 75 Paris, etc.). These numbers are also used
on French car number plates and indicate where the car is registered.

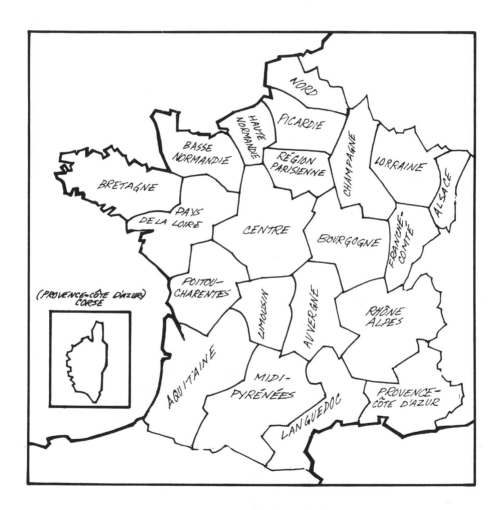

French is the official language of twenty-one nations, including eighteen
former French colonies in Africa. In addition, French is one of the official
languages of four other countries: Belgium, Switzerland, Luxemburg,
Canada. The French-speaking Walloons live mainly in southern Belgium
and the 20% French-speaking Swiss nationals live mainly in the west of
Switzerland. French is also learnt as a first or second foreign language in
many other countries, so with English and French under your belt you have
a good chance of making yourself understood in many parts of the world.

Your turn to speak

In the conversation on the tape you will take the part of a young Parisian woman. Pierre will prompt you. You will need to understand **mon anniversaire** (my birthday).

And finally Don't forget to play through all the dialogues again without looking at the book.

Answers

Practise what you have learnt p. 29 Exercise 1 (a) 7 (b) 13 (c) 17 (d) 15 (e) 8 (f) 16 (g) 12.

p. 29 Exercise 2 (a) Je suis professeur de gymnastique. (b) Je suis secrétaire. (c) Je suis facteur. (d) Je suis dentiste. (e) Je suis plombier. (f) Je suis médecin. (g) Je suis comptable. (h) Je suis réceptionniste. (i) Je suis en retraite.

p. 30 Exercise 3 (a) English (b) very badly (c) England (d) Paris (e) secretary (f) civil servant.
p. 30 Exercise 4

```
                    Denise═Robert
        ┌──────────────────┼──────────────────┐
Brigitte═Claude    Michèle═Pierre      Odette═Philippe
        │                               ┌──────┴──────┐
    Monique                         Bertrand      Jean-Luc
```

Grammar p. 31 Exercise 1
(a) Je ne sais pas.
(b) Nous ne sommes pas mariés.
(c) Je ne suis pas célibataire.
(d) Vous n'habitez pas chez vos parents.
(e) Vous ne travaillez pas bien.
(f) Vous n'avez pas dix francs.
(g) Je ne connais pas Henri.
(h) Je ne suis pas fonctionnaire.

p. 32 Exercise 2 Vous êtes/je suis/Vous avez/j'ai/Vous habitez/J'habite/je travaille/Vous parlez/Je recommence.

Read and understand p. 32 (a) French (b) 15 avenue Pompidou (c) Paris (d) accountant (e) a school (f) civil servant (g) two (h) secretary (i) a school (j) Fabienne.

3 Ordering drinks and snacks

What you will learn

- understanding what drinks and snacks are available
- understanding questions about what type of drink or snack you prefer
- ordering drinks and snacks
- something about typical drinks and snacks in France
- some metric/imperial equivalents

Before you begin

The study-pattern for this unit is similar to those you followed in Units 1 and 2. Try, as far as possible, to work aloud – you are much more likely to be able to say the correct word when you need it if you have practised saying it beforehand. Remember that you do not have to do the whole unit at one sitting; in fact the best advice for language learners is 'little and often' – ten minutes a day is better than an hour once a week. There will be an opportunity for revision at the end of this unit, but you should also get into the habit of looking back over what you have learnt – and re-doing exercises that you are not sure of.

Study guide

To obtain the maximum benefit from the material in this unit, work through the stages set out below. If you wish, tick them off as you complete each one.

	Dialogues 1–4: listen straight through without the book
	Dialogues 1–4: listen, read and study one by one
	Dialogues 5–9: listen straight through without the book
	Dialogues 5–9: listen, read and study one by one
	Study the *Key words and phrases* and the numbers from 21–30
	Do the exercises in *Practise what you have learnt*
	Study *Grammar* and do the exercise
	Do *Read and understand*
	Read *Did you know?*
	Do the tape exercise in *Your turn to speak*
	Listen to all the dialogues again without the book

Dialogues

1 *Breakfast by telephone*

Réceptionniste Oui? Alors deux petits déjeuners. Qu'est-ce que vous prenez? Alors un lait – chaud ou froid? Un lait chaud et un café-lait? Et tous les deux complets? D'accord.

alors well, then
un lait one milk
♦ **chaud** hot

♦ **froid** cold
ou or
♦ **d'accord** OK, fine, agreed

2 *Choosing what you want for breakfast*

Jeanne Bonjour, Monsieur.
Garçon Bonjour, Madame. Qu'est-ce que vous désirez?
Jeanne Euh . . . Qu'est-ce que vous avez?
Garçon Pour le petit déjeuner nous avons du café, du café au lait, du lait, du chocolat et du thé.
Jeanne Un thé, s'il vous plaît.
Garçon Oui. Citron? Nature?
Jeanne Avec du lait froid.
Garçon Avec du lait froid. Parfait.
Jeanne Merci.

un garçon (de café/de restaurant) a waiter (in a café/in a restaurant)
♦ **un chocolat** a chocolate
♦ **un thé** a tea
parfait perfect, fine

3 *Ordering drinks in the hotel bar*

Jeanne Qu'est-ce que vous avez comme bière, s'il vous plaît?
Garçon Comme bière nous avons de la pression et de la Kronenbourg en bouteilles.
Jeanne Bon . . . euh . . . deux pressions, s'il vous plaît.
Garçon Deux pressions? Des petits, des grands . . . ?
Jeanne Des petits.
Garçon Des petits – d'accord.
Jeanne Merci. Et pour les enfants, qu'est-ce que vous avez?
Garçon Pour les enfants: Orangina, Coca-Cola, Schweppes – euh – du lait, lait-fraise et tout ça.
Jeanne Ben . . . deux Orangina, s'il vous plaît.
Garçon Deux Orangina.
Jeanne Merci.

ben um
une bière a beer
une Kronenbourg trade name for a beer
en in
une bouteille a bottle

un Orangina trade name for an orangeade
du lait-fraise strawberry flavoured milk drink
un Schweppes a tonic water

1 ♦ **deux petits déjeuners** two breakfasts. **Un déjeuner** is lunch and **un petit déjeuner** (lit. a little lunch) is breakfast.

♦ **qu'est-ce que vous prenez?** what will you have? (lit. what are you taking?) **Qu'est-ce que** . . . means 'what. . .?' There is more about it in the *Grammar* section (p. 45).

♦ **un café-lait** usually **un café <u>au</u> lait** a white coffee.

tous les deux both.

♦ **complets** with continental breakfasts. If you want continental breakfast with tea, ask for **un petit déjeuner complet avec du thé au lait.** You must specify **au lait** (with milk) unless you want **un thé au citron** (a tea with lemon).

2 qu'est-ce que vous désirez? what would you like? (lit. what do you desire?)

pour le petit déjeuner for breakfast.

du café coffee. If you ask for **du café** you will be given just that – coffee, without milk.

du some (in front of masculine nouns). 'Some' is often used in French when we wouldn't use anything in English (as in this list of drinks).

citron? nature? (with) lemon? on its own? French people usually drink tea without milk. If you ask for milk, specify that you want **du lait froid** (cold milk) or you may be given hot milk!

3 ♦ **qu'est-ce que vous avez comme bière?** what have you in the way of beer? Note also **qu'est-ce que vous avez comme vin?** (What do you have in the way of wine?).

de la pression (some) draught. **De la** means 'some' in front of a feminine noun just as **du** means 'some' in front of a masculine noun.

des petits, des grands . . .? small ones, large ones. . .? This refers to small and large *glasses* of beer. **Un verre** = a glass.

pour les enfants for the children. **Les** will be explained in the *Grammar* section (p. 45).

et tout ça and all that.

4 *Ordering an apéritif*

Jacques	Une vodka-orange – euh – un Byrrh, un kir.
Serveuse	Merci.
Serveuse	La vodka-orange.
Marguerite	C'est pour moi.
Serveuse	Le Byrrh.
Jeanne	C'est pour moi.
Serveuse	Madame. Et le kir pour Monsieur. Voilà.
Jeanne	Merci.

une serveuse a waitress
une vodka-orange a vodka and orange (juice)

5 *Taking the children out for a snack*

Bernadette	Bon, moi je prends un café noir . . . vous prenez un café crème?
Jeanne	Un café noir, s'il vous plaît.
Bernadette	Café noir. Alors deux cafés noirs.
Garçon	Alors deux noirs.
Bernadette	Deux noirs. Pour les enfants . . . euh . . .
Philippe	Un Orangina.
Barbara	Un Coca.
Garçon	Orangina et un Coca?
Bernadette	Attendez! Attendez! Et – et – et à manger, qu'est-ce que vous avez?
Garçon	A manger, maintenant? Alors, maintenant, hot-dog, croque-monsieur, pizza, sandwichs (camembert, gruyère, jambon, pâté, saucisson, rillettes). . .

un café crème a coffee with cream
noir black
attendez! wait!
à manger to eat

♦ **maintenant** now
du jambon ham
du saucisson salami

6 *Ordering ice-creams*

Lisette	Alors – un café liégeois.
Garçon	Alors un café liégeois.
Claude	Une glace antillaise, s'il vous plaît.
Garçon	Une antillaise.
Jeanne	Un sorbet, s'il vous plaît.
Garçon	Un sorbet cassis ou citron, s'il vous plaît?
Jeanne	Euh – cassis, s'il vous plaît.
Garçon	Cassis. Un sorbet cassis. Merci.

♦ **une glace** an ice-cream
un sorbet a sorbet, a water ice
cassis blackcurrant

4 **un Byrrh** is a popular apéritif, NOT beer.

un kir is a mixture of white wine and blackcurrant liqueur, named after Canon Kir, who invented it.

la vodka-orange . . . le Byrrh. La is the word for 'the' before a feminine noun and **le** the word for 'the' before a masculine noun (see *Grammar*, p. 45).

♦ **c'est pour moi** that's for me.

♦ **voilà** here it is, there you are.

5 ♦ **je prends** I'll have (lit. I am taking). You have already met **qu'est-ce que vous prenez?** (what will *you* have?).

croque-monsieur is a toasted sandwich of cheese and ham.

♦ **un sandwich** – the name is the same, but remember that in France it may be made from a split French loaf (**une baguette**) or a roll (**un petit pain**) and will be very substantial.

camembert, gruyère are two types of cheese: **camembert** is a soft, often strong cheese and **gruyère** is hard with holes in it.

rillettes are a type of potted meat, usually pork, similar to pâté.

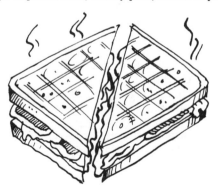

6 **un café liégeois** is a coffee ice with Chantilly cream.

une glace antillaise is an ice with West Indian fruit and rum; **antillais(e)** means 'from the West Indies'.

7 *The bill*

Claude   S'il vous plaît, Monsieur – l'addition.

◆ **l'addition** the bill

8 *Ordering savoury pancakes*

Serveuse   Madame, vous désirez?
Danielle   Trois galettes, s'il vous plaît, une galette au jambon et au fromage, une galette à la saucisse et une galette aux œufs et au jambon.
Serveuse   Et vous voulez boire quelque chose?
Danielle   Oui – du cidre, s'il vous plaît.
Serveuse   Une grande bouteille, une petite . . .?
Danielle   Une grande bouteille, je pense, s'il vous plaît.
Serveuse   Très bien, Madame.

   du cidre cider
◆ **je pense** I think
   très bien very good, certainly

9 *Pierre-Yves likes his cup of tea!*

Nadine   Tu veux jouer?
Pierre-Yves   Boire du thé.
Nadine   Tu veux boire du thé.
Pierre-Yves   Mm – c'est bon, Maman.
Nadine   Oui. Tu aimes bien le thé, alors?
Pierre-Yves   C'est sucré.
Nadine   Qu'est-ce que tu as dans le thé?
Pierre-Yves   Citron.

   sucré sweet
   dans in

7   **Monsieur** – note that it is no longer considered polite to address a waiter as **Garçon**.

8   ◆ **galettes** are savoury pancakes made from buck-wheat flour. A sweet pancake is **une crêpe**.

    ◆ **une galette au jambon et au fromage** a ham and cheese pancake. In the same way you would say:
    un sandwich au jambon a ham sandwich
    un sandwich au fromage a cheese sandwich.

    une galette à la saucisse a sausage pancake.

    une galette aux œufs et au jambon an egg(s) and ham pancake. **Au**, **à la** and **aux** are explained later in Unit 6.

    vous voulez boire quelque chose? would you like something to drink? (lit. do you want to drink something?)

9   **tu veux jouer?** do you want to play? **Tu veux?** (do you want?) is the intimate form of **vous voulez?** which you met in the last unit.

    boire du thé (want to) drink some tea. Pierre-Yves is still using baby-talk.

    tu aimes bien le thé, alors? you like tea don't you?

Key words and phrases

je prends (un lait)	I'll have (a milk)
qu'est-ce que vous prenez?	what will you have?
un petit déjeuner complet	a continental breakfast
un café	a coffee
un café au lait	a white coffee
un lait (chaud/froid)	a (hot/cold) milk
un chocolat	a chocolate
un thé (au citron/avec du lait froid)	a tea (with lemon/with cold milk)
. . . s'il vous plaît	. . . please
qu'est-ce que vous avez comme (bière)?	what do you have in the way of (beer)?
qu'est-ce que vous avez à manger?	what do you have to eat?
je pense. . .	I think. . .
une glace	an ice-cream
une galette	a savoury pancake
un sandwich	a sandwich
au fromage	with cheese
au jambon	with ham
c'est pour moi	that's for me
l'addition, s'il vous plaît	the bill, please
maintenant	now
d'accord	OK, right
voilà	here you are
bien	good

Now turn to p. 225 and learn the numbers from 21–30. You haven't yet met them in the dialogues, but you will have a chance to practise them in Exercise 4, p. 44.

Practise what you have learnt

1 On the tape you will hear Yves and Carolle ordering snacks in a bar. Below each picture write the initial of the person who is ordering that item. (Answers p. 48).

a. ☐   b. ☐   c. ☐   d. ☐

e. ☐   f. ☐   g. ☐   h. ☐

2 See if you can un-muddle each of the sentences below. (Answers on p. 48.) You won't need your tape recorder.

a. au sandwich prends un jambon je.

JE PRENDS UN SANDWICH AU JAMBON

b. comme avez vous qu'est-ce que bière?

QU'EST-CE QUE VOUS AVEZ COMME BIÈRE?

c. voulez déjeuner qu'est-ce que le petit pour vous?

QU'EST-CE QUE VOUS VOULEZ POUR LE PETIT DEJEUNAC?

d. du froid thé votre prenez avec vous lait?

VOUS PRENEZ VOTRE THÉ AVEC DU LAIT FROID?

e. le apprendre je à français recommence.

JE RECOMMENCE APPRENDRE À LE FRANCAIS

3 A teacher is taking his class on an outing. Listen to the tape and write in on the menu below the number of orders they place for each item. (Answers p. 48)

Hot-dog	....	Coca Cola	....
Sandwich (fromage)	....	Orangina	....
Pizza	....	Lait-fraise	....
Glace au chocolat	....	Chocolat	....
Sorbet au citron	....	Café	....
Schweppes	....		

4 On the tape you will hear Yves and Carolle deciding on a meal from the menu. Listen as many times as you like to their conversation and answer the questions below in English. (Answers p. 48.)

A MANGER		A BOIRE
Galettes		Café
– au jambon	– aux oeufs	Café crème
– à la saucisse	– aux oeufs et	Thé au citron
– au fromage	au jambon	Thé au lait
Sandwichs		Lait-fraise
– jambon	– camembert	Orangina
– rillettes	– gruyère	Coca Cola
Glaces		Schweppes
– café	– cassis	
– chocolat	– antillaise	Bière
– citron	– café liégeois	Cidre
		Martini
Sorbet au cassis		Whisky
Sorbet au citron		Cognac
		Vodka
		Kir

a. What savoury dish does she order?
....

b. What savoury dish does he order? ....

c. What sweet does he want? ....

d. What will she drink? ....

e. What will he drink? ....

f. Will they be served by a waiter or a waitress? ....

Grammar

Le, la, les

In French there are three words for 'the'. Before a masculine singular noun it is **le** e.g. **le citron** (the lemon). Before a feminine singular noun it is **la** e.g. **la vodka** (the vodka). If the noun begins with a vowel sound both **le** and **la** are shortened to **l'** e.g. **l'adresse** (the address), **l'enfant** (the child). Before a plural noun, masculine *or* feminine, 'the' is **les** e.g. **les enfants** (the children), **les sœurs** (the sisters).

From now on, all nouns in the vocabulary lists after the dialogues will be in the singular with **le** or **la** to indicate their gender. If the noun begins with a vowel, gender will be indicated by (m.) or (f.).

Du, de la, des

Du is used before a masculine singular noun to mean 'some' e.g. **du café** (some coffee).

Before a feminine singular noun 'some' is **de la** e.g. **de la bière** (some beer). The plural of both **du** and **de la** is **des** e.g. **des œufs** (some eggs), **des galettes** (some savoury pancakes).

Note that **du**, **de la** and **des** are used in French where 'some' would not be needed in English. In dialogue 2 the waiter said **nous avons du café** where in English we should say 'we have coffee' (leaving out the 'some').

Prendre to take

Most French verbs are regular, however some of the most frequently used ones are irregular and this is why you have to learn them early on. Here is another very common irregular verb.

je prends I am taking / I take	**nous prenons** we are taking / we take
tu prends you are taking / you take	**vous prenez** you are taking / you take
il/elle prend he/she is taking / he/she takes	**ils/elles prennent** they are taking / they take

Remember you use **prendre** rather than **avoir** when ordering food and drink: **je prends un café** I'll have a coffee

The verbs **comprendre** (to understand) and **apprendre** (to learn) follow exactly the same pattern as **prendre**.

Qu'est-ce que?

Qu'est-ce que. . .? though tiresome to spell, is easy enough to pronounce and use, as you heard in dialogues 1, 2, 3, 5 and 9. The whole expression means simply 'what. . .?' e.g.

qu'est-ce que vous avez comme glaces? what do you have in the way of ice-creams?

qu'est-ce que vous prenez? what will you have?

Exercise

Write **du**, **de la** or **des** in the gaps below. Check the gender of the nouns in the vocabulary list at the back of the book if you are not sure. (Answers p. 48)

a. Vous prenez ..DU.. lait?
b. Je prends ..DU.. thé.
c. Vous voulez ..DE LA.. bière?

d. Les enfants prennent ..DES.. œufs.
e. Monsieur prend ..DE LA.. vodka.

Read and understand

This is a take-away menu (**vente à emporter** literally means 'sale for taking away'). Many of the items are familiar to you and some of them you can guess. Answer the questions below in English. (Answers p .48.)

CELLE (M)
CELUÌ (F)

THE ONE

OR
C'EST CELLE
AU JAMBON
ET FROMAGE

1 What is the most expensive savoury pancake?
→ C'EST LA GALETTES JAMBON ET FROMAGE

2 Is the drinking chocolate hot or cold?
C'EST DU COHOCALAE FROÌD

3 Which is dearer, a chocolate pancake or an orange juice?
LA CRÈPES AU CHOCALAT EST PLUS CHÈRE QUE
LE JUÌS D'ORANGE

4 Is a cheese pancake cheaper than a strawberry ice?
LA GLACE À LA FRAÌSE EST MOÌNS CHÈRE QUE LA GALLETTE AU FROMAGE

5 Are there any alcoholic drinks on the menu?
IL N'Y A PAS DE BOÌSSONS ALCOOLISÉES
AUCUME

Did you know?

Un petit déjeuner in France usually consists of a pot of black coffee and a pot of hot milk with **croissants**. **Un petit déjeuner complet** is a full continental breakfast: bread, butter and jam as well as croissants and coffee, tea or hot chocolate.

French cafés stay open from early morning until late at night. They serve all kinds of soft drinks, hot drinks, wines and spirits and often snacks as well. Most imported drinks (e.g. whisky, Guinness and even tea) tend to be expensive. Coffee, French beer and Cognac are better value. In summer popular drinks are **un panaché** (a shandy), **un citron pressé** (the juice of a lemon, served with ice, cold water and sugar to taste) and **un diabolo-menthe** (lemonade mixed with green peppermint cordial and served with ice). Drinks are cheaper if you stand at the counter inside and more expensive if you sit at a table or outside on the **terrasse**.

In Brittany, Normandy and increasingly in other parts of the country, you can find excellent **crêperies** serving wafer-thin **galettes** and **crêpes** (sweet pancakes). In the south of France **pizzerias** serve delicious pizzas (no resemblance to the frozen variety sold in Britain) which you can often have as a take-away.

Metric weights and measures

Here are some useful approximations:

Metric	Imperial	Metric	Imperial
Length		*Volume*	
1 centimetre (cm)	0.4 inch	5 millilitres (mls) *or*	1 teaspoon
2.5 cms	1 in	cubic centimetres (ccs)	
10 cms	4 ins	1 litre (l)	1.75 pints
30 cms	1 foot	10 litres	2.2 gallons
1 metre (m)	39.5 ins		
1 kilometre (km)	0.625 mile		
Weight		*Speed*	
100 grams (gms)	3.5 ounces	50 kms per hour	31 mph
250 gms	9 ozs	80 kmph	50 mph
500 gms	1.1 pounds	100 kmph	62 mph
1 kilo(gram) (kg)	2.2 lbs	120 kmph	75 mph

Your turn to speak

On the tape, the receptionist will ask you what you want for breakfast tomorrow. Pierre will whisper suggestions to you in English. You should say them aloud in French and then listen to the correct reply. Revise the key phrases on p. 42 before you start.

And finally Remember to listen to all the dialogues again, straight through.

Revision

Now a chance to go over again some of the important language you have learnt in Units 1–3. Turn to the back of your book p. 213 for what to do. You will also need your tape recorder.

Pronouncing numbers

You will have a lot of practice with numbers in this course. Here is a detail of pronunciation which has not yet been pointed out. Take the number six. You have learnt it as **six** (with the final **-x** pronounced like a double 'ss'), but if the word coming after it begins with a consonant (e.g. t, p, b etc.), the **six** will be pronounced **si'**, as in **si' francs** or **si' bières**. Most of the numbers between one and ten are pronounced in a slightly different way when they are followed by a vowel. Only **quatre** and **sept** have exactly the same pronunciation.

Answers

Practise what you have learnt p. 43 Exercise 1 (a) Y (b) C (c) Y (d) C (e) Y (f) C (g) Y (h) C.

p. 43 Exercise 2 (a) Je prends un sandwich au jambon. (b) Qu'est-ce que vous avez comme bière? (c) Qu'est-ce que vous voulez pour le petit déjeuner? (d) Vouse prenez votre thé avec du lait froid? (e) Je recommence à apprendre le français.

p. 44 Exercise 3 21 hot-dogs, 7 sandwichs, 8 pizzas, 29 glaces, 6 sorbets, 2 Schweppes, 14 Coca-Cola, 5 Orangina, 3 laits-fraise, 11 chocolats, 1 café.

p. 44 Exercise 4 (a) a ham and egg pancake (b) a sausage pancake (c) a lemon ice (d) cider (e) beer (f) a waiter.

Grammar p. 45 (a) du lait (b) du thé (c) de la bière (d) des œufs (e) de la vodka.

Read and understand p. 46 (1) ham and cheese (2) cold (3) a chocolate pancake (4) no (5) no.

4 Getting information

What you will learn

- asking questions
- booking in at hotels and camp-sites
- asking where things are
- coping with numbers up to 100
- the alphabet in French
- something about French money, banks, hotels and camp-sites

Before you begin

Most conversations involve asking for and understanding information of one kind or another. With a foreign language it is important to develop the skill of listening for the *gist* of what someone is saying – all too often people panic because they don't understand every word when in fact they do understand as much as they need to for practical purposes.

Follow the study guide below to make sure you make the most effective use of the unit.

Study guide

	Dialogues 1–4: listen straight through without the book
	Dialogues 1–4: listen, read and study one by one
	Dialogues 5–8: listen straight through without the book
	Dialogues 5–8: listen, read and study one by one
	Learn the *Key words and phrases* and the numbers up to 100
	Do the exercises in *Practise what you have learnt*
	Study the *Grammar* section
	Do *Read and understand*
	Read *Did you know?*
	Do the tape exercise in *Your turn to speak*
	Listen to all the dialogues again without the book

Dialogues

1 *The Palym Hotel receptionist takes a telephone booking for a room*

Réceptionniste Allô, Palym Hôtel . . . Bonjour . . . Le 18 septembre oui, ne quittez pas . . . oui – euh – avec cabinet de toilette, oui, d'accord, à quel nom? . . . Rodriguez . . . Vous pouvez me confirmer par lettre? . . . Non , P–A–L–Y–M . . . Oui, 4, rue Émile-Gilbert, dans le douzième. . .G–I–L–B–E–R–T . . . Voilà . . . C'est ça. C'est entendu.

septembre September
entendu agreed

2 *Full up!*

Réceptionniste Allô, Palym Hôtel . . . Bonjour . . . Ah non, nous sommes complets, Monsieur . . . Oui . . . Au revoir.

♦ **complets (m. pl.)** (*here*) full up.

3 *Jeanne books a hotel room*

Jeanne Bonsoir, Monsieur.
Hôtelier Bonsoir, Madame.
Jeanne Vous avez des chambres pour ce soir, s'il vous plaît?
Hôtelier Oui, nous avons des chambres, oui. Vous êtes combien de personnes?
Jeanne Deux personnes.
Hôtelier Deux personnes. Pour combien de temps?
Jeanne Une nuit seulement.
Hôtelier Une nuit.
Jeanne C'est combien?
Hôtelier Euh – nous avons trois catégories de chambre: la première, qui fait soixante-deux francs, la seconde, avec douche, quatre-vingts, et la troisième, avec WC et salle de bains, qui fait cent vingt-six francs.
Jeanne Avec douche, alors.
Hôtelier Avec douche. Bon je vais vous donner la treize.

l'hôtelier (m.) hotel manager
la chambre room, bedroom
♦ **la personne** person
♦ **la nuit** night
seulement only
la catégorie category
♦ **première (f.)** first
soixante-deux 62
seconde (f.) second
♦ **la douche** shower
quatre-vingts 80
♦ **troisième** third
♦ **la salle de bains** bathroom
cent vingt-six 126

1 ◆ **allô** hello. Used only on the telephone.

ne quittez pas hold on (lit. don't leave) – telephone jargon.

◆ **avec cabinet de toilette** with washing facilities. This means there will be a wash-basin and possibly a bidet 'en suite'. It does not mean there will be private lavatory.

à quel nom? in what name?

vous pouvez me confirmer par lettre? can you confirm (for me) by letter? Hotels also often ask for **des arrhes** (a deposit).

dans le douzième (lit. in the twelfth.) Paris is divided into twenty numbered **arrondissements** (districts).

◆ **c'est ça** that's right.

3 ◆ **vous avez des chambres pour ce soir?** do you have any rooms for tonight?

◆ **vous êtes combien de personnes?** for how many people? (lit. You are how many people?). **Combien de. . .?** means 'how many. . .?' or 'how much. . .?'

pour combien de temps? for how long? (lit. for how much time?)

◆ **c'est combien?** how much is it?

qui fait which costs. The verb **faire**, normally translated 'to do' or 'to make' has a variety of meanings, e.g.

◆ **ça fait combien?** is the usual way of asking a shopkeeper how much your purchases come to.

WC should be pronounced **double vé-cé** but people invariably shorten it to **vé-cé**.

je vais vous donner I'm going to give you. You will be learning to use this way of expressing the future in Unit 14. You will come across it frequently in the dialogues from now on.

Hôtel Napoléon
★ ★ ★ nn
05100 *Montgenèvre*   **montgenèvre**

You will find details of the cost of the hotel room and services on the back of the door of the room.

Chambre N° *105* *102*

Nombre de personnes *2*

Prix de la Chambre *160,⁰⁰*

Prix Pension complète *230,⁰⁰*

Petit Déjeuner *18,⁰⁰ᶠ*

Ces prix s'entendent taxes et service compris

4 *Marie-Claude books in at a camp-site*

Réceptionniste	Bonjour, Madame. Que désirez-vous?
Marie-Claude	Est-ce qu'il reste encore des places pour deux personnes?
Réceptionniste	Combien de jours vous voulez rester?
Marie-Claude	Trois semaines (je pense).
Réceptionniste	Trois semaines. Bon. Je vais regarder . . . Bon, d'accord. Trois semaines – c'est d'accord. Est-ce que vous pouvez me donner votre nom et votre adresse, s'il vous plaît?
Marie-Claude	Oui, bien sûr.

encore (*here*) still
la place (*here*) space
le jour day
la semaine week
bien sûr certainly

5 *Jeanne asks an important question*

Jeanne	Où sont les toilettes, s'il vous plaît?
Réceptionniste	Euh – première porte ici à gauche.
Jeanne	Bon, merci.

◆ **la porte** door
◆ **ici** here
◆ **à gauche** on the left

6 *Danielle wants to change her travellers' cheques*

Danielle	Pardon, Monsieur – où peut-on changer des chèques de voyage, s'il vous plaît?
Homme	Excusez-moi, Madame, je ne comprends pas – je suis anglais.

◆ **l'homme (m.)** man
◆ **pardon** sorry, excuse me

4 que désirez-vous? can I help you? (lit. what do you desire?)

♦ est-ce que . . . ? is a simple way of starting any question that can be answered by yes or no. (See p. 59 for further notes on how to ask questions.)

il reste there remains or there remain. e.g. il reste une place; il reste des places.

est-ce qu'il reste encore des places? are there any spaces left?

combien de jours vous voulez rester? how many days do you want to stay?

je vais regarder I'll have a look (lit. I'm going to look).

est-ce que vous pouvez me donner . . . ? can you give me . . . ?

5 ♦ où sont les toilettes? where are the toilets? Les toilettes (i.e. plural) is generally used instead of la toilette even when there is only one. You will learn more directions in Unit 5.

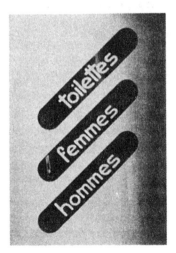

6 ♦ où peut-on changer des chèques de voyage? where can one change travellers' cheques? Chèques de voyage are also often called simply travellers (with the stress on the final syllable).

♦ excusez-moi, Madame, je ne comprends pas – je suis anglais I'm sorry, Madame, I don't understand – I'm English. A very useful set of phrases to know! Remember if you are a woman to say je suis anglaise (or écossaise Scots, galloise Welsh or irlandaise Irish).

7 *Now for a change, Pierre-Yves on animals*

Nadine	Qu'est-ce qu'il fait, Sam?
Pierre-Yves	Ouâou!
Nadine	Mm mm. Et qu'est-ce qu'elle fait, Isis?
Pierre-Yves	Maou!
Nadine	Oui. Qu'est-ce qu'ils font, les oiseaux?
Pierre-Yves	Maou!
Nadine	Non! Qu'est-ce qu'ils font, les oiseaux?
Pierre-Yves	Tou-ite!

l'oiseau (m.) (**pl. les oiseaux**) bird

8 *Pierre-Yves says what he eats for lunch*

Nadine	Et Pierre-Yves, qu'est-ce qu'il mange?
Pierre-Yves	. . .
Nadine	De la viande?
Pierre-Yves	Oui.
Nadine	Avec quoi?
Pierre-Yves	. . .
Nadine	De la purée?
Pierre-Yves	Oui.
Nadine	Et puis, comme dessert?
Pierre-Yves	Hein?
Nadine	Qu'est-ce que tu manges?
Pierre-Yves	La soupe!
Nadine	De la soupe? Non!
Pierre-Yves	Ah?
Nadine	On mange la soupe d'abord. Et qu'est-ce qu'on mange comme dessert?
Pierre-Yves	Vanille-citron.
Nadine	Une glace à vanille-citron?
Pierre-Yves	Oui.
Nadine	Oui. Mm mm.
Pierre-Yves	Et à framboise.
Nadine	A la framboise aussi?
Pierre-Yves	Tout ça!
Nadine	Tout ça?
Pierre-Yves	Oui.
Nadine	Tu vas être malade!
Pierre-Yves	. . . ?
Nadine	Oh oui.

puis then
comme as
le dessert dessert
hein? what?
d'abord first of all
vanille-citron vanilla-lemon
à la framboise raspberry-flavoured
tout ça all that

7   **qu'est-ce qu'il fait, Sam?** what does Sam do? (i.e. say).

♦ For **qu'est-ce que?** (what?) see p. 59. **Il fait** comes from the verb **faire** (to do, to make) which is written out on p. 59. Sam is the dog's name.

Isis the name of their (female) cat. The word for 'cat' is masculine: **le chat**.

ils font they do (say). This is also from **faire**.

8   **et Pierre-Yves, qu'est-ce qu'il mange?** and what does Pierre-Yves eat?

de la viande? some meat? In French you cannot just say 'meat'. The same applies for **de la purée** and **de la soupe** below.

avec quoi? with what? Whereas **qu'est-ce que. . .?** is used for 'what. . .?' at the beginning of a sentence, **quoi?** is used mainly after prepositions, e.g. **avec quoi?** (with what?) **dans quoi?** (in what?) **sur quoi?** (on what?)

de la purée? mashed potato? This is always more liquid than its British equivalent.

on mange one eats. **On** is used much more frequently in French than 'one' is in English, e.g. a notice saying **Silence! On dort** (lit. Silence! One is sleeping) could be translated 'Silence! People are sleeping,' 'I am sleeping' *or* 'we are sleeping'.

tu vas être malade! you're going to be ill! Another example of the way of expressing the future which you will be learning in Unit 14.

Key words and phrases

These are the most important phrases from the dialogues. The ones in brackets are those you will need to understand only.

(qu'est-ce que vous voulez?)	(what would you like?)
vous avez des chambres pour ce soir?	do you have any rooms for this evening?
avec cabinet de toilette	with washing facilities
avec douche	with a shower
avec salle de bains	with a bathroom
(pour combien de personnes/nuits?)	(for how many people/nights?)
pour (quatre) personnes	for (four) people
pour (deux) nuits	for (two) nights
est-ce que vous avez encore des places?	do you still have any spaces?
(pour combien de temps?)	(for how long?)
pour (trois) jours	for (three) days
pour une semaine	for one week
(nous sommes complets)	(we're full)
c'est combien?/ça fait combien?	how much is it?/how much does that come to?
où sont les toilettes?	where are the toilets?
où peut-on changer des chèques de voyage?	where can one change travellers' cheques?
qu'est-ce que c'est?	what is it?
pardon	excuse me
je ne comprends pas	I don't understand
excusez-moi	I'm sorry
c'est ça	that's right
bien sûr	certainly

At this stage, learn the numbers up to 100. They are set out on p. 225. The difficult ones are those from 70 to 99. Seventy is **soixante-dix** (literally) 'sixty-ten'), eighty is **quatre-vingts** (literally 'four twenties') and ninety is **quatre-vingt-dix** (literally 'four twenties ten'). In Switzerland and Belgium it is easier. They have the much simpler forms **septante (70), octante** or **huitante (80)** and **nonante (90)**.

Practise what you have learnt

1 You can turn almost any phrase or sentence into a question by putting a
question – a rising intonation – into your voice. On the tape you will hear
each of the phrases and sentences below said twice – as a statement and as a
question. Listen to them and identify whether the first or the second is the
question and put a question mark in the space. (Answers p. 62).

a. Oui ………   **b.** Oui ………

c. C'est ça ………   **d.** C'est ça ………

e. C'est complet ………   **f.** C'est complet ………

g. Vous êtes anglais ………   **h.** Vous êtes anglais ………

i. Vous aimez la France ………   **j.** Vous aimez la France ………

For some extra pronunciation practice wind back and repeat after the tape.
It's a good idea to do this several times.

2 This exercise will help you to understand numbers in French. On the tape
you will hear Barbara counting money (100 centimes = 1 franc). You will
notice that she leaves out the word **centimes** in, for instance, **vingt-huit
francs vingt**, just as we leave out the word 'pence' from 'twenty-eight
pounds twenty'. Write down in figures (e.g. **28F 20**) each of the amounts
mentioned. Stop and rewind the tape as often as you like – you will
certainly need to play it several times. Use the space below to write your
answers and then check them on p. 62. Barbara starts at **14F**.

3 You heard in the first dialogue at the Palym Hotel how useful it can be to
know the French names for the letters of the alphabet. The confusing ones
are E, G, I, J, W and Y. Listen to the alphabet on the tape and then repeat
after the speaker until you know it. Test yourself by spelling your own
name aloud.

4 Below is a dialogue between a hotel receptionist and a client. The client's lines have been left out and put in the box below – in the wrong order. Decide which line belongs where and write it in the gap. Then check your answers by listening to the tape which gives you the dialogue in full.

Réceptionniste   Bonjour, Monsieur.

Client   BONJOUR, MADAME

Réceptionniste   Qu'est-ce que vous désirez?

Client   VOUS AVEZ DES CHAMBRES, S'IL VOUS PLAÎT?

Réceptionniste   Oui, nous avons des chambres. C'est pour combien de personnes?

Client   POUR DEUX PERSONNES

Réceptionniste   Et pour combien de temps?

Client   POUR DEUX NUITS

Réceptionniste   J'ai une chambre avec douche on une chambre avec cabinet de toilette.

Client   C'EST COMBIEN AVEC DOUCHE

Réceptionniste   Cent francs.

Client   BON, D'ACCORD

Réceptionniste   Alors, je vais vous donner la vingt-huit.

Client   LA 28? TRÈS BIEN; MERCI.

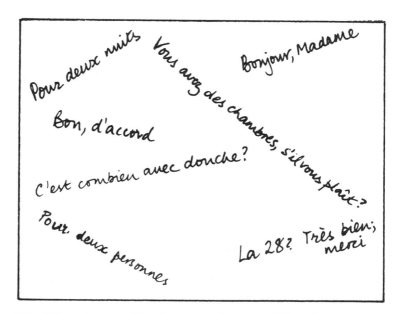

Pour deux nuits
Vous avez des chambres, s'il vous plaît?
Bonjour, Madame
Bon, d'accord
C'est combien avec douche?
Pour deux personnes
La 28? Très bien; merci

This dialogue is a model for the conversations you will have if ever you have to book hotel rooms in France, so do make the most of it! Play it through several times saying the client's lines with him.

Grammar

Questions

You have already practised the simplest way of asking a question: saying something with a rising intonation. Another way is to put **est-ce que. . .?** at the beginning of a sentence. (If you don't remember how to pronounce it, go back and listen again to dialogue 4.) Look at these examples.

la clé est dans la chambre	the key is in the room
est-ce que la clé est dans la chambre?	is the key in the room?

When the word following it begins with a vowel sound, **est-ce que. . . ?** runs into it to become **est-ce qu'. . . ?**

elle est dans la chambre	she/it is in the room
est-ce qu' elle est dans la chambre?	is she/it in the room?

Question-words

Est-ce que. . .? is only used in questions which can be answered by 'yes' or 'no'. Other types of questions are introduced by other question-words. You met **qu'est-ce que. . .?** (what?) in Unit 3. In this unit you have also met **où?** (where?) and **combien?** (how much? how many?).

Exercise **Où est . . . ?** where is . . . ?
Où sont . . . ? where are . . . ?

Which of the above should you use in each of the following questions? Write your answers in the gaps (don't forget the accent on **où** because without an accent it means 'or'!) and then check them against the answers on p. 62.

1 ...*OÙ EST*... le bar?
2 ...*OÙ EST*... la chambre?
3 ...*OÙ SONT*... les enfants?
4 ...*OÙ EST*... la rue Émile-Gilbert?
5 ...*OÙ EST*... la salle de bains?
6 ...*OÙ SONT*... Monsieur et Madame Fleury?

Faire

You have already met some parts of the present tense of the verb **faire** (to do, to make). Now you should learn all of them – it is one of the most useful of all French verbs.

je fais	**nous faisons**
tu fais	**vous faites**
il/elle fait	**ils/elles font**

Vendre

Another useful verb to learn is **vendre** (to sell) – useful because it is the model for a whole group of verbs with infinitives ending in -re e.g. **rendre** (to give up, to give back), **tendre** (to hold out), **pendre** (to hang).

je vends	**nous vendons**
tu vends	**vous vendez**
il/elle vend	**ils/elles vendent**

Read and understand

Below is an extract from the kind of list of hotels issued free by most tourist offices in France. The questions will give you practice at interpreting them. (Answers p. 62).

Nom de l'hôtel	Nombre de chambres			Prix des chambres		Petit déjeuner	Pension par personne
	Total	Avec bains ou douches		1 personne	2 personnes		
		Avec WC	Sans WC	mini/ maxi	mini/ maxi		
Hôtel Métropole	25	6	6	53/85F	90/137F	11F	–
Hôtel de Paris	38	25	13	137F	137F	13F	–
Hôtel Terminus	67	67	–	105/170F	105/170F	12F	205/270F
Hôtel de la Poste	36	7	7	53/125F	65/150F	10F	–
Hôtel de France	33	3	8	50/75F	75/135F	–	–
Grand Hôtel	56	15	13	85F	125F	13F	–
Hôtel Molière	10	–	4	50/75F	50/75F	10F	210/235F
Hôtel du Midi	40	4	8	80/105F	105/120F	9F	137F

le nombre number   **sans** without
le prix price   **la pension** full board
par per

1 Where can you get the cheapest breakfast?

....

2 In which two hotels can you get the cheapest single room?

....

3 Which hotels charge the same for a single room as for a double?

....

4 How many rooms at the Hôtel Métropole have neither bath nor shower?

....

5 At which hotel do all the rooms have a private lavatory?

....

6 What is the least that two people could pay for full board at any of these hotels?

....

7 Can you get a private lavatory at the hôtel Molière?

....

8 What is the least and what is the most you could pay for a double room in this town?

....

Did you know?

Money

The unit of currency in France, Belgium and Switzerland is the **franc**, which is divided into 100 **centimes**. In France life is complicated by people who still insist on talking in *old* **francs** (1 old franc = 1 new centime) even though they were abolished in 1960. So, if people ask you for what seem to be ridiculous sums of money, try dividing by 100 and seeing if they make more sense. It is useful to remember that 1,000 old francs **mille (anciens) francs** = ten new francs **dix (nouveaux) francs**.

Banks and bureaux de change

You can change money and travellers' cheques either in a **bureau de change** or in a bank displaying the sign **change**. The exchange rate in small **bureaux de change** may often be better than that of the **banques**. Remember to take your passport with you if you are changing travellers' cheques. Bank opening hours vary from town to town, but they are generally open from 9 a.m–12 noon and 2–4 p.m. on weekdays and 9.30 a.m.–12 noon on Saturdays. In many towns banks are closed all day Saturday or all day Monday. All banks are closed on Sundays and public holidays (see p. 89).

Hotels

Hotels are officially graded one-star, two-star, three-star, four-star and four-star de luxe. In general, the standard of accommodation within any one category will be better in the provinces than in Paris. The prices quoted are usually per room rather than per person and they do not include breakfast. If you stay at a **pension** rather than an **hôtel** you will be expected to have **pension** (full board), or **demi-pension** (half-board). The standard of accommodation is usually similar to that in hotels. An indispensable publication if you are going to stay at French hotels is the red *Guide Michelin* which classifies the hotels and restaurants of every town and village in France, giving an indication of their prices and facilities. A guide to good, inexpensive hotels and restaurants is published by *Relais Routiers* (354 Fulham Road, London SW10 9UH). In general French hotels are more reasonably priced than British ones.

Camping and caravanning

Camp-sites too have their official star-rating. More than a third of them are in the top three- or four-star categories and you would be well advised to aim for one of these, as facilities on the one- and two-star sites may be minimal. Camp-sites run by local authorities are often good value; look for the sign **camping municipal**. If you are going to camp near the sea in the summer months you should book well in advance or you are likely to meet **complet** (full up) signs wherever you go. Crowding is not nearly so bad on inland sites and many of them offer water-sports on lakes and rivers. **Le camping sauvage** (camping on unauthorized land) is frowned upon by the authorities. Probably the easiest way to go camping in France – though not the cheapest – is to hire a ready-pitched tent and equipment from one of the many operators now offering this service through the Sunday newspapers. The standards of these companies are generally high. Michelin have a good publication for campers too: a green paperback called *Camping Caravaning France* which gives the same kind of information about camp-sites as its red counterpart does for hotels. If you write to the *French Government Tourist Office* (178 Piccadilly, London W1V 0AL) enclosing a stamped addressed envelope: they will supply an information sheet called *A key to your trip to France* which includes some useful information for campers.

Your turn to speak

This section will give you the opportunity to practise booking in at a hotel. You will need the expression **j'ai réservé une chambre** (I've booked a room). On the tape you will hear Carolle taking the part of the hotel receptionist. Pierre will tell you in English what to say to her; you should stop the tape to give yourself time to say it in French and then start it again to hear the correct reply.

And finally You should wind the tape back and listen to all the dialogues again without the book, stopping to look up any words you have forgotten. Test yourself on the *Key words and phrases* by covering up the French and translating the English. Be sure you know the verbs **faire** and **vendre**. Most important of all, you should practise the numbers – read prices in French when you are shopping, and practise counting while you are doing odd jobs.

Answers

Practise what you have learnt p. 57 Exercise 1 (b)? (c)? (f)? (h)? (i)?

p. 57 Exercise 2 14F, 19F, 20F, 21F, 26F, 28F, 28.20F, 28.40F, 28.60F 28.80F, 29F, 29.05F.

Grammar p. 59 (1) Où est (2) Où est (3) Où sont (4) Où est (5) Où est (6) Où sont

Read and understand p. 60 (1) Hôtel du Midi (2) Hôtel de France and Hôtel Molière (3) Hôtel de Paris, Hôtel Terminus and Hôtel Molière (4) 13 (5) Hôtel Terminus (6) 274F (2×137F) (7) no (8) 50F and 170F.

5 Directions

What you will learn

- asking for information in a tourist office
- asking the way
- explaining how you are travelling
- understanding directions
- asking if there is a bus or a train
- asking and understanding which floor rooms are on
- numbers from 100–1000
- something about the French underground system
- something about French tourist services

Before you begin

Asking the way is relatively easy: it is understanding the answer that tends to prove more of a problem! The best way round this is to listen over and over again to the directions given in the dialogues, so that you will understand the *key* phrases (*straight on*, *first left* etc.), even if they are obscured by a lot of other words that you do not know. It is usually a good idea to repeat directions as soon as you are given them, so that you can be corrected if you have misunderstood anything.

Study guide

	Dialogues 1–4: listen straight through without the book
	Dialogues 1–4: listen, read and study one by one
	Dialogues 5–7: listen straight through without the book
	Dialogues 5–7: listen, read and study one by one
	Dialogues 8, 9: listen straight through without the book
	Dialogues 8, 9: listen, read and study one by one
	Learn the *Key words and phrases*
	Do the exercises in *Practise what you have learnt*
	Study *Grammar* and do the exercises
	Do *Read and understand*
	Read *Did you know?*
	Do the tape exercise in *Your turn to speak*
	Listen to all the dialogues again without the book

Dialogues

1 *Getting a map and directions at the tourist office*

Michel Bonjour, Madame.
Hôtesse Bonjour, Monsieur.
Michel Vous avez un plan de la ville, s'il vous plaît?
Hôtesse Oui, bien sûr – voilà.
Michel Merci. Oui. Pour aller à . . . à la gare?
Hôtesse Alors, vous prenez tout droit, jusqu'au bout; après le pont, vous tournez à gauche . . . la troisième sur la gauche . . . vous avez la gare.
Michel Bon, merci. On est *où* exactement ici?
Hôtesse Alors, au numéro un sur le plan, en face de l'église Saint-Pierre.
Michel Ah bon. Au centre de la ville, au fond?
Hôtesse C'est ça, oui.
Michel Oui.

l'hôtesse (f.) receptionist in a tourist office
le plan de la ville map of the town
bien sûr certainly

après after
le pont bridge
en face de facing, opposite
l'église Saint-Pierre (f.) Saint Peter's church

2 *More directions to the station*

Michel Pour aller à la gare?
Dame Oui. Vous voulez aller en voiture ou (en autobus)?
Michel Non, je suis à pied.
Dame Pour aller à pied. Alors, nous sommes ici. Vous prenez la rue Saint-Jean, vous traversez le pont.
Michel Oui.
Dame Et un petit peu après le pont, la troisième rue sur votre gauche.
Michel Merci, Madame.
Dame Et là vous trouverez la gare.
Michel Bon.

la dame lady
en voiture by car
en autobus by bus

la rue Saint-Jean Saint John's Street
là there

3 *How to get to Bayeux*

Michel Et pour aller à Bayeux?
Hôtesse Vous prenez le train, et c'est très rapide, hein, très facile.
Michel Bon, combien de temps?
Hôtesse Je crois que c'est un quart d'heure.
Michel Pas plus?
Hôtesse Non, non, non.
Michel Très bien, merci.

le train train
rapide quick
facile easy

1 ♦ **pour aller à la gare?** how do I get to the station? (lit. to go to the station?). This is the standard way to ask for directions.

♦ **vous prenez tout droit** you take (the street) straight ahead.

♦ **jusqu'au bout** right to the end. **Jusqu'à** = as far as, **le bout** = the end; when **à** and **le** come together they become **au**.

♦ **vous tournez à gauche** you turn left. From **tourner** (to turn).

la troisième sur la gauche the third on the left. She could equally well have said **la troisième à gauche**. **La troisième** refers to **la troisième rue** (the third street).

on est *où* exactement ici? where are we exactly here? (lit. one is *where* exactly here?). It is very common to use **on** (one) instead of **nous** (we), as you learnt in Unit 4, dialogue 8.

au numéro un sur le plan at number one on the map.

au centre de la ville, au fond in the centre of the town, in fact. Sign-posts
♦ use the abbreviation **centre-ville**.

2 **vous voulez aller . . .?** do you want to go. . .?

♦ **je suis à pied** I'm on foot. Or you might want to say **je suis en voiture** (I'm travelling by car).

vous traversez le pont you cross the bridge. From **traverser** (to cross).

♦ **un petit peu après le pont** a little bit after the bridge. Note also:
♦ **un petit peu plus loin** (a little bit further on).

sur votre gauche on your left. This is the same as **sur la gauche** or **à gauche**.

vous trouverez you will find.

3 **hein** is a 'filler word' with no real meaning, rather like 'you see' or 'you know' in English.

je crois que c'est un quart d'heure I think it's a quarter of an hour. **Je crois que . . .** (I think that . . .) is a useful way of starting a sentence.

pas plus? not more?

4 *Directions at the camp-site*

Réceptionniste Alors vous êtes ici. Vous allez tout droit. Vous tournez à la deuxième à droite – là. A côté de vous, vous avez le restaurant, le bar, le bazar . . .

Marie-Claude Attendez. On est ici – là . . .

Réceptionniste Alors vous allez aller tout droit . . .

Marie-Claude Je prends la route tout droit . . .

Réceptionniste Voilà.

Marie-Claude Et je tourne à droite.

Réceptionniste Oui.

la deuxième second
♦ **à côté de** next to
la route road

5 *Going by underground to the Eiffel Tower*

Bernadette Alors – euh – pour aller à la Tour Eiffel, vous allez prendre le métro, direction Nation. Vous descendez à Trocadéro et c'est à deux cents mètres.

6 *By underground to Notre Dame*

Barbara Pour aller à Notre Dame?

Bernadette Pour aller à Notre Dame il faut changer. Tu prends donc à l'Étoile la direction Vincennes et tu changes à Châtelet. Tu reprends la direction Porte d'Orléans – euh – et tu descends à Cité.

Barbara D'accord.

donc so, then

4
* **vous allez tout droit** you go straight on.

* **à droite** on the right. Notice the difference between **à droite** and **tout droit.**

  le bazar is a store selling a variety of goods other than foodstuffs.

  vous allez aller you're going to go.

5 **la Tour Eiffel** the Eiffel Tower (named after the designer Gustave Eiffel 1832–1923). Notice the pronunciation.

* **vous allez prendre le métro, direction Nation** you're going to take the underground (on the line going in the) direction of Nation. (See also p. 75)

  vous descendez you get off, get down. From **descendre** (to get off).

* **c'est à deux cents mètres** it is two hundred metres (away). e.g. also **c'est à un kilomètre** (it's one kilometre away).

6
* **il faut changer** you have to change. See p. 73 for an explanation of **il faut.**

  l'Étoile is the site of the Arc de Triomphe. The full official name is now Charles de Gaulle-Étoile.

  tu changes à Châtelet you change at Châtelet. From **changer** (to change). Note that Bernadette uses 'tu' because Barbara is her daughter. If you were talking to a stranger you would say **vous prenez, vous changez, vous reprenez, vous descendez** etc.

  tu reprends you take another (train).

7 *The RER*

Henri   Vous allez par le train?
Anna   Oui, le train ou le métro.
Henri   Vous ne prenez pas le RER?
Anna   Si, je prends le RER – euh – surtout pour aller travailler.
Henri   C'est un transport très rapide.
Anna   Très rapide, oui, très pratique, et qui peut transporter beaucoup de voyageurs.

surtout especially
le transport (means of) transport
pratique handy, convenient

8 *Where is Jean-Claude's bank?*

Michèle   Où se trouve ta banque?
Jean-Claude   Ah, ma banque? Ma banque se trouve du côté de la rive gauche. Et – euh – c'est situé en plein milieu d'un carrefour avec une très grande enseigne. Elle s'appelle la BICS.

situé situated
l'enseigne (f.) sign
du côté de on the side of
la rive gauche the left bank (of the Seine in Paris)

9 *Finding out where things are in the hotel*

Jeanne   Où sont les toilettes, s'il vous plaît?
Réceptionniste   Euh – première porte ici à gauche.
Jeanne   Bon, merci. Et ma chambre est à quel étage?
Réceptionniste   Alors, votre chambre est au troisième étage.
Jeanne   Et il y a des toilettes là?
Réceptionniste   Oui, oui, oui. A l'étage il y a des toilettes.
Jeanne   Et la douche?
Réceptionniste   La douche – alors il y a une douche au deuxième étage, hein.
Jeanne   D'accord. Et on est au premier?
Réceptionniste   Non, nous sommes au rez-de-chaussée.

7 ♦ **par le train** by train. Be careful, if you were to say 'on the train' in French, people would assume you were sitting on the roof!

le RER is **le Réseau Express Régional** (lit. the regional express network) – the fast underground train service connecting the suburbs with the centre of Paris. (See also p. 75)

pour aller travailler to go to work.

qui peut transporter beaucoup de voyageurs which can transport a lot of travellers. **Beaucoup** (a lot) is used frequently e.g.
♦ **merci beaucoup** (thanks a lot, thank you very much).

MÉTRO LES HALLES →
CORRESPONDANCE AVEC LE RER

8 **où se trouve ta banque?** where is your bank? (lit. where does your bank find itself?). The word for 'your' (when you know someone well and address them as **tu**) is **ta** before a feminine singular noun e.g. **ta banque** (your bank), and **ton** before a masculine singular noun e.g. **ton jardin** (your garden). Before a plural noun (masculine or feminine) the form is **tes** e.g. **tes yeux** (your eyes).

en plein milieu d'un carrefour right in the middle of a crossroads.

elle s'appelle it's called (lit. it calls itself). Learn also
♦ **je m'appelle** (my name is – lit. I call myself) and **comment vous appelez-vous?** (what's your name? – lit. what do you call yourself?).

9 ♦ **à quel étage?** on what floor?

♦ **il y a des toilettes là?** are there toilets there?
il y a means both 'there *is*' and 'there *are*', so when you are asking the way you can say: **il y a un autobus?** (is there a bus?); **il y a des trains pour Bayeux?** (are there any trains for Bayeux?).

à l'étage on the floor (i.e. the third floor)

au premier (étage) on the first (floor)

au rez-de-chaussée on the ground floor. On lift buttons this is abbreviated to **RC** or **RCh**.

Key words and phrases

When asking the way you don't need to *say* very much yourself, but you do need to understand directions.

What to ask

vous avez un plan de la ville?	do you have a map of the town?
pour aller à (la gare)?	how do I get to (the station)?
je suis en voiture/à pied	I'm in the car/on foot
je vais (à Paris) en autobus	I'm going (to Paris) by bus
je vais (à Paris) par le train	I'm going (to Paris) by train
il y a (un autobus/des trains)?	is there/are there (a bus/some trains)?
à quel étage?	on which floor?

Directions to understand

vous allez. . .	you go. . .
tout droit	straight on
jusqu'à (la banque)	as far as (the bank)
vous prenez le métro, direction. . .	you take the underground, in the direction of. . .
il faut changer	you have to change
vous tournez à gauche/à droite	you turn left/right
c'est. . .	it's. . .
là	there
à deux cents mètres	two hundred metres away
à côté de (l'église)	next to (the church)
en face de (la banque)	opposite (the bank)
après (le pont)	after (the bridge)
un petit peu plus loin	a little bit further on
le centre-ville	the town centre
au premier étage	on the first floor
au deuxième étage	on the second floor
au troisième étage	on the third floor

Learn also

comment vous appelez-vous?	what's your name?
je m'appelle (Suzanne)	my name is (Suzanne)
merci beaucoup	thank you very much

Before going on, learn the numbers between 100 (**cent**) and 1000 (**mille**). They follow exactly the same pattern as 1–99 (see p. 225).

Practise what you have learnt

1 Yves is visiting a town for the first time so he goes to the tourist office (**le syndicat d'initiative**) for some information. Listen to his conversation with the employee on the tape and answer the following questions. Tick in the box where there is a choice. (Answers p. 76)

1 What is the first thing he asks for?

....

2 Is the tourist office at **a.** number ten? ☐
b. number seven? ☐

3 Is the tourist office **a.** opposite the station? ☐
b. next to the station? ☐

4 Where does Yves want to go?

....

5 Will he find it if he goes **a.** straight on, first left? ☐
b. straight on, third right? ☐
c. straight on, third left? ☐

6 Is it **a.** opposite the bank, on the left? ☐
b. a little after the bank, on the left? ☐

7 He could take bus number **a.** 113? ☐
b. 213? ☐
c. 203? ☐

2 You are a motorist in a strange town and want to get to the tourist office. First select your phrases from the box below and write them into the appropriate spaces in the conversation. (Answers on p. 76.) You won't need your tape recorder.

Merci beaucoup. Au revoir, Monsieur.   Non, en voiture.   Je vais tout droit, jusqu'au cinéma.   Pardon, Monsieur – pour aller au syndicat d'initiative, s'il vous plaît?   Je tourne à droite et le syndicat d'initiative est à cent mètres.

Vous: ....

....

Homme: Vous voulez aller en autobus ou à pied?
Vous: ....
Homme: Alors, vous allez tout droit, jusqu'au cinéma . . .
Vous: ....
Homme: Vous tournez à droite et le syndicat d'initiative est à cent mètres.
Vous: ....

....

Homme: C'est ça.
Vous: ....

3 a. Follow these directions on the map below and see where you arrive. Your starting-point is the Hôtel des Anglais. (Answer p. 76.)

Vous traversez la rue. Vous tournez à gauche. Vous prenez la première à droite et puis la deuxième à droite. Vous tournez à la première à gauche. Vous traversez le carrefour et vous allez tout droit. Sur votre gauche il y a un hôtel. Un petit peu après l'hôtel vous allez trouver . . . quoi?

b. Now listen to the tape where you will hear another set of directions relating to the same map. This time the starting-point is the Syndicat d'Initiative. Where do you finish up? (Answer p. 76.)

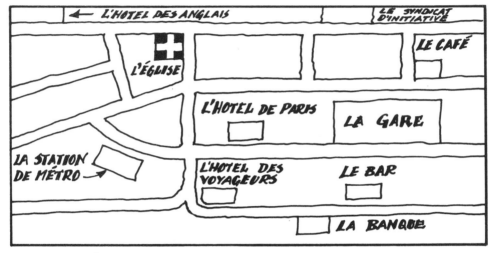

4 Now why not see if you could give clear directions in French for getting from your own home to the nearest church? Try and say them out loud and ask someone you know who speaks French to check them if possible.

Grammar

Aller

It is always the really common verbs that are irregular and although when you're learning them there seem to be a lot, in fact there aren't all that many. Here is the present tense of **aller** (to go).

je vais	nous allons
tu vas	vous allez
il/elle va	ils/elles vont

Il faut

The phrase **il faut** is very easy to use. **Il faut travailler** means all of the following, depending on the context: *I must work, you must work, he must work, she must work, one must work, we must work, they must work* and *it is necessary to work.* **Il faut** is followed by the infinitive, which always keeps the same ending (see p. 221), so no need to worry about verb endings.

Prepositions

You have by now met a number of prepositions (words like *on, at, above* etc.) Here is a list of them, together with a few new ones.

sur on	**après** after	**en** in (e.g. **en France,**
sous under	**devant** in front of	**en français**)
à at, to	**derrière** behind	**près de** near to
de of, from	**chez** at the house of	**à côté de** next to
pour for, in order to	**par** by (means of),	**en face de** opposite
entre between	through	**jusqu'à** as far as
avant before	**dans** inside (e.g. **dans**	
	la chambre)	

Look at the way **près de** joins nouns which come after it:

près de + **le restaurant** becomes **près *du* restaurant** (de + le = du)
près de + **la gare** → **près *de la* gare**
près de + **l'église** → **près *de* l'église**
près de + **les hôtels** → **près *des* hôtels** (de + les = des)

En face de and **à côté de** follow the same pattern.

Exercises 1 Le carrefour (Answers p. 76)

Working from the map at the foot of page 72 opposite, complete the following sentences using **dans**, **entre**, **devant** and **derrière**.

a. Le parc est .... le restaurant.
b. Il y a des toilettes .... la gare.
c. Le syndicat d'initiative est .... la rue St. Jean.
d. Le bar se trouve .... le café de Paris et le syndicat d'initiative.
e. L'école est située .... le garage et la banque.

2

Still working from the map, use **à côté de**, **près de** and **en face de** to complete the sentences below. Remember to use **du, de la, de l'** and **des** as appropriate.

a. La banque et le restaurant sont .... gare.
b. Le garage est .... café de Paris.
c. Le bazar est .... hôtel.
d. Le bar se trouve .... syndicat d'initiative.
e. Le syndicat d'initiative est situé .... restaurant.

Read and understand

If you make an advance booking at a French hotel you will probably receive a letter similar to this. Answer the questions below in English. (Answers p. 76.)

---

le Grand Hôtel,
Avenue Amélie,
33780 Soulac-sur-Mer

Soulac-sur-Mer, le 13 mai

Madame,
Monsieur,

Je vous remercie de votre lettre du 2 mai. Je confirme votre réservation pour une chambre avec douche pour deux personnes du 5 au 15 septembre. La chambre est très agréable et elle se trouve au deuxième étage.

Si vous arrivez par le train, la gare est à 500 mètres de l'hôtel. Il faut tourner à gauche et prendre la rue Gambetta; l'avenue Amélie est la quatrième rue sur votre droite.

Si vous êtes en voiture, il y a un grand parking pour nos clients derrière l'hôtel.

Je vous prie, Madame, Monsieur, d'agréer mes salutations distinguées,*

P. Thierry

P. Thierry
Directeur

---

* This is a standard letter-ending, equivalent to 'yours faithfully' or 'yours sincerely'.

je vous remercie de I thank you for
agréable pleasant
le parking the car-park
le client the customer

1 What was the date of *your* letter to the hotel?

....

2 Will your room have a shower or a bath? ....

3 How many of you will be staying there? ....

4 On what floor is your room? ....

5 What are the dates of your holiday? ....

6 How far is the hotel from the station? ....

7 Once you are in the rue Gambetta, how do you find the avenue Amélie? ....

8 Where can you park your car? ....

Did you know?

Every French town and almost every village of any size has its own **syndicat d'initiative** (tourist office) also called **office de tourisme** or **bureau du tourisme**. The receptionist, often called **l'hôtesse**, will be able to give you free information on the town (remember to ask for **un plan de la ville**). The office should also have information on the area (**une carte de la région** is a map of the area, which may not be free) and on local places of interest. They can tell you about hotels and restaurants and may be willing to make a booking for you, for the price of the telephone call. **Syndicats d'initiative** also have bus timetables (buses are called **bus** for urban services and **cars** for services between towns). You can often buy tickets for local events such as concerts at the **syndicat d'initiative** – altogether a very useful institution!

The Paris **métro** (or **métropolitain**, to give it its full name) is cleaner, more pleasant and much cheaper than the London underground. There is a flat rate for travel in the centre of Paris and it is much more economical to buy your tickets ten at a time. Ask for **un carnet** if you want ten tickets and **un ticket** if you only want one. Do not be lured into buying from the illegal ticket-touts who prey on unwary foreigners – their prices are generally high and their tickets often invalid. Smoking is forbidden in all carriages, as official notices everywhere remind you. **Métro** lines take their name from the station (**la station**) that is the terminus in the direction in which you are travelling. When you go in the opposite direction you will find the line has a completely different name. This avoids the London hazard of getting an east-bound train when you want a west-bound one. When you change trains the sign to look out for, if your next line is not indicated, is **correspondance** (connections).

The **RER** is the high-speed underground service connecting the suburbs with the centre of Paris. **Métro** tickets are valid for it within the central Paris area, but longer journeys cost more. The **RER** stations are brightly coloured, futuristic works of art and worth a visit for their own sake.

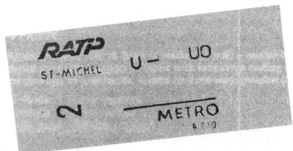

Your turn to speak

In this exercise imagine you are a businessman who has just arrived in a strange town and you are looking for your hotel. Pierre will tell you what to say on the tape. You won't need your book this time but you'll need to remember the expression you learnt in Unit 4: **pardon** (excuse me). Remember to add **Monsieur**, or **Madame**: **pardon Monsieur, pardon Madame**.

You will also be practising: **pour allez à** . . . ?, **il y a**, and understanding directions.

And finally   Make sure you have worked through all the stages on your study-guide on p. 63, and then go back and listen to all the dialogues in this unit again, this time without stopping.

Answers

Practise what you have learnt p. 71 Exercise 1 (1) a map of the town (2) b (3) a (4) to the Hotel Métropole (5) c (6) b (7) b.

p. 71 Exercise 2 Pardon, Monsieur – pour allez au syndicat d'initiative, s'il vous plaît?/Non, en voiture./Je vais tout droit, jusqu'au cinéma./Je tourne à droite et le syndicat d'initiative est à cent mètres./Merci beaucoup. Au revoir, Monsieur.

p. 72 Exercise 3 (a) la gare (b) la banque.

Grammar p. 73 Exercise 1 (a) derrière (b) devant (c) dans (d) entre (e) derrière.

p. 73 Exercise 2 (a) près de la (b) en face du (c) à côté de l' (d) à côté du (e) en face du.

Read and understand p. 74 (1) 2nd May (2) shower (3) two (4) second (5) 5th-15th September (6) 500m. (7) it is the fourth street on your right. (8) in the large hotel car park behind the hotel.

6 Time

What you will learn

- telling the time
- the days of the week
- the months of the year
- other useful expressions of time
- coping with timetables
- something about French holiday patterns
- the opening hours of shops

Before you begin

Being able to ask and understand *when* things are happening/open/available is essential to the smooth running of a holiday or business trip. Asking the questions is fairly simple: **quand?** (when?) and **à quelle heure?** (at what time?) will cover most eventualities. There is little in the way of new grammar in this unit, but there is a good deal of new vocabulary. Learn days, dates and times carefully, and practise them aloud. For example, whenever you look at your watch you could try saying the time to yourself in French.

Before you listen to the dialogues, revise the following numbers. Say them out loud in French and then check them on p. 90.

61 2 5 18 90 54 200 1000 7 15

Study guide

	Dialogues 1–4: listen straight through without the book
	Dialogues 1–4: listen, read and study one by one
	Dialogues 5–7: listen straight through without the book
	Dialogues 5–7: listen, read and study one by one
	Learn the *Key words and phrases*
	Study p. 84: *The date* and *Telling the time*
	Do the exercises in *Practise what you have learnt*
	Study *Grammar* and do the exercises
	Do *Read and understand*
	Read *Did you know?*
	Do the tape exercise in *Your turn to speak*
	Finally, listen to all the dialogues again without the book.

Dialogues

1 *Off to a bad start at the airport!*

Employée Monsieur, vous avez une heure de retard au départ de l'avion.

l'avion (m.) aeroplane

2 *What time is the last bus to the concert?*

Michel Euh – est-ce qu'il y a des moyens de communication (pour s'y rendre?)
Hôtesse Oui, vous avez des bus.
Michel Des bus . . .
Hôtesse Le problème, c'est que le dernier bus rentre à vingt heures ou vingt heures trente, alors pour le concert c'est difficile . . .

le problème problem
que that
♦ **le dernier** last
le concert concert
difficile difficult

3 *Train times from La Roche-sur-Yon to Nice*

Employée Alors départ tous les soirs de La Roche à 18 heures 48 et arrivée à Nice à 8 heures 37.
Robert 18 heures 48, ça fait 6 heures 48?
Employée C'est ça. Sept heures moins le quart.
Robert Sept heures moins le quart. Oui, merci. Et on arrive à Nice à quelle heure?
Employée A 8 heures 37.
Robert Ah, c'est bien – le matin, oui. Ça fait une bonne nuit dans le train pour dormir.

l'arrivée (f.) arrival
dormir to sleep

4 *Times at the camp-site*

Réceptionniste C'est chaud de six heures à dix heures le matin et ensuite de quatre heures à huit heures le soir.
Marie-Claude Et le portail – à quelle heure ferme le . . .
Réceptionniste Alors le portail est ouvert le matin à six heures et fermé à onze heures, sauf le samedi, où il est fermé à . . . à minuit.

ensuite then
le portail gate
ferme (from fermer) shuts
♦ **ouvert** open
♦ **fermé** shut
♦ **minuit** midnight

1   **une heure de retard** an hour's delay.

♦ **le retard** = the delay; **en retard** = late.

au départ to the departure: **à** + **le** = **au.**

2   **des moyens de communication (pour s'y rendre)** means of communication (for getting oneself there). He might have said more simply: **des moyens de transport** (means of transport).

rentre à vingt heures returns at 8 p.m. (lit. twenty hours). All timetables in France use the 24-hour clock and the French abbreviation of the English 8 p.m. or 8.30 p.m. would be 20h and 20h 30. (How to tell the time will be explained on p. 84.) **Rentre** is from **rentrer** (to come back, to return).

3 ♦ **tous les soirs** every evening (lit. all the evenings).

de La Roche from La Roche(-sur-Yon).

♦ **ça fait** that makes, that is. **Ça fait** is often used when shopping: **ça fait combien?** (How much does it come to?) **ça fait dix francs** (that comes to ten francs).

sept heures moins le quart quarter to seven (lit. seven hours less the quarter, see p. 84).

♦ **on arrive à Nice** it gets to Nice. From **arriver** (to arrive).

♦ **à quelle heure?** at what time?

♦ **le matin** in the morning (lit. the morning).

4 ♦ **de six heures à dix heures** from six o'clock to ten o'clock. Marie-Claude has asked when the water is hot.

♦ **le soir** in the evening (lit. the evening).

à onze heures meaning 11 o'clock at night.

♦ **sauf le samedi** except on Saturdays (lit. except the Saturday). On Saturdays/Fridays etc is translated simply as <u>le</u> **samedi,** <u>le</u> **vendredi.**

⬜ 5 *The school week*

Isabelle Alors – euh – les écoliers français travaillent le lundi, le mardi, le jeudi et le vendredi toute la journée. En général on commence à huit heures et demie le matin et on termine le soir vers quatre heures et demie, cinq heures, quelquefois plus tard. Et le mercredi matin on travaille et l'après-midi est libre. Les écoliers travaillent aussi le samedi matin. Donc en général les gens partent en week-end le samedi à midi et ils reviennent le dimanche soir.

l'écolier (m.) schoolchild
en général in general
vers around
l'après-midi (m.) afternoon
libre free
donc so
midi midday, noon
ils reviennent (from **revenir**) they come back

⬜ 6 *School holidays*

Françoise Euh – fin-octobre – euh – début-novembre il y a les . . . les vacances de la Toussaint, qui durent une semaine. Euh – il y a des vacances – euh – de Noël, qui sont en général du 21 décembre jusqu'au 4 janvier. Il y a les vacances de février, qui durent une semaine. Il y a aussi les vacances de Pâques, qui durent deux semaines pleines, qui sont – euh – vers les mois de mars, avril, et les grandes vacances, qui durent deux mois et demi, du 30 juin jusqu'au 15 septembre.

qui which
durent (from **durer**) last
Noël Christmas
◗ **décembre** December
◗ **janvier** January
◗ **février** February
Pâques Easter
pleines (f. pl.) full
◗ **le mois** month
◗ **mars** March
◗ **avril** April
◗ **juin** June
◗ **septembre** September

5 ◆ **lundi, mardi, mercredi, jeudi, vendredi, samedi, dimanche** Monday, Tuesday, Wednesday, Thursday, Friday, Saturday, Sunday.

◆ **toute la journée** all day (lit. all the day). Note that a 'journey' is **un voyage** in French.

on commence à huit heures et demie they begin at half past eight. Here again is the useful little word **on** which is used all the time in French to mean 'one', 'we' or (as here) 'they'. **Commence** is from **commencer** (to begin).

on termine le soir they finish in the evening. **Termine** is from **terminer** (to end, finish).

quelquefois plus tard sometimes later (lit. sometimes more late).

◆ **les gens partent** people leave. You will certainly need the verb **partir** (to leave) e.g. **à quelle heure part l'autobus?** (what time does the bus leave?), **le train part à six heures** (the train leaves at six o'clock).

en week-end for the week-end.

6 **fin-octobre, début-novembre** (at the) end of October, beginning of November. The months of the year do not require a capital letter in French.

la Toussaint All Saints'. The 1st November is a traditional bank holiday.

◆ **du 21 décembre jusqu'au 4 janvier** from the 21st December until the 4th January. Note that in French you say literally 'four January' and 'twenty-one December'.

les grandes vacances is the usual term for the long summer holiday.

7 *The summer holidays*

Isabelle Euh – les Français aiment bien prendre leurs vacances – euh –
vers le 14 juillet, la Fête Nationale. Et il y a un jour de départ en
vacances en France – c'est le premier (1ᵉʳ) août. Là il faut éviter
les routes parce que vraiment on peut pas . . . on peut pas rouler.
Et après le 15 août – euh – c'est assez calme sur la côte. Euh –
c'est l'idéal pour les – pour les Anglais pour venir chez nous.

> **leurs (pl.)** their
> **éviter** to avoid
> ◆ **parce que** because
> ◆ **vraiment** really
> ◆ **assez** fairly
> **calme** quiet
> **la côte** coast
> **venir** to come

7

aiment bien are very fond of

le 14 juillet, la Fête Nationale the 14th July is Bastille Day and a national holiday.

un jour de départ a day when everyone leaves (lit. a departure day).

le premier (1ᵉʳ) août 1st August. The **t** of **août** is sometimes pronounced and sometimes not.

là usually means 'there', but in this case it means 'then'.

on peut pas rouler you can't move, i.e. the traffic jams are so bad. In certain phrases, in spoken French *only*, you will find that **ne** is omitted. **Rouler** is the verb used to describe the flow of traffic and you will see signs on the road such as **ne roulez pas trop vite!** (don't drive too fast!).

c'est l'idéal it's the ideal (time).

Key words and phrases

For the days of the week (**les jours de la semaine**), see the first note with dialogue 5, p. 81.

Les mois de l'année	*The months of the year*
janvier	January
février	February
mars	March
avril	April
mai	May
juin	June
juillet	July
août	August
septembre	September
octobre	October
novembre	November
décembre	December

à quelle heure . . .?	at what time . . .?
quand . . .?	when . . .?
est-ce que le train arrive?	does the train arrive?
est-ce que l'autobus part?	does the bus leave?
est-ce que c'est ouvert/fermé?	is it open/closed?
est-ce qu'on arrive/part?	do we arrive/leave?

il y a un train . . .?	is there a train. . .?
le soir?	in the evening?
tous les soirs?	every evening?
le matin?	in the morning?
l'après-midi?	in the afternoon?
le (lundi)?	on (Mondays)?
à minuit?	at midnight?
à midi?	at midday?
à (deux) heures?	at (two) o'clock?

c'est en retard?	is it late?
c'est le dernier?	is it the last?
ça fait combien?	how much does that make?

je travaille . . .	I work . . .
de (neuf heures) à (cinq heures)	from (nine) to (five)
toute la journée	all day
sauf (le samedi)	except (Saturdays)

je suis en vacances . . .	I'm on holiday . . .
du (17 juillet) jusqu'au (3 août)	from the (17th July) until the (3rd August)
pendant le mois de (mai)	during the month of (May)

parce que	because
vraiment	really
assez	fairly

The date

Whereas in English we talk about the *fifth of May*, the French say the equivalent of *the five May*, **le cinq mai**. Other examples: June 12th, **le douze juin**; August 30th, **le trente août**; November 11th, **le onze novembre** (for some reason it is **le onze** and not **l'onze**). The only exception to this pattern is for the first of the month, which is **le premier** (abbreviated to **1ᵉʳ**) **janvier, février**, etc. For practice, work out today's date and the date of your birthday (and if today happens to be your birthday, **joyeux anniversaire!** – happy birthday!)

Telling the time
The 24-hour clock

The 24-hour clock is used more widely in France than it is in Britain. To give the time on the hour you simply say **il est** followed by the number of hours o'clock, e.g. **il est une heure** (it is one o'clock), **il est huit heures** (it is eight o'clock), **il est vingt-trois heures** (it is twenty-three hours i.e. 11 p.m.). In between hours you add the number of minutes after the word **heures**: e.g. **une heure quinze** (1h 15), **huit heures trente** (8h 30), **vingt-trois heures quarante-cinq** (23h 45). The word **minutes** is almost always omitted.

The 12-hour clock

The reply to the question **quelle heure est-il?** (what time is it?) is more likely to use the twelve-hour clock, as in English. So **il est onze heures** would be used whether it is morning or evening. Noon and midnight, however, are distinguished from each other: **il est midi** means 'it is noon' and **il est minuit** means 'it is midnight'. Study the following:

Il est dix heures cinq
Il est dix heures dix
Il est dix heures et quart
il est dix heures vingt
il est dix heures vingt-cinq
il est dix heures et demie

il est onze heures moins vingt-cinq
il est onze heures moins vingt
il est onze heures moins le quart
il est onze heures moins dix
il est onze heures moins cinq

Practise what you have learnt

1 Listen to the tape. Yves is talking about what he's going to do this week. Fill in the gaps below with the correct days of the week – in English. (Answers p. 90)

a. On.................he's going to the cinema in the evening.

b. On.................he's working.

c. On.................he's going on holiday.

d. On.................he has a meeting at the bank.

e. On.................he's going to Rouen by train.

f. On.................he's going to the restaurant with the whole family.

g. On.................he's going to buy some wine.

Yves has pronounced all the days of the week in this exercise, so practise saying them aloud to yourself.

2 Listen to the tape and fill in the clock faces below with the times spoken. (Answers p. 90.)

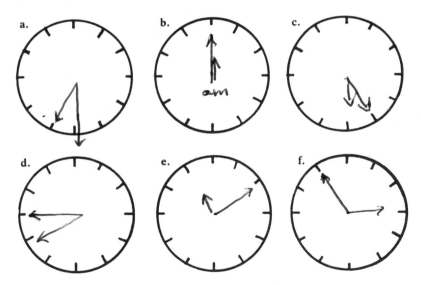

3 Translate the following dates. (Answers on p. 90.)

a. 10th July _LE DIX JUILLET_

b. 12th August _LE DOUZE AOÛT_

c. February 29th _LE VINGT-NEUF FÉVRIER_

d. 23rd November _LE VINGT-TROIS NOVEMBRE_

e. 1st January _LE PREMIÈRE JANVIER_

f. April 16th _LE SEIZE AVRIL_

g. 22nd October _LE VINGT-DEUX OCTOBRE_

4 Listen to the tape where you will hear Yves and Carolle discussing the dates of their holidays. Answer the following questions about their plans – in English.

a. What date is Carolle going on holiday? ....

b. How long will she be in Marseilles? ....

c. What date is she going to her parents in Brittany? ....

d. What date is she coming home? ....

e. Between which dates is Yves going to work in Nice?

....

....

Grammar

Venir

You have already met some parts of **venir** (to come). You should learn the rest of it, both because it is such a useful verb in itself and because so many other common verbs follow the same pattern e.g. **revenir** (to come back), **devenir** (to become), **tenir** (to hold), **retenir** (to hold back), **maintenir** (to maintain) and **soutenir** (to hold up, keep up).

je viens	**nous venons**
tu viens	**vous venez**
il/elle vient	**ils/elles viennent**

Exercise Reply by using **Oui, je. . .** and a full sentence to each of the questions below, e.g.
Est-ce que vous devenez riche? (Are you getting rich?)
Oui, je deviens riche (Yes, I'm getting rich)
(Answers on p. 90)

1 Est-ce que vous venez souvent à Lyon?

....

2 Est-ce que vous tenez un restaurant? (Do you keep a restaurant?)

....

3 Est-ce que vous revenez samedi?

....

4 Est-ce que vous soutenez la conversation?

....

5 Est-ce que tu viens au cinéma ce soir?

....

Au, à la, à l', aux

Look at the way **à** (at, to) joins to nouns which come after it:

à + **le restaurant** becomes **au restaurant** (à + le = au)
à + **la gare** → **à la gare**
à + **l'église** → **à l'église**
à + **les hôtels** → **aux hôtels** (à + les = aux)

Read and understand

HORAIRES DES VISITES

DE PAQUES AU 31 MAI : MERCREDI
SAMEDI, DIMANCHE ET JOURS FÉRIÉS
DE 14H30 A 18H30

DU 1ER JUIN AU 15 SEPTEMBRE
LES APRES-MIDI 〈 SAUF MARDI ET VENDREDI 〉
DE 14H30 A 18H30

DU 16 SEPT AU 15 OCT : MERCREDI
SAMEDI, DIMANCHE ET JOURS FÉRIÉS
DE 14H30 A 18H30

DU 16 OCTOBRE A PAQUES
DIMANCHE ET JOURS FÉRIÉS
DE 14H A 18H

l'horaire (m.) timetable
le jour férié bank holiday

This is a typical notice giving the opening times (**heures d'ouverture**) of a château. See if you can understand it well enough to answer the following questions. You can check your replies on p. 90.

1 Can you visit the château on a Friday in July? ....
2 Can you visit on 1st October if it is a bank holiday? ....
3 Can you visit on the Saturday after Easter? ....
4 Can you visit in the morning in November? ....
5 What is the earliest you can go in if you visit on a Monday in August? ....
6 Between what times can you visit on a Sunday in December?
....

Did you know?

Opening times of shops

French shops stay open much longer in the evening than is normal in
Britain. All but the big stores compensate for this by closing for up to three
hours at midday. Many shops are shut for all or part of Monday: rather
than an early-closing day it tends to be a late-opening day.

The baker's (**la boulangerie**) often opens as early as 7.30 a.m. and does not
close until 7–8 p.m. The baker's and the cake shop (**la pâtisserie**) also
usually open on Sunday mornings. Most French people still shop for bread
twice a day in order to have it fresh for the midday and evening meals.

The French on holiday

If you are going to France in the summer you should avoid travelling on
1st, 14th, 15th and 31st July and on 1st, 15th and 31st August as those are
the traditional dates for what the French call the July and August
'migrations': the trains are very crowded and traffic jams build up. This
occurs because many factories shut down completely for the month of July
or the month of August, so that large numbers of people with exactly the
same holiday period want to make the most of it. This custom is now being
changed and staggered holidays are on the increase. The public holidays on
14th July and 15th August are also traditional landmarks in the holiday
calendar: the period between them is when resorts are at their most
crowded and, particularly on the south coast, at their most expensive. Bank
holidays in France are as follows:

New Year's Day (1st January)	**le jour de l'an**
Easter Monday	**le lundi de Pâques**
Labour Day (1st May)	**le premier mai**
Ascension Day (in May)	**l'Ascension**
Whit Monday (in May)	**le lundi de la Pentecôte**
Bastille Day (14th July)	**la Fête Nationale**
Assumption Day (15th August)	**l'Assomption**
All Saints' Day (1st November)	**la Toussaint**
Remembrance Day (11th November)	**le onze novembre**
Christmas Day (25th December)	**Noël**

Your turn to speak

You need to get to the station to catch a train. Pierre will help you to ask the right questions of a man standing at a bus stop. The only new word will be **le taxi** which should not be too difficult!

And finally Go through the dialogues again – and remember to practise putting times and dates into French at every opportunity.

Revision

Now turn to p. 214 and complete the revision section on Units 4–6. On the cassette the revision section follows straight after this unit.

Answers

Revision p. 77 soixante-et-un; deux; cinq; dix-huit; quatre-vingt-dix; neuf; cinquante-quatre; deux cents; mille; sept; quinze.

Practise what you have learnt p. 85 Exercise 1 (a) Thursday (b) Monday (c) Sunday (d) Wednesday (e) Tuesday (f) Saturday (g) Friday.

p. 86 Exercise 2 (a) 7h30 (b) 12h (midday) (c) 5h25 (d) 7h45 (e) 11h10 (f) 2h55.

p. 86 Exercise 3 1 (a) le dix juillet (b) le douze août (c) le vingt-neuf février (d) le vingt-trois novembre (e) le premier janvier (f) le seize avril (g) le vingt-deux octobre.

Exercise 4 (a) 17th July (b) one week (c) 24th July (d) 7th August (e) 1st October to 21st November.

Grammar p. 87 (1) Oui, je viens souvent à Lyon. (2) Oui, je tiens un restaurant. (3) Oui, je reviens samedi. (4) Oui, je soutiens la conversation. (5) Oui, je viens au cinéma ce soir.

Read and understand p. 88 (1) no (2) yes (3) yes (4) no (5) 2.30 p.m (6) 2–6 p.m.

7 Shopping – part 1

What you will learn

- asking for common items in shops
- understanding and responding to questions of clarification
- making appointments
- where to buy bus-tickets
- something about types of shop
- something about the French post-office
- how to use the telephone in France

Before you begin

Once again, there is very little new grammar in this unit, but there is a fair amount of vocabulary, all of it very useful on a French holiday. Learn it as thoroughly as you can now; you may find that it does not all 'stick', so come back and revise it later on – particularly just before your holiday!

Do you remember what the following foods are? (Answers p. 104.)

le saucisson	**le fromage** ....
le lait	**les œufs** ....
le jambon	**la glace** ....

Study guide

	Dialogues 1–4: listen straight through without the book
	Dialogues 1–4: listen, read and study one by one
	Dialogues 5–7: listen straight through without the book
	Dialogues 5–7: listen, read and study one by one
	Learn the *Key words and phrases* and the extra vocabulary
	Do the exercises in *Practise what you have learnt*
	Study *Grammar*
	Do *Read and understand*
	Read *Did you know?*
	Do the tape exercise in *Your turn to speak*
	Finally, listen to all the dialogues again without the book

Dialogues

1 *Trying to buy English newpapers*

Robert Monsieur, avez-vous des journaux anglais?
Vendeur Ah non.
Robert Merci.

le vendeur sales assistant (man)

2 *Buying stamps*

Robert Trois timbres pour des lettres pour l'Angleterre et deux timbres pour des cartes postales. Merci.
Employée Alors pour les lettres c'est 1.70 et . . . cartes postales . . . ça doit être 1 franc 20.
Robert C'est ça.

♦ **le timbre** stamp
♦ **la carte postale** post card

3 *Buying bread*

Simone Euh – je voudrais une baguette.
Boulangère Oui, Madame.
Simone Et cinq croissants.
Boulangère Cinq croissants – ordinaires ou beurre?
Simone Euh – ordinaires.
Boulangère Ordinaires.

la boulangère baker (woman)

1 ◆ **avez-vous des journaux anglais?** have you any English newspapers?
Le journal = the newspaper, **les journaux** = the newspapers. Most words
form their plural by adding an **-s**, but words ending in **-al** form theirs in
-aux e.g. **un anim<u>al</u>** (an animal), **des anim<u>aux</u>** (animals)

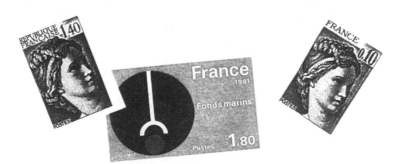

2 **ça doit être** that must be.

◆ **pour l'Angleterre** for England. Note also **pour les États-Unis** (for the
USA), **pour le Canada** (for Canada).

3 ◆ **je voudrais une baguette** I'd like a French stick. You will find **je voudrais**
a very useful, courteous phrase for asking for what you want. There are
several different types of French bread – **une baguette** is a medium-size
stick, **une ficelle** is smaller and thinner and **un gros pain** is a large round
loaf.

ordinaires ou beurre plain or (made with) butter? **Ordinaire** also means
'ordinary', e.g. **vin ordinaire** ordinary wine (i.e. not vintage).

<table>
<tr><td>☐ **4**</td><td>*Buying a bottle of wine*</td></tr>
</table>

Simone	Une bouteille de vin – euh – appellation contrôlée. . .
Vendeuse	Oui.
Simone	Euh – un vin pas trop . . . pas trop fort en alcool.
Vendeuse	J'ai un Bordeaux, qui fait 9F 80, un '79.
Simone	Très bien – on va essayer.
Vendeuse	Bien, Madame.

    la vendeuse sales assistant (woman)
♦ **le vin** wine

<table>
<tr><td>☐ **5**</td><td>*Buying cream cheeses and eggs*</td></tr>
</table>

Simone	Une boîte de petits suisses.
Vendeuse	Des petits ou des gros?
Simone	Euh – des gros.
Vendeuse	4.90. Avec ça?
Simone	Et – six œufs.
Vendeuse	Ce sera tout, Madame?
Simone	Oui, c'est tout.

    gros large, big, fat

4 **appellation contrôlée,** often abbreviated to **AC**: the official guarantee of both geographical origin and quality, and the opposite of **un vin ordinaire.**

pas trop fort en alcool not too alcoholic (lit. not too strong in alcohol).

on va essayer let's give it a try (lit. one is going to try).

5 ◆ **une boîte de petits suisses** a box of small cream cheeses. **Une boîte** can also mean a 'tin' or 'container'. Note as well **un paquet** (a packet).

◆ **six œufs** six eggs. In **un œuf** the final 'f' is pronounced, but not in the plural.

avec ça? anything else? (lit. with that?)

ce sera tout? will that be all?

◆ **c'est tout** that's all.

Extra note: when buying food for a picnic try to go to a **charcuterie** (delicatessen) where you can buy all sorts of cold meats as well as prepared dishes such as stuffed tomatoes, pizzas and various salads.

6 *Buying fruit and vegetables*

Simone	Un kilo de tomates – bien mûres.
Vendeuse	Bien mûres – il y a un petit peu moins?
Simone	Oui, très bien.
Vendeuse	Très bien comme ça?
Simone	Une livre de raisin.
Vendeuse	Une livre de raisin. Du blanc ou du noir?
Simone	Du blanc.
Vendeuse	Oui. Vous avez 50 grammes en plus.
Simone	Oui.
Vendeuse	Ça va aller comme ça? Alors 3F 20.
Simone	Et quatre artichauts.
Vendeuse	Quatre artichauts. Alors – euh – 7F 45.
Simone	Merci.
Vendeuse	Voilà.
Simone	Ce sera tout.
Vendeuse	Ce sera tout? 15F 30, Madame.

♦ **le kilo** kilogram
la tomate tomato
l'artichaut (m.) an artichoke

7 *Making a hair appointment*

Simone	Je voudrais un rendez-vous pour shampooing-mise en plis . . .
Coiffeuse	Oui.
Simone	. . . euh – vendredi après-midi si possible.
Coiffeuse	Vendredi après-midi. A quelle heure?
Simone	Euh – vers deux heures ou trois heures . . .
Coiffeuse	Oui, deux heures. C'est pour une mise en plis?
Simone	Oui.
Coiffeuse	Mise en plis-coupe ou . . .
Simone	Non, mise en plis simplement.
Coiffeuse	Mise en plis.
Simone	Shampooing et mise en plis.
Coiffeuse	Bon. Deux heures, alors, vendredi.
Simone	D'accord.
Coiffeuse	Voilà.

la coiffeuse (woman) hairdresser
le shampooing shampoo
la coupe cut
simplement simply, only

6   **bien mûres** nice and ripe.

un petit peu moins? a little under?

▶ **comme ça?** like that? You can also answer **oui, comme ça.**

▶ **une livre** (lit. a pound) now taken to mean 500 grams (**un demi-kilo** or **cinq cents grammes**).

une livre de raisin a pound of grapes. **Le raisin** means grape*s*.

du blanc ou du noir? white or black?

en plus over.

ça va aller comme ça? will that do like that?

7 ▶ **un rendez-vous** an appointment, meeting. Here it is a hair appointment but it can be used for *any* appointment.

une mise en plis a set. You may also need **un brushing** (a blow-dry).

▶ **si possible** if possible. (For **si** meaning 'yes', see p. 27.)

Key words and phrases

avez-vous . . .?	do you have. . .?
un journal anglais?	an English newspaper?
un timbre?	a stamp?
pour l'Angleterre?	for England?
pour le Canada?	for Canada?
pour les États-Unis?	for the United States?
pour des lettres?	for letters?
pour des cartes postales?	for post-cards?
je voudrais . . .	I'd like. . .
une baguette	a French stick
une bouteille de vin	a bottle of wine
six œufs	six eggs
une livre de (beurre)	a pound (500 g) of (butter)
un kilo de (raisin)	a kilo of (grapes)
une boîte de (sardines)	a tin of (sardines)
un paquet de (sucre)	a packet of (sugar)
comme ça	like that
c'est tout	that's all
je voudrais un rendez-vous	I'd like an appointment/meeting

You can always point to something on display which you want to buy, but it's best if you know its name. Here are the names of some common foodstuffs which you may like to learn.

les fruits	*fruit*
la banane	banana
la pomme	apple
l'orange (f.)	orange
la poire	pear
le melon	melon
les légumes	*vegetables*
la pomme de terre	potato
la carotte	carrot
le chou	cabbage
les petits pois	peas
le concombre	cucumber
la salade	lettuce, *but*
la salade de tomates	tomato salad
les viandes	*meats*
le bœuf	beef
le steak	steak
le veau	veal
l'agneau (m.)	lamb
le porc	pork
le cheval	horsemeat
la volaille	poultry
le poulet	chicken
le jambon	ham
le pâté	pâté
le poisson	fish

Practise what you have learnt

1 On the tape you will hear a conversation in **un bureau de tabac** (a tobacconist's shop). Listen carefully and then answer the following questions in English. (Answers p. 104.)

a. Which English newspaper(s) does the shop stock? ....

b. How many post-cards does the shopper buy? ....

c. Where is he sending them? ....

d. How many letters is he posting? ....

e. Where are the letters going? ....

f. How much is the total bill? ....

2 The conversation below takes place in a baker's shop (**une boulangerie**). Put the words in each sentence in the right order and then listen to the correct version on the tape.

le boulanger baker (man)
la boucherie butcher's shop

Boulanger   désirez   vous   qu'est-ce que? ....
Cliente   voudrais   croissants   s'il vous plaît   je   quatre

....

Boulanger   croissants   quatre ....
Cliente   baguette   voudrais   je   et   s'il vous plaît   une

....

Boulanger   voilà   tout   c'est? ....
Cliente   tout   c'est ....
Boulanger   soixante   francs   ça   Madame   sept   fait

....

Cliente   voilà   boucherie   s'il vous plaît   aller   pour   la   et   à?

....

Boulanger   nous   face   est   en   de   boucherie   la

....

Cliente   au   merci   revoir ....

3 Listen to the tape where you will hear Yves shopping for a picnic. As he is in a hurry, he buys everything at the same shop. Put a tick in the box if he buys the goods shown in the pictures below, and fill in the amount of the final bill. (Answer p. 104.)

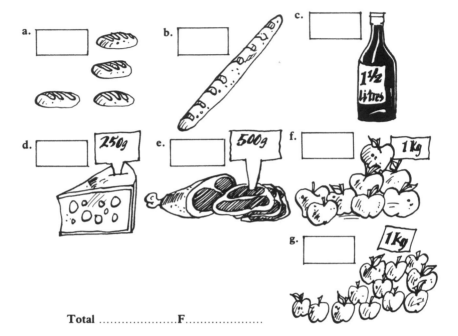

Total ....F....................

Grammar

Je voudrais

Je voudrais is a most useful expression. It can be translated by 'I'd like', 'I would like' or 'I should like'. It can be followed by the infinitive of a verb (see glossary p. 221.)

je voudrais parler I should like to speak
je voudrais manger des escargots I'd like to eat snails
or by a noun
je voudrais une glace I'd like an ice-cream
je voudrais une voiture I would like a car

Study these useful verbs. (The best way to learn them is to recite them aloud.)

pouvoir to be able

je peux I can	**nous pouvons** we can
tu peux you can	**vous pouvez** you can
il/elle peut he/she/it can	**ils/elles peuvent** they can

je ne peux pas sortir ce soir I can't come out this evening
où peut-on changer des chèques de voyage? where can one change travellers' cheques?
Note when you ask a question you must say **puis-je?** (can I? may I?) e.g.
puis-je venir avec vous? may I come with you?

savoir to know (a fact)/to know how to

je sais I know	**nous savons** we know
tu sais you know	**vous savez** you know
il/elle sait he/she knows	**ils/elles savent** they know

je sais que vous aimez le vin I know that you like wine
elle sait faire le café she knows how to make coffee

connaître to know (a person or place)

je connais	**nous connaissons**
tu connais	**vous connaissez**
il/elle connaît	**ils/elles connaissent**

je connais Marseille I know Marseilles
Lloyd George connaît mon père Lloyd George knows my father
reconnaître (to recognize) follows exactly the same pattern.

Adjectives

Look at the following adjectives which all occurred in the dialogues. **anglais** (English) **fort** (strong) **petit** (small) **blanc** (white) **ordinaire** (ordinary) **mûr** (ripe) **gros** (big, fat) **noir** (black).

Adjectives describe nouns (big, small, white, strong etc.) and in French they also 'agree' with nouns, that is they have a different form in the masculine, feminine, singular, plural e.g. **un chien noir** (a black dog), **une maison noire** (a black house), **des taxis noirs** (some black taxis), **des voitures noires** (some black cars).

As a general rule, French adjectives add an **-e** in the feminine and an **-s** in the plural e.g. singular **petit** (masc) **petite** (fem)
plural **petits** **petites**
Adding an **-e** often changes the pronunciation (as with **petit, petite**) but not always e.g. **mûr, mûre; noir, noire.** The final **-s** is not usually pronounced.

Some adjectives are irregular, so you will have to learn them when you meet them e.g. **gros** (masc), **grosse** (fem); **blanc** (masc), **blanche** (fem).

Most adjectives *follow* the noun in French e.g. **du vin blanc** (white wine); **un journal anglais** (an English newspaper) but some of the most common e.g. **grand** and **petit** come in front e.g. **une grande boîte** (a big box); **un petit sac** (a small bag).

Read and understand

Le bureau de tabac the tobacconist's

Les 'tabacs' se trouvent souvent dans un café ou un bar: alors il y
a devant l'entrée l'enseigne CAFÉ-TABAC ou BAR-TABAC, avec
le grand cigare rouge qui est l'emblème des bureaux de tabac.
    Dans les bureaux de tabac, on peut acheter, bien sûr, des
cigares, des cigarettes, des pipes et des allumettes. Ils ont aussi des
cartes postales, des timbres, du chocolat et quelquefois des
journaux. Et si vous allez prendre le bus, achetez votre ticket à
l'avance dans un bureau de tabac.

acheter to buy
l'allumette (f.) match
à l'avance in advance
souvent often
l'entrée (f.) entrance

Can you answer the following questions? (Answers p. 104.)

1 In what premises do you often find a **bureau de tabac?**

....

2 What is the emblem of French tobacconists' shops?

....

3 Where will you see it?

....

4 What reading-matter is likely to be on sale there?

....

5 What other things can a non-smoker buy there?

....

Did you know?

Les magasins shops

The local **marché** (market) is likely to have the freshest and cheapest fruit, vegetables, meat, fish, cheeses and pâtés. For groceries, look for shops called **alimentation** (food), **épicerie** (grocer's), **supermarché** (supermarket) or **libre-service** (self-service). You will find bread in a **boulangerie** and cakes in a **pâtisserie**, which may or may not be part of the same shop. Picnic food such as ham, pâté etc can be bought in a **charcuterie** (delicatessen, pork butcher's). On the outskirts of larger towns look for **un hypermarché** (a hypermarket), where you can buy almost anything, usually at good value.

Post-offices

Post-offices are known as **postes, PTT (Postes-Télégraphes-Téléphones)** or **P et T (Postes et Télécommunications)**. They are open from 8 a.m.–7 p.m. on week-days and 8 a.m.–12 noon on Saturdays. Letter-boxes are yellow in France and Switzerland and red in Belgium. At the post-office, use the slot marked **étranger** (abroad) for your mail home.

Telephones

It is possible to make a telephone call from a public call-box, from the post-office or (more expensive) from a café or your hotel. Public telephone boxes take coins (the coins needed will be indicated on the slots). You pick up the receiver, put in your coins and wait for the dialling tone. Any unused coins will be returned to you when you hang up. The code for international calls from France is 19; wait for a second dialling tone, then dial 44 for the UK (to be found on Post-Office lists as **le Royaume-Uni**) or 353 for Eire or 1 for the USA. This should be followed by the area code number *without* the first zero (e.g. for Brighton dial 273 instead of 0273), and then the subscriber's number.

Most French telephone numbers have six digits, e.g. 24–46–51, which you read **vingt-quatre** (twenty-four), **quarante-six** (forty-six), **cinquante-et-un** (fifty-one). Numbers in the Paris area have seven figures, e.g. 854–00–15. For 0 say **zéro**.

To telephone from one department of France to another you have to dial 16 and then wait briefly for a second dialling tone before continuing with the number. If you call from a post-office, a telephonist will dial the number for you and then tell you which booth (**la cabine**) to go to. You pay when the call is finished.

Dial 12 for enquiries: this is not a free call.

Your turn to speak

Carolle is going to do the week-end shopping at the market (**le marché**).
She asks you what you would like to eat. Pierre will suggest what you say.
Pause the tape before replying as usual.
You will hear these new words and phrases:
rouge red
à tout à l'heure see you later

And finally   Test yourself on the verbs you learned in the *Grammar* section and on the
shopping vocabulary on p. 98. (Cover the French and see if you can
translate the English.) And remember to play through all the dialogues
again without the book.

Answers

Revision p. 91 le saucisson = salami, le lait = milk, le jambon = ham, le
fromage = cheese, les œufs = eggs, la glace = ice-cream.

Practise what you have learnt p. 99 Exercise **1** (**a**) the Daily Telegraph (**b**)
three (**c**) England (**d**) five (**e**) France (**f**) 21F 40.

p. 100 Exercise **3** (**b**), (**d**), (**f**), Total 26F 70.

Read and understand p. 102 (**1**) in a café or bar (**2**) a large red cigar (**3**)
in front of the entrance (**4**) newspapers (**5**) post-cards, stamps, chocolate
and bus-tickets.

8 Shopping – part 2

What you will learn

- asking for some common medicines
- explaining your ailments to the pharmacist
- buying clothes: getting the right size
- specifying the colour
- saying something is bigger/smaller etc.
- saying something is too big/too small etc.
- finding out about prices and special offers

Before you begin

When you are shopping you need to be able to specify precisely what you want, and also to be sure that you are getting the best value for your money. This unit will help you – and will also stand you in good stead if you suffer from any of the usual holiday ailments and need the help of a chemist.

Study-tip When you are doing odd jobs around the house, tune your radio to a French station. You will probably not understand much of it to start with (except perhaps the English pop songs and adverts) but you will be listening to the rhythm and intonation of the language. As these become more familiar, you will find it easier to understand what people are saying in French, and to have less of a foreign accent yourself.

Remember these useful phrases for shopping:
je voudrais I'd like . . .
est-ce que vous avez . . .? do you have . . .?
c'est tout that's all
ça fait combien? how much is that?

Study guide

Dialogue 1: listen straight through without the book
Dialogue 1: listen, read and study
Dialogues 2, 3: listen straight through without the book
Dialogues 2, 3: listen, read and study one by one
Dialogues 4, 5: listen straight through without the book
Dialogues 4, 5: listen, read and study one by one
Learn the *Key words and phrases*
Do the exercises in *Practise what you have learnt*
Study *Grammar* and do the exercise
Read *Did you know?* and study the vocabulary
Do the tape exercises in *Your turn to speak*
Finally, listen to all the dialogues again without the book.

Dialogues

1 *Shopping at a chemist's*

Isabelle	Bon, j'aimerais quelque chose contre le mal de tête.
Pharmacien	Euh – en comprimés?
Isabelle	Oui, en comprimés.
Pharmacien	Vous avez mal – euh – comment?
Isabelle	Des migraines, enfin . . .
Pharmacien	Vous voulez de l'aspirine?
Isabelle	Oui.
Pharmacien	Vous n'avez pas de problème rénal?
Isabelle	Non, ça va.
Pharmacien	Voilà. Six francs, s'il vous plaît.
Isabelle	Oui, et puis aussi quelque chose pour après le soleil.
Pharmacien	. . . Une crème. Une huile?
Isabelle	(Une crème.) Une crème, oui.
Pharmacien	D'accord.
Isabelle	Et alors un médicament contre les diarrhées.
Pharmacien	Contre la diarrhée?
Isabelle	Oui.
Pharmacien	Vous avez mal au ventre?
Isabelle	Oui.
Pharmacien	Oui. En comprimés aussi?
Isabelle	Oui, en comprimés.
Pharmacien	En comprimés. 5F 10.
Isabelle	Voilà. C'est tout.

le comprimé tablet	**la crème** cream
la migraine migraine	**l'huile (f.)** oil
l'aspirine (f.) aspirin	♦ **le médicament** medicine
♦ **le soleil** sun	**la diarrhée** diarrhoea

2 *Buying socks for Pierre-Yves*

Nadine	Pour aller avec cette chemise, s'il vous plaît: bordeaux ou vert foncé . . . du beige, peut-être.
Pierre-Yves	C'est quoi?
Nadine	Ça c'est du fil, mais on n'a pas besoin de fil, hein?
Pierre-Yves	Hein?
Nadine	On va acheter des chaussettes, pas du fil. On enlève la chaussure?
Pierre-Yves	Non!
Nadine	Si, pour regarder les chaussettes, dis-donc.
Nadine	Bon, je vais prendre ça, alors; je prends les beiges.
Vendeuse	Mm.
Nadine	D'accord.

vert green	**le fil** thread
foncé dark	**regarder** to look at
beige beige	**la chaussette** sock
♦ **peut-être** perhaps	

1   **j'aimerais** I'd like. From the verb **aimer** (to like, to love). This is an alternative to **je voudrais.**

quelque chose contre le mal de tête something for (lit. against) headaches.

♦ **en comprimés** in tablets. The French make far more use than we do of **suppositoires** (suppositories) – so be careful what you swallow!

vous avez mal you have a pain, **comment?** lit. how? He is asking her to describe the pain.

enfin lit. at last, but used here like the meaningless but very common 'you know' in English.

vous n'avez pas de problème rénal? you haven't any kidney trouble?

♦ **ça va** that's all right. Often used familiarly as a question: **ça va?** (everything all right?), to which the answer is **ça va** (yes, fine).

♦ **vous avez mal au ventre?** do you have pain in your stomach? (lit. in *the* stomach?). You should learn **j'ai mal** (I have a pain). You may also need **j'ai mal au dos** (I have a backache), **j'ai mal aux dents** (I have toothache), **j'ai mal à l'oreille** (I have ear-ache), **j'ai mal à la gorge** (I have a sore throat), and **j'ai mal à la tête** (I have a headache).

2   **pour aller avec cette chemise** to go with this shirt. (For **cette**, see p. 115.)

bordeaux this is the colour burgundy, though Burgundy (the area and its wine) is actually Bourgogne.

♦ **on n'a pas besoin de fil** we don't need any thread. Learn **j'ai besoin de** (I need – lit. I have need of).

on va acheter des chaussettes, pas du fil we are going to buy socks, not thread. Children's socks are smarter in France than in Britain.

on enlève la chaussure let's take off your shoe.

dis-donc is a persuasive 'come on then'.

♦ **je vais prendre ça** I'll take that.

Some other useful clothes vocabulary is illustrated on p. 109.

Note that **le pantalon** is singular in French and means 'trousers' or 'pair of trousers'.

3 *Buying a sweater*

Nadine   Bonjour, Madame. J'aurais voulu un . . . un pull, s'il vous plaît.
Vendeuse   Qu'est-ce que vous faites comme taille?
Nadine   40 . . . 40/42, enfin ça dépend de la . . . de la coupe.
Vendeuse   Oui. Alors j'ai plusieurs modèles – euh – comme ça, marine avec une encolure blanche . . .
Nadine   Oui. Ça, ça va être trop petit pour moi.
Vendeuse   On a ça, en blanc avec des grosses côtes.
Nadine   Mm mm. C'est le pull de tennis, ça?
Vendeuse   Oui.
Nadine   D'accord. Je vais essayer.
Vendeuse   Oui.

Nadine   Je crois que c'est la bonne taille, oui . . . je peux essayer le bleu?
Vendeuse   Oui.
Nadine   Oui?

Nadine   Non, je crois que le . . . le bleu est plus grand, hein? Il est trop grand, là.
Vendeuse   Il est plus grand que le blanc, hein?
Nadine   Oui. Oui, c'est trop grand. Je crois que je . . . je préfère le blanc. Il vaut combien?
Vendeuse   220 francs.
Nadine   Je peux vous régler par chèque?
Vendeuse   Oui, bien sûr.
Nadine   D'accord.

     le pull (pullover) sweater
♦ **ça dépend (de)** that depends (on)
     la coupe cut
     le modèle style
     marine navy
     l'encolure (f.) neck (of a garment)
     blanche (f.) white
♦ **trop petit** too small
     le tennis tennis
     en blanc in white
     (le) bleu (the) blue (one)

3   **j'aurais voulu** means the same as **je voudrais**.

qu'est-ce que vous faites comme taille? what size are you? (lit. What do you make as size?) (See p. 117 for clothes sizes.)

ça va être trop petit pour moi that is going to be too small for me.

des grosses côtes with wide ribbing (the pattern in which it is knitted.)

▶ **je vais essayer** I'm going to try it on: **je peux essayer?** (may I try it on?).

je crois que I think that.

▶ **la bonne taille** the right size.

plus grand bigger (lit. more big), **trop grand** too big.

▶ **il est plus grand que le blanc** it is bigger than the white. See p. 115 for **plus . . . que**.

▶ **je préfère** I prefer. From **préférer** (to prefer).

il vaut combien? how much is it? (lit. it is worth how much?)

je peux vous régler par chèque? can I pay by cheque? (lit. settle with you?)

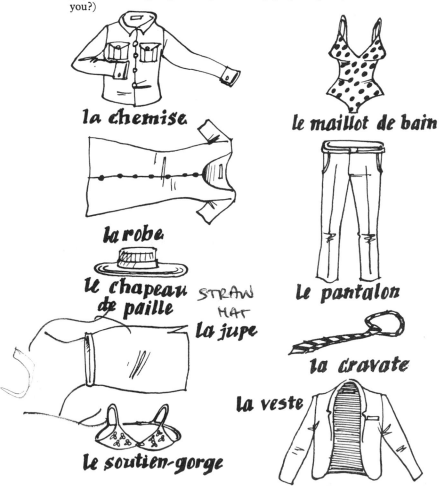

la chemise

le maillot de bain

la robe

le chapeau de paille   STRAW HAT

le pantalon

la jupe

la cravate

la veste

le soutien-gorge

4 *Shopping for flowers*

Fleuriste	Les roses? Alors vous avez les dix roses qui vous font quinze francs la botte.
Nadine	Oui. A la pièce c'est combien?
Fleuriste	La pièce, 3F 50.
Nadine	D'accord. Et autrement, qu'est-ce que vous avez comme fleurs en ce moment?
Fleuriste	En ce moment, alors, vous avez les chrysanthèmes, qui sont les fleurs de saison, à dix francs la botte.
Nadine	Oui – combien dans une botte?
Fleuriste	Euh – alors, ça dépend – environ – euh – dix fleurs.
Nadine	D'accord.

la fleuriste florist
la rose rose
la botte bunch
autrement otherwise
la fleur flower
le chrysanthème chrysanthemum
♦ **de saison** in season
environ about, approximately

5 *Buying fruit-juice on special offer*

Vendeuse	J'ai des promotions en ce moment. Vous avez dix pour cent sur les vins – euh – et les jus de fruits.
Simone	Vous avez – euh – jus d'orange?
Vendeuse	Jus d'orange, oui.
Simone	Oui. Un jus d'orange et un jus de . . .
Vendeuse	Pamplemousse, ananas . . .
Simone	Euh – ananas.

♦ **le jus de fruit** fruit-juice
♦ **le pamplemousse** grapefruit
l'ananas(m.) pineapple

4   **qui vous font quinze francs la botte** which cost you fifteen francs the bunch. Here the verb **faire** is used to mean 'to make' i.e. 'to cost'.

à la pièce separately

♦ **la pièce** each

qu'est-ce que vous avez comme fleurs? what have you got in the way of flowers? Remember this useful construction which you learnt in Unit 3.

combien dans une botte? how many in a bunch?

5   **j'ai des promotions en ce moment** I have some special offers at the moment (lit. at *this* moment – for **ce**, see p. 115.)

vous avez dix pour cent sur les vins you have 10% off wines (lit. *on* wines).

ananas pineapple, the final 's' can be pronounced or not, as you prefer.

soldes sale
entrée libre free to come in and look around

Key words and phrases

j'ai mal . . .	I have a pain . . .
à la tête	in my head (i.e. a headache)
à la gorge	in my throat (a sore throat)
au ventre	in my stomach (a stomach-ache)
je voudrais un médicament . . .	I'd like some medicine . . .
quelque chose . . .	something . . .
contre le soleil	for (lit. against) the sun
en comprimés	in tablet form
j'ai besoin d' . . .	I need . . .
un pull	a jumper
une chemise	a shirt
un maillot de bain	a swimming costume
plus grand(e) que ça	bigger than that
petit(e)	smaller
je peux essayer?	may I try it on?
(il/elle est) trop grand(e)	(it's) too big
petit(e)	small
peut-être	perhaps
c'est la bonne taille	it's the right size
je vais prendre ça	I'll take that
qu'est-ce que vous avez comme (vins)?	what have you got in the way of (wines)?
je préfère . . .	I prefer . . .
le jus de fruit	fruit juice
le pamplemousse	grapefruit
les fleurs/fruits de saison	flowers/fruit in season
c'est combien la pièce?	how much are they each?
ça dépend	that depends
ça va? ça va	how are things? fine

Practise what you have learnt

1 Beneath each of the pictures below, write the letter of the sentence which applies to it. You won't need your tape recorder. (Answers p. 118.)

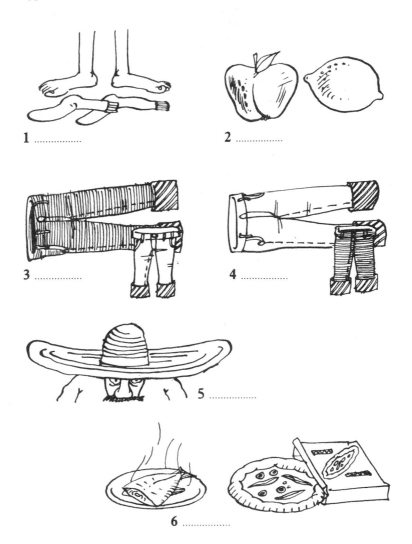

a. Le bleu est plus grand que le blanc.
b. C'est trop grand pour moi.
c. On enlève les chaussettes.
d. Le bleu est plus petit que le blanc.
e. Le poisson est plus chaud que la pizza.
f. La pomme est plus sucrée que le citron.

2 On the tape you will hear Yves shopping. Listen to the conversation as many times as you like and then answer the questions below, in English. (Answers p. 118.)

a. What does Yves want to buy?

....

b. What does he think his size is?

....

c. What shade of blue does he ask for?

....

d. How many styles does the saleswoman offer him to start with?

....

e. What is wrong with the first garment he tries on?

....

f. What is wrong with the next one?

....

g. How much is the one he buys?

....

3 Listen to another conversation in a chemist's shop on the tape and then answer the following questions. New word **une grippe** ('flu). (Answers p. 118.)

1. Carolle a mal seulement à la tête? oui ☐
non ☐

2. Elle voudrait un médicament (a) en suppositoires? ☐
(b) une comprimés? ☐

3. Elle a la diarrhée? oui ☐
non ☐

4. Contre le soleil, elle préfère (a) une crème? ☐
(b) une huile? ☐

5. Le pharmacien n'a pas de crème. vrai ☐
faux ☐

6. Carolle achète de l'huile? oui ☐
non ☐

7. Combien vaut le médicament? 23F ☐
26F ☐
25F ☐

Grammar

Ce, (cet), cette, ces

j'ai des promotions en ce moment   pour aller avec cette chemise

Ce, cet and cette all mean 'this' or 'that'.

Ce is used with most masculine nouns e.g. ce pull (this jumper), ce médicament (this medicine). If the noun begins with a vowel or an 'h' which is not pronounced, you use cet e.g. cet enfant (this child), cet homme (this man).

In front of feminine nouns the word is always cette, (which sounds the same as cet) e.g. cette pomme (this apple), cette orange (this orange).

Ces is the plural i.e. 'these', whether the noun is masculine or feminine e.g. ces médicaments (these medicines), ces pommes (these apples).

Exercise (Answers p. 118.)

Put ce, cet, cette or ces, as appropriate, in front of each of the following nouns and then translate the phrase.

1 ...Ce.... soleil ....

2 ..Ces... comprimés *tablets* ....

3 ..Ce.... chapeau ....

4 ..Cette taille *SIZE* ....

5 ..Cet... avion ....

6 ..Ce.... samedi ....

7 ....Ces.. citrons ....

8 ..Cette chemise ....

More ... than

With most adjectives you get over the idea that something is *more ... than* something else by using plus ... que, e.g.

Londres est plus grand que Paris London is bigger than Paris
Jean est plus âgé que Pierre Jean is older than Pierre.

Just as in English we say *better* (not 'gooder'), the French also use a different word, so bon and bonne (good) become meilleur and meilleure (better) e.g.

votre anglais est meilleur que mon français your English is better than my French

la viande est meilleure que le poisson ici the meat is better than the fish here

Note that you pronounce the -ll in meilleur like the 'y' in 'yacht'.

Read and understand

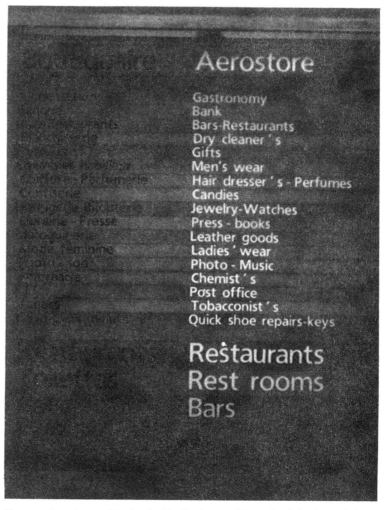

You are shopping at Charles de Gaulle airport. For each of the items below, write down the French name of the shop that you need to look for:

1 Un journal ....

2 Des cigarettes ....

3 Du chocolat ....

4 Une robe ....

5 De l'eau de cologne ....

6 Quelque chose à boire ....

7 Une cassette ....

8 Des timbres ....

Did you know?

Clothes

French clothes are renowned for their quality and style and should you feel tempted into buying, here are some equivalent sizes:

	Men's clothes								
GB	34	36	38	40	42	44	46	48	50
France	44	46	48	50	52	54	56	58	60

	Men's shirts						
GB	14	14½	15	15½	16	16½	17
France	36	37	38	39	40	41	42

	Women's clothes								
GB	8	10	12	14	16	18	20	22	24
France	34	36	38	40	42	44	46/48	50	52

	Shoes												
GB	1	2	2½	3	4	5	6	7	7½	8	9	9½	10½
France	33	34	35	36	37	38	39	40	41	42	43	44	45

You may find the following extra vocabulary useful:

Vêtements	*Clothes*
un collant	a pair of tights
des bas	stockings
un jupon	a petticoat
un foulard	a scarf
un manteau	a coat
un short	a pair of shorts
un slip	a pair of underpants

Note that **un short** is singular in French, like **un pantalon** (see p. 107).

Couleurs	*Colours*
jaune	yellow
orange	orange
marron	brown
rose	pink
vert(e)	green
gris(e)	grey

The chemist's

You will recognize the chemist's, **la pharmacie**, by the green neon cross sign outside. The **pharmacien** (pharmacist) is fully trained and will be able to advise you on minor ailments. A French **pharmacie** sells medicines and medicated beauty products only. For films and development you have to go to a photographic shop usually called simply **photo**, and for perfumes and cosmetics you should go to a **parfumerie**.

Your turn to speak

1 You are in a flower shop. On the tape Pierre will suggest what you should say to the florist. You now know three ways of asking questions:
est-ce que vous avez . . . ?
avez-vous . . . ?
and **vous avez . . . ?**
We recommend using the third form in this section as it is the simplest and quite correct.

2 You are at a chemist's. Pierre will prompt you again. The chemist will tell you how many tablets to take per day:
il faut prendre quatre comprimés par jour
il faut prendre sept ou huit pastilles par jour

And finally Make sure you have completed all the steps in the *Study guide* and finish off the unit by listening once again to all the dialogues. Only use the book to check up on anything that you have forgotten.

Answers

Practise what you have learnt p. 113 Exercise **1** 1c, 2f, 3a, 4d, 5b, 6e.

p. 113 Exercise **2** (**a**) a shirt (**b**) 41 (**c**) not too dark (**d**) three (**e**) it is too big (**f**) it is too dark (**g**) 240 francs

p. 114 Exercise **3** (**1**) non (**2**) b (**3**) non (**4**) a (**5**) vrai (**6**) non (**7**) 25F

Grammar p. 115 (**1**) ce soleil, this sun (**2**) ces comprimés, these tablets (**3**) ce chapeau, this hat (**4**) cette taille, this size (**5**) cet avion, this plane (**6**) ce samedi, this Saturday (**7**) ces citrons, these lemons (**8**) cette chemise, this shirt.

Read and understand p. 116 (**1**) (Librairie-)Presse (**2**) Tabacs (**3**) Confiserie (**4**) Mode féminine (**5**) (Coiffure-)Parfumerie (**6**) Bar (**7**) (Photo-)Son (**8**) PTT.

9 Making travel arrangements

What you will learn

- understanding travel information (means of transport, times, platforms, airports)
- understanding questions about your travel requirements
- asking for single and return tickets
- specifying your travel requirements
- reserving seats and couchettes
- asking for petrol and getting your oil and tyres checked
- some useful information about driving and public transport in France

Before you begin

If you can, make your own travel arrangements, as you will have far more independence and flexibility on your holiday. It is also so much easier if you have to change your plans because of illness or harbour strikes. Travel arrangements necessarily involve times and dates, so you may find it helpful to revise Unit 6 before going on with this unit.

Also, do you remember these verbs of movement which have occured over several units?

partir	to leave
arriver	to arrive
rentrer	to go back
sortir	to go out
se rendre à	to get to (a place)
aller	to go

Study guide

	Dialogues 1, 2: listen straight through without the book
	Dialogues 1, 2: listen, read and study one by one
	Dialogues 3–5: listen straight through without the book
	Dialogues 3–5: listen, read and study one by one
	Dialogues 6, 7: listen straight through without the book
	Dialogues 6, 7: listen, read and study one by one
	Learn the *Key words and phrases*
	Do the exercises in *Practise what you have learnt*
	Study *Grammar* and do the exercise
	Study *Read and understand* and do the exercise
	Read *Did you know?* and note the vocabulary
	Do the tape exercise in *Your turn to speak*
	Finally, listen to all the dialogues again

Dialogues

1 *Booking a flight*

Employée	Vous voulez partir quel jour?
Jeanne	Lundi prochain.
Employée	Le 15 septembre, alors.
Jeanne	C'est ça.
Employée	Euh – c'est un billet aller et retour ou aller simple?
Jeanne	Aller simple.
Employée	D'accord. Euh – vous voyagez en quelle classe?
Jeanne	Oh – deuxième, hein.
Employée	En classe économique. Et vous voulez partir au départ de Roissy ou au départ d'Orly?
Jeanne	Roissy c'est Charles de Gaulle, c'est ça?
Employée	C'est cela même.
Jeanne	Oh, Charles de Gaulle, oui.
Employée	Charles de Gaulle. Vous voulez partir le matin ou l'après-midi?
Jeanne	Vers midi.
Employée	Il y a un vol qui part à midi de Roissy et qui arrive à 11h 55 à Londres. C'est un vol sur British Caledonian. Ça irait?
Jeanne	Oh, c'est très bien, oui.

◧ **prochain** next
  le billet ticket
◧ **(un) aller simple** (one) single
  vous voyagez (from **voyager**) you travel
  la classe économique economy class
  Orly Orly International Airport, Paris

2 *Means of transport*

Michel	Et Bayeux, est-ce facile d'y aller?
Employée	Oui, pas de problème – vous avez des trains et des bus. Les trains sont plus pratiques, hein, beaucoup plus rapides – et moins chers. En France le train est moins cher que le bus.

  y there
  chers (m. pl.)
◧ **cher** (m. sing.) dear, expensive
  chère (f. sing.)
  chères (f. pl.)

1   **vous voulez partir quel jour?** which day do you want to leave?

♦ **un billet aller et retour** we call it a return ticket; the French more logically say 'a go and return ticket'.

partir au départ de Roissy to leave by departure from Roissy.

Roissy c'est Charles de Gaulle the ultra-modern Charles de Gaulle airport is situated near the village of Roissy. (See photo opposite.)

c'est cela même that's it exactly. **Même** can also mean 'same' e.g. **la même chose** (the same thing).

ça irait? would that do?

Note that there is one hour's difference between French and British time which explains the midday departure and 11.55 arrival.

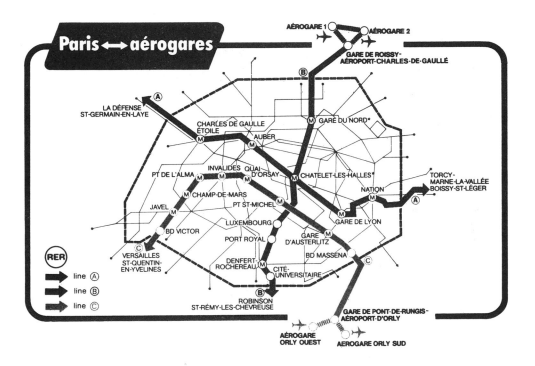

2   **est-ce facile d'y aller?** is it easy to go there? **Est-ce** is **c'est** inverted to make clear that it is a question.

♦ **pas de problème** no problem. This is a very common expression and is used when you would say 'don't worry' in English.

♦ **moins . . . que** less . . . than, used in the same way as **plus . . . que** (more than) which you learned in Unit 8.

3 *Buying a train ticket*

Robert   Alors, pour moi un aller Soulac pour demain.
Employé   Souillac?
Robert   Soulac. Soulac en Gironde.
Employé   *(looking up the fare)* Soulac, Soulac.
Robert   Il y a bien une gare.
Employé   Soulac-sur-Mer?
Robert   Oui – c'est ça.
Employé   Pas de réduction, Monsieur?
Robert   Pas de réduction, mais avec une réservation. On peut prendre une réservation jusqu'à Bordeaux?
Employé   Oui, alors ce sera au bureau Renseignements à côté.
Robert   Bien.

♦ **demain** tomorrow
♦ **la réservation** reservation (for a seat)

4 *To travel by day or by night*

Robert   Je voudrais les horaires pour aller à Nice, s'il vous plaît.
Employée   Oui – c'est pour quel jour, Monsieur?
Robert   Bien, je pars demain.
Employée   Il y a deux possibilités: ou vous voyagez de jour avec le changement à Bordeaux ou vous avez un train direct de nuit.
Robert   S'il y a un train direct c'est plus intéressant.
Employée   Alors vous pouvez donc voyager en couchette – le prix est de 48 francs.
Robert   Ce n'est pas cher une couchette, en plus.

     je pars (from **partir**) I leave
     la possibilité possibility
     le changement change
♦ **le prix** price
     en plus moreover, as well

3   un aller Soulac a single (for) Soulac. **Un aller** is the same as **un aller simple**.

il y a **bien** une gare there *is* a station.

pas de réduction? no reduction? Many French people have a right to reduced fares on account of disability or military service.

ce sera au bureau Renseignements à côté that will be at the Information office alongside. Information offices are labelled
♦ **Renseignements** or **Informations**.

SUD-EST

							Station							
6 41	7 17	12 08	13 11	14 29	17 00	19 36	PARIS-Gare de Lyon •	10 00	11 56	13 23	17 00	a18 52	21 32	23 02
8 54	10 00	14 18	15 31	16 51	19 25	21 45		7 48	9 41	10 54	14 48	15 58	18 48	20 28
10 06	11 32	...	16 52	17 58	20 37	22 37	BESANÇON •	6 58	8 22	9 42	13 09	14 35	17 48	19 04

							Station	26	21	23	24	22		
...	7 52	9 58	13 11	14 29	16 48	...	PARIS-Gare de Lyon •	c 6 12	6 33	6 30	7 45	8 22	8 25	8 28
10 09	10 12	12 20	15 31	16 51	19 08	19 20	DIJON •		3 18		4 21	5 21	5 24	
11 44	11 50	13 58	17 05	18 39		20 55	LYON-Perrache •	1 06	1 20					
12 43	12 47	14 58	18 00	19 38	21 38	21 55	VALENCE •	23 59	0 07					
13 45	13 48	15 59	18 59	20 39	22 42	23 08	AVIGNON •	22 48	23 01		23 59			
14 53	14 53	17 09	20 00	21 48	23 51	0 17	MARSEILLE •	21 38	21 49		22 35		23 53	
b15 40	b15 40	17 59	20 48	22 37	1 28	1 28	TOULON •	20 37	20 44	21 48			22 58	23 16
b17 30	b17 30	19 57	22 27	0 18	...	...	NICE •	18 40	18 17	19 55		21 15	20 45	21 20

21		22		23	24	25	Station							
20 42	20 48	21 48	21 49	22 17	22 30	c22 57	PARIS-Gare de Lyon •	13 33	14 14	16 57	19 00	19 00	21 54	23 48
23 48					1 40	2 25	DIJON •	10 55		14 32	16 36	16 36	19 28	21 26
						4 11	LYON-Perrache •	9 12	10 21	12 55	14 59	14 59	17 53	19 56
			4 54			5 11	VALENCE •	8 12	9 25	11 46	13 50	13 59	16 53	18 57
			6 09		6 10	6 20	AVIGNON •	6 59	8 21	10 44	12 38	12 57	15 47	17 57
5 08			7 32	6 59	7 45	7 48	MARSEILLE •	5 47	7 06	9 31	11 30	11 48	14 42	16 57
6 14	5 58					8 41	TOULON •	4 28	5 44	8 40	10 28	10 56	13 49	16 03
8 23	8 00	7 55	9 35	9 10		10 30	NICE •	...	...	6 59	8 35	8 56	12 08	14 27

						TEE	Station		(A)					TEE
6 00	6 27	8 00	10 48	13 30	15 17	16 46	MARSEILLE •	6 45	7 43	8 44	9 23	11 39		13 44
6 45	7 19	8 41	11 31	14 15	16 04	17 24	TOULON •	5 44	6 52	7 59	8 40	10 56	12 17	12 59
8 39	9 26	10 30	13 30	16 10	18 00	19 02	NICE •			6 10	6 59	8 56	d10 15	11 25

							Station							
17 17	18 40	19 25	20 08	21 56	0 25	...	MARSEILLE •	16 49	19 05	20 18	21 41	22 15	23 26	0 26
17 59	19 45	20 07	20 48	22 37	1 28	...	TOULON •	16 03	18 20	19 32	20 44	21 32	22 39	23 41
19 57		22 18	22 27	0 18	...	...	NICE •	14 27	17 25	17 48	18 17	19 30	20 22	21 47

(A) *Sauf samedis, dimanches et fêtes*
(a) *Paris-Bercy*
(b) *Arrivée plus tardive certains jours*
(c) *Paris-Nord*
(d) *du 22 avril au 19 mai : départ 10 h 05.*

4 ♦ **ou ... ou ...** either ... or ...

de jour ... de nuit by day ... by night.

intéressant the basic meaning of the word is 'interesting', but it is also used, as here, to describe a proposition as 'attractive'. When it is applied to a price it means 'good value' or 'a bargain'.

♦ **en couchette** there are normally six couchettes to a compartment, each with clean bedding. They provide an economical alternative to the more luxurious sleepers known as **wagons-lits** or **voitures-lits**.

5 *Booking a couchette*

Robert Je prends le train demain soir pour Nice.
Employé Je peux vous faire votre billet et votre réservation couchette en même temps.
Robert Oh, mais c'est très bien.
Employé Une couchette de deuxième classe?
Robert Oui, oui, oui, en deuxième classe.
Employé Bien. Supérieure, inférieure – vous avez une préférence?
Robert Ah – je préfère être en haut.
Employé Vous préférez être en haut. Bien.
Robert Dans les couchettes ce sont des compartiments non fumeurs, j'espère?
Employé Toujours non fumeurs.
Robert Ah, c'est très bien.

◆ **la préférence** preference
◆ **le compartiment** compartment

non fumeurs no smoking
◆ **j'espère** (from **espérer**) I hope
◆ **toujours** always

6 *Tickets, platform numbers and train times*

Femme Un aller Nantes, s'il vous plaît.
Employé Oui, voilà; vingt-quatre, s'il vous plaît.
Femme C'est sur quel quai?
Employé Alors quai numéro deux, 12h 21.
Femme Est-ce que vous pouvez me dire les horaires pour revenir de Nantes ce soir?
Employé Ce soir, alors vous avez un départ à 17h 34.
Femme Oui, bon . . . Très bien.
Employé La Roche à 18h 30.
Femme Merci.
Employé Voilà. Bonsoir, Madame.
Femme Au revoir.

revenir to come back

7 *Buying petrol and checking oil and tyres*

Bernadette Bon, alors, vous me mettez le plein.
Pompiste Entendu, Madame . . . . Voilà.
Bernadette Est-ce que vous pouvez vérifier aussi le niveau de l'huile?
Pompiste Oui, bien sûr. Alors, ça c'est à l'arrière de la voiture.

Bernadette Et vous pouvez vérifier la pression des pneus?
Pompiste Sûrement. Cela ne vous dérange pas de vous mettre devant la pompe de gonflage? Merci.

le pompiste petrol-pump attendant
◆ **vérifier** check
le niveau level
l'arrière (f.) back

la pression pressure
le pneu tyre
sûrement surely, certainly
la pompe de gonflage air-pump

5 **je peux vous faire votre billet** I can do you your ticket.

en même temps at the same time. Usually you have to buy your ticket first and then go to a different counter (**le guichet des réservations**) to reserve a seat or couchette. If it is a direct train, however, you may be able to get both from the reservations desk.

supérieure, inférieure upper, lower. The adjectives are feminine (they end with an **-e**) because they refer to **une couchette**.

en haut on the top. Notice the pronunciation.

ce sont they are. This is the plural of **c'est**.

6 **un aller Nantes** a single (for) Nantes. Normally you would say **un aller pour Nantes** – remember a *return* ticket is **un aller et retour**.

♦ **quel quai?** which platform? She might equally well have asked **quelle voie?** (which track?). Like other adjectives, **quel . . . ?** (which . . . ? what . . . ?) has masculine (**quel?**), feminine (**quelle?**), and plural (**quels? quelles?**) forms, but they all sound exactly the same.

est-ce que vous pouvez me dire? can you tell me?

7 ♦ **vous me mettez le plein** fill her up for me (lit. you put me the full).

♦ **cela ne vous dérange pas . . . ?** would you mind . . . ? (lit. that doesn't bother you?). This is a polite formula, e.g. also:
ça ne vous dérange pas de payer maintenant? would you mind paying now?
ça ne vous dérange pas de bouger votre voiture? would you mind moving your car?

de vous mettre to put yourself. He means to put the car.

Key words and phrases

un billet aller et retour pour (Nice)	one return ticket to (Nice)
un aller simple pour (Bordeaux)	one single to (Bordeaux)
avec une réservation	with a reservation
(lundi) prochain	next (Monday)
demain	tomorrow
première classe	first class
deuxième classe	second class
en couchette	with a couchette
en haut	on the top
un compartiment (non) fumeurs	a (non-)smoking compartment
c'est moins cher que (l'avion)?	is it cheaper than (the plane)?
j'espère partir <u>ou</u> ce soir <u>ou</u> demain	I hope to leave *either* this evening *or* tomorrow
c'est quel prix?	what's the price?
c'est quel quai?	what platform is it?
vous me mettez le plein	fill her up
vous pouvez vérifier l'huile?	could you check the oil?
les pneus?	the tyres?
cela ne vous dérange pas?	would you mind? (if it's no bother)
pas de problème	no problem
toujours	always

Extra vocabulary

la sortie	exit
l'entrée (f.)	entrance
les bagages (NB plural in French)	luggage
la valise	suitcase
le sac	bag
la consigne	left-luggage
objets trouvés	lost property (lit. objects found)
Renseignements	Information (office)

Practise what you have learnt

1 Write out each of the sentences below underneath the appropriate picture. Then translate them into English. You will not need your tape recorder. (Answers p. 132.)

a. Cela ne vous dérange pas?
b. Il y a des toilettes ici?
c. On peut acheter quelque chose à boire ici?
d. Vous me mettez le plein, s'il vous plaît.
e. Vous avez des cartes de la France?
f. Vouz pouvez vérifier la pression des pneus?

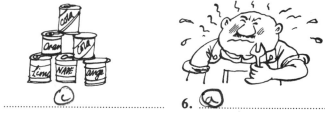

1. VOUS ME METTEZ LE PLEIN, SIL VOUS PLAIT

2. IL Y A DES TOILETTES ICI?

3. VOUZ POUVEZ VERIFIER LA PRE (f)

4. (e)

5. (c)

6. (a)

2 On the tape you will hear Carolle buying a train ticket. Listen to the conversation as many times as you like and see if you can answer the following questions. (Answers p. 132.)

a. Which day is she travelling? ....
b. Does she ask for a first or a second class ticket? ....
c. Does she buy a single or a return? ....
d. Is she a smoker? ....
e. At what time does the train leave La Roche-sur-Yon? ....
f. Where will she have to change trains? ....
g. At what time does the train reach Soulac-sur-Mer? ....
h. How much does the ticket cost? ....

3 Choose the correct sentence from the list below to complete the following dialogue. When you have filled in the spaces, listen to the tape where you will hear the whole conversation.

Mme Gerbier Bonjour, Monsieur. A quelle heure part le prochain train pour Toulouse?

Employé ....

Mme Gerbier C'est combien un aller simple pour Toulouse?

Employé ....

Mme Gerbier Il y a des couchettes?

Employé ....

Mme Gerbier C'est moins cher la couchette que le wagon-lit, j'espère?

Employé ....

Mme Gerbier C'est trop tard pour une réservation?

Employé ....

Mme Gerbier Alors, trois allers simples pour Toulouse, en couchette et en compartiment non fumeurs, s'il vous plaît.

Employé ....

Mme Gerbier Deux adultes et un enfant.

Employé ....

Mme Gerbier Voilà Monsieur. C'est quel quai?

Employé ....

Alors, c'est moins cher pour l'enfant; ca fait 519F.
Oui, c'est un train de nuit, il y a des couchettes et des wagons-lits.
Non, vous êtes combien?
A 20h 30, Madame.
Bien, pas de problème, trois adultes?
Oui, c'est moins cher . . . la couchette c'est 48F.
Quai numéro 12. Merci Madame.
173F train direct, deuxième classe.

Grammar

Your and our

Votre is the word for 'your' for one item belonging to a person you call **vous**, e.g. **votre chambre** (your room), **votre père** (your father).

Vos is used for 'your' when the person has more than one of the items, e.g. **vos chambres** (your rooms), **vos parents** (your parents).

The words for 'our' are very similar. **Notre** is used if there is only one item, as in **notre village** (our village), **notre mère** (our mother).

Nos is used when there is more than one item, e.g. **nos passeports** (our passports), **nos enfants** (our children).

Exercise Insert **votre** or **vos** as appropriate in each of the gaps below. (Answers on p. 132.)

1 VOTRE anniversaire est le 14 juillet.
2 Vous faites ..VOS. exercices.
3 Est-ce que VOTRE mari est là?
4 VOS. fleurs sont très belles.
5 ...VOS bagages sont dans VOTRE chambre.

Two verbs together

Such verbs as **espérer, pouvoir, préférer, aimer** and **savoir** are often followed by another verb. *If you have two verbs together like this the second one must always be in the infinitive e.g.*

j'espère venir demain I hope to come tomorrow

pouvez-vous vérifier le niveau de l'huile? can you check the level of the oil?

je préfère toujours **voyager** par le train I always prefer travelling by train

je sais parler français I know how to (i.e. I can) speak French

est-ce que **vous aimez apprendre** le français? do you like learning French?

Dire

Here is the present tense of another useful, slightly irregular verb: **dire** (to say, to tell).

je dis   **nous disons**
tu dis   **vous dites**
il/elle dit **ils/elles disent**
Note: **dites-moi** (tell me).

Partir

And another useful but slightly irregular verb is **partir** (to leave). You have already met some parts of the present tense in Unit 6; here is the full present tense.

je pars   **nous partons**
tu pars   **vous partez**
il/elle part **ils/elles partent**

Read and understand

The following is taken from a French Railways (SNCF) brochure about sleeping compartments. It contains some words that you do not know, but with the help of the vocabulary at the bottom you should be able to understand the general gist well enough to answer the questions below.

Il y a des gens qui voyagent de jour. D'autres préfèrent partir de nuit et profiter de leur voyage pour dormir et gagner ainsi du temps. Ces personnes réservent un lit dans une voiture-lit TEN (Trans Euro Nuit). Les voitures-lits TEN circulent sur beaucoup des grandes lignes en France et à l'étranger. C'est comme à l'hôtel: vous allez trouver un lit confortable avec de vrais draps, des couvertures et un oreiller. Il y a de l'eau chaude et froide, du savon, des serviettes de toilette et une prise de courant pour le rasoir. Vous êtes comme chez vous!

Il y a cinq types de compartiment:
Avec un billet de 1ère classe:
1 Le très grand confort d'une vraie chambre individuelle.
2 Une petite cabine pour une personne.
3 Un confort de 1ère classe dans une cabine à deux lits.

Avec un billet de 2ème classe:
4 Avec deux lits – la solution économique pour un voyage à deux.
5 Cabine avec 3 lits pour des voyageurs du même sexe ou pour une famille. C'est la solution la moins chère.

gagner to gain	**l'eau (f.)** water
à l'étranger abroad	**le savon** soap
le drap sheet	**la serviette de toilette** hand towel
la couverture blanket	**la prise de courant** power point
l'oreiller (m.) pillow	**le rasoir** razor

1 What is the advantage of travelling by night?
....

2 What is the best way of travelling by night, according to this brochure?
....

3 Do you find TEN carriages outside France?
....

4 Which of the following will you find in your compartment – sheets, soap, a toilet, a razor, hand towels?
....

5 Can you get a one-bedded compartment if you have a second-class ticket?
....

6 Which type of sleeping compartment is cheapest per person?
....

Did you know?

En voiture   If you intend to travel through France by car, you should buy some good maps. You can buy them in book-shops (**librairies**) or very often in petrol stations (**stations-service**). Michelin maps are probably the best known: the red ones cover the whole or half of France and the 84 yellow ones each cover a different area of the country. When buying petrol the word to use is **essence** (NOT **pétrole** which is paraffin); it will be assumed that you want **normale** (3-star) unless you specify **super**.

It is compulsory to wear seat-belts in France, Belgium and Switzerland. You should also display a nationality plate at the rear of your vehicle.

Roads in France are classified as **nationales** (main roads) or **départementales** (minor roads). You will know which is which because there is always an N or a D before a road number (e.g. N27, D44). This is like the British system of A and B roads. There are many motorways (**autoroutes**) in France but you have to pay for most of them. You usually pick up a computer card at the entrance and then pay at your chosen exit (**sortie**), at a **péage** (toll). On some motorways, if you have the right change (**la monnaie**) you simply throw the necessary coins into a wire basket. If you have no change you drive through a separate channel. Useful multi-lingual lists of motoring vocabulary are available from the AA (*The Car Components Guide*) and the RAC (*The Motorist's Interpreter*).

Par avion   Air Inter, the French internal airline can fly you between the main cities.

Par le train   **La gare SNCF** is the railway station, not to be confused with **la gare routière** (the bus station). French trains are generally comfortable and very punctual but crowded, so if you are travelling any distance you would be well advised to book a seat – this is not expensive. If you will be travelling a great distance by train, you will probably find the **France Vacances** rail rover ticket saves you money. Details from French Railways, 179 Piccadilly, London W1V 0AL. (Tel. 01–493–9731). You should also note that children aged eleven upwards are charged the full adult rate.

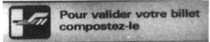 To validate your ticket, punch it.

Your ticket, although paid for, is not valid (**en règle**) until you have had it punched by the machine (an orange-red pillar) at the entrance to the platform. Do not do this until just before you travel.

la grande ligne (main line)
la banlieue (suburb)

Par le metro   You need **un billet** to travel by train but **un ticket** to travel by tube or bus. In Paris the same tickets are valid for both. You buy them in advance at a **métro** station, a bus station, a bar or a **tabac**. (See also p. 102.)

Taxi!   If you need a taxi, look for the blue and white sign **station de taxis** or telephone for a **radio-taxi**.

Your turn to speak

You want to book couchettes on the train to Biarritz. Follow Pierre's prompts on the tape. You will need the word **un adulte** (an adult).

And finally As usual, play through all the dialogues again, this time noting down in English as many of the travel details as you can. (You will probably have to keep stopping the tape in order to do this.)

Revision

Now turn to p. 216 and complete the revision section on Units 7–9. On the cassette the revision section follows straight after this unit.

Answers

Practise what you have learnt p. 127 Exercise 1 (1) **d** Fill her up, please; (2) **b** Are there any toilets here? (3) **f** Can you check the tyre pressure? (4) **e** Do you have any maps of France? (5) **c** Can we buy anything to drink here? (6) **a** If it's not too much bother?

p. 127 Exercise 2 (a) next Friday (b) second (c) return (d) no (e) 10.09 (f) Bordeaux (g) 15.19 (h) 151 francs.

Grammar p. 129 (1) votre (2) vos (3) votre (4) vos (5) vos . . . votre.

Read and understand p. 130 (1) you sleep and gain time (2) in a TEN sleeper (3) yes (4) sheets, soap and hand towels (5) no (6) type 5.

10 Food and drink

What you will learn

- understanding some of the items on a menu
- ordering food and drinks
- understanding and answering the waiter's questions
- the difference between a **menu** and a **carte**
- something about French eating habits and eating places

Before you begin

At the end of this unit, you will have acquired the necessary language for coping with all the basic tourist situations. As well as learning how to order a meal, this unit also includes 'talking about food' because the French do so much of it! They take food far more seriously than we do, with superb results. Restaurant meals are generally much better value in France than in Britain – more about this in *Did you know?*. A word of advice about French menus: they tend to use unnecessarily complicated vocabulary just as we do in English – compare 'fresh fillet of cod in breadcrumbs with French fried potatoes' and 'fish and chips'. So don't be shy about asking the waiter **Qu'est-ce que c'est?**, **C'est du poisson?** or **C'est quelle viande?**

Try to write down all the food and drink vocabulary you have learnt. (See Units 3 and 7 if you're stuck.) Do you remember these three useful phrases?

moi, je prends . . . c'est pour moi l'addition, s'il vous plaît

Study guide

Dialogue 1: listen straight through without the book
Dialogue 1: listen, read and study
Dialogues 2–4: listen straight through without the book
Dialogues 2–4: listen, read and study one by one
Learn the *Key words and phrases* and the extra vocabulary
Do the exercises in *Practise what you have learnt*
Study *Grammar* and do the exercise
Do *Read and understand*
Read *Did you know?*
Do the exercise in *Your turn to speak*
Listen to all the dialogues again and test yourself on the *Key words and phrases*.

Dialogues

1 *Ordering a meal from a fixed-price menu*

Sylviane Bon, alors menu à 28 francs: sardines à l'huile et au citron ou pâté de campagne. Ensuite, côte de porc grillée aux herbes avec pommes frites ou bien chipolatas grillées et pommes frites. Ensuite fromage ou dessert. Ah – il est bien celui-là.

Marc Oui.

Sylviane Bon, qu'est-ce que tu choisis, sardines à l'huile ou pâté de campagne?

Marc Moi je vais prendre un pâté.

Sylviane Alors pâté . . . euh . . . moi aussi, pâté de campagne, alors . . .

Serveuse Un pâté, une sardine, d'accord.

Marc Non, deux pâtés.

Serveuse Deux pâtés – pardon.

Sylviane Ensuite, moi je prendrai une côte de porc grillée aux herbes.

Marc Ah – moi aussi.

Sylviane Alors deux côtes de porc grillées.

Serveuse Deux côtes de porc.

Sylviane Mais bien grillées, hein?

Serveuse Bien grillées, bien sûr.

Sylviane Et ensuite nous verrons si on prend un fromage ou une glace?

Marc Moi je prendrai du fromage . . .

Serveuse (Du fromage.)

Marc . . . avec un verre de vin.

Serveuse Oui. Je vous ai donné la carte des vins.

Sylviane Euh . . . nous prendrons . . . un Saint-Estèphe?

Marc Ah oui.

Sylviane Allez – un Château Marbuzet, s'il vous plaît. 1976.

Marc Un '76.

Serveuse Il en reste un.

Sylviane Bon. Très bien. Merci.

Serveuse On s'occupe de vous tout de suite.

à l'huile et au citron with oil and lemon
le menu set menu
la sardine sardine
le pâté de campagne country pâté
 ♦ **ensuite** then
la côte de porc pork chop
grillée (f.) grilled
la chipolata chipolata
 ♦ **le dessert** dessert
tu choisis (from **choisir**) you choose
la carte des vins wine list
 ♦ **tout de suite** straightaway (pronounced **tout<u>e</u> suite**)

♦ **aux herbes** with herbs

♦ **avec pommes frites** with chips. **Pommes frites** is the accepted abbreviation of **pommes de terre frites** (fried potatoes), often shortened to **frites**. On signs you will often find the simpler **steack frites** (steak and chips).

celui-là that one, i.e. the menu.

pardon sorry. This is also the usual way to ask somebody to repeat something: **pardon?** (sorry? what did you say?).

je prendrai I'll have. This and the phrase which occurs later **nous prendrons** (we'll have) are both parts of the future tense of **prendre**. You will be learnimg how to express things in the future in Unit 14.

bien grillées well grilled. French people tend to eat their meat rarer than we do, so you may find this expression, along with **bien cuit** (well cooked, well done) very useful.

nous verrons we'll see. Another future, this time from the verb **voir**.

je vous ai donné I've given you. A past which you will learn in Unit 13.

Saint-Estèphe is the **appellation contrôlée**. Château Marbuzet is a good wine from that area. (See p. 95.)

allez 'come on' (lit. go). They are going to choose an expensive wine. This is the expression used by fans to cheer on a sports team e.g. **allez Toulouse!**

il en reste un there's one left (lit. there remains one of them). For **en** (of it, of them), see p. 143.

on s'occupe de vous we'll see to your order. The verb **s'occuper de** is heard a lot, e.g. **je m'occupe de vous** (I'll see to you, I'll look after you).

Le Menu

28 frs.

Sardines à l'huile et au citron
Pâté de campagne.

Côte de porc grillée aux herbes avec pommes frites
Chipolatas grillées et pommes frites
...

Fromage ~ Dessert

2 *Set menu or à la carte?*

Michel Il y a un bon petit restaurant par ici?

Christian Il faut aller dans le village d'à côté où il y a un petit restaurant pas cher qui donne à manger – euh – juste un menu surtout pour les gens qui passent et qui sont pressés.

Michel Un menu ou . . . on peut manger à la carte aussi?

Christian An non, non, non. Uniquement le menu, hein?

Michel Est-ce que les boissons sont comprises dans le menu?

Christian Les boissons sont comprises dans le prix du menu. Par contre quand – euh – on mange à la carte il faut payer les boissons en sus.

le village village
juste just
◗ **pressés (pl.)** in a hurry
uniquement only
la boisson drink
par contre on the other hand
payer to pay (for)
en sus extra, in addition

3 *Deciding on what to eat in a bar*

Bernadette Qu'est-ce que tu voudrais manger?

Barbara Qu'est-ce qu'il y a?

Bernadette Ils ont des croque-monsieur, sans doute des sandwichs au jambon . . . euh . . . saucisson, rillettes, fromage . . . Ils ont également des tartes maison, des omelettes . . .

Barbara Est-ce qu'il y a aussi des croque-madame?

Bernadette Alors des croque-madame avec un œuf, c'est cela?

Barbara Oui, c'est ça.

Bernadette Eh bien, je ne sais pas s'ils ont des croque-madame. On demandera – on verra bien.

Barbara Parce que s'il y en a, je veux bien essayer.

Bernadette (Un croque-dame.)

Barbara S'il n'y en a pas, je prends un croque-monsieur.

Bernadette Entendu.

sans doute doubtless, certainly
également as well
l'omelette (f.) omelet

2 ♦ **il y a un bon petit restaurant par ici?** is there a good little restaurant round here? This is a very useful phrase e.g.
il y a une banque par ici?
il y a un hôtel par ici?
il y a une boulangerie par ici?

♦ **pas cher** not expensive

donne à manger provides food.

les gens qui passent people who drop in. From **passer** (to pass).

♦ **un menu . . . à la carte** **Un menu** is a fixed-price menu for a set meal, usually at least three courses. If you wish to eat **à la carte** and have more choice you must ask for **la carte** rather than **le menu.**

est-ce que les boissons sont comprises? are the drinks included?
♦ You will need to know **service compris** (service included).

3 **des tartes maison** home-made tarts. Note that **vin de la maison** means 'house wine'.

des croque-madame are **croque-monsieur** (see p. 39) with an egg. Notice that these two words are irregular in the plural – they do not add an **-s.**

c'est ça (that's right) which you have now met several times, is the abbreviated form of **c'est cela.**

s'ils ont if they have. Before a vowel **si** (if) becomes **s'.**

on demandera – on verra bien we'll ask – we'll see. Here are more examples of the future tense.

♦ **s'il y en a** if there are any. **En** (any) goes in front of the verb (here **a**).

♦ **je veux bien essayer** I'd like to try. **Je veux** (I want) is, on its own, rather rude, so the **bien** modifies it to something with the impact of 'I would like'. If you are offered food and wish to accept, **je veux bien** is the phrase to use: **vous voulez de la salade? oui, je veux bien.** Similarly, if someone asks you if you would like to do something: **vous voulez boire quelque chose? oui, je veux bien.**

s'il n'y en a pas if there aren't any. Like many people, Barbara swallows some of her syllables, so that what she says sounds more like **s'y en a pas.**

4 *What did you have for lunch?*

Michèle   Et qu'est-ce que tu as mangé à midi?

Jean-Claude   Des radis, un bifteck et des choux-fleurs. Et comme dessert, une pomme.

Michèle   Moi j'ai mangé un sandwich en un quart d'heure avec des Coca-Cola.

Jean-Claude   Quoi?

Michèle   Sandwich-Coca Cola en un quart d'heure, tellement j'étais pressée.

le radis radish

4

qu'est-ce que tu as mangé? what did you eat? (lit. what have you eaten?).

◗ **un bifteck** is from the English 'beefsteak'.

des choux-fleurs cauliflowers. The more usual expression is **du chou-fleur** (cauliflower) i.e. in the singular as in English.

j'ai mangé I ate (lit. I have eaten).

quoi? what? He is astonished that she has eaten so little because lunch is usually a very substantial meal in France.

tellement j'étais pressée I was in such a hurry (lit. so much I was in a hurry). You will be learning **j'étais** (I was) in Unit 11.

Key words and phrases

il y a un bon petit restaurant	is there a good little restaurant
un hôtel	a hotel
par ici?	round here?
pas cher	not expensive
le menu (à 45 francs)	the set menu (at 45 francs)
la carte . . . s'il vous plaît	the à la carte menu . . . please
un bifteck	a steak
bien cuit	well cooked
avec des (pommes) frites	with chips
s'il y en a	if there are any/there is any
tout de suite, s'il vous plaît	straightaway, please
je suis pressé(e)	I'm in a hurry
ensuite (du fromage)	then (some cheese)
et comme dessert (une glace)	and for dessert (an ice-cream)
le service est compris?	is service included?
(*written on menus*) service compris	service included
(*as an answer*) je veux bien	(yes, please) I'd like some
	I'd like to
pardon/pardon?	sorry/sorry? (what did you say?)

Some more useful vocabulary

(*of meat*) saignant/à point	rare/medium
c'est garni?	is there anything with it?
l'eau minérale (f.)	mineral water
. . . gazeuse/non gazeuse	. . . fizzy/still
la carafe	carafe
l'assiette (f.)	plate
le couteau	knife
la fourchette	fork
la cuillère (also spelt cuiller)	spoon
le pain	bread
le sel	salt
le poivre	pepper
la moutarde	mustard
commander	to order (food)
le couvert	cover charge
bon appétit	enjoy your meal (lit. good appetite)

Practise what you have learnt

1 On the tape you will hear Jacques ordering a meal for three from the menu below in one of the **Bistros de la Gare** in Paris.

a. Tick on the menu the items he orders.

b. Does he want his beef rare? ☐
or medium? ☐

c. Does he order Bistro wine? ☐   Answers on p. 146.
Breton cider? ☐
or Pilsner lager? ☐

Le Bistro de la Gare

kir 4,80 frs   Menu 34,90 frs s.n.c.

La Bouillabaisse froide en gelée
Mousse chaude du bord de la mer
Soupe du jour
La terrine de légumes
La salade variée aux Pignons de Pins
(au choix)

Suggestion du jour: 37 frs s.n.c.
Suprême de volaille

Filet de Poisson frais du Bistro
Le steak au Poivre
Le Coeur d'Aloyau "sauce boeuf"
(au choix)
Les Pommes Allumettes fraîches
Le chou-fleur au gratin
Dessert ~ Fromage ~ Fruit

snc = service non compris service not included

la bouillabaisse froide en gelée cold fish soup in gelatine

mousse chaude au bord de la mer hot seafood mousse (lit. on the sea-shore)

variée (f.) mixed

aux pignons de pins with pine kernels

au choix choice

du jour of the day

suprême de volaille poultry supreme (with cream sauce)

filet fillet

frais (m.), fraîche (f.) fresh

le cœur d'Aloyau 'sauce bœuf' middle-cut sirloin with 'beef sauce'

les pommes allumettes finely cut (lit. matchstick) chips

2 The sentences below come from a conversation between a waiter and a customer. Write them out in the correct order and then check your answers on p. 146. You won't need your tape recorder. New word: **voici** here is.

Cliente	Un jus de tomate, s'il y en a.
Garçon	Très bien, Madame; on s'occupe de vous tout de suite.
Garçon	Saignant? A point?
Cliente	Pas de dessert, merci.
Garçon	Bonsoir, Madame. Voici la carte.
Cliente	De l'eau minérale, non-gazeuse.
Garçon	Oui, il y a du jus de tomate.
Cliente	Bien cuit.
Garçon	Pas de dessert, mais à boire?
Cliente	Je voudrais commander tout de suite, s'il vous plaît – je suis pressée.
Garçon	Et comme dessert?
Cliente	Ensuite un bifteck avec des pommes frites.
Garçon	Très bien, Madame. Pour commencer?

Garçon ....

Cliente ....

Garçon ....

Cliente ....

Garçon ....

Cliente ....

Garçon ....

Cliente ....

Garçon ....

Cliente ....

Garçon ....

Cliente ....

Garçon ....

3 **a.** On the tape you will hear Yves working at the till in a self-service snack bar. Listen to what he says and fill in the correct prices in the white circles on the menu.

b. How would you ask for a ham sandwich, a glass of red wine and a pastry? (Answers to both parts of the exercise on p. 146.)

....

....

4 Listen to the tape where you will hear a couple ordering a meal in a restaurant, then answer the questions below. (Answers p. 146)

New words you will hear on tape:
la soupe du jour soup of the day
l'oignon(m) onion
le rôti roast

la côtelette d'agneau lamb cutlets
la truite trout
vanille vanilla
le plateau de fromages cheese board

a. The wine is included in the price of meals. true ☐ false ☐

b. The couple choose the 40F menu? ☐ the 60F menu? ☐

c. The soup of the day is tomato? ☐ onion? ☐

d. The woman orders meat ☐ or fish? ☐

e. The man orders steak? ☐ roast pork? ☐ lamb cutlet? ☐

f. The main course is served with chips, mixed salad or ....

g. Underline those ice-creams and fruits that are offered on the menu:
chocolate, strawberry, coffee, vanilla
bananas, apples, peaches, grapes, pears

h. The couple choose a bottle of red wine. true ☐ false ☐

Grammar

En

En can mean 'of it', 'of them', 'some/any of it' or 'some/any of them'. You can't leave it out as we do in English in sentences like 'I have five'. **En** comes before the verb in any sentence except a straightfoward command like **prenez-en!** (take some) or **goûtez-en!** (taste some).

s'il y en a if there are any (of them)
il en reste un there is one (of them) left

combien de frères avez-vous? how many brothers have you?
j'en ai cinq I have five (of them).

prenez-vous de l'aspirine? do you take aspirin?
oui, j'en prends quelquefois yes, I take some sometimes.

Exercise Translate the following sentences into French using **en** in each.

1 I have three (of them) ....

2 I am taking two of them ....

3 He eats some (of it) ....

4 Take some! ....

5 I am buying some ....

6 I am sure of it ....

(Answers on p. 146.)

Here are two more useful verbs:

Voir to see

je vois	nous voyons
tu vois	vous voyez
il/elle voit	ils/elles voient

As with so many verbs, all the forms except those for **nous** and **vous** sound exactly the same. **Revoir** (to see again) follows the same pattern as **voir**.

Finir to finish

je finis	nous finissons
tu finis	vous finissez
il/elle finit	ils/elles finissent

Here the **ils/elles** form sounds different from the singular because the double 's' has to be pronounced.

Other verbs following the same pattern as **finir:**
choisir (to choose)
grossir (to grow fat)
grandir (to grow taller)
réussir (to succeed)
maigrir (to grow thin)

Read and understand

Here is a recipe from a children's cookery book. The drawings and the questions below will help you understand it. (Answers on p. 146.)

Mousse au citron
(6 personnes)
SÉPAREZ DANS 2 GRANDS BOLS LES
BLANCS ET LES JAUNES DE 3 OEUFS.

SUR LE BOL CONTENANT LES JAUNES
RAPEZ LE ZESTE D'UN CITRON.
AJOUTEZ LE JUS DU CITRON, 3 PETITS
SUISSES ET ¾ DE TASSE DE SUCRE.
MÉLANGEZ BIEN AVEC LE FOUET.

DANS L'AUTRE BOL MONTEZ LES
BLANCS D'OEUF EN NEIGE *très ferme*.
AJOUTEZ-LES AU CONTENU DU 1ᵉʳ BOL.
MÉLANGEZ *très vite* AVEC LE FOUET.
METTEZ AU RÉFRIGÉRATEUR.

1 How many eggs do you need? ....

2 Why do you need two bowls for them? ....

3 Into which bowl do you grate the zest of the lemon? ....

4 How much sugar do you use? ....

5 How thoroughly should the ingredients in the first bowl be mixed?

   ....

6 What do you do with the contents of the other bowl?

   ....

7 When you have added the contents of the second to the first, what

   do you do?

   ....

Did you know?

French eating habits

After a light breakfast, most French people take a substantial meal at midday, so the standard lunch-break is from noon to 2 p.m. to give them time to eat it. There is, however, a move towards shorter lunch-breaks and a main meal in the evening.

A main meal, whether at home or in a restaurant, has more courses in France than in Britain. It is often preceded by an **apéritif** and most people drink wine with the meal. There is always a starter such as pâté or soup, the vegetables are often served on a separate plate and lettuce (**salade**) is eaten to freshen the palate before the cheese or dessert. Cheese and dessert are often alternatives on many set **menus**. Choosing from a **menu** usually gives much better value for money than eating **à la carte.**

Where to eat

The signs to look out for when you want somewhere to eat are **restaurant, bistro(t)** or **brasserie,** and **auberge** (inn). In Paris and other large cities you will even find **drugstore** and **self,** but these are not typically French! If you want a meal at an odd time of day, try a **brasserie,** though it will have a limited range of dishes, usually grills and so on. **Crêperies** sell pancakes with different flavourings. Snacks are available from a **snack-bar** and sometimes from a **bistro(t),** a **café** or a **bar,** but French snacks are not nearly as good value as the set menus.

Be warned that bars and cafés often operate two price lists: it will cost you more to sit outside on the **terrasse** than inside at the bar.

Bills will always include service, unless they are specifically stamped **service non compris** (sometimes shortened to **snc**), but the prices on the menu may be **service compris** or **service en sus** (service extra). It is normal to leave only a little small change by way of a tip when the service is included.

Regional specialities

There are hundreds of regional dishes throughout France. If you want to know what to look out for you could send off for a little book entitled *La France à votre table: The gastronomic routes of France,* available from SOPEXA, 43–45 rue de Naples, 75008 Paris.

Your turn to speak

Your camp-site take-away has the menu below. You go in the morning to order your evening meal. Study the menu carefully and then listen to the tape. Follow Pierre's suggestions for your order.

plats à emporter take-away dishes
les moules marinière mussels cooked in a
   liquid with garlic and parsley, like a soup
frites means **et frites** with chips

And finally Listen to the dialogues again without the book. Test yourself on the *Key words and phrases* and on the verbs in the *Grammar* section. There is quite a lot of new vocabulary in the unit, some with the *Key phrases* and some given in the exercises; most of the words are very useful, so you would do well to learn them.

Answers

Practise what you have learnt p. 140 Exercise **1** (**a**) bouillabaisse, terrine and salade, then volaille, filet de poisson and aloyau (**b**) rare (**c**) bistro wine.

p. 141 Exercise **2** Bonsoir, Madame. Voici la carte./Je voudrais commander tout de suite, s'il vous plaît – je suis pressée./Très bien, Madame. Pour commencer?/Un jus de tomate, s'il y en a./Oui, il y a du jus de tomate./ Ensuite un bifteck avec des pommes frites./Saignant? A point?/Bien cuit./Et comme dessert?/Pas de dessert, merci./Pas de dessert, mais à boire?/De l'eau minérale, non-gazeuse./Très bien, Madame; on s'occupe de vous tout de suite.

p. 142 Exercise **3** (**a**) sandwichs 5F; salade 20F; assiette de charcuterie 20F; assiette de fromages 15F; ballon de vin du Tarn 4F; pâtisserie 8F; glace 8F (**b**) un sandwich au jambon, un ballon (*or* un verre) de vin rouge et une pâtisserie (s'il vous plaît).

p. 142 Exercise **4** (**a**) true (**b**) 40F menu (**c**) onion (**d**) meat (**e**) lamb cutlet (**f**) cauliflower (**g**) chocolate, vanilla, apples, grapes, pears (**h**) true.

Grammar p. 143 (**1**) J'en ai trois. (**2**) J'en prends deux. (**3**) Il en mange. (**4**) Prenez-en! (**5**) J'en achète. (**6**) J'en suis sûr/sûre.

Read and understand p. 144 (**1**) three (**2**) one for the whites and one for the yolks (**3**) the bowl containing the yolks (**4**) ¾ cup (**5**) well (**6**) whisk the egg-whites until they are very firm (**7**) mix very fast with the whisk and put in the fridge.

11 Likes and dislikes

What you will learn

- expressing your likes and dislikes
- more vocabulary to do with food
- saying what you like about your town or village
- more about the past
- understanding some important signs
- something about the geography of France

Before you begin

As soon as you get on friendly terms with a French person, you will find yourself wanting to express likes and dislikes. In this unit you will meet the following ways of doing so:

j'adore	I adore, I love
j'aime beaucoup	I like very much
j'aime	I love, I like
j'aime bien	I like
je n'aime pas beaucoup	I don't much like
je n'aime pas	I don't like
je déteste	I hate
j'ai horreur de	I can't stand

Listen out for them in the dialogues.

Study guide

Dialogues 1–7: listen straight through without the book
Dialogues 1–7: listen, read and study one by one
Dialogues 8–11: listen straight through without the book
Dialogues 8–11: listen, read and study one by one
Learn the *Key words and phrases*
Do the exercises in *Practise what you have learnt*
Study *Grammar* and do the exercises
Do *Read and understand*
Read *Did you know?*
Do *Your turn to speak*
Listen to all the dialogues again and test yourself on the *Key words and phrases*.

Dialogues

What do you like to eat and drink?

1 *Chewing-gum and lollipops*

Élise J'aime bien des chewing-gums et . . . et puis j'aime bien les sucettes.

> **le chewing-gum** chewing-gum
> **la sucette** lollipop

2 *Anything except jelly!*

Martin Dans la nourriture française j'aime tout . . . dans la nourriture anglaise, à peu près tout, sauf la gelée.

> ♦ **tout** everything, all
> ♦ **à peu près** almost, approximately

3 *A few of my favourite – and not so favourite – things*

Fabienne J'aime – euh – beaucoup le riz, les pommes de terre, les fruits rouges: les fraises, les framboises, les cerises . . . Euh – je n'aime pas beaucoup les bananes et les oranges, les fruits que l'on mange l'hiver . . .

> **le riz** rice
> **la fraise** strawberry
> **la framboise** raspberry
> **la cerise** cherry

4 *Wines*

Lisette Je déteste les vins doux – ils me font mal. Je préfère les vins secs.

> **sec (m.), sèche (f.)** dry

1 ♦ **j'aime bien** I like. She could equally have said simply **j'aime** . . . . 'I like very much' is **j'aime beaucoup**.

2 **la nourriture** food. He might equally well have said
♦ **dans la cuisine française** (French *cooking*). Note that **la cuisine** also means 'kitchen'.

sauf la gelée except for jelly. Most French people dislike English jelly – be warned if you have visitors!

3 **les fruits que l'on mange l'hiver** the fruit that one eats in the winter. An **l'** is sometimes inserted before **on**. It is a refinement to avoid saying **qu'on** which sounds like a French swear word.

♦ Note **l'hiver** for 'in winter'. The other seasons will be introduced in Unit 12, p. 165.

♦ You might also need the phrase **je n'aime pas du tout** . . . (I don't like . . . at all) e.g. **je n'aime pas du tout les bananes** (I don't like bananas at all). Used on its own **pas du tout** means 'not at all'.

4 ♦ **les vins doux** sweet wines. **Doux (f. douce)** also means 'soft' or 'gentle'.

♦ **ils me font mal** they make me ill (lit. they do bad to me). If you want to say that *one* thing makes you ill, the verb **faire** must be in the singular e.g. **le fromage me <u>fait</u> mal (cheese makes me ill)**.

Anna   J'adore les plats très consistants, où il y a beaucoup de choses à manger, comme la paëlla, le couscous, les lasagne, le cassoulet. J'ai horreur de la triperie. J'adore toutes les viandes. J'aime beaucoup les pâtisseries. Je déteste les alcools et les vins . . .

♦ **le plat** dish
   consistants (pl.) substantial, filling
♦ **la chose** thing
   la paëlla paëlla
   les lasagne lasagne
   la triperie tripe
♦ **toutes (f. pl.)** all
♦ **l'alcool (m.)** spirit (alcoholic)

□□ **6** *Sweet and sour*

Guylaine   Moi, j'aime beaucoup de choses, sauf le mélange salé-sucré. C'est très difficile de manger la viande et des fruits, par exemple – sinon j'aime la viande.

par exemple for example   **sinon** otherwise
salé salted

□□ **7** *Eat, drink and be merry*

Henri   J'aime bien manger et j'aime surtout bien boire. J'aime la viande, bien sûr, mais je préfère le poisson. J'aime aussi les crustacés: les huîtres, les langoustes, les homards . . . Avec le crustacé en France on boit du vin blanc.

♦ **bien sûr** of course   **la langouste** crayfish
   l'huître (f.) oyster   **le homard** lobster

5 ♦ **j'adore** lit. I adore, but used more extensively in French than in English.

le couscous is a North African dish which is very popular in France. It is something like an Irish stew made with a type of semolina.

le cassoulet is a casserole of beans and goose, pork or mutton.·

♦ **j'ai horreur de** I can't stand.

6 **le mélange salé-sucré** the mixture of savoury and sweet. Try not to give French visitors apple sauce, cranberry jelly or pineapple rings with meat.

7 ♦ **j'aime bien manger et . . . bien boire** I like eating well and . . . drinking well. Notice that 'I like eat*ing*' is translated in French by **aimer + the** infinitive; **j'aime man<u>ger</u>.** Here are some other examples: **j'aime <u>boire</u>** (I like drink*ing*), **nous aimons dans<u>er</u>** (we like danc*ing*).

♦ **les crustacés** shellfish. You should learn the general term **les fruits de mer** (seafood).

What do you like about your town or village?

8 *My village*

Marie-Odile Dans ce village il y a une église du onzième siècle, un café – euh – beaucoup de maisons neuves, quelques fermes, beaucoup de champs, une ligne de chemin de fer . . .

Jeanne Vous vous plaisez ici?

Marie-Odile Ah oui, beaucoup. J'ai les vaches en voisines . . .

- **la maison** house
  neuves (f. pl.) (m. sing.
  neuf) new
- **quelques** a few
  la ferme farm
  le champ field

- **la ligne** line
  le chemin de fer railway
  la vache cow
- **la voisine** and
  le voisin neighbour

9 *The village where I was born*

Michèle Moi je suis née à Paris. Paris c'est mon village natal. C'est beau, et en plus on est libre – on est complètement libre à Paris. C'est une très, très belle ville. Il y a toujours quelque chose à faire et c'est intéressant pour ça.

- **beau (m.), belle (f.)** beautiful
  complètement completely

10 *The anonymity of the big city*

Jean-Claude J'adore Paris. Je me sens anonyme. Personne ne me connaît et personne n'a envie de savoir qui je suis.

What do you like about your friends?

11 *Staying with a musical family in London*

Michèle Tout le monde était musicien. Le père, c'était son métier, la mère était très, très musicienne et les filles étaient très musiciennes aussi. Alors c'était très agréable, parce que . . . on faisait de la musique – euh – tous ensemble . . . et avec mes amis musiciens du lycée, aussi.

- **tout le monde** everyone
  le métier profession
- **agréable** pleasant, nice
  tous ensemble all together

- **mes (pl.)** my
- **un ami (f. amie)** friend
  le lycée (grammar) school

8   **du onzième siècle** of the eleventh century. For'some reason it is **du onzième siècle** and not **de l'**. (See also p. 84 **le onze novembre**.)

vous vous plaisez ici? do you like it here? (lit. you please yourself here?)

en voisines as neighbours. Note that the word **en** is very versatile, it can mean 'some' (as in Unit 10), 'as' and also sometimes 'in'.

9   **je suis née** I was born. This verb form will be explained in Unit 15.

mon village natal the village where I was born. Although Paris is hardly a village, this indicates the affection she feels for the city.

♦ **libre** free. But for 'free' when you mean 'at no cost' use **gratuit**.

10   **je me sens anonyme** I feel anonymous (lit. I feel myself anonymous).

personne ne (+ verb) nobody. e.g. **personne ne va au cinéma le lundi** (nobody goes to the cinema on Mondays), **en France personne n'aime la gelée** (in France nobody likes jelly).

a envie de wants. This is from **avoir envie de** (lit. to have desire to) which can be used instead of **vouloir**, e.g. **les enfants ont envie d'aller à la plage** (the children want to go to the beach), **j'ai envie de voir Paris** (I want to see Paris).

11   **était musicien** was musical. Note the feminine, **musicienne**. For **était** and **étaient** see p. 157.

on faisait de la musique we used to make music. You do not need to learn this past tense of the verb **faire**.

Key words and phrases

As well as the following words and phrases, look back at p. 147 and learn the important phrases for expressing likes and dislikes.

j'aime (bien) . . .	I like . . .
la cuisine (française)	(French) cooking
à peu près tout	almost everything
tout	everything
beaucoup de choses	a lot of things
mon ami/mon amie	my (boy) friend/my (girl) friend
tout le monde	everyone
je n'aime pas . . .	I don't like . . .
quelques plats	a few dishes
le vin doux/sec	sweet/dry wine
l'hiver	winter (*also* in winter)
mon voisin	my neighbour
j'ai envie de (bien manger et bien boire)	I want to (eat well and drink well)
(l'alcool) me fait mal	(alcohol) makes me ill
(les fruits de mer) me font mal	(shellfish) make me ill
personne ne (boit l'eau salée)	nobody (drinks salt water)
bien sûr	of course
pas du tout	not at all
(une chaise) libre	a free (chair)
(un musée) gratuit	a free (museum)
la maison	house
agréable	pleasant, nice
beau (m.), belle (f.)	handsome, beautiful
tout (m.), toute (f.)	all, every

Practise what you have learnt

1 On the tape you will hear Yves telling you some of his likes and dislikes. Put a tick beside the drawing of anything he likes and a cross beside whatever he dislikes. (Answers on p. 160.)

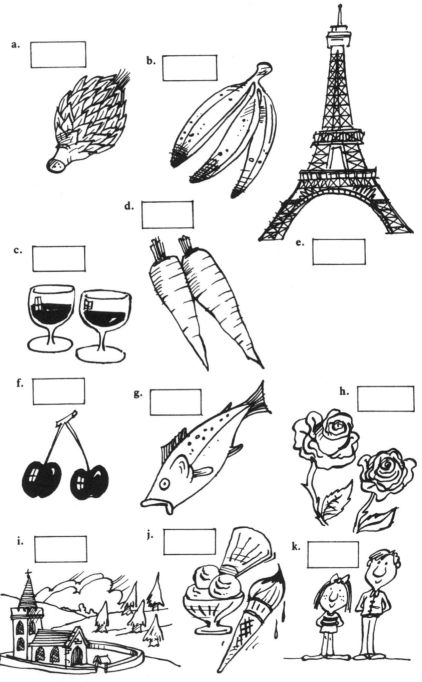

a.

b.

c.

d.

e.

f.

g.

h.

i.

j.

k.

2 On tape you will hear Carolle telling you about her likes and dislikes. Listen carefully and then put a tick in the appropriate box below. (Answers p. 160)

		likes a lot	likes	doesn't like	hates
a.	travelling by train				
b.	travelling by plane				
c.	tea				
d.	coffee				
e.	going to the cinema				
f.	going to the theatre				
g.	cheese				
h.	English jelly				
i.	dry white wine				
j.	whisky				
k.	the neighbours				

3 First find an appropriate gap in the passage below for each of the words from the following list. When you have filled in the gaps, check your answers by listening to Carolle reading the passage on the tape.

Arc   quelque chose   belle   théâtre   monuments   Notre   libre   la nuit   aller   Eiffel   hiver

Paris est une très .... ville. Il y a toujours .... à faire, même l' ....; on peut s'amuser toute la journée et toute .... De jour, on peut visiter les .... historiques: la Tour ...., bien sûr, l' .... de Triomphe, ... Dame; de nuit, on peut .... au restaurant, au ...., au night-club. Et en plus, on est complètement .... à Paris.

s'amuser to enjoy oneself

Here, just for fun, is the French equivalent of the English chant 'he (she) loves me, he (she) loves me not . . .'

à la folie....pas du tout.....un peu....beaucoup......passionnément.....

Il m'aime....
Elle m'aime.....

Grammar

Mon, ma, mes; ton, ta, tes

There are three words for 'my' in French. If I own something feminine the word for 'my' is **ma**, e.g. **ma mère, ma maison**. If I own something masculine, the word to use is **mon**, e.g. **mon père, mon crayon**. Also, if the feminine word begins with a vowel, **mon** is used, simply because it sounds better, e.g. **mon amie, mon orange**. The third word is **mes**. This is used in the plural in all cases, e.g. **mes parents, mes chemises, mes amies**.

Ton, ta and **tes** (your), for a person you call **tu**, follow exactly the same pattern e.g. **c'est ton fils? c'est ta fille? ce sont tes enfants?**

Exercise 1 Write **mon, ma** or **mes**, as appropriate, in each of the gaps below:

a. Je préfère .... maison aux maisons neuves.

b. J'aime aller au cinéma avec .... amis.

c. .... amie est secrétaire.

d. J'aime bien .... professeurs.

e. Je n'aime pas beaucoup .... voisin.

Personne

Une personne means 'a person', but **personne** on its own means 'nobody':
e.g. **qui est là? – personne**. who is there? – nobody.
When it is used in a sentence it requires a **ne** before the verb.
e.g. **personne n'aime Georges** nobody likes George
  Georges n'aime personne George likes nobody
  Personne ne me connaît nobody knows me

Était, étaient

In dialogue 11 you met **était** and **étaient**. They come from a past tense (sometimes called the 'imperfect') of the verb **être** and they mean 'was', 'were' or 'used to be'.

j'étais I was	**nous étions** we were
tu étais you were	**vous étiez** you were
il/elle était he/she/it was	**ils/elles étaient** they were

Note that **étais, était** and **étaient** all sound the same.

Exercise 2 Write the correct form of the past tense of **être** in each of the gaps below:

a. Georges .... chez nous à Noël.

b. Mes soeurs .... là aussi.

c. J'..................... très content.

d. Nous .... tous musiciens.

e. C'..................... très agréable.

f. Hélas: Vous n'..................... pas là!

UNIT 11   157

Read and understand

l'issue de secours (f.)   emergency exit

See if you can work out from the pictures above how to say the following:
(Answers on p. 160.)

1. No smoking ....

2. No parking (2 ways) ....

   ....

3. Dogs are forbidden in the shop ....

   ....

4. Garage exit ....

5. No way down ....

6. For your safety ....

7. Car exit ....

8. No parking in front of emergency exits ....

   ....

Did you know?

France is divided into geographical **régions** (see Unit 2), each with its own special character, culture and cuisine and, in some cases, such as Brittany and Provence, with its own local language. France is a land of many contrasts, but you will not find the 'real' France on the main roads or in the big cities: instead you will have to explore the old provinces like the Auvergne, Burgundy or the Basque country. There are many prehistoric monuments and paintings in Britanny and the Dordogne, Gallo-Roman remains in Provence, rich architecture in Normandy, more than a hundred châteaux in the Loire valley, quiet little villages in the Pyrenees and natural beauty in the Limousin. Wherever you go, the local **syndicat d'initiative** will be able to tell you what there is to see in the area and give you details of local events from folklore festivals to firework displays.

French addresses now end in a five-digit postal code, e.g. rue de la Couronne, 13100 Aix-en-Provence. The first two figures in this code are the number of the **département**. So Aix-en-Provence has the postal code 13 100, from which one can tell that it is in **département** number 13, i.e. les Bouches-du-Rhône. The map below will enable you to identify and locate **départements** from their postal codes. You can also work out where French cars come from – the **département** number is shown on the car number plate.

Your turn to speak

In this first exercise you are in a restaurant having lunch with Yves.
Unfortunately, you're rather fussy about your food. You'll be practising the
phrases you have learnt for expressing likes and dislikes (see p. 147) and
you will also need the food vocabulary you have met.

And finally Listen to the dialogues again and test yourself on the *Key words and phrases.*
Then give yourself some extra practice by seeing how many of your own
likes and dislikes you can express in French.

Answers

Practise what you have learnt p. 155 Exercise 1 (a) dislikes (b) dislikes
(c) likes (d) dislikes (e) likes (f) likes (g) dislikes (h) likes (i) likes (j)
dislikes (k) likes.

p. 156 Exercise 2 (a) likes a lot (b) doesn't like (c) hates (d) likes
(e) likes (f) likes a lot (g) doesn't like (h) hates (i) likes a lot (j) likes
(k) likes a lot.

p. 156 Exercise 3 belle/quelque chose/hiver/la nuit/monuments/Eiffel/Arc/
Notre/aller/théâtre/libre.

Grammar p. 157 Exercise 1 (a) ma (b) mes (c) mon (d) mes (e) mon.

p. 157 Exercise 2 (a) était (b) étaient (c) étais (d) étions (e) était
(f) étiez.

Read and understand p. 158 (1) Défense de fumer. (2) Défense de
stationner, ne stationnez pas, (prière de) ne pas stationner. (3) Les chiens
sont interdits dans le magasin. (4) Sortie de garage. (5) Descente interdite.
(6) Pour votre sécurité. (6) Sortie de voitures. (8) Ne stationnez pas devant
les issues de secours.

12 Your town – the weather

What you will learn

- describing a town
- talking about life there
- talking about a seaside resort
- asking about the weather
- describing the weather
- more about questions
- something about the climate in France

Before you begin

This unit will help you both to talk about your own town and to understand some of what you read about French towns in leaflets and guide-books. Remember if you are planning to go to France, write to the **syndicat d'initiative** of a town you hope to visit. If you enclose an international reply coupon (obtainable from post offices) they will almost certainly be willing to send you a tourist leaflet (**un dépliant touristique**) and **un plan de la ville**.

Talking about the weather is a peculiarly British preoccupation, but it is useful to be able to ask about the weather forecast if you are planning to go sailing or skiing or to walk or climb in the mountains.

Study guide

Dialogues 1–5: listen straight through without the book
Dialogues 1–5: listen, read and study one by one
Dialogues 6, 7: listen straight through without the book
Dialogues 6, 7: listen, read and study one by one
Learn the *Key words and phrases*
Do the exercises in *Practise what you have learnt*
Study *Grammar* and do the exercises
Do *Read and understand*
Read *Did you know?*
Do *Your turn to speak*
Listen to all the dialogues again without the book

Dialogues

1 *Paris and the provinces*

Jacques Dans l'ensemble, les Parisiens ont des salaires un peu plus élevés
. . . que les provinciaux, mais – euh – ils vivent d'une façon . . .
plus . . . tendue. Le temps est très précieux à Paris, alors que
. . . en province – euh – on a peut-être un peu plus le temps de
vivre. La qualité de la vie est peut-être supérieure – euh – en
province.

le Parisien (f. la Parisienne) Parisian
le salaire pay
élevé high
ils vivent (from **vivre**) they live
précieux (f. précieuse) precious
alors que whereas
la qualité de la vie quality of life
supérieure (*here*) superior, better

2 *Life in la Roche-sur-Yon*

Denise C'est très calme. Il n'y a pas beaucoup de . . . de vie, mais la ville
est très agréable parce que, en général, les gens sont gentils,
sont restés simples, et les commerçants sont très agréables – oui
– et la vie n'est pas trop chère encore . . . enfin – ça peut aller.
Le dimanche, les gens ne restent pas à la Roche, parce que la mer
est très proche; alors, ils passent leur dimanche aux Sables
d'Olonne ou bien . . . sur la côte.

◆ **calme** quiet
◆ **la vie** life, the cost of living
◆ **gentils (m. pl.), gentille (f. sing)** nice, kind
ils passent (from **passer**) they spend (time), they pass

3 *The seaside resort of Soulac-sur-Mer*

Claire Maintenant, ça devient un petit peu trop fréquenté – il y a un
peu trop de monde. Enfin, ça reste une plage pas dangereuse, une
belle plage de sable – euh – où le climat est agréable, le sable est
propre, la mer n'est pas dangereuse, pas trop . . .

◆ **maintenant** now
◆ **la plage** beach
◆ **le sable** sand
le climat climate
◆ **propre** clean

1   **les provinciaux** people from the provinces. The provinces are referred to collectively as **la province**. In France there is often a gulf – and sometimes animosity – between the capital and the provinces.

d'une façon plus . . . tendue under more stress (lit. in a more stretched way).

le temps in this case means 'time' in a general sense. Note that **temps** is never used in asking the time (remember **quelle heure est-il?** in Unit 6).

2 ◆   **il n'y a pas beaucoup de vie** there's not a lot of life i.e. it's not very exciting.

sont restés simples have remained unpretentious. You will be learning this variation of the past tense in Unit 15.

encore yet. It can also mean 'again'.

ça peut aller it's all right (lit. that can go).

◆   **la mer est très proche** the sea is very near. She could have said **la Roche est près de la mer** (la Roche is near the sea).

aux Sables d'Olonne ou bien . . . sur la côte at les Sables d'Olonne or (somewhere else) on the coast. **Ou bien** means 'or else'.

3   **un peu trop fréquenté** a bit too popular i.e. (in this case) crowded. **Un restaurant très fréquenté** would be a popular restaurant, i.e. one visited by a lot of people.

◆   **un peu trop de monde** rather too many people. Remember **tout le monde** (everyone). **Le monde** means literally 'the world'.

pas dangereuse not dangerous. You can make any adjective negative by putting **pas** in front of it, e.g. **pas gentil** (not nice, not kind), **pas vrai** (not true), **pas bon** (not good). Note: dangerous = **dangereux (m.), dangereuse (f.)**.

◆   **pas trop** i.e. **pas trop dangereuse.**

A verb you might find useful when describing a holiday by the sea is **nager** (to swim).

4 *The rebuilding of Caen*

Michel   Bien, c'est une ville très ancienne qui a été restaurée et, de l'avis général, bien restaurée, parce que . . . à la fois il reste – euh – des monuments intéressants, et puis, il y a une reconstruction aussi qui a été bien faite.

ancienne (f.) (**m. ancien**) ancient	**le monument** monument
l'avis (m.) opinion	⬧ **intéressant** interesting
à la fois at the same time	

5 *The old town of Senlis*

Marie-Lise   La ville de Senlis, c'est une ville – euh – intéressante car elle est très vieille. Il y a une cathédrale, il y a des remparts romains, il y a – euh – pas mal de . . . maisons moyenâgeuses . . .

car because	**la cathédrale** cathedral
⬧ **vieille (f.)** (**m. vieux**) old	**le rempart** rampart
romains (pl.) Roman	

6 *What's the weather like?*

Jeanne   Quel temps fait-il normalement ici?

Michel   Eh bien, vous voyez, en ces semaines d'été, il fait un temps agréable – il fait assez chaud et, cependant, il y a toujours de l'air.

normalement normally

7 *A mock weather forecast*

Anna   Guylaine, à ton avis, quel temps fera-t-il demain?

Guylaine   Je vais te dire la météo de la France. Sur la Bretagne il est prévu un temps pluvieux, parce qu'il pleut toujours en Bretagne. Dans le sud-ouest, temps nuageux, parce qu'il y a souvent des nuages dans le sud-ouest. Sur la Côte d'Azur, ensoleillé, parce que le soleil brille toujours. Dans le Massif Central, des averses, parce qu'il pleut beaucoup. Dans les Alpes, des éclaircies, entre deux nuages. Dans la région parisienne, brouillard – il y a toujours du brouillard dans la région parisienne. Et dans le nord de la France, des éclaircies – entre deux flocons de neige!

te to (you)	**brille** (from **briller**) shines, is shining
la météo weather forecast	**l'averse (f.)** shower, downpour
⬧ **il pleut** it rains, it is raining	**l'éclaircie (f.)** bright period
nuageux cloudy	**le brouillard** fog
le nuage cloud	**le flocon** flake
ensoleillé sunny	⬧ **la neige** snow

4   **qui a été restaurée** which has been restored. The past (perfect) tense will be explained in the next unit.

une reconstruction a reconstruction. Caen was one of the first towns to be liberated after the Normandy invasion of France by the Allies in 1944, and was badly damaged in the fighting.

qui a été bien faite which has been well done.

5   ▸ **pas mal de** quite a lot of. e.g. **pas mal de musées** (quite a lot of museums), **pas mal de discothèques** (quite a lot of discos).

moyenâgeuses medieval. From **le moyen âge** (the Middle Ages).

▸ Other vocabulary you may find useful for describing your town: **la piscine** (swimming pool), **les distractions** (amusements, entertainment).

6   ▸ **quel temps fait-il?** what's the weather like? (lit. what weather does it make?) See p. 169 for further details on weather.

▸ **en ces semaines d'été** in these weeks of summer. You met **l'hiver** or **en hiver** (in winter) in Unit 11. It is also useful to know **en été** (in summer), **en automne** (in autumn) and **au printemps** (in spring).

▸ **il fait un temps agréable** the weather is nice. See also p. 169.

cependant il y a toujours de l'air yet there is always a breeze (lit. some air).

7   ▸ **quel temps fera-t-il demain?** what will the weather be like tomorrow? (lit. what weather will it make tomorrow?). You will find this phrase very useful on holiday.

sur la Bretagne, il est prévu un temps pluvieux over Brittany rainy weather is forecast (lit. it is forecast rainy weather). Guylaine is copying the style and tone of voice of a typical radio or television weather forecaster!

▸ **le sud-ouest** the south-west.

la Côte d'Azur (lit. the Blue Coast) is the Mediterranean coast, often called the French Riviera in English.

▸ **le nord** the north. You may also need **l'est** (the east), which is pronounced like the English word 'lest'.

Key words and phrases

Describing your town

le village est . . .	the village is . . .
beau	beautiful
agréable	nice
intéressant	interesting
calme	quiet
vieux	old
propre	clean
pas trop (grand)	not too (big)

la ville est . . .	the town is. . .
belle	beautiful
agréable	nice
intéressante	interesting
calme	quiet
vieille	old
propre	clean
pas trop (grande)	not too (big)

il y a . . .	there's . . .
une cathédrale	a cathedral
une piscine	a swimming pool
une belle plage de sable	a beautiful sandy beach

il y a pas mal de . . .	there are quite a lot of . . .
distractions	entertainments
musées	museums
discothèques	discos

la mer est proche	the sea is near
les gens sont gentils	the people are nice
maintenant, il y a un peu trop de monde	now, there are rather too many people
il n'y a pas beaucoup de vie	there's not much life
la vie n'est pas trop chère	the cost of living is not too high

The weather

quel temps fait-il . . . ?	what's the weather like . . . ?
dans le nord?	in the north?
dans le sud?	in the south?
dans l'est?	in the east?
dans l'ouest?	in the west?

quel temps fera-t-il demain?	what will the weather be like tomorrow?

il fait un temps agréable	the weather is nice
il pleut	it's raining
il y a beaucoup de neige	there's a lot of snow

Practise what you have learnt

1 You have a correspondent in Dinan and are planning to visit the town. You write asking for information. Put each of the following words into the appropriate gap in the letter below. You don't need your tape recorder for this exercise. (Answers on p. 172.) New vocabulary: **envoyer** (to send)

plan   cher   renseignements   manger   avril   normalement
où   comme   plaît   il y a

Bradford
le 1er février

Cher Jean-Pierre,

Merci de votre lettre. Oui – je viens enfin à Dinan au mois d'...... Pouvez-vous me donner quelques ...., s'il vous .....?

Quel temps fait-il .... en avril? Pouvez-vous me recommander un hôtel pas trop ....? Qu'est-ce qu'il y a ..... distractions à Dinan? Est-ce qu'.... une piscine? Pouvez-vous m'envoyer un .... de la ville? .. est-ce qu'on peut bien...... à Dinan? Je vous invite!

Excusez-moi de vous déranger. Merci d'avance.

Meilleurs souvenirs,   Mike

---

2 When he receives his letter (see exercise 1), Mike's friend Jean-Pierre telephones him from France. Listen to the tape two or three times. Can you write down (in English) answers to the questions below? Your answers will give the information Mike wanted about Dinan. (Answers p. 172.)
New vocabulary: **la patronne** (the woman owner of the hotel)

a. What's the weather like in April? ....

....

b. Why does he recommend the Hôtel de la Poste? ....

....

c. What is the hotel's phone number? ....

....

d. What attractions does Dinan have? ....

....

e. What will Jean-Pierre mark on the map he is sending?

....

f. Which dates do you guess Mike is hoping to arrive?

....

3 On the tape you will hear Carolle telling you about the seaside town of Cabourg in Normandy. Read the questions below, listen to the tape two or three times and then see if you can answer the questions. You can check your answers on p. 172.

a. How far is Cabourg from Caen? ....

b. Is the beach sandy or pebbly? ....

c. Is the sea dangerous? ....

d. Would you need to book in advance if you wanted a hotel room

during the summer? ....

e. What is the population of Cabourg in the off-season? ....

f. Is it a noisy town then? ....

g. Name three kinds of entertainment available in Cabourg. ....

....

4 Prepare and read aloud a description of your own town or village, mentioning its size, its position, its amenities, its weather and why you like or do not like it. Obviously we cannot give you the exact vocabulary, but the questions below will help you. You will find it very useful to be able to tell a French person about your background.

- c'est . . . une grande/petite ville?   un grand/petit village?
- c'est à combien de kilomètres de Londres/Cardiff/Edimbourg?
- c'est . . . près de la côte/près des montagnes/dans le nord/dans
  le sud/dans l'est/dans l'ouest?
- il y a . . . une cathédrale/une piscine/un musée/une plage?
- normalement le temps est . . . agréable/froid/chaud? (see also
  p. 169)
- vous l'aimez parce que . . . c'est beau/intéressant/vieux/calme/
  propre?
  parce que. . .les gens sont gentils/la vie n'est pas chère/il y a pas
  mal de distractions?
- vous ne l'aimez pas parce que . . . c'est trop grand/il y a un peu
  trop de monde/il n'y a pas beaucoup de vie?

Grammar

The weather

When you are speaking of weather conditions, use **il fait** for 'it is':

il fait beau it is fine
il fait mauvais it is bad (weather)
il fait chaud it is hot
il fait froid it is cold

For comparisons:
il fait plus chaud aujourd'hui it is hotter today (lit. more hot)
il fait moins froid aujourd'hui it is not so cold today (lit. less cold)

Learn also:
il fait du brouillard it is foggy
il fait du vent it is windy

il pleut it is raining
il neige it is snowing
le soleil brille the sun is shining

Exercise Describe the weather in each of the pictures below:

a.

b.

c.

d.

e.

More question forms

où? (where?) **quand?** (when?) **comment?** (how?)
pourquoi? (why?) **combien?** (how many? how much?)

Each of these question-words can be followed EITHER by **est-ce que?** e.g.
quand est-ce que vous partez? (when are you leaving?) OR by an 'inverted'
verb, e.g. **quand partez-vous?** You won't need to use an inverted verb
yourself but it is useful to be able to understand it.

Here are the inverted forms of **avoir**:
ai-je?   **avons-nous?**
as-tu?   **avez-vous?**
a-t-il? a-t-elle?   **ont-ils? ont-elles?**

The **t** in **a-t-il?** and **a-t-elle?** is merely to make it easier to pronounce. Note
that the question-form of **il y a** is **y a-t-il?**

Read and understand

The following text has been adapted from a tourist brochure describing some of the villages in the **département** of the Loire-Atlantique (see p. 159). See if you can understand enough of it to answer the questions below. (Answers p. 172)

PAULX
Paulx est situé à l'intersection des routes départementales Nos 13 et 73, à 40 kilomètres au sud de Nantes. D'origine romaine, cette ancienne paroisse agréable et tranquille est située sur les deux rives du Falleron. Le touriste peut visiter quelques belles propriétés, en particulier le château de la Caraterie; il faut voir également l'église et les sculptures de la chapelle. Et it faut essayer le bon vin de Paulx!

LA MARNE
La Marne, village de 788 personnes, est située à 35 kilomètres au sud-ouest de Nantes et à 6 kilomètres à l'est de Machecoul. La paroisse de Notre-Dame de la Marne date de l'an 1062. Aujourd'hui la principale activité du village est l'agriculture: on y produit du lait, du bœuf et des vins de bonne qualité.

---

la paroisse parish

1 Which direction would you take from Nantes to get to

 a. Paulx? ....

 b. La Marne? ....

2 Which of them is further from Nantes? ....

3 Which parish has Roman origins? ....

4 Which parish dates from the time of William the Conqueror? ....

5 What is there to see at Paulx? ....

 ....

6 What are the main products of La Marne? ....

 ....

Did you know?

You may like to know a little more about the places mentioned in the dialogues.

Paris et la province

Paris is at the heart of French life in a way that none of the British capitals can match. It is pre-eminent in finance, in administration and in the arts. The partial devolution of local government was introduced by François Mitterand in response to the growing resentment of people living in the provinces who felt that all their local issues were decided by Parisians who knew nothing about them. This resentment that **tout passe par Paris** is only one facet of the complex love-hate relationship that many people in the provinces (particularly the south) have for Paris: they are immensely and justly proud of its monuments, its art, its music and its theatre and yet they feel alienated by the way it has come to dominate the rest of the country and by the **vie de dingue** (rat-race) of its inhabitants.

La Roche-sur-Yon

La Roche-sur-Yon is a quiet little town of some 48,000 people in the department of **la Vendée** (see p. 159). You may well pass through it if you are going to les Sables d'Olonne on the Atlantic Coast. You will be reading more about la Roche-sur-Yon in Unit 15.

Soulac-sur-mer

Soulac is a charming little seaside town some 60 miles north-west of Bordeaux near the estuary of the Gironde. It has only about 2,000 inhabitants in the winter, but its excellent sandy beaches attract as many visitors as its hotels and camp-sites can accommodate in the summer, when there is one direct train a day to Paris. A favourite activity for visitors is to hire a bicycle and ride on some of the specially made cycle tracks through the local forest.

Caen

75% of Caen was destroyed in 1944, but its most important monuments remain, surrounded by a beautifully reconstructed new city which houses some 123,000 people. The main monuments are: the Abbaye-aux-Dames, a convent that is now a hospital (Michel works there); the Abbaye-aux-Hommes, once an abbey and now the Hôtel de Ville; the churches of Saint-Pierre and Saint-Jean (both restored); the castle and its ramparts. The town has a university and is an important commercial centre.

Senlis

Senlis is an old town of some 14,000 people about 30 miles north of Paris. It has a Gothic cathedral and some fine ramparts, some of them Gallo-Roman. There are some picturesque old streets and the names conjure up the town's history: **la Place des Arènes** (Amphitheatre Square) and **le Rempart des Otages** (Hostages' Rampart) for instance.

Your turn to speak

Imagine you come from York. On the tape a new French acquaintance is asking you about the city. Pierre will prompt you. You won't find the questions difficult even if you have never visited the city. Remember though **il faut** (p. 73) which means 'you should' etc. (lit. it is necessary).

And finally   As usual, listen to all the dialogues again. You should then test yourself on the *Key words and phrases* and on the various expressions you need to describe the weather.

Revision

Now turn to p. 217 and complete the revision section on Units 10–12. On the cassette the revision section follows straight after this unit.

Answers

Practise what you have learnt p. 167 Exercise 1 avril . . . renseignements . . . plaît . . . normalement . . . cher . . . comme . . . il y a . . . plan . . . où . . . manger.

p. 167 Exercise 2 (a) nice, not very hot, rains sometimes (b) it's close to his house, clean and he knows the owner (c) 28–16–98 (d) beach, museums, two or three discos, swimming pool (e) his house, the Hôtel de la Poste, and two restaurants he recommends (f) Friday 17th or Saturday 18th April.

p. 168 Exercise 3 (a) 24 km. (b) sandy (c) no (d) yes (e) 4,000 (f) no (g) casino, cinéma, restaurants, cafés.

Grammar p. 169 Exercise 1 (a) il pleut (b) il fait du vent (c) il fait du brouillard; (d) il fait froid; il neige (e) il fait beau; il fait chaud; le soleil brille.

Read and understand p. 170 (1a) south (1b) south-west (2) Paulx (3) Paulx (4) Notre-Dame de la Marne (Our Lady of La Marne) (5) the château de la Caraterie, the church and the sculptures in the chapel (6) milk, beef and wine of good quality.

13 More about yourself

What you will learn

- describing your home
- the names of rooms in a house
- talking about the past
- talking about learning a language
- something about French housing
- something about French history

Before you begin

The first four dialogues are descriptions of people's homes; the last three all contain examples of the past (perfect) tense, which is explained in the grammar section. Take your time studying this tense. It's not difficult but it is new and you want to avoid saying the equivalent of 'I have tooken' and 'I haved'. When you learn verbs there really is no substitute for chanting them aloud, over and over again, until they stick!

- Here are some verbs you have already met; can you remember their present tense? To check, look back at the pages in brackets.
  être (p. 17), **avoir** (p. 31), **prendre** (p. 45), **faire** (p. 59), **aller** (p. 73), **venir** (p. 87), **vendre** (p. 59).

- How would you translate the following? (The answers are directly below.)

  the first floor, the lavatory, the ground floor, the bedroom, the bathroom, the shower, the kitchen

  le premier étage, les toilettes, le rez-de-chaussée, le chambre, la salle de bains, la douche, la cuisine

Study guide

	Dialogues 1–4: listen straight through without the book
	Dialogues 1–4: listen, read and study one by one
	Dialogues 5–7: listen straight through without the book
	Dialogues 5–7: listen, read and study one by one
	Learn the *Key words and phrases*
	Do the exercises in *Practise what you have learnt*
	Study the *Grammar* section carefully and do the exercise
	Do *Read and understand*
	Read *Did you know?*
	Do *Your turn to speak*
	Listen to all the dialogues again
	Test yourself on the *Key words and phrases* and *Grammar*

Dialogues

1 *Denise's house*

Jeanne Elle est comment, la maison?
Denise Au rez-de-chaussée, il y a une entrée, le bureau de mon mari, deux chambres, une salle d'eau, des toilettes, des placards de rangement, et au premier étage, nous avons la cuisine, la slle de séjour, la salle de bains, trois chambres, un débarras, des toilettes.

- **l'entrée (f.)** entrance hall
- **le bureau** study, office
- **le placard** cupboard
  le rangement storage
  le débarras junk-room

2 *Michel's apartment*

Michel J'ai un appartement de quatre pièces: une pièce au rez-de-chaussée, qui est mon bureau professionel, et trois pièces au premier étage: salle de séjour et deux chambres.

- **l'appartement (m.)** flat, apartment
  professionnel (m.) professional

3 *Barbara's house*

Barbara Nous avons – euh – un petit pavillon. Nous avons un grand salon où . . . une partie est salon et une partie salle à manger. Il y a une cuisine. Chacun a sa chambre et il y a aussi la chambre des invités et il y a des salles de bains . . . Et nous avons aussi un grenier qui, pour le moment, est vide, parce que . . . il faut le nettoyer – et une cave aussi, où on met des choses . . . des conserves . . . certaines choses comme ça.

  le pavillon detached house
- **la partie** part
- **la salle à manger** dining-room
- **la chambre des invités** guest-room
  le grenier attic
- **vide** empty
  la cave cellar
  on met (from mettre) we put, one puts
  la conserve preserve – jam, bottled fruit etc.
  certaines (f. pl.) certain

1 une salle d'eau lit. a water-room; usually a shower-room as opposed to a bathroom.

la salle de séjour the sitting-room. You will also hear
 ♦ le salon and le living (from the English 'living-room').

2 ♦ quatre pièces four rooms (excluding kitchen and bathroom) – a flat like this is often referred to as un F4. Pièce is the general word for 'room', une chambre is a bedroom. Une salle on its own means a large (public) room; in a private house you always specify salle de séjour, salle de bains etc.

3 chacun a sa chambre each (of us) has his own room.

il faut le nettoyer we must clean it (lit. it is necessary to clean it). You have probably noticed that le and la are often used to mean 'him', 'her' or 'it'. You use le when *it* refers to a masculine word and la when *it* refers to a feminine word, e.g. je le connais (I know *him*, I know *it*), je la vois (I see *her*, I see *it*). Similarly, les is used for *them*, e.g. je les aime (I like *them* – people or things).

4 *Sylvie's bed-sit*

Jeanne Où est-ce que tu habites?

Sylvie A Paris – euh – dans le 12ᵉ – à un quart d'heure de mon travail.

Jeanne Et tu as un appartement?

Sylvie Un studio, au huitième étage, avec un ciel, quand il fait beau, merveilleux . . .

Jeanne Un studio, c'est quoi?

Sylvie C'est en général une pièce simplement, mais là j'ai la chance d'avoir une vraie cuisine, et pas un placard qui sert de cuisine, une salle d'eau, qui n'est pas une salle de bains parce qu'il n'y a pas de . . . de baignoire, et des toilettes.

> ◗ **le studio** bed-sitter
> **huitième** eighth
> ◗ **merveilleux** marvellous
> **la chance** luck
> ◗ **vraie (f.)** real
> **sert de** (from **servir de**) serves as
> **la baignoire** bath (tub)

5 *Pierre-Yves' present*

Nadine C'est à qui, ça?

Pierre-Yves A moi.

Nadine Qui est-ce qui a donné ça?

Pierre-Yves Mm – euh – euh – Fafanie.

Nadine C'est un cadeau?

Pierre-Yves Oui.

Nadine Stéphanie est gentille, alors?

Pierre-Yves Oui.

Nadine Tu as dit merci à Stéphanie?

Pierre-Yves Euh – merc(i).

> ◗ **le cadeau** gift

4   **12ᵉ = douzième** 12ᵗʰ arrondissement (district) of Paris.

à un quart d'heure de mon travail a quarter of an hour away from my job.

avec un ciel . . . merveilleux with a marvellous skyscape. **Le ciel** = the sky.

5 ♦ **c'est à qui, ça?** whose is that? (lit. that's to whom, that?).

♦ **à moi** mine (lit. to me). Learn also **c'est à moi** (it is mine), and **c'est à vous** (it is yours).

qui est-ce qui a donné ça? who's given (you) that? (lit. who is it who has given that?). As in English, the past tense in French can be formed with **avoir** and the 'past participle' of the verb: **qui a donné?** (who *has given*?). This will be explained in more detail on p. 183.

Fafanie is Pierre-Yves' pronunciation of the name **Stéphanie**.

tu as dit? have you said? (lit. you have said?). This is the past tense of **dire** (to say).

6 *Michel's trip to the Ivory Coast*

Michel Euh – j'ai quitté Caen par le train, jusqu'à Paris. A Paris, j'ai pris l'avion à Roissy-Charles de Gaulle, un vol direct sur Abidjan, capitale de la Côte d'Ivoire. A Abidjan, là, je n'ai pas pu utiliser les lignes intérieures. J'ai pris l'autocar.

j'ai quitté (from **quitter**) I left
j'ai pris (from **prendre**) I took
la capitale capital
la Côte d'Ivoire Ivory Coast
l'autocar (m.) coach

7 *Bernadette's experience of learning languages*

Barbara Qu'est-ce que tu as commencé par faire comme langue?
Bernadette En premier j'ai appris l'allemand – euh – à l'âge de onze ans à l'école – pas de magnétophones à l'époque! Et puis plus tard l'anglais, et puis plus tard j'ai appris aussi l'italien, mais – euh – en vivant en Italie.
Barbara Combien – euh – d'années as-tu habité en Italie?
Bernadette Alors, en Italie, j'ai vécu dix ans, et là j'ai appris l'italien.

en premier in the first place
▸ **j'ai appris** (from **apprendre**) I learnt
▸ **l'allemand (m.)** German
▸ **le magnétophone** tape recorder
▸ **l'italien (m.)** Italian
as-tu habité? (from **habiter**) did you live?
j'ai vécu (from **vivre**) I lived

6   un vol direct sur Abidjan a direct flight to Abidjan. When talking of flight destinations, the French say **sur** where we say 'to', e.g. **je voudrais un vol direct sur Londres** (I'd like a direct flight to London).

je n'ai pas pu utiliser les lignes intérieures I couldn't use the internal (air) routes. **Je n'ai pas pu** is part of the past tense of **pouvoir** (to be able). 'I could' would be **j'ai pu**.

7   qu'est-ce que tu as commencé par faire comme langue? what did you start by doing in the way of languages?

pas de magnétophones à l'époque! no tape recorders in those days! (lit. at the time).

en vivant while living

♦   en Italie in Italy. You have already met en **Angleterre, en France,** note also en **Allemagne** (in Germany).

Key words and phrases

Your home

(See also p. 173, the first page of this unit.)

dans la maison il y a . . .	in the house/there is/are . . .
l'appartement	the flat
quatre pièces (f.)	four rooms
l'entrée (f.)	the hall
le salon	the sitting-room
le bureau	the study
la salle à manger	the dining-room
la salle d'eau	the shower-room
la chambre des invités	the guest-room
dans le salon il y a . . .	in the sitting room there is . . .
un placard	a cupboard
un magnétophone	a tape recorder
j'ai un studio	I have a bed-sit

The languages you speak

j'ai appris . . .	I learnt . . .
l'allemand, en Allemagne	German, in Germany
l'italien, en Italie	Italian, in Italy
le français, en France	French, in France

Other useful words and phrases

la partie	part
la chose	thing
le cadeau	present
vide	empty
vrai	true
merveilleux	marvellous

Practise what you have learnt

1 Below is the plan of a flat.
Write the names of the various rooms against the appropriate letters below.
(Answers p. 186.) You won't need your tape recorder.

a. ....

b. ....

c. ....

d. ....

e. ....

f. ....

g. ....

h. ....

i. ....

2 Look at the plan of the flat in Exercise 1 on p. 181 and then listen to the tape. Yves and Carolle will make eight statements about this flat. Decide whether these statements are true (**vrai**) or false (**faux**). The first one has been done for you. (Answers p. 186).

a. *vrai* .... e. ....

b. .... f. ....

c. .... g. ....

d. .... h. ....

3 On the tape you will hear Marie-Odile talking about her home. Listen carefully and see if you can answer the following questions. (Answers on p. 186.)

a. Does she live in a house or a flat? ....

b. How many main rooms are there, excluding the kitchen and bathroom?

....

c. How many bedrooms are there? ....

d. Which of the following does she have (tick in the box):
a study? ☐   a cellar? ☐   an attic? ☐   a junk-room? ☐

4 Complete the following sentences from the list below and then listen to the tape where you will hear the full sentences.

On travaille ....

On regarde la télévision ....

On mange ....

On prépare le dîner ....

On met les conserves ....

On prend une douche ....

On dort ....

dans la cuisine   dans la chambre
dans la salle d'eau   dans la salle à manger
dans le bureau   dans un placard ou dans la cave
dans le salon

Grammar

The past tense

Look at these two examples from the dialogues:

j'ai quitté Caen par le train   tu as dit merci à Stéphanie?

J'ai quitté is, literally, 'I *have* left', but it is also used to mean 'I left'. Look at the full past tense of **quitter** (to leave).

j'ai quitté I have left/I left	**nous avons quitté** we have left/we left
tu as quitté you have left/you left	**vous avez quitté** you have left/you left
il/elle a quitté he/she has left	**ils/elles ont quitté** they have left
he/she left	they left

In the negative this becomes:

je n'ai pas quitté	**nous n'avons pas quitté**
tu n'as pas quitté	**vous n'avez pas quitté**
il/elle n'a pas quitté	**ils/elles n'ont pas quitté**

As you see, this tense is made up of the verb **avoir** (to have) plus a new form called the 'past participle'. The past participle for -er verbs is easy to learn as it sounds exactly the same as the infinitive but is spelt with a final -é. Here are some of the commonest examples.

infinitive	*past*	*infinitive*	*past*
acheter (to buy)	**j'ai acheté**	**parler** (to speak)	**j'ai parlé**
casser (to break)	**j'ai cassé**	**penser** (to think)	**j'ai pensé**
commencer (to begin)	**j'ai commencé**	**regarder** (to look at)	**j'ai regardé**
fermer (to close)	**j'ai fermé**	**téléphoner** (to telephone)	**j'ai téléphoné**
grimper (to climb)	**j'ai grimpé**	**travailler** (to work)	**j'ai travaillé**
manger (to eat)	**j'ai mangé**	**visiter** (to visit)	**j'ai visité**
oublier (to forget)	**j'ai oublié**	**voyager** (to travel)	**j'ai voyagé**

Of course, not all verbs have infinitives ending in -er and you will need to know the commonest past participles from other verbs:

infinitive	*past*	*infinitive*	*past*
être (to be)	**j'ai été**	**comprendre** (to understand)	**j'ai compris**
avoir (to have)	**j'ai eu** (pronounced like the u in **tu**)	**perdre** (to lose)	**j'ai perdu**
		voir (to see)	**j'ai vu**
faire (to do, to make)	**j'ai fait**	**boire** (to drink)	**j'ai bu**
écrire (to write)	**j'ai écrit**	**lire** (to read)	**j'ai lu**
dire (to say)	**j'ai dit**	**pouvoir** (to be able)	**j'ai pu**
mettre (to put)	**j'ai mis**	**dormir** (to sleep)	**j'ai dormi**
prendre (to take)	**j'ai pris**	**finir** (to finish)	**j'ai fini**
apprendre (to learn)	**j'ai appris**	**ouvrir** (to open)	**j'ai ouvert**

Exercise   In the following account of a trip to France, many of the verbs are given in the infinitive in brackets. Write them in the past tense. (Answers p. 186.)

A Pâques nous (passer) . . . . huit jours à Paris. Nous (visiter) . . . . la Tour Eiffel, bien sûr, Notre Dame et les autres monuments importants. Nous (voir) . . . . le Château de Versailles et son magnifique parc. Aux grands magasins, nous (acheter) . . . . des cadeaux pour nos amis et nous (admirer) . . . . les belles robes. Malheureusement, j' (perdre) . . . . mon passeport, mais j' (finir) . . . . par le trouver à l'hôtel. Nous (faire) . . . . la connaissance d'une famille française – ils étaient très gentils et nos enfants (jouer) . . . . ensemble.

Read and understand

Read through this account of part of the life of Louis Blériot, a famous French aviator. Then read the questions below. Re-read the passage and then see if you can answer the questions in English. (Answers p. 186)

BLÉRIOT Louis (1872–1936)

Louis Blériot a été un des plus grands pilotes de l'histoire de l'aviation. Il a eu une formation d'ingénieur, et, très jeune, il a commencé à s'intéresser à la nouvelle science de l'aéronautique. En 1900, il a fabriqué un petit modèle d'avion qui a réussi à voler. Ensuite, il a construit une succession de grands avions, mais il n'a pas pu les faire voler. Puis, en 1907, il a eu un succès: son nouvel avion a volé pendant 8 minutes 24 secondes. Blériot a continué à expérimenter et à construire de nouveaux avions, et en 1909, il a construit une belle machine où il a mis le premier levier de commande. Cette année-là, le journal anglais le Daily Mail a offert mille livres sterling pour la première traversée de la Manche en avion. Le 25 juillet, l'avion de Blériot a quitté Les Baraques (à quelques kilomètres de Calais) sans carte et sans compas. Il a fait du brouillard mais Blériot a réussi à trouver Douvres. Quand il a vu le château, il a coupé le moteur pour atterrir; il a un peu cassé l'avion, mais lui-même n'a pas eu de mal. Cette première traversée de la Manche (50 km. via Margate) a duré 37 minutes.

jeune young
nouvelle (f.), nouveau (m.) new
réussi (from réussir) succeeded
construit (from construire) built
nouvel (m.) new (used before a vowel)
pendant for
continué à + infin continued to

le levier de commande joystick
offert (from offrir) offered
la Manche the Channel
Douvres Dover
atterrir to land
coupé (from couper) cut, turned off

1 What was Blériot's professional training? ....

2 Did the model aeroplane he made in 1900 actually fly? ....

3 What about the full-sized ones he made between 1900 and 1906?

....

4 What was his success of 1907? ....

....

5 What spurred him to attempt the Channel crossing? ....

....

6 Did he take a map and a compass? ....

7 What was the weather like? ....

8 What land-mark helped him identify Dover? ....

9 Was his plane damaged in the landing? ....

10 Was he himself hurt? ....

Did you know?

Housing   Most French city-dwellers live in flats. The entrance to each block is watched over by the janitor (**le/la concierge**). Modern blocks naturally have a lift (**un ascenseur**), but there are many old buildings of four storeys or so which do not. The French equivalent to a council house or flat is **une HLM** (**habitation à loyer modéré** – lit. dwelling with moderated rent). By the doorbell of French houses you will usually find the name of the occupant.

Inside a French home, you will probably be struck by the number of labour-saving gadgets in the kitchen (note that it's best not to insist on helping to wash up unless you know people well – many French people do not like their guests to invade their kitchen). The bathroom is likely to be **une salle d'eau**, with a shower instead of a bath, and there will almost certainly be a bidet – for refreshing the parts that wet flannels don't easily reach! French flannels are rectangular bags into which you put your hand; they are known as **gants de toilette** (lit. toilet or washing gloves). Most homes have a living room in which, as Barbara said, **une partie est salon et une partie salle à manger**. When you go to bed you are likely to find you have **un traversin** (a cylindrical bolster) instead of a pillow (**un oreiller**); a hotel will often put a square pillow in the wardrobe in case you prefer it.

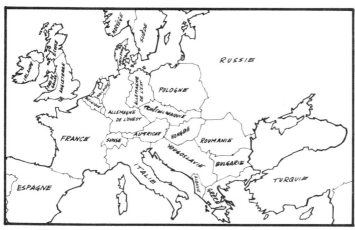

Here are some more names of countries you may need.

l'Australie (f.) Australia
le Canada Canada
la Chine China
les États-Unis The United States
l'Inde (f.) India
le Japon Japan
la Nouvelle-Zélande New Zealand

A thumb-nail sketch of French history

5th Century AD The transformation of Gaul into a modern nation began in this century. The Franks, a barbarian tribe from the east, invaded Gaul and gave their name to France.

843 AD Clovis (Charles le Chauve) was the first French king and he spent most of his reign trying to unify the country.

1661–1715 The most famous monarchs belong to the house of Bourbon; the best known of all is Louis XIV, the Sun King, who ruled France with great splendour for fifty-four years.

1789 The French Revolution signified the end of the old monarchist regime and Louis XVI was executed in 1793.

1804 Napoleon Bonaparte crowned himself emperor in 1804. He is probably the most influential character in the whole of French history; he completely centralised the administration of the country, and imposed a new code of civil law which is still the basis of French law today.

20th Century France today is, of course, a republic – the fifth republic since the Revolution of 1789. Charles de Gaulle was its first president.

Your turn to speak

On the tape Yves will put some questions to you, using the past tense. You should answer them all in the negative, giving a full sentence each time. e.g. if he says **Avez-vous vu la Tour Eiffel?** you should answer **Non, je n'ai pas vu la Tour Eiffel**. You will then hear Carolle giving the correct version.

And finally As usual, before you go on, listen to the dialogues again and test yourself on the *Key words and phrases*. If possible, spend some extra time making sure that you know the past tense of the verbs given in the *Grammar* section. Test yourself by covering up the *past* columns and seeing whether you can remember the past tense for each infinitive. For extra practice, choose two or three and say the whole tense out loud, then try putting them in the negative.

Answers

Practise what you have learnt p. 181 Exercise **1** (a) l'entrée (b) la salle à manger (c) une chambre (d) un placard (e) le salon/la salle de séjour (f) une chambre (g) la salle de bains (h) les toilettes (i) la cuisine.

p. 182 Exercise **2** (a) L'appartement a quatre pièces – vrai (b) La salle à manger est à côté du salon – faux (c) Le placard est ouvert – vrai (d) Les toilettes sont dans la salle de bains – faux (e) La salle à manger est plus grande que le salon – faux (f) Une des chambres est plus grande que l'autre – vrai (g) C'est une vraie salle de bains avec une baignoire – vrai (h) La cuisine est en face de la salle à manger – vrai.

p. 182 Exercise **3** (a) a house (b) five (c) three (d) a cellar and an attic.

Grammar p. 183 avons passé . . . avons visité . . . avons vu . . . avons acheté . . . avons admiré . . . ai perdu . . . ai fini . . . avons fait . . . ont joué.

Read and understand p. 184 (**1**) as an engineer (**2**) yes (**3**) they did not fly (**4**) his new 'plane flew for 8 minutes 24 seconds (**5**) the Daily Mail's offer of £1,000 to the first person to achieve it (**6**) no (**7**) foggy (**8**) the castle (**9**) yes, slightly (**10**) no.

14 Stating your intentions

What you will learn

- asking questions about the future
- talking about the future
- talking about age
- using **son**, **sa** and **ses**
- using reflexive verbs
- something about French leisure activities

Before you begin

In English we can talk about the future EITHER by making statements like 'he will leave' (using the future *tense* of the verb) OR by saying 'he is going to leave' (using *to go* + the infinitive). This is the same in French, but, as the future tense is used less frequently and has many irregular forms, it is simpler to use *aller* + the infinitive. You have already come across this form a number of times in earlier units and will be meeting it again in four of the five dialogues in this unit.

Study hint: remember the motto 'little and often'. It is more valuable to spend a few minutes every day thinking in French than to have a blitz once every few weeks. When you have finished studying this unit, why not try every evening to give an account in French of what you have done during the day – and what your plans are for the next day.

Study guide

Dialogues 1–3: listen straight through without the book
Dialogues 1–3: listen, read and study one by one
Dialogues 4, 5: listen straight through without the book
Dialogues 4, 5: listen, read and study one by one
Learn the *Key words and phrases*
Do the exercises in *Practise what you have learnt*
Study *Grammar* and do the exercise
Do *Read and understand*
Read *Did you know?*
Do the exercises in *Your turn to speak*
Listen to all the dialogues again
Test yourself on the *Key phrases* and reflexive verbs

Dialogues

1 *Ambitions*

Jeanne   Qu'est-ce que tu espères faire dans la vie, alors?

Isabelle   J'espère devenir journaliste, faire des reportages dans les pays étrangers sur – euh – l'actualité.

Jeanne   Et qu'est-ce que tu vas faire pour devenir journaliste?

Isabelle   Je vais faire des stages – euh – dans une école – euh – à Paris.

Jeanne   Quand ça?

Isabelle   Dans un an ou deux ans, après ma licence à l'université.

    le/la journaliste journalist
    faire des reportages to report on
◆ **le pays** country (geographical, not country-side)
    l'actualité (f.) news, what is going on
    le stage course
◆ **l'école (f.)** school, college
    la licence degree
    l'université (f.) university

2 *Plans for tomorrow*

Christian   Alors, demain matin, je vais me lever comme d'habitude à l'aube. Je vais – euh – faire ma toilette. Je vais aller chercher – euh – un collègue qui habite pas très loin d'ici. Je vais – euh – l'emmener à son travail avant de regagner le mien, qui se trouve – euh – dans la même ville mais à environ cinq kilomètres.

◆ **comme d'habitude** as usual
    l'aube (f.) dawn
    le/la collègue colleague
◆ **loin** far
    emmener to take (someone somewhere)
    se trouve is (lit. finds itself)

1 ◆ **qu'est-ce que tu vas faire?** what are you going to do? Just as in English we can express the future by saying 'I am going to . . . eat/speak/write' in French you just use the appropriate part of the verb **aller** (to go) with the infinitive of the verb you need. e.g.

je vais . . . manger/parler/écrire
tu vas . . . manger/parler/écrire
il/elle va . . . manger/parler/écrire
nous allons . . . manger/parler/écrire
vous allez . . . manger/parler/écrire
ils/elles vont . . . manger/parler/écrire

2 ◆ **je vais me lever** I'll get up (lit. get myself up). 'To get up' is a reflexive verb in French. These verbs will be explained on p. 197.

◆ **je vais faire ma toilette** I'll wash and dress.

◆ **je vais aller chercher** I'll go and fetch. **Chercher** means 'to look for' but **aller chercher** means 'to go and fetch', e.g. **allez chercher votre manteau** (go and fetch your coat). Similarly, **venir chercher** means 'to come and fetch', e.g. **venez me chercher à la gare** (come and fetch me from the station).

l'emmener to take him. The **l'** is short for **le** (him). Look back at the notes on dialogue 3, Unit 13, p. 175.

avant de regagner le mien before getting back to mine. Note that French uses **avant de** + an infinitive where we say 'before . . . ing', e.g. **j'étais à l'université avant de devenir journaliste** (I was at university before becoming a journalist). **Le mien** (mine) refers to **mon travail**; the feminine form for 'mine' would be **la mienne**, e.g. **vous n'avez pas votre voiture aujourd'hui? . . . prenez la mienne!** (haven't you got your car today? . . . take mine!).

3 *Changing jobs*

Christian A la rentrée donc – euh – je vais changer de lieu de travail. Je vais en effet – euh – passer d'un travail d'un côté de la ville à un lieu de travail de l'autre côté de la ville.

Jeanne Et qu'est-ce que vous allez faire dans ce nouveau lieu de travail?

Christian Je vais être responsable d'une – euh – maison de quartier, qui est le . . . le centre d'animation du quartier – un lieu où toutes les personnes peuvent se rencontrer pour – euh – y trouver différents services administratifs, sociaux, médicaux – pour discuter, pour – euh – boire un verre – ou se distraire.

le lieu de travail place of work
en effet in fact
responsable de responsible for
le quartier district (of a town)
différents (m. pl.) different, various
administratifs (m. pl.) administrative
sociaux (m. pl.) social (m. sing.) social
médicaux (m. pl.) médical (m. sing.) medical
discuter to chat
se distraire to amuse oneself

4 *Jobs that will need doing*

Claire Vous me demandez ce que je vais faire à Paris, quand je vais rentrer à Paris? Eh ben, qu'est-ce que je vais faire? Je vais prendre le train, pour commencer, et, arrivée chez moi, mm – j'y ai beaucoup de choses à faire, puisque mon fils va rentrer en classe. Alors je vais aller avec lui dans les grands magasins pour – euh – acheter ce qui lui manque comme vestiaire. Je vais préparer – euh – ses livres, ses cahiers – euh – ça fait déjà pas mal de choses . . . Et puis, personnellement, j'ai un autre problème: je dois me trouver un nouvel appartement. Alors, je vais chercher, je vais visiter, je vais grimper des étages, je vais téléphoner à des . . . des agences . . . à des agences immobilières, qui vont me convoquer, et je vais aller visiter, arpenter des rues – euh – pour comparer les appartements.

  ◆ **vous demandez** (from **demander**) you ask
  puisque since
  ◆ **le fils** son
  préparer to prepare
  ◆ **le livre** book
  le cahier exercise book
  l'agence immobilière (f.) estate agent's
  convoquer to call to an appointment
  arpenter to tramp up and down
  comparer to compare

3 ◆ **à la rentrée** when I get back after the holiday (lit. at the return). **La rentrée** is the name given to both the period when everyone returns from their holidays, when the roads are very crowded, and to the beginning of term.

une maison de quartier a community centre.

le centre d'animation the social centre. Literally, **animation** means 'putting life into something' and the leader of any group is often known as the **animateur**.

◆ **se rencontrer** meet up or meet each other. Another reflexive verb – see p. 197.

Part of Christian's community centre: a day centre for old people (**le troisième âge** is old age). **Un foyer** can also be a hostel attached to a college or university.

4 **ce que** what (lit. that which). This is the object of **je vais faire**.

arrivée chez moi (having) arrived home.

rentrer en classe to go back to school (lit. to go back in class).

avec lui with him. 'With her' would be **avec elle**; you have already met **avec moi** (with me) and **avec vous /avec toi** (with you).

ce qui lui manque comme vestiaire whatever he needs in the way of clothes (lit. that which is lacking to him in the way of clothing). There is no verb 'to miss' or 'to lack' in French: you can't say 'he lacks clothes' – it has to be 'clothes are lacking to him'. Here are some further examples:
l'argent me manque I lack money (lit. money is lacking to me)
tu me manques I miss you (lit. you are lacking to me)

ce qui what (lit. that which). This is the subject of **manque**.

nouvel new. You cannot use **nouveau** before a masculine noun beginning with a vowel. Other examples: **un nouvel autobus** (a new bus), **un nouvel ami** (a new friend).

5 *How old are you?*

Nadine	Tu as quel âge?
Pierre-Yves	...
Nadine	Quel âge tu as?
Pierre-Yves	...
Nadine	Quel âge as-tu?
Pierre-Yves	Deux!
Nadine	Deux ans.
Pierre-Yves	Deux ans.

5   **tu as quel âge** how old are you? (lit. you have what age?). You must use
the verb **avoir**, not **être**, for giving and asking about age, e.g.

‣ **quel âge avez-vous? j'ai soixante ans**. Try to work out how *you* would tell
someone your age.

Key words and phrases

The future

qu'est-ce que vous allez/espérez faire?	what are you going/do you hope to do?
aujourd'hui/demain?	today/tomorrow?
à la rentrée?	at the end of the holidays/the beginning of term

je vais . . .	I'm going to/I'll . . .
me lever	get up
faire ma toilette	wash and dress
aller chercher mon fils à l'école	go and fetch my son from school
sortir avec lui/avec elle	go out with him/with her
acheter un livre	buy a book
chercher un nouvel appartement	look for a new flat
visiter un pays étranger	visit a foreign country

comme d'habitude, ils vont . . .	as usual, they're going to . . .
demander (une grande chambre)	ask for (a big room)
se rencontrer (au restaurant)	meet each other (at the restaurant)

j'espère aller au restaurant	I hope to go to the restaurant
c'est loin?	is it far?

Age

quel âge avez-vous?	how old are you?
j'ai (soixante) ans	I'm (sixty)

Extra vocabulary

The names for most sports are the same in French as in English and they are all masculine. You may like to know:
jouer au football to play football
and **jouer au rugby/tennis/cricket/badminton/ping-pong**
One slight difference from the English is **jouer au basket** (to play basketball).
Other sporting activities include:
faire du ski to go skiing
faire de la natation to go swimming
nager to swim
se baigner to bathe
faire du cheval to go horse riding
(also **faire de l'équitation**)

Practise what you have learnt

1 Choose from **B** the phrase you need to complete each of the sentences begun in **A** and write it in the gap provided. Then listen to the tape where you will hear the answers, which together describe a day-trip to the seaside.

A Demain, nous allons passer ....

....

Nous allons nous lever ....

....

Nous allons prendre ....

....

Nous allons boire ....

....

Nous allons arriver à Cabourg ....

....

S'il fait beau ....

....

A midi nous allons trouver ....

....

Nous espérons manger ....

....

Pendant l'après-midi, les enfants ....

....

Puis le train du retour ....

....

Arrivés chez nous ....

....

B   va partir à huit heures du soir.   des fruits de mer.
le train de sept heures.   à l'aube.
nous allons jouer sur la plage.   un restaurant.
la journée à Cabourg.   vers neuf heures du matin.
vont se baigner dans la mer.   du café dans le train.
nous allons nous coucher tout de
  suite.

2 Imagine you are the woman whose morning routine is illustrated below. Answer the questions you will hear on the tape about what you will be doing tomorrow morning. Say your answer out loud and also write it in the gap provided. (Answers on p. 200.)

1. ....

2. ....

3. ....

4. ....

5. ....

6. ....

7. ....

....

3 You have received the letter below from a French acquaintance who is going to visit England soon. Write each of the following words in the appropriate gap in the letter. You won't need your tape recorder. (Answers on p. 200.)

arriver	rencontrer	venir	besoin	allons
demander	vol	va	28	
loin	chez	rentrer	vers	
cher	merci	plus tard	ont-ils	
a	prendre	gentille	quitter	

                                                        Chartres

                                                        le 5 juin

            Chère Madame,

                        ....beaucoup de

votre....................lettre - et félicitations pour votre français!

    Oui, nous....................visiter votre pays - enfin! Mon fils va

....................à l'école le 15 septembre, alors, je dois être de

retour vers le 12. Si possible, je voudrais....................en

Angleterre avec lui. (Il....................douze ans. Et vos enfants,

quel âge....................?)

    Nous allons....................Chartres (qui n'est pas

........de Paris) le....................août, ...midi.

Notre avion....................partir d'Orly à 15h. pour....................

une heure....................à Heathrow. C'est un....................

sur Air France.

    Puis-je vous....................de nous recommander un hôtel pas

trop....................à Londres?

    Quand est-ce qu'on peut se....................? Vous n'avez pas

....................de venir nous chercher: nous pouvons très bien

....................un train pour aller....................vous.

    Amicalement à vous,

            Madeleine Louis

Grammar

Son, sa, ses

Son, sa and ses mean EITHER 'his' OR 'her' and the form to use is determined by the gender of the *following noun*, not by the sex of the owner, e.g.

il aime son père   he loves his father
elle aime son père   she loves her father

In these examples **son** is used in both cases because **père** is masculine.

However, **son** is also used before a feminine singular noun when it begins with a vowel. (See also **mon** and **ton** Unit 11, p. 157.), e.g.

il aime bien son amie   he is fond of his (girl)friend
elle aime bien son amie   she is fond of her friend

Before all other feminine singular nouns you should use **sa**, e.g.

il aime sa mère   he loves his mother
elle aime sa mère   she loves her mother

Ses is the plural for both masculine and feminine nouns, e.g.

il aime ses parents   he loves his parents
elle aime ses parents   she loves her parents

Exercise

Write **son**, **sa** or **ses**, as appropriate, in each of the gaps below.

1 Il mange .... petit déjeuner.

2 Elle regarde .... frère.

3 A-t-il lu tous .... livres?

4 Elle parle avec .... grand-mère.

5 A-t-il vu .... lettre?

6 A-t-elle mangé .... orange?

7 Aime-t-il .... cadeaux?

Reflexive verbs

In English if you say 'I'm going to get up' you mean you are going to get *yourself* up; if you say you are going to wash, it is understood that you will be washing yourself. In French you have to specify that it is yourself by using a 'reflexive' verb. This is just the grammatical term used when you are doing something to or for yourself, e.g. **se lever**/to get (oneself) up, **se laver**/to wash (oneself). Here is the pattern followed by all reflexive verbs in the present tense:

je me lave   **nous nous lavons**
tu te laves   **vous vous lavez**
il/elle se lave **ils/elles se lavent**

In the negative this becomes **je ne me lave pas** etc.

Perhaps the most useful reflexive verb is **s'appeler** (lit. to call oneself) which you met already in Unit 5. You should learn the phrase **comment vous appelez-vous?** (what's your name? lit. how do you call yourself?) and **je m'appelle . . .** (my name is . . .).

Here are some reflexive verbs used in common requests for someone to do something:

asseyez-vous   sit down
adressez-vous (au bureau 'Informations')   go and ask (at the Information office)
approchez-vous   come closer

You may sometimes hear an ordinary verb used in a reflexive form, to give the idea of people doing something together, e.g. **nous nous regardons** (we look at each other), **elles s'écrivent** (they write to each other).

Read and understand

Read this letter and then check your understanding by answering the questions below in English

                                          Lille
                                          le 10 juillet
                      Ma chère Julie,
                              Je te remercie de ta
gentille lettre. La mienne va être moins longue parce que je vais
partir en vacances demain matin - il faut faire les bagages ce
soir.
                              Nous allons passer quinze
jours à Aix-en-Provence - et c'est au moment du Festival! J'ai
toujours eu envie d'aller au Festival d'Aix, et maintenant - pour
la première fois de ma vie - je vais y aller! Georges n'aime pas
beaucoup l'opéra, mais il va m'accompagner jeudi à 'Elisabetta
Regina d'Inghilterra' de Rossini - c'est au théâtre antique d'Arles,
mais ça fait partie du Festival d'Aix. Puis vendredi il va y avoir
un concert de Mozart en plein air. Samedi j'ai envie d'aller au
'Requiem' de Verdi au Théâtre de l'Archevêché, mais Georges m'a
dit "Vas-y, toi. Moi, samedi soir, je préfère aller au bar." J'ai
déjà réservé des places pour le 'Requiem', alors je vais y aller
toute seule. C'est cher, toutes ces réservations!
                              Georges m'appelle - il
commence à faire ses bagages et il ne trouve pas ses chaussettes!
                      Je t'embrasse,
                                  Hélène

longue (f.) (m. long) long
plein air open air
je t'embrasse the quivalent of 'much love' (lit. I kiss you)

1 When is Hélène going on holiday? ....

2 What job does she have to do this evening? ....

3 How long will she spend in Aix-en-Provence? ....

4 Is it the first time she has been to the Festival? ....

5 Is her husband Georges keen on opera? ....

6 Who composed the opera they will be seeing in the ancient Roman

   theatre in Arles? ....

7 When is the open air concert? ....

8 Where will Georges be going on Saturday evening? ....

9 Will Hélène be with him? ....

10 What has George not been able to find to put in his suitcase? ....

   ....

Did you know?

Leisure activities

The French working day tends to be long, leaving little time over for relaxation. The great escape is the annual four-week holiday. Nearly two million families have a second home to go to during this holiday or at weekends. Camping has also become very popular over the last few years.

A much loved national pastime is the weekly gamble on the horses. Betting is not in special 'betting shops' but in cafés and bars with the sign **PMU**. Every Sunday, many French families place a bet on horses running in a race called **le tiercé** in which you have to guess the first three past the post. The largest amount of money is won by people who have also predicted the first three in the correct order; smaller amounts are won by those who have the first three horses, but in the wrong order.

Every week many French people also buy **un billet de la loterie nationale** – a ticket in the national lottery. The winnings vary; they are always high, but even higher on particular occasions such as Christmas and 14th July. You can also buy **un dixième** (a tenth share of a ticket). A warning for would-be punters: you will not be sent your winnings automatically, you will have to look up the prize-winning numbers in the newspaper and then make a claim.

The most popular team-sports are soccer and rugger. (**Le rugby** is the great game in the south-west.) Organized competition in both games is avidly followed by fans all over the country. Cycling is another favourite and the Tour de France, which takes place in the summer and lasts for three weeks, is the most important sporting event of the year. The overall winner wears **le maillot jaune** (the yellow jersey) and is awarded large prizes.

Fishing, hunting, skiing, sailing, wind-surfing and **boules** are other favourite activities. The game of **boules** – called **pétanque** in the south – consists of first throwing **le cochonnet** (the jack) and then throwing your bowls as near as possible to it. **Boules** should be made of metal, but you can buy coloured wooden ones quite cheaply for playing on the beach or at a camp-site.

If you enjoy festivals you are spoiled for choice in France (or, as the French say, **vous avez l'embarras du choix**). Probably the most famous of all is the Festival of Aix-en-Provence, a three-week orgy of classical music held every July/August. The charm of Aix is exploited to the full in the choice of venues, many of them open-air, with opera and ballet in the courtyard of the old Archbishop's Palace and early music in the cathedral cloister. Some items from the programme are put on outside Aix: the spectacular Roman theatre at Arles is a favourite setting. There is also a fringe programme to cater for non-classical tastes, in particular for those who like folk music (**la musique folklorique**).

Festival tickets should generally be booked in advance. If you are alarmed by the price there is a very attractive – and free – alternative to the Festival. This is **la musique dans la rue**, which takes place for about three weeks before the start of the Festival. It is, quite literally, music in the street – music of all kinds – in the tree-lined Cours Mirabeau and in the many quiet little squares with fountains that one finds all over Aix.

You can obtain a programme for the Festival and for **la musique dans la rue** by sending an international reply coupon (available at post offices) to: Le Bureau du Festival, 32 place des Martyrs de la Résistance, 13100 Aix-en-Provence   Tel. (010 33) (42) 23–05–02

Be warned that accommodation is much more expensive during the pre-Festival and Festival period. It is also likely to be fully booked, so do not trust to luck.

Your turn to speak

1 An exercise to practise reflexive verbs. Yves will ask the questions. Pause the tape and answer, using a full sentence starting with **oui** . . . Carolle will then give the correct replies. Here is an example.

Carolle **Vous vous levez à l'aube quelquefois?**

You **Oui, je me lève à l'aube quelquefois.**

2 Next a conversation. Take the part of a woman dealing with a persistent admirer! He'll want to know what you are going to be doing in the near future. Pierre will prompt you and Carolle will give you the correct replies. When you have tried this exercise a couple of times, try stopping the tape *before* Pierre's prompt and give your own answers.

3 Lastly, on tape you will hear some open-ended questions for you to answer as you wish. Pause the tape after each to give yourself time to reply. If you find the questions difficult to understand, they are printed below in the *Answers* section.

And finally Listen to the dialogue again and test yourself on the *Key words and phrases* and (if you are at all interested in sport) on the extra vocabulary. To check that you understand reflexive verbs, try to write out **se coucher** (to go to bed). Then write it in the negative as well (**je ne me couche pas** etc.). You can check your answers below.

Answers

Practise what you have learnt p. 195 Exercise **2 (1)** Je vais me lever. **(2)** Je vais faire ma toilette. **(3)** Je vais préparer le/mon petit déjeuner. **(4)** Je vais manger mon petit déjeuner. **(5)** À huit heures dix. **(6)** A huit heures vingt-cinq. **(7)** Je suis médecin.

p. 196 Exercise **3** Merci . . . gentille . . . allons . . . rentrer . . . venir . . . a . . . ont-ils . . . quitter . . . loin . . . 28 . . . vers . . . va . . . arriver . . . plus tard . . . vol . . . demander . . . cher . . . rencontrer . . . besoin . . . prendre . . . chez.

Grammar p. 197 **(1)** son **(2)** son **(3)** ses **(4)** sa **(5)** sa **(6)** son **(7)** ses.

Read and understand p. 198 **(1)** tomorrow morning **(2)** pack **(3)** fifteen days **(4)** yes **(5)** no **(6)** Rossini **(7)** Friday **(8)** to a bar **(9)** no **(10)** his socks.

Your turn to speak (open-ended questions) **(1)** Comment vous appelez-vous? **(2)** Qu'est-ce que vous aimez comme sports? **(3)** Et vous allez souvent au cinéma et au théâtre? **(4)** Quels pays avez-vous visité? **(5)** Et quels pays est-ce que vous voulez visiter? **(6)** Pour aller en France, quel est le moyen de transport que vous préférez? **(7)** Qu'est-ce que vous allez faire pendant les vacances? **(8)** Que pensez-vous de la langue française?

And finally (above) je me couche, tu te couches, il/elle se couche, nous nous couchons, vous vous couchez, ils/elles se couchent.
je ne me couche pas, tu ne te couches pas, il/elle ne se couche pas, nous ne nous couchons pas, vous ne vous couchez pas, ils/elles ne se couchent pas.

15 Talking about the past

What you will learn

- describing past holidays
- describing past leisure activities
- talking about an accident
- saying you are hungry, thirsty, hot or cold
- something about EEC health agreements
- something about overseas French **départements**

Before you begin

As you will be learning more about the past tense in this unit, can you remember how to say the following? (Answers below.)
At Easter I visited Paris.
I saw the Eiffel Tower.
I took the underground.
I spoke French every day
Everyone understood my French.
Also, look back at p. 119 and revise the verbs of movement.

This is, of course, the last unit of the course. You should find the language you have learnt here of value if you go to a French-speaking country, but don't give up French when you have finished this course. Even if you don't have a chance to practise speaking regularly with French people, try not to let your language skills get rusty. Take every opportunity to read or speak French, even if only for a few minutes at a time.

Answers

A Pâques j'ai visité Paris. J'ai vu la Tour Eiffel. J'ai pris le métro. J'ai parlé français tous les jours. Tout le monde a compris mon français.

Study Guide

	Dialogues 1–3: listen straight through without the book
	Dialogues 1–3: listen, read and study one by one
	Dialogues 4, 5: listen straight through without the book
	Dialogues 4, 5: listen, read and study one by one
	Learn the *Key words and phrases*
	Do the exercises in *Practise what you have learnt*
	Study *Grammar* and do the exercise
	Do *Read and understand*
	Read *Did you know?*
	Do *Your turn to speak*
	Listen to the dialogues again
	Test yourself on the *Key words* and the verbs from *Grammar*
	Do the revision exercises on p. 218–219.

Dialogues

1 *A trip to England*

Isabelle Alors, je suis partie – euh – par – euh – Boulogne et j'ai pris le car-ferry jusqu'à Douvres. On est allé jusqu'à Maidstone. Je suis restée une semaine à Maidstone. Après, je suis allée à Londres. J'ai visité Londres . . . les musées . . . j'ai vu un peu toutes les curiosités de la ville. Et puis, je suis retournée dans le Kent. J'ai fait du tennis et de la natation. Le temps était assez beau.

le car-ferry car ferry
la curiosité interesting thing, sight

2 *What Barbara did yesterday*

Barbara Euh – hier – euh – nous avons un peu joué à la maison avec – euh – nos voisins. Après, – euh – nous sommes allés ensemble – euh – à la piscine. On a joué, on a nagé, on a fait des courses. Après, – euh – on est allé boire une petite boisson parce que . . . on avait soif. Et après – euh – on a essayé d'avoir un court de tennis, mais on n'a pas pu. Alors, nous avons pris nos vélos . . . nous avons fait un grand tour dans le bois . . . et . . . puis après, – euh – on est rentré à la maison.

◆ **hier** yesterday
le court de tennis tennis court
◆ **le vélo** (also **la bicyclette**) bicycle
◆ **faire un tour** to go for a ride or walk
le bois wood

3 *Sailing to Morocco*

Brigitte Euh – je suis allée au Maroc en voilier. Nous sommes partis de France – euh – à la fin de juillet en bateau et nous sommes arrivés – euhm – cinq jours plus tard en Espagne. Nous sommes repartis mais nous avons dû faire escale – euh – une centaine de kilomètres plus loin, de nouveau en Espagne. Et . . . de là nous avons réussi à avoir des vents plus favorables et . . . nous sommes allés directement à Casablanca au Maroc.

le Maroc Morocco
le voilier sailing-boat, yacht
◆ **le bateau** boat
◆ **une centaine de** about 100
◆ **de nouveau** again
favorables (pl.) favourable
directement directly

1

◆ **je suis partie** I left. In this last unit comes a tricky point: some verbs make their past tense with **être** instead of **avoir**, and their past participles are spelt differently according to the subject, e.g. **parti** (masculine sing.), **partie** (feminine sing.), **partis** (m. pl.), **parties** (f. pl.). This does *not* alter the pronunciation. (See p. 209)

◆ **on est allé** we went. Another past with **être**.

◆ **je suis restée** I stayed. Note **je suis resté à la maison** (I stayed at home).

je suis retournée I returned.

2

on a fait des courses we had races

◆ **Faire des courses** can also mean 'to run errands' or 'to go shopping' e.g. **je vais faire des courses** (I'm going to go shopping).

on avait soif we were thirsty (lit. one had thirst). **Avait**, from the verb **avoir**, belongs to the same continuous past tense as **était**, from the verb **être**.

◆ Whereas in English we say 'I am thirsty', and 'I am hungry', in French you say 'I have thirst' and 'I have hunger': **j'ai soif** and **j'ai faim**. Similarly, **j'ai chaud** means 'I am hot' and **j'ai froid** means 'I am cold'.

on est rentré à la maison we went home.

3

nous sommes arrivés we arrived.

en Espagne in Spain. **En** is used for 'in' or 'to' with the names of most countries. One of the few exceptions is **au Maroc** in line 1.

nous sommes repartis we set off again.

◆ **nous avons dû** we had to. This is the past tense of **devoir** (to have to).

faire escale put into port. This can also mean 'to stop over', for example on a long flight.

The boss's motorcycle accident

Jean-Claude Et ton patron? Tu m'as dit qu'il a eu un accident . . .
Michèle Ah oui, en ce moment c'est la mode! Il a eu un accident de moto. Alors, il est tombé; il s'est cassé le coude, en plusieurs morceaux; on l'a conduit à l'hôpital et on l'a opéré tout de suite.
Jean-Claude Et sa moto?
Michèle Elle est complètement cassée. Alors il a été obligé de . . . de prendre un taxi et d'arriver – euh – à Paris, le bras tout pendant, avant d'aller consulter. Enfin, c'était une catastrophe, quoi!

le patron boss
le morceau piece
cassée (f.) broken
obligé de obliged to
la catastrophe catastrophe

☐ **5** *Michèle's holiday on the Côte d'Azur*

Michèle Alors, cet été, je suis allée en vacances sur la Côte d'Azur, chez des amis, et j'en ai profité pour visiter un petit peu la . . . la Côte d'Azur, qui est un des plus beaux endroits de France. Nous sommes allés à la plage évidemment presque tous les jours, mais nous avons changé de plage. Donc, nous avons visité pas mal d'endroits, et des endroits moins fréquentés que . . . que les grandes plages, qui sont bondées. Et puis, – euh – en ce moment il y a des modes – euh – sur la Côte d'Azur, donc, nous avons fait de la planche à voile, comme tout le monde, et nous avons joué à tous ces jeux de raquette qui ressemblent au tennis mais qui sont des tennis sous-developpés. Et puis, nous avons mangé dans des petits restaurants sur la plage, des petits restaurants très simples . . . et – euhm – vraiment c'était très agréable.

évidemment obviously
♦ **presque** nearly
bondées (f. pl.) crowded out
la planche à voile wind-surfing
♦ **le jeu** game
la raquette racquet
sous-developpés (m. pl.) under-developed

4   **tu m'as dit** you told me.

♦ **c'est la mode!** it's the fashion! it's all the rage!

♦ **un accident de moto** a motorbike accident. A car accident is **un accident de voiture.**

♦ **il est tombé** he fell. (Again, see p. 209)

il s'est cassé le coude he broke his elbow. This is the past tense of a reflexive verb (see p. 197). Notice that in French you say '*the* elbow' and not 'his elbow' because the reflexive verb makes it quite clear whose elbow is referred to. If you are unlucky you might also need to say:

♦ **je me suis cassé le bras** I have broken my arm or
♦ **je me suis cassé la jambe** I have broken my leg

on l'a conduit à l'hôpital they took him to hospital. From **conduire** (to drive, to take).

on l'a opéré they operated on him.

le bras tout pendant (with) his arm hanging down.

avant d'aller consulter before going to consult (a doctor).

quoi lit. what? Here it is used to finish the exclamation and has no particular meaning.

5   **j'en ai profité** I took advantage of it.

♦ **endroits** places, spots. **Endroit** is a more usual word than **lieu**.

nous avons changé de plage we changed beaches.

qui ressemblent au tennis which are like tennis. From **ressembler** à (to be like, to resemble).

Key words and phrases

hier	yesterday
je suis resté(e) à la maison	I stayed at home
je suis parti(e)	I left
nous avons dû . . .	we had to . . .
faire des courses	do some shopping
on est allé . . .	we went . . .
faire un tour	for a walk/for a ride
j'ai eu un . . .	I've had a . . .
accident de moto	motorbike accident
accident de voiture	car accident
je me suis cassé . . .	I've broken . . .
le bras	my arm
la jambe	my leg
il a eu un accident	he had an accident
avec le bateau	with the boat
avec le vélo	with the bicycle
c'était un jeu	it was a game
il est tombé	he fell
il s'est cassé (le coude)	he broke (his elbow)
on l'a conduit à l'hôpital	they drove him to the hospita
j'ai faim	I'm hungry
j'ai soif	I'm thirsty
j'ai chaud	I'm hot
j'ai froid	I'm cold
c'est la mode!	it's the fashion
une centaine (de)	about a hundred
presque	nearly
le morceau	bit, piece
l'endroit (m.)	place

Practise what you have learnt

1 Listen as many times as you like to the recording on tape of Claire saying where she has been on holiday this year and then answer the following questions. (Answers on p. 212).

a. Why does she say she has been lucky?

....

b. When did she first leave Paris?

....

c. How long did she stay in Soulac then?

....

d. With whom did she go to the Alps? ....

e. What did she do there?

....

f. Where did she meet the person she is talking to?

....

2 Below is the description of an accident. Fill in the gaps in the passage with the appropriate word from this list. (Answers on p. 212.) You won't need your tape recorder.

endroit	tombé	vélo	tour	parti	s'est cassé	a
accident	hier	conduit	centaine	hôpital	allé	presqu'

.... matin, Georges est ....

vers dix heures. Il a pris son .... et il est

.... faire un .... dans le

bois qui se trouve à une .... de mètres de la

maison. Il etait dans un .... qui n'était pas

fréquenté quand il a eu un .... Un chien est

sorti du bois et Georges n'a pas pu l'éviter. Il est ....

de son vélo et il .... le coude en plusieurs

morceaux. Il avait très mal, mais il .... dû

marcher .... un kilomètre pour rentrer à

la maison. Là, on l'a .... tout de suite

à l' ...., où on l'a opéré.

3 Listen to Yves on tape describing a disastrous journey and then answer the questions below.

a. What do Yves and his family usually do during the Christmas

holidays? ....

b. Where did they go this time? ....

c. In which town do their friends live? ....

d. What does Yves say is the big national holiday in England?

....

e. On what date did they start the return journey?

....

f. Where did it start to snow? ....

g. At what time did they arrive in Dover? ....

h. When was the next boat to sail? ....

i. At what time did Yves come out of the hotel in the morning?

....

j. What did he do then? ....

....

k. How long did he stay in the hospital? ....

....

l. Where did his family stay meanwhile? ....

m. What did his friends think? ....

....

n. And what does he think? ....

....

Grammar

Past tense with être

A very few verbs, notably those of movement (e.g. to come, go, arrive, leave etc), form their past tense with **être** instead of **avoir**. *All* reflexive verbs also form their past with **être**.

Here is the full form of the past tense of **aller**.

je suis allé(e)	I went I have gone	**nous sommes allé(e)(s)**	we went we have gone
tu es allé(e)	you went you have gone	**vous êtes allé(e)(s)**	you went you have gone
il est allé	he went he has gone	**ils sont allés** **elles sont allées** }	they went they have gone
elle est allée	she went she has gone		

And here is the past tense of a reflexive verb **se réveiller** (to wake up)

je me suis réveillé(e)   **nous nous sommes réveillé(e)s**
tu t'es réveillé(e)   **vous vous êtes réveillé(e)(s)**
il s'est réveillé   **ils se sont réveillés**
elle s'est réveillée   **elles se sont réveillées**

As you can see, with past tenses formed with **être**, the past participle behaves like an adjective, i.e. it is feminine if the person it refers to is feminine, and plural if it refers to more than one person. So a man would write **je suis allé** for 'I went' but a woman would write **je suis allée**. This is only important if you want to *write* accurately as there is no difference in the sound of the word.

The other verbs which form their past tense with **être** are:

venir (to come) **je suis venu(e) etc.**   **rester** (to stay) **je suis resté(e)**
arriver (to arrive) **je suis arrivé(e)**   **tomber** (to fall) **je suis tombé(e)**
partir (to leave) **je suis parti(e)**   **naître** (to be born) **je suis né(e)**
entrer (to enter) **je suis entré(e)**   **mourir** (to die) **il est mort** (here th
sortir (to go out) **je suis sorti(e)**   sound *does*
monter (to go up) **je suis monté(e)**   change) **elle est**
descendre (to go down) **je suis descendu(e)**   **mor<u>te</u>**

It's worth learning this list; it contains all the verbs you need to know.

Exercise   Write out the correct form of the past tense for each of the verbs below.

e.g. Il (tomber)   *il est tombé* ....(Answers p. 212)

1   Il (arriver) ....

2   Elle (entrer) ....

3   Nous (venir) ....

4   Je (rester) ....

5   Tu (descendre) ....

6   Il (naître) ....

7   Elle (mourir) ....

8   Elles (sortir) ....

9   Ils (monter) ....

Read and understand

Here is an extract from a tourist brochure for la Roche-sur-Yon. See if you can answer the questions below. (Answers p. 212)

'**La Roche Loisirs'** journal en vente le premier du mois dans toutes les librairies – 1F.

Musée Municipal: rue Clémenceau, ouvert tous les jours juillet-août 10–12h et 14–18h (entrée 2F); gratuit hors saison mais fermé dimanche et lundi.

Théâtre restauré. Le théâtre municipal de l'époque Louis-Philippe accueille les troupes en tournée, les concerts et les réunions diverses.

Concerts dans l'ancien Palais de Justice; le Conservatoire de Musique et d'Art Dramatique offre une salle de 240 places et accueille 900 élèves. Des concerts se donnent aussi au théâtre et dans des églises.

Expositions: le musée municipal en accueille plusieurs chaque année, mais les artistes exposent aussi, assez fréquemment, dans les Foyers de Jeunes Travailleurs et les centres socio-culturels.

Bibliothèque: l'une des plus fréquentées de France, la bibliothèque municipale (avec salles de travail) se trouve rue Lafayette mais il y a une annexe pour les jeunes au centre socio-culturel des Pyramides. L'emprunt est gratuit. Ouvert l'après-midi sauf lundi.

Marché aux Puces: deuxième dimanche matin du mois devant l'église du Bourg-sous-la-Roche.

les loisirs (m.) leisure activities
la librairie book-shop
hors saison out of season
accueille (from **accueillir**) welcomes
en tournée on tour
la réunion meeting

l'élève (m. and f.) pupil, student
l'exposition (f.) exhibition
chaque each
la bibliothèque library
l'emprunt (m.) loan
le marché aux puces flea-market

1 When is the guide to local activities published?

....

2 Where can you buy it? ....

3 Between what times is the municipal museum closed for lunch in

July and August? ....

4 Is it open every day of the week in November? ....

5 What is the theatre used for?

....

6 Where else are concerts given, other than at the Conservatoire and

the theatre? ....

7 Where can you see art exhibitions? ....

....

8 Can you go to the library to work? ....

9 Is it open on Monday afternoons? ....

10 How much does it cost to borrow a book? ....

Did you know?

Health

A few weeks before you travel to any other country in the EEC, you should obtain from your local DHSS office a copy of leaflet SA 30, *Medical treatment during visits abroad*. You will need to fill out the form at the back of the leaflet and send it in to the DHSS office at least two weeks before you travel. The form will then be stamped and returned to you. You should take it abroad with you – it is your certificate of entitlement to a refund on emergency medical or dental treatment. In France you will receive 80% refund on hospital expenses, about 75% of medical or dental fees and 70% of prescribed medicines, provided you supply all the relevant documentation, including the **vignettes** from the medicine containers (these are detachable seals showing the name and cost of the medicine). The problem with the system is that you have to pay first and then claim your refund afterwards. See leaflet SA 30 for how to claim a refund. Note the verb **rembourser** (to reimburse, to refund).

French departments overseas

In addition to the ninety-five **départements** of the **métropole** (mainland France), there are four overseas **départements**, collectively referred to as **la France d'outre-mer** (overseas France). They are French Guyana (in the north of South America), the islands of Martinique and Guadeloupe in the West Indies, and La Réunion, which is a small island east of Madagascar. These overseas territories are full **départements**, not colonies: people there vote in French elections and send their own members of parliament to Paris. The education system, syllabuses and text-books are the same as those used in mainland France.

Martinique, known as the island of flowers, was the birthplace of Josephine, the first wife of Napoleon. Guadeloupe is formed of two islands, Grande-Terre and Basse-Terre. Both islands are covered in tropical rain-forests and are renowned for their beautiful sandy beaches. The mother-tongue of most people on the islands is Creole, a mixture of French and the original native language which was spoken before the arrival of Europeans. The islanders too are generally of mixed races and are known as Creoles.

Cayenne, the capital of French Guyana, is well known for its pepper. French convicts condemned to hard labour used to be transported to the penitentiary there.

From each of these overseas territories, tropical products like sugar, bananas, rum and cocoa are exported to mainland France. In return the tropical paradises are supplied with subsidised French products, so that you can buy, for instance, a **camembert** for no more than you would pay in mainland France, whereas a few miles away, in the British West Indies, the same **camembert** would be prohibitively expensive.

Your turn to speak

1 First a chance to practise the past tense with both **être** and **avoir**. On tape Carolle will ask you some questions about things you have done, e.g.
a. **Etes-vous venu à Londres l'année dernière?**
b. **A quelle heure avez-vous joué au tennis?**
Pierre will then give you a brief suggestion for your answer:
a. **Oui. . .**
b. **A dix heures. . .**
Pause the tape and give your answer aloud using a full sentence:
a. **Oui, je suis venu à Londres l'année dernière.**
b. **J'ai joué au tennis à dix heures.**
Then listen on and Yves will repeat the correct answer.

2 Next on the tape you will hear Carolle playing the part of a doctor. Yves will be one of her patients. Listen to their conversation three or four times, concentrating particularly on what Yves says. Then play the tape again, this time saying Yves' part with him. To understand Carolle's **après on vous rembourse à 80%** (afterwards they reimburse you (to the tune of) 80%) see *Did you know?* p. 211.

And finally Now listen to the dialogues through once again and test yourself on the *Key phrases*. Go through the past tense forms on p. 209 very carefully and try saying the whole verb aloud (**je suis parti, tu es parti**, etc.) Finish the course by doing the *Revision* section on p. 215 and 219 and on the tape.

You should now have a good basic knowledge of French and the ability to cope in most of the situations likely to come your way on holiday – an ability that will improve with practice. **Bon courage!**

Answers

Practise what you have learnt p. 207 Exercise 1 (a) because she has been on holiday several times this year (b) in July (c) a month (d) with her husband (e) walked and climbed (f) at Soulac.

p. 207 Exercise 2 Hier/parti/vélo/allé/tour/centaine/endroit/accident/ tombé/s'est cassé/a/presqu'/conduit/hôpital.

p. 208 Exercise 3 (a) ski (b) to England (c) Birmingham (d) Christmas (e) 2nd January (f) in London (g) at 6 p.m. (h) in the morning (i) 9 a.m. (j) fell in the snow and broke his leg (k) 10 days (l) in the hotel (m) that it was a skiing accident (n) that skiing is less dangerous than the English climate!

Grammar p. 209 (1) Il est arrivé. (2) Elle est entrée. (3) Nous sommes venu(e)s. (4) Je suis resté(e). (5) Tu es descendu(e). (6) Il est né. (7) Elle est morte. (8) Elles sont sorties. (9) Ils sont montés.

Read and understand p. 210 (1) on the 1st of the month (2) in bookshops (3) 12–2 (4) no (5) touring companies, concerts and meetings (6) in churches (7) in Young Workers' Hostels and socio-cultural centres (8) yes (9) no (10) nothing

Revision   Units 1–3

Revision is vital. Before you go on to Unit 4, we suggest you first:

1 Play through the dialogues from Unit 1 reading them aloud from the book at the same time.
2 Re-read the *Grammar* notes from Unit 1.
3 Play through the dialogues from Unit 2, stopping the tape at the end of every sentence to allow yourself time to repeat it aloud. (There are only three minutes of dialogue in each unit, so this should not take too long.)
4 Re-read the *Grammar* notes from Unit 2.
5 Make sure you know the *Key phrases* from Units 1–3.
6 Do the following crossword. It has been designed specifically to help you revise, so do look back through Units 1–3 as much as you like.
7 Do the revision exercises which follow straight after Unit 3 on the tape. You won't need your book. There are no set answers to the first exercise; the answers to the second are on tape.

Mots croisés

Here are the jumbled answers to the clues. The correct answers are printed at the foot of p. 214.

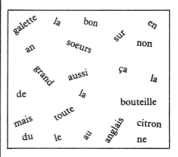

galette   la   bon   en
an   soeurs   sur   non
grand   aussi   ça   la
de   la   bouteille
mais   toute   citron
du   le   au   anglais   ne

Horizontalement

1 365 jours. (2)
5 Une .... aux oeufs et au jambon, s'il vous plaît. (7)
7 Vous êtes ...., Monsieur? Moi, je ne sais pas. (3)
8 Non, je ne suis pas français, je suis .... (7)
9 Nous avons .... chocolat. (2)
10 Non, nous n'avons pas de pizzas, ... nous avons des sandwichs. (4)
13 Une grande .... de cidre, s'il vous plaît. (9)
16 Un sandwich .... gruyère, s'il vous plaît. (2)
17 Vous .... prenez pas de café? (2)
19 Un thé au ...., s'il vous plaît. (6)
20 C'est *le* ou *la* vodka? (2)

Verticalement

New word: **le contraire** (the opposite)
1 Vous travaillez demain? Moi .... je travaille. (5)
2 C'est *le* ou *la* pression? (2)
3 Du café, du thé et .... la bière. (2)
4 C'est *le* ou *la* sandwich? (2)
5 Le contraire de petit. (5)
6 Un emploi. (7)
11 Non, je n'ai pas de frères, mais j'ai deux .... (6)
12 Le thé sucré, c'est ...., Maman! (3)
14 Vous êtes avec un groupe ou vous êtes .... seule? (5)
15 C'est *le* ou *la* pizza? (2)
17 Le contraire de *oui*. (3)
18 Vous êtes .... vacances? (2)
19 'Je suis secrétaire.' 'Où ....?' (2)

Revision   Units 4–6

You have covered a great deal of ground so far and should already be able to cope with quite a range of transactions if you go to France. Before you go any further with the course, consolidate what you have learnt by doing revision as follows:

1. Play through the dialogues from Unit 4, reading them aloud from the book at the same time.

2. Re-read the *Grammar* notes from Unit 4.

3. Play through the dialogues from Unit 5, stopping the tape at the end of each sentence to allow yourself time to repeat it aloud.

4. Re-read the *Grammar* section of Unit 5.

5. Test yourself on the *Key words and phrases* from Units 4, 5 and 6 by covering up the French and seeing if you can translate the English.

6. Do the crossword which follows selecting the answers to the clues from those jumbled in the box (p. 215). Look back at the dialogues and vocabulary as much as you need.

7. Do the revision exercises on the tape. They start after the last exercise of *Your turn to speak* Unit 6. The answers are printed upside down on p. 215.

Mots croisés

Crossword answers

(Units 1–3)

Horizontalement **1** an **5** galette **7** sûr **8** anglais **9** du **10** mais **13** bouteille **16** au **17** ne **19** citron **20** la

Verticalement **1** aussi **2** la **3** de **4** le **5** grand **11** soeurs **12** bon **14** toute **15** la **17** non **18** en **19** ça

Here are the jumbled answers to the clues. (Correct answers below.)

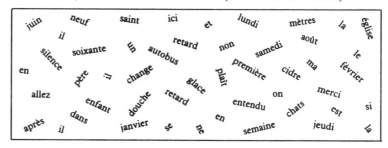

Horizontalement

1 Moyen de transport. (7)
6 Numéro entre huit et dix. (4)
8 On mange le dessert ...... la viande. (5)
9 Le mois des roses. (4)
10 "Un homme .... une femme" (film). (2)
12 Premier mois de l'année. (7)
13 17h 45, ... fait 5h 45. (2)
15 Est-ce que c'est *le* ou *la* chambre? (2)
17 Vous ne voulez pas manger? ..., je veux manger. (2)
18 On peut dormir .... le train. (4)
19 Premier jour de travail. (5)
20 Où nous sommes. (3)
21 On va ... vacances. (2)
24 Le cinéma est à 500 ...... de la Tour Eiffel. (6)
25 La catégorie de luxe. (8)
29 Bonne comme dessert. (5)
32 Après le sport il faut prendre une .... (6)
35 Le mari de la mère. (4)
36 Combien de minutes y a-t-il dans une heure? (8)
37 Non adulte. (6)
39 Est-ce que c'est *le* ou *la* rue? (2)
41 On va à l' ...... le dimanche. (6)
43 Où peut-... changer des chèques de voyage? (2)
44 Un homme respecté par 41. (5)
45 ʻEst-ce que c'est *le* ou *la* train? (2)

Verticalement

New word: **voir** (see)

1 Un des mois des grandes vacances. (4)
2 .., deux, trois. (2)
3 Sept jours. (7)
4 Jour de liberté. (6)
5 Au revoir et ..... . (5)
7 Mois avant mars. (7)
9 Deux jours après mardi. (5)
11 S'.. vous 28. (2)
14 D'accord. (7)
16 Je vais; vous ..... . (5)
17 Il 22 faut pas parler. (7)
22 Voir 17. (2)
23 Où ..... trouve ta banque?
26 Ah, .. banque? (2)
27 Avec des galettes il faut boire du ..... . (5)
28 Voir 11. (5)
30 Un bureau de .... (Voir 43) (6)
31 Vous avez une heure de ...... au départ de l'avion. (6)
33 Ils font miaou. (5)
34 Il ... midi. (3)
35 Crois. (5)
38 Vous êtes français? (3)
40 Normalement, .. général. (2)
42 Quelle heure est-..? (2)

Answers (Crossword and tape exercise)

Horizontalement 1 autobus 6 neuf 8 après 9 juin 10 et 12 janvier 13 ça
15 la 17 si 18 dans 19 lundi 20 ici 21 en 24 mètres 25 première 29 glace
32 douche 35 père 36 soixante 37 enfant 39 la 41 église 43 on 44 saint 45 le

Verticalement 1 août 2 un- 3 semaine 4 samedi 5 merci 7 février 9 jeudi
11 il 14 entendu 16 allez 17 silence 22 ne 23 se 26 ma 27 cidre 28 plaît
30 change 31 retard 33 chats 34 est 35 pense 38 non 40 en 42 il

Tape exercise 1 1 sept 2 douze 3 trente 4 le vingt-cinq décembre
Tape exercise 2 PHILIPS, GEORGE, JACKSON.

Revision   Units 7–9

1   First answer the questions below based on the station board. (Answers below)

```
┌─────────────────────────────────────────────────────────────────────┐
│                      INFORMATIONS VOYAGEURS                           │
│                                                                        │
│  SORTIE        [i]  INFORMATION       SORTIES      [taxi] TAXIS        │
│  Bercy-Rapée                          Diderot                         │
│                [taxi] TAXIS RADIO     Tour de l'horloge [bus] AUTOBUS URBAINS │
│                                                                        │
│                [P]  PARKING                         [bus] AUTOBUS SNCF │
│                                                      SNCF              │
│                     POSTE DE POLICE                                   │
│                                       Quai A   WC [.] [wc] RELAIS TOILETTES │
│  SORTIE Bercy  [.]  BAGAGES A L'ARRIVÉE                               │
│                                                [.] SALLE D'ATTENTE     │
│                [.]  OBJETS TROUVÉS                                    │
│                                                [.] TÉLÉPHONE           │
│                [.]  CONSIGNE                                          │
│                                       Voies 3 à 19 [.] SALLE D'ATTENTE │
│                     BUREAU MILITAIRE                                  │
│  SORTIE Chalon [.][.] RÉSERVATION              WC TOILETTES           │
│                                                                        │
│                [.]  BILLETS                    [.] BAR COMESTIBLES     │
│                                                                        │
│                [.]  CHANGE                                            │
│                                       87, rue du Charolais            │
│                [.]  BAGAGES AU DÉPART                                 │
│                                                                        │
│                [.]  CONSIGNES AUTOMATIQUES  144, rue de Bercy          │
│                                                                        │
│                [.]  BAR COMESTIBLES           COMMISSARIAT SPÉCIAL DE POLICE │
│                                                                        │
│                     BOUTIQUES                 POLICE DE L'AIR ET DES FRONTIERES │
└─────────────────────────────────────────────────────────────────────┘
```

a.   What sign would you look for if you wanted an automatic left-luggage locker? ....

b.   What is the French for 'lost property'? ....

c.   Near which platform will you find telephones? ....

d.   Near which exit is the reservations office? ....

e.   Near which exits are the bus-stops? ....

f.   Near which exit is the ticket office? ....

2   Do the revision exercise on the tape which follows straight after Unit 9. (You will not need your book.) It is set in a clothes shop.

3   Revise the *Key words and phrases* and the extra vocabulary in Unit 7 and then make up a dialogue of your own in which you ask a shop-keeper for as many foodstuffs as you can. Remember to specify the quantities.

4   Go over the verbs in the *Grammar* section of Unit 7 and then try to write them out, with their translations, without looking at the book.

5   Revise the *Grammar* section, the *Key phrases* and the extra vocabulary in *Did you know?*, Unit 8. Then practise by looking at the clothes you are wearing and making statements about the colours of the different garments e.g. **ce pantalon est gris, cette chemise est verte** etc.

6   Be sure you know the *Key words and phrases* and the *Grammar* from Unit 9. Plan an imaginary journey and write out all the phrases you would need to buy your ticket, ask the train times etc. Test yourself on the verbs by writing them out in full with their translations, without looking at your book.

7   Finally, play through all the dialogues from Units 7 and 8 one by one, and at the end of each, try to repeat it aloud from memory. You need not be word-perfect – just recapture the general drift of the conversation.

Answers   (a) consignes automatiques (b) objets trouvés (c) platform A (d) the Chalon exit (e) Diderot and Tour de l'horloge (f) Chalon.

Revision   Units 10–12

1 Complete this crossword, selecting the answers to the clues from the box below. Look back at the previous units as much as you need.

2 Do the exercises which follows Unit 12 on tape.

Here are the jumbled answers to the clues. The correct answers are at the foot of the next page (p. 218.

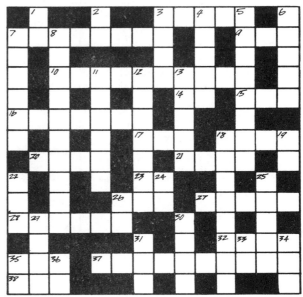

Horizontalement

3 Dessert préféré des enfants. (5)
7 Beaucoup de. (3,3,2)
9 Je suis ... à Paris. (3)
10 Tarte. (10)
14 Je vais .. dire la météo de la France. (2)
15 Je vais téléphoner à ... parents, parce que mon père est malade. (3)
16 Je déteste: j'ai .... de. (7)
17 Moi, j'adore le salé; ... tu préfères le sucré. (3)
18 Le contraire de *moins*. (4)
20 Au mois de mars, il fait du .... .(4)
21 Pour ouvrir une porte, on pousse ou on .... . (4)
23 ½ + ½ = ...(2)
26 Saison où le soleil brille. (3)
27 Si on désire le calme, on ..... les plages trop fréquentées. (5)
28 ...... de fer – pour les trains. (6)
32 On .... dans une piscine. (4)
35 . ... y en a, j'en prends un. (1,2)
37 Le soleil brille – mais pas toute la journée. (10)
38 Des vaches? Oui il y .. . beaucoup dans les champs. (2,1)

Verticalement

1 and 2 Oh!..! ..! Phrase typiquement française! (2,2)
3 Personnes. (4)
4 Aime passionnément. (5)
5 En général: dans l'........ .(8)
6 Cartes à prix fixe dans un restaurant. (5)
7 Près. (6)
8 Plus élevée. (10)
11 Combien de minutes y a-t-il dans une demi-heure? (6)
12 En particulier. (7)
13 Tout le monde ..... musicien. (5)
18 Les provinciaux habitent en ....(8)
19 'Tu ne le vois pas?' '.., je le vois!' (2)
22 Le vin peut être ... ou doux. (3)
24 Personne .. me comprend! (2)
25 Mon appartement est au 2e ..... . (5)
26 Il .. reste un. (2)
29 Quoi? (4)
30 Baguette. (4)
31 Pour fermer la porte. (3)
33 Avoir: j'.. .(2)
34 Le contraire d'ouest. (3)
35 Où .. trouve ta banque? (2)
36 Est-ce que c'est *le* ou *la* plage? (2)

Revision Units 13–15

1. A chance to practise verbs. Fill in all the missing tenses below:

	Demain/tomorrow	**Aujourd'hui**/today	**Hier**/yesterday
e.g.	*je vais visiter*	*je visite*	*j'ai visité*
	....	vous jouez	....
	....	....	nous avons vu
	tu vas manger	....	....
	....	....	elle a préparé
	elle va monter	....	....
	....	tu descends	....
	....	tu tombes	....
	....	il écrit	....
	....	ils sortent	....
	elle va venir	....	....
	....	il a	....

2. Do the exercises on the tape.

Answers

vous allez jouer, vous avez joué/nous allons voir, nous voyons/tu manges, tu as mangé/elle va préparer, elle prépare/elle monte, elle est montée/ tu vas descendre, tu es descendu(e)/tu vas tomber, tu es tombé(e)/il va écrire, il a écrit/ils vont sortir, ils sont sortis/elle vient, elle est venue/il va avoir, il a eu.

Crossword answers (Units 10–12)

Horizontalement **3** glace **7** pas mal de **9** née **10** pâtisserie **14** te **15** mes **16** horreur **17** toi **18** plus **20** vent **21** tire **23** un **26** été **27** évite **28** chemin **32** nage **35** s'il **37** éclaircies **38** en a

Verticalement **1** la **2** là **3** gens **4** adore **5** ensemble **6** menus **7** proche **8** supérieure **11** trente **12** surtout **13** était **18** province **19** si **22** sec **24** ne **25** étage **26** en **29** hein **30** pain **31** clé **33** ai **34** est **35** se **36** la

The poem below is by Jacques Prévert, one of the best known of modern French poets. There is a recording of it on the tape. See if you can learn it by heart – apart from anything else this is an excellent way of making sure you know the many past tense forms used in it!

Déjeuner du Matin

Il a mis le café
Dans la tasse
Il a mis le lait
Dans la tasse de café
Il a mis le sucre
Dans le café au lait
Avec la petite cuiller
Il a tourné
Il a bu le café au lait
Et il a reposé la tasse   **reposé**   put down again
Sans me parler
Il a allumé   **allumé**   lit
Une cigarette
Il a fait des ronds   **des ronds**   rings
Avec la fumée   **la fumée**   smoke
Il a mis les cendres   **les cendres**   ash
Dans le cendrier   **le cendrier**   ash-tray
Sans me parler
Sans me regarder
Il s'est levé
Il a mis
Son chapeau sur sa tête
Il a mis
Son manteau de pluie   **pluie**   rain
Parce qu'il pleuvait   **il pleuvait**   it was raining
Et il est parti
Sous la pluie
Sans une parole   **une parole**   a word
Sans me regarder
Et moi j'ai pris
Ma tête dans ma main
Et j'ai pleuré.   **pleuré**   cried

Jacques Prévert *Paroles* © Éditions Gallimard

Grammar in the course

Grammar summary

For easy reference, the most useful grammar points are set out below.

Definitions of grammatical terms

A VERB denotes action or being, e.g.
the man *goes*;
I *am*;
Mary *hates* football.

The INFINITIVE is the form of the verb preceded in English by 'to', e.g.
to go; to be; to hate.

The SUBJECT of the verb is the person or thing who acts or is, e.g.
the man goes;
I am;
Mary hates football.

The OBJECT of the verb is the person or thing on the receiving end e.g.
'Mary hates *football*',
'John hates *it*' and
'Mary loves *Fred*.'

The basic rules for French

There are three main groups of regular verbs

1 those with infinitives ending in -er,
e.g. **parler, donner** (see Unit 2, p. 31)

2 those with infinitives ending in -re,
e.g. **vendre, attendre** (see Unit 4, p. 59)

3 those with infinitives ending in -ir,
e.g. **finir, choisir** (see Unit 10, p. 143)

Unfortunately some of the most commonly used verbs are irregular and you need to learn them individually. The present tenses given in this course are: être (Unit 1), **avoir** (Unit 2), **prendre** (Unit 3), **faire** (Unit 4), **aller** (Unit 5), **venir, tenir** (Unit 6), **pouvoir, savoir, connaître** (Unit 7), **dire, partir** (Unit 9) and **voir** (Unit 10).

Remember that simple present tenses such as **je mange** can be translated in two ways, EITHER 'I eat' OR 'I am eating', so there is only one present tense to learn in French.

As well as saying what you are doing, you need to be able to talk about what you have done (in the *past*) and what you are going to do (in the *future*).

The past tense known sometimes as the *perfect* or *passé composé* is explained in Units, 13 and 15. Most verbs form this tense by adding the appropriate past participle to the present of **avoir**, e.g. **j'ai fini; nous avons parlé**. In the negative this is **je n'ai pas fini; nous n'avons pas parlé**. A list of commonly used past participles is given in Unit 13, p. 183.

Some verbs, reflexive verbs and those usually described as 'verbs of movement', form their past tense with the present tense of être instead of avoir, e.g. **je suis entré; elle est partie; nous sommes tombés**. With être the past participle behaves like an adjective and agrees with the subject of the verb. See Unit 15, p. 209 for further explanation and a list of these verbs.

There is also a past tense called the *continuous past tense*, but only the verb être need be learnt at this stage. You will find the forms j'étais etc. in Unit 11, p. 157.

To express *future* intentions, translate 'I am going to . . .' by using the present tense of **aller** and the infinitive of the relevant verb, e.g. **je vais venir; ils ne vont pas rester**. (See Unit 14, p. 189.)

When two verbs come together, unless the first one is **avoir** or **être**, the second one is always in the infinitive, e.g. **je vais venir; il espère aller en Amérique; nous ne pouvons pas manger à midi**.

A NOUN is the name of a person or thing, e.g. *James, child, dog, book.*

All French nouns are masculine or feminine. Most nouns add an **-s** to form their plural. The four exceptions you should note are

1 those ending in **-s, -x** or **-z** in the singular remain unchanged in the plural, e.g.
le fils son   **les fils** sons
le choix choice   **les choix** choices
le nez nose   **les nez** noses

2 those ending in **-eau** have a plural in **-eaux**, e.g.
le seau bucket   **les seaux**
le tableau picture **les tableaux**

3 those ending in **-al** have a plural in **-aux**, e.g.
le journal newspaper **les journaux**
le cheval horse   **les chevaux**

4 those ending in **-eu** have their plural in *-eux*, e.g.
le jeu game   **les jeux**
le cheveu a single hair **les cheveux**
(Where we talk about someone's 'hair' the French logically talk of their 'hairs'.)

The ARTICLES in English are *the, a, an* and *some.*

The word for 'the' in French is **le** before a masculine noun, **la** before a feminine noun, and **l'** before a word beginning with a vowel sound. Before any plural noun the word for 'the' is **les**.
e.g. **le taxi, les taxis; la pomme, les pommes; l'enfant, les enfants.**

The word for 'a' is **un** before a masculine noun and **une** before a feminine noun, e.g. **un taxi, une pomme, un ami, une amie.**

The word for 'some' is **du** before a masculine noun, **de la** before a feminine noun, and **de l'** before a noun beginning with a vowel sound. Before any plural noun it is **des**, e.g. **du courage** (some courage), **de la chance** (some luck), **de l'eau** (some water), **des oranges** (some oranges), **des dictionnaires** (some dictionaries).

We very often leave out the word 'some' in English and talk about 'courage', 'luck' etc. In French you must always put in **du, de la, de l'** or **des**, e.g. 'coffee, please' – <u>du</u> café, s'il vous plaît.

An ADJECTIVE describes a noun or pronoun, e.g.
beautiful, green, small, comfortable.

In French an adjective 'agrees' with the noun or pronoun it describes, i.e. it is feminine when describing something feminine and plural when describing something plural. The feminine singular form is usually made by adding an **-e** to the masculine, e.g.
le garçon est grand the boy is tall
sa sœur est grande aussi his sister is tall too.
The plurals are made in the same way as the plurals of nouns (see above) – generally by adding an **-s**.

1 If the adjective already ends in an **-e** it does not change in the feminine. e.g. **le garçon est jeune; sa soeur est jeune aussi.**

2 When the masculine ends in **-er**, the feminine ends in **-ère**, e.g. **cher, chère; premier, première.**

3 When the masculine ends in **-eux**, the feminine ends in **-euse**, e.g. **heureux, heureuse** (happy).

4 When the masculine ends in **-f**, the feminine ends in **-ve**, e.g. **veuf, veuve** (widowed).

5 When the masculine ends in **-el**, **-en**, **-et** or **-on**, the feminine is formed by doubling the final consonant and adding an **-e**, e.g. **visuel, visuelle; ancien, ancienne; net, nette** (clear); **bon, bonne.**

Irregular adjectives

beau, belle (masc. sing. **bel** before a vowel)
nouveau, nouvelle (masc. sing. **nouvel** before a vowel)
vieux, vieille (masc. sing. **vieil** before a vowel)
blanc, blanche
sec, sèche
gentil, gentille
gros, grosse
bas, basse (low)

An ADVERB describes the way something happens, e.g. 'She reads *well*', 'She runs *quickly*' and 'She sings *beautifully*'.

The usual way of forming an adverb in French is to add **-ment** to the feminine of the corresponding adjective, e.g. **heureusement** (happily), from **heureuse**; **doucement** (gently, sweetly), from **douce**.
BUT adjectives ending in **-ent** and **-ant** give adverbs ending in **-emment** and **-amment** (both pronounced the same: **-amment**). e.g. **violent, violemment; évident, évidemment; constant, constamment.**

An adverb can also qualify another adverb or an adjective, e.g. 'She reads *very* well' 'She runs *quite* quickly' 'She is *extremely* beautiful'.

Irregular adverbs

1 **bien** (well)   **mieux** (better)
  mal (badly)   **souvent** (often)

2 The adjectives **soudain** (sudden), **bref** (brief) and **fort** (strong) are used as adverbs to mean 'suddenly', 'briefly' and 'strongly' (or 'very').

PREPOSITIONS in English are such words as *near, by, to, for, with, over, through* and *into*

The two most common prepositions in French are **de** (from, of) and **à** (to, at, in), e.g.
je suis de Londres   I am from London
le départ de l'avion   the departure of the aeroplane
je vais à Paris   I am going to Paris
nous sommes à la gare   we are at the station

Le and **les** change their form when used with these prepositions

de + le → du   je viens du café
de + les → des   les cris des enfants

à + le → au   on va au cinéma
à + les → aux   il est aux États-Unis

There is a list of other prepositions in Unit 5 (p. 73). Remember that those which end in **de** or **à** (e.g. **près de** and **jusqu'à**) change their form with **le** and **les** in the same way as above.

A PRONOUN stands for a noun, e.g. 'Mary loves Fred
– *she* loves *him*'
She is a subject pronoun and *him* is an object pronoun.

The subject pronouns in French are je, **tu, il, elle, on, nous, vous, ils** and **elles**.

The object pronouns come immediately before the verb and are as follows.

il **me** comprend	he understands me
il **te** comprend	he understands you
il **le** comprend	he understands him or it
il **la** comprend	he understands her or it
il **nous** comprend	he understands us
il **vous** comprend	he understands you
il **les** comprend	he understands them

Pronouns can refer to people or things, e.g.
'The man frightened the children
– *he* frightened *them*';
'The cars damaged the lawn
– *they* damaged *it*'.

Some verbs take an 'indirect' object rather than a 'direct' object, e.g. 'he speaks *to* me,' not 'he speaks *me*'.

The French for 'me' and 'to me' is the same; 'you' and 'to you' are the same, as are 'us' and 'to us', but there are differences with 'to him', 'to her' and 'to them';

il **me** parle	he speaks to me
il **te** parle	he speaks to you
il **lui** parle	he speaks to him OR to her
il **nous** parle	he speaks to us
il **vous** parle	he speaks to you
il **leur** parle	he speaks to them

Y means 'there' or 'to it' e.g.
elle y est   she is there
elle y va   she is going there, she is going to it

En (some, any, of it, of them) is explained on p. 143, Unit 10.

POSSESSIVE ADJECTIVES are words like *my, your* and *his*.

For **mon, ma, mes** see p. 157, Unit 11.
For **ton, ta, tes** see p. 157, Unit 11.
For **son, sa, ses** see p. 197, Unit 14.
For **notre** and **nos** see p. 129, Unit 9.
For **votre** and **vos** see p. 129, Unit 9.
You will also need the words for 'their'; **leur** (singular) and **leurs** (plural), e.g. **leur père, leur mère, leurs enfants**.

Numbers

1	un	70	soixante-dix
2	deux	71	soixante et onze
3	trois	72	soixante-douze
4	quatre	73	soixante-treize
5	cinq	74	soixante-quatorze
6	six	75	soixante-quinze
7	sept	76	soixante-seize
8	huit	77	soixante-dix-sept
9	neuf	78	soixante-dix-huit
10	dix	79	soixante-dix-neuf
11	onze	80	quatre-vingts
12	douze	81	quatre-vingt-un
13	treize	82	quatre-vingt-deux
14	quatorze	83	quatre-vingt-trois
15	quinze		
16	seize	90	quatre-vingt-dix
17	dix-sept	91	quatre-vingt-onze
18	dix-huit	92	quatre-vingt-douze
19	dix-neuf	93	quatre-vingt-treize
20	vingt	94	quatre-vingt-quatorze
		95	quatre-vingt-quinze
21	vingt et un	96	quatre-vingt-seize
22	vingt-deux	97	quatre-vingt-dix-sept
23	vingt-trois	98	quatre-vingt-dix-huit
24	vingt-quatre	99	quatre-vingt-dix-neuf
25	vingt-cinq		
26	vingt-six	100	cent
27	vingt-sept	101	cent un
28	vingt-huit	102	cent deux *etc*
29	vingt-neuf	1000	mille
30	trente		
31	trente et un		
32	trente-deux		
40	quarante		
41	quarante et un		
42	quarante-deux		
50	cinquante		
60	soixante		

Numbers from 101–199 are made up of **cent** followed immediately by the rest of the number (with no **et** in between), e.g.

101 cent un
118 cent dix-huit
199 cent quatre-vingt-dix-neuf

200, 300, 400 etc. are straightforwardly

deux cents, trois cents, quatre cents etc.

and numbers in between follow the same pattern as 101–199, e.g.

751 sept cent cinquante-et-un
876 huit cent soixante-seize
992 neuf cent quatre-vingt-douze

Vocabulary

The feminine ending of adjectives is given in brackets, e.g. **bon(ne)** means that the masculine is **bon** and the feminine **bonne**. Where nothing is given in brackets, the feminine form is the same as the masculine, e.g. **jeune**.

abord see **d'abord**
accident(m.) accident
accord see **d'accord**
accueillir to welcome
acheter to buy
actualité(f.) the news, what is going on
addition(f.) bill
administratif(ive) administrative
adorer to adore, to love
adresse(f.) address
adressez-vous à go and ask at
adulte(m. and f.) adult
aéronautique(f.) aeronautics
âge(m.) age; **troisième âge(m.)** old age
âgé(e) aged
agence immobilière(f.) estate agent's
agneau(m.) lamb
agréable nice, pleasant
agréer to accept, to approve of
aimer to like, to love; **aimer bien** to like
air (m.) air
ajouter to add
Albanie(f.) Albania
alcool(m.) alcohol, spirit
alimentation(f.) food
allemand(e) German
aller to go; **aller et retour(m.)** return (ticket); **aller simple(m.)** single (ticket)
allô hello (on the telephone)
allumette(f.) match
alors then, well then
aloyau(m.) sirloin (of beef)
américain(e) American
Amérique(f.) America
ami(e) (m. and f.) friend
amicalement in a friendly way
s'amuser to enjoy oneself
an(m.) year
ananas(m.) pineapple
ancien(ne) ancient, former
andouillette(f.) small sausage made of chitterlings
anglais(e) English (often used for British)
animateur(m.) leader of a group
anniversaire(m.) birthday
anonyme anonymous
août August
apéritif(m.) drink, aperitif
appartement(m.) flat, apartment
s'appeler lit. to call oneself; **je m'appelle** my name is
appellation contrôlée(f.) lit. controlled name – the guarantee of a wine's origin and quality
appétit(m.) appetite; **bon appétit!** have a good meal!
apprendre to learn
approchez-vous come closer

après after; **après-midi(m.)** afternoon
argent(m.) money
arpenter to tramp up and down
arrière(f.) back
arrivée(f.) arrival
artichaut(m.) artichoke
artiste(m. and f.) artist
aspirine(f.) aspirin
asseyez-vous (do) sit down
assez enough
assiette(f.) plate
attendre to wait (for)
atterrir (of a plane) to land
aube(f.) dawn
auberge(f.) inn
aujourd'hui today
au revoir goodbye
aussi also, too, as well
autobus(m.) bus; **en autobus** by bus
autocar(m.) coach
automatique automatic
automne(m.) autumn
autre other
autrement otherwise
Autriche(f.) Austria
à l'avance in advance
avant (de) before
avec with
avenue(f.) avenue
averse(f.) shower, downpour
aviation(f.) aviation
avion(m.) aeroplane
avis(m.) opinion, notice
avoir to have
avril April

bagages(m. pl.) luggage
baguette(f.) 'French stick' (bread)
se baigner to bathe
ballon(m.) ball, brandy glass
banane(f.) banana
banlieue(f.) suburbs
banque(f.) bank
bar(m.) bar
bas(m.) bottom, lower part
basket(m.) basket-ball
bateau(m.) boat
bazar(m.) cheap stores
beau (belle) handsome, beautiful
beaucoup a lot
beige beige
Belgique(f.) Belgium
belle see **beau**
ben well, um
besoin(m.) need
beurre(m.) butter
bibliothèque(f.) library
bicyclette(f.) bicycle
bien well; **bien sûr** certainly
bière(f.) beer
bifteck(m.) steak

billet(m.) ticket
bistro(t)(m.) small restaurant
blanc(he) white
bleu(e) blue
boeuf(m.) beef, ox, bullock
bol(m.) bowl
boire to drink
bois(m.) wood
boisson(f.) drink
boîte(f.) box, can, tin
bon(ne) good
bondé(e) crowded
bonjour good day, hello
bonne see bon
bonsoir good evening
bordeaux Bordeaux (wine), burgundy
   (colour)
botte(f.) bunch, boot
boucher(m.) butcher
boucherie(f.) butcher's shop
bouillabaisse(f.) Provençal fish-soup,
   -stew, -chowder
boulanger(m.), boulangère(f.) baker
boulangerie(f.) baker's shop
boulevard(m.) boulevard
bout(m.) end
bouteille(f.) bottle
boutique(f.) small shop
bras(m.) arm
brasserie(f.) pub-restaurant
bref (brève) brief, briefly
briller to shine
britannique British
brushing(m.) blow-dry
brouillard(m.) fog
Bulgarie(f.) Bulgaria
bungalow(m.) holiday hut, bungalow
bureau(m.) office, study
bus(m.) bus

ça that; ça va? how are things?; ça
   va things are OK
cabine(f.) booth
cabinet de toilette(m.) small room/
   cupboard containing wash-basin
cadeau(m.) present
café(m.) café, coffee; café au lait (also
   café-lait)(m.) white coffee; café
   crème(m.) coffee with cream
cahier(m.) exercise book
calamar(m.) squid
calme calm, quiet
camping(m.) camping, camp-site
capitale(f.) capital
car as, for, since
carafe(f.) carafe
car-ferry(m.) car-ferry
carnet(m.) book (of tickets), 10 metro
   tickets
carotte(f.) carrot
carrefour(m.) crossroads
carte(f.) map, card, 'à la carte' menu;
   carte d'identité(f.) identity card;
   carte postale(f.) post-card; carte des
   vins(f.) wine-list
casser to break

cassis(m.) blackcurrant, blackcurrant
   liqueur
cassoulet(m.) dish with beans and meat
catastrophe(f.) catastrophe
cathédrale(f.) cathedral
catégorie(f.) category
cave(f.) cellar
ce, cet, cette this, that (adjective); ce
   qui that which (subject); ce que that
   which (object)
cela that (prounoun)
célibataire single, bachelor
celui-là that one
cent a hundred
centaine(f.) about a hundred
centre(m.) centre; centre
   d'animation(m.) community centre
cependant however
cerise(f.) cherry
certain(e) certain
ces these, those (adjective)
c'est it is, this is
cet, cette see ce
chacun(e) each one
chambre(f.) (bed)room; chambre des
   invités(f.) guest-room
champ(m.) field
chance(f.) luck
changement(m.) change
changer to change
chaque each (adjective)
charcuterie(f.) pork-butcher's shop, cold
   meats, delicatessen
château(m.) stately home, palace, castle
chaud(e) hot; avoir chaud to be hot
chaussette(f.) sock
chemin(m.) way, road, track; chemin de
   fer(m.) railway
chemise(f.) shirt
chèque de voyage(m.) travellers'
   cheque
cher (chère) dear, expensive
chercher to look for; aller chercher to
   go and fetch; venir chercher to come
   and fetch
cheval(m.) horse, horsemeat; faire du
   cheval to ride
chevalin(e) horse- (adj.)
chewing-gum(m.) chewing gum
chez at the home of; chez moi at my
   house
chien(m.) dog
chipolata(f.) chipolata
chocolat(m.) chocolate (eating or
   drinking)
choisir to choose
choix(m.) choice
chose(f.) thing
chou(m.) cabbage
chou-fleur(m.) cauliflower
choucroute(f.) sauerkraut
chrysanthème(m.) chrysanthemum
cidre(m.) cider
ciel(m.) sky
cinq five
citron(m.) lemon

classe(f.) class; **classe
économique(f.)** economy class
client(e) (m. and f.) client, customer
climat(m.) climate
coiffeur(m.), **coiffeuse(f.)** hairdresser
collant(m.) tights
collègue (m. and f.) colleague
combien? how much? how many?
commander to order
comme as, like, in the way of; **comme
ça** like that; **comme d'habitude** as
usual
commencer to start
comment? what? how?
commerçant(m.) shopkeeper
communication(f.) communication
comparer to compare
compartiment(m.) compartment
compas(m.) compass
complet (ète) full; **petit déjeuner
complet(m.)** full continental breakfast
complètement completely
composter to punch (a ticket to validate
it)
comprendre to understand, to include
comprimé(m.) tablet
compris included, understood
comptable(m.) accountant, book-keeper
compter to count
concert(m.) concert
concierge (m. and f.) caretaker
concombre(m.) cucumber
conduire to drive, to take (someone
somewhere)
confiance(f.) confidence
confirmer to confirm
connaissance(f.) knowledge,
acquaintance
connaître to know (a person or place)
conserve(f.) preserve, jam
consigne(f.) left luggage, deposit (on
bottle etc.)
consistant(e) substantial
construire to build
consulter to consult
contenant containing
contenu(m.) contents
continuer to continue
contraire(m.) opposite
contre against; **par contre** on the other
hand
convoquer to summon to a meeting
correspondance(f.) connection (trains),
correspondence
côte(f.) coast; **côte de porc(f.)** pork
chop
côté side; **à côté de** beside; **du
côté de** on the side of, in the
direction of
couchette(f.) couchette
coude(m.) elbow
couleur(f.) colour
coupe(f.) cut
courage(m.) courage
course(f.) race, errand; **faire ses
courses** to do one's shopping

court de tennis(m.) tennis court
couscous(m.) couscous (Arab dish)
couteau(m.) knife
couverture(f.) cover, blanket
cravate(f.) tie
crayon(m.) pencil
crème(f.) cream
crêpe(f.) pancake; **crêperie(f.)** pancake
house
croire to believe
croissant(m.) croissant
croque-monsieur(m.) toasted cheese
sandwich with ham; **croque-
madame(m.)** croque-monsieur, with
an egg
crustacé(m.) shellfish
cuiller/cuillère(f.) spoon
cuisine(f.) kitchen, cooking
curiosité(f.) curiosity, place of interest

d'abord first of all
d'accord OK, agreed
dame(f.) lady
Danemark(f.) Denmark
dangereux, (-euse) dangerous
dans in
de of, from
débarras(m.) junk-room
début(m.) beginning
décembre December
défense de (it is) forbidden to
déjeuner to lunch, to breakfast; **(m.)**
lunch; **petit déjeuner(m.)** breakfast
demain tomorrow
demander to ask (for)
demi(e) half; **demi-kilo(m.)** half a
kilogram
dent(f.) tooth
dentiste (m. and f.) dentist
départ(m.) departure
département(m.) department, county
départementale(f.) departmental (road),
B-road
dépendre de to depend on
dépliant(m.) leaflet
depuis since, **je suis mariée depuis 36
ans** I have been married for 36 years
déranger to inconvenience, to disturb
dernier, (-ère) last
derrière behind
des some, of the (see also **du**)
descendre to go down
descente(f.) descent
désirer to wish for
dessert(m.) dessert
détester to detest
deux two
deuxième second
devant in front of
devenir to become
devoir should, ought, must
diarrhée(f.) diarrhoea
différent(e) different
difficile difficult
dimanche Sunday
dire to say

direct(e) direct; **directement** directly
direction(f.) direction, management
se diriger vers to direct oneself towards,
   to head for
discuter to discuss, argue
dis-donc come on, look here
distingué(e) distinguished
distraction(f.) amusement, entertainment
se distraire to amuse onself
dix ten
doit, ça doit see **devoir**
donc then
donner to give
dormir to sleep
dos(m.) back
douche(f.) shower
doute(f.) doubt; **sans doute** certainly,
   doubtless
Douvres Dover
doux, (douce) sweet, gentle
drap(m.) sheet
droit(e) straight; **tout droit** straight on
droite right (hand)
durer to last

eau(f.) water
éclaircie(f.) bright period
école(f.) school, college
écolier(m.) schoolchild
écossais(e) Scottish
Écosse(f.) Scotland
écrire to write
en effet indeed
également also
église(f.) church
élève (m. and f.) pupil
élever to raise
emmener to take (someone somewhere)
emploi(m.) a job
employé(e) employed
emporter to take away
emprunt(m.) loan
en in, on, of it, of them; **en face**
   de facing
encolure(f.) neck (of dress)
encore again, still, yet
endroit(m.) place
enfant (m. and f.) child
enfin at last, well
enlever to take off
enseigne(f.) sign
enseignement(m.) teaching
ensemble together; **dans l'ensemble** on
   the whole
ensoleillé(e) sunny
ensuite then
entendu agreed
entre between
entrecôte(f.) rib of beef
entrée(f.) entrance, entrance-hall,
   entrée
envie(f.) desire; **avoir envie de** to want
environ about, approximately
envoyer to send
épicerie(f.) grocer's shop
époque(f.) era, period

équitation(f.) riding
escale(f.) port of call; **faire escale à** to
   put in at, stop over at
escargot(m.) snail
Espagne(f.) Spain
espérer to hope
essayer to try
essence(f.) petrol
est(m.) east
est-ce que? lit. is it that? (introduces a
   question)
et and
établissement(m.) establishment
étage(m.) floor, storey
j'étais I was
été (from être) been; (m.) summer
étranger, (-ère) foreign (adjective); à
   l'étranger abroad
être to be
évidemment obviously
éviter to avoid
exactement exactly
excusez-moi excuse me
expérimenter to experiment, to
   experience
exposer to expose, to exhibit
exposition(f.) exhibition

fabriquer to make, to manufacture
en face de facing
facile easy
façon(f.) way
facteur(m.) postman
faim(f.) hunger; **avoir faim** to be hungry
faire to do, to make
famille(f.) family
il faut it is necessary, one must
faux (fausse) false
favorable favourable
félicitations! congratulations
femme(f.) woman, wife
férié, jour férié(m.) bank-holiday
ferme(f.) farm; (adjective) firm
fermé(e) closed
fermer to close
fête(f.) feast-day, celebration
février February
fil(m.) thread
filet(m.) fillet (also net, string bag)
fille(f.) girl, daughter
fils(m.) son
fin(f.) end
fleur(f.) flower
flocon(m.) flake
fois(f.) time; **une fois** once; **à la fois** at
   the same time
folie(f.) madness, extravagance
foncé(e) dark (colour)
fonctionnaire (m. and f.) administrator,
   civil servant
fond(m.) bottom, depths, far end
formation(f.) training
fort(e) strong (adj.); **fort** (adv.) very,
   strongly
fouet(m.) whisk, whip
foulard(m.) scarf

fourchette(f.) fork
foyer(m.) hearth, day-centre, hostel
fraise(f.) strawberry
framboise(f.) raspberry
franc(m.) franc
français(e) French
fréquemment frequently
fréquenté(e) crowded, often visited
frère(m.) brother
fricassée(f.) fricassée (meat and
    vegetables in white sauce)
frite(f.) chip; (adjective) fried
froid(e) cold; avoir froid to be cold
fromage(m.) cheese
fruit(m.) fruit; fruits de mer(m. pl.) sea-
    food
fumer to smoke
fumeurs smoking (compartment); non
    fumeurs non-smoking

gagner to gain, to win, to arrive at
galette(f.) savoury buckwheat pancake
gallois(e) Welsh
garage(m.) garage
garçon(m.) boy, waiter
gare(f.) station; gare routière(f.) bus
    station; gare SNCF(f.) railway station
garni(e) garnished, served with
    vegetables
gauche left
gazeux, (-euse) fizzy
gelée(f.) jelly
en général in general
gens (m. pl.) people
gentil(le) nice, kind
glace(f.) ice, ice-cream, mirror
gorge(f.) throat
grand(e) big, tall
grandir to grow taller
gratuit(e) free (of charge)
Grèce(f.) Greece
grenier(m.) attic
grillé(e) grilled
grimper to climb
gris(e) grey
gros(se) fat
grossir to grow fatter, larger
groupe(m.) group
guichet(m.) counter, desk, window
guide(m.) guide
gymnastique(f.) gymnastics

habiter to live (in)
habitude(f.) habit; comme
    d'habitude as usual
hamburger(m.) hamburger
haut(e) high
hein? what? (often meaningless)
herbe(f.) herb, grass
heure(f.) hour; quelle heure est-il? what
    time is it?
heureux (-euse) happy
hier yesterday
histoire(f.) history, story
historique historic
hiver(m.) winter

HLM council housing, council flat
Hollande(f.) Holland
homme(m.) man; homme
    d'affaires(m.) businessman
homard(m.) lobster
Hongrie(f.) Hungary
hôpital(m.) hospital
horaire(m.) timetable
horreur(f.) horror; j'ai horreur de
    I can't bear
hors outside
hot dog(m.) hot dog
hôtel(m.) hotel; hôtel de
    ville(m.) town hall
huile(f.) oil
huit eight; huitième eighth
huître(f.) oyster
hygiène(f.) hygiene
hypermarché(m.) hypermarket

ici here
idéal(e) ideal
île(f.) island
importance(f.) importance, size
important(e) important
inférieur(e) inferior, lower
informations (f. pl.) information, news
ingénieur(m.) engineer
interdit(e) forbidden
intéressant(e) interesting, worthwhile,
    good value
s'intéresser à to be interested in
intérieur(e) internal
international(e) international
Irlande(f.) Ireland
Italie(f.) Italy
italien(ne) Italian

jambon(m.) ham
janvier January
jaune yellow
je I
jeu(m.) game
jeudi Thursday
jeune young
jouer to play
jour(m.) day
journal(m.) newspaper
journaliste (m. and f.) journalist
journée(f.) day, day-time
joyeux, (-euse) joyful, happy
juillet July
juin June
jupe(f.) skirt
jupon(m.) petticoat
jus(m.) juice
jusqu'à until, as far as
juste just

kilo(gramme)(m.) kilogram

la the, her, it
là there, then
laisser to leave
lait(m.) milk
lait-fraise(m.) strawberry milk-shake

langouste(f.) crayfish
langue(f.) tongue, language
lasagne (f. pl.) lasagne
laver to wash; se laver to wash oneself
le the, him, it
légume(m.) vegetable
les the, them
lettre(f.) letter
leur their, to them
lever to lift; se lever to get (oneself) up
librairie(f.) book-shop
libre free (but for 'free of charge' use
  gratuit); libre service(m.) small
  supermarket
licence(f.) (university) degree
lieu(m.) place
ligne(f.) line
limonade(f.) lemonade
lire to read
living(m.) living room
livraison(f.) delivery
livre(f.) pound; (m.) book
loin far
loisirs (m. pl.) leisure activities
Londres London
loyer(m.) rent
lui he, as for him, to him, to her
lui-même himself
lundi Monday
lycée(m.) grammar school

ma see mon
machine(f.) machine
Madame Madam, Mrs.
Mademoiselle Miss
magasin(m.) shop
magnétophone(m.) tape recorder
mai May
maigrir to grow thinner
maillot de bain(m.) swimming costume
maintenant now
maintenir maintain
mais but
maison(f.) house; maison de
  quartier(f.) community centre; tarte
  maison(f.) home-made tart
mal badly; avoir mal to have a pain;
  mal de tête(f.) headache
malade ill
Maman Mummy
Manche(f.) Channel
manger to eat
manquer to be lacking, missing; cela me
  manque I miss that
manteau(m.) coat
marché(m.) market; Marché
  Commun(m.) Common Market;
  marché aux puces(m.) flea-market
mardi Tuesday
mari(m.) husband
marié(e) married
marine, bleu(e) marine navy blue
marinière cooked with onion sauce
Maroc(m.) Morocco
marron brown
mars March

matin(m.) morning, in the morning
me me, to me, myself
médecin(m.) doctor
médical(e) medical
médicament(m.) medicine
meilleur(e) better
mélange(m.) mixture; mélanger to mix
melon(m.) melon
même same, even
menu(m.) (set) menu
mer(f.) sea
merci thank you
mercredi Wednesday
mère(f.) mother
mériter to deserve
merveilleux, (-euse) marvellous
mes see mon
Messieurs-dames ladies and gentlemen
mesure(f.) mesure
météo(f.) weather forecast
métier(m.) trade, profession
mètre(m.) metre
métro(m.) underground (train)
métropole(f.) mainland France
mettre to put; se mettre to place oneself
micro(phone)(m.) microphone
midi noon
mien(m.), mienne(f.) mine
migraine(f.) migraine
milieu(m.) middle, milieu
mille a thousand
minéral(e) mineral
minuit midnight
minute(f.) minute
mise en plis(f.) set (hair)
mode(f.) fashion
modèle(m.) model, style
moi I, me, as for me
moins less
mois(m.) month
moment(m.) moment
mon, ma, mes my
monnaie(f.) change
Monsieur Sir, Mr.
monter to go up; monter en neige to
  whisk until firm
monument(m.) monument
morceau(m.) bit
moteur(m.) motor
moto(f.) motorbike
moule(f.) mussel
mourir to die
mousse(f.) mousse
moutarde(f.) mustard
moyen(m.) means, average; moyen
  âge(m.) Middle Ages; moyenâgeux,
  (-euse) medieval
municipal(e) municipal
mûr(e) ripe
musée(m.) museum
musicien(ne) musical
musique(f.) music

nager to swim
naître to be born
natal(e) natal, native

natation(f.) swimming
nationalité(f.) nationality
nature(f.) nature
né(e) born
neige(f.) snow
neiger to snow
ne . . . pas not
nettoyer to clean
neuf nine
neuf, (neuve) new
night-club(m.) night-club
niveau(m.) level
Noël Christmas
noir(e) black
nom(m.) name, surname
non no
non fumeurs no-smoking (compartment etc.)
nord(m.) north
normalement normally
Norvège(f.) Norway
notre, nos our
nourriture(f.) food
nouveau, (-elle) new; de nouveau again
novembre November
nuage(m.) cloud; nuageux, (-euse) cloudy
nuit(f.) night
numéro(m.) number

objets trouvés (m. pl.) lost property (lit. objects found)
obliger de to oblige to
s'occuper de to deal with, to attend to
octobre October
œuf(m.) egg
offert(e) offered, given
offrir to offer, to give
oiseau(m.) bird
on one (used also for 'we' and 'I')
opérer to operate
orange(f.) orange
ordinaire ordinary
oreille(f.) ear
ou or; ou bien or else; ou . . . ou either . . . or
où where, when
oublier to forget
ouest(m.) west
oui yes
outre-mer overseas
ouvert(e) open
ouverture(f.) opening
ouvrir to open

paella(f.) paëlla
pain(m.) bread
palais de justice(m.) law-courts
pamplemousse(m.) grapefruit
pantalon(m.) trousers
papiers (m.pl.) papers
Pâques Easter
par by; par ici this way
parc(m.) park
parce que because

pardon pardon, sorry, excuse me
parent(m.) parent, relative
parfait(e) perfect
parfumerie(f.) perfume-shop, beauty-shop
Parisien(ne) (m. and f.) Parisian
parking(m.) parking, car park
parler to speak
partie(f.) part
partir to leave
pas not; pas du tout not at all; pas mal de quite a lot of
passeport(m.) passport
passer to pass
passionnément passionately
pâté(m.) pâté; pâté de campagne(m.) country pâté
pâtisserie(f.) cake-shop, pastry (cake)
patron(m.) boss
pavillon(m.) detached house, pavilion
payer to pay (for)
pays(m.) country, area; Pays de Galles(m.) Wales
péage(m.) toll
pendant during; (from pendre) hanging
penser to think
perdre to lose
père(m.) father
personne(f.) person; personne (+ ne) nobody
petit little; petit déjeuner(m.) breakfast; un petit peu a little bit
pétrole(m.) paraffin
P et T Post Office
un peu a little; un petit peu a little bit; à peu près more or less
peut-être perhaps
je peux see pouvoir
pharmacie(f.) pharmacy, chemist's
pharmacien(ne) (m. and f.) pharmacist
pièce(f.) room; 5F la pièce 5 francs each; à la pièce individually
pied(m.) foot
piéton(m.) pedestrian
pilote(m.) pilot
piscine(f.) swimming pool
pizza(f.) pizza
placard(m.) cupboard
place(f.) space, seat (in theatre etc.)
plage(f.) beach
se plaire to enjoy oneself
planche à voile(f.) windsurfing board
plan de la ville(m.) a street-map of the town
plat(m.) dish
plateau(m.) board
plein(e) full; le plein, s'il vous plaît (in a garage) fill it up, please
il pleut it is raining
plombier(m.) plumber
plus plus, more; plus . . . que more . . . than; en plus in addition, moreover
plusieurs several
pluvieux, (-euse) rainy
pneu(m.) tyre

à point medium (of steak)
poire(f.) pear
pois, petits pois (m. pl.) peas
poisson(m.) fish
poivre(m.) pepper
Pologne(f.) Poland
pomme(f.) apple; pomme de
  terre(f.) potato; pommes frites (f.
  pl.) chips
pompe de gonflage(f.) air-pump
pont(m.) bridge
porc(m.) pork
portail(m.) gate
porte(f.) door
possible possible
possibilité(f.) possibility
poste(f.) post, post office
poulet(m.) chicken
pour for; pour cent per cent
pourquoi? why?
pousser to push
pratique handy, convenient
précieux, (-euse) precious
préférence(f.) preference
préférer to prefer
premier, (-ière) first
prendre to take
prénom(m.) forename
préparer to prepare
près nearby; près de near to
presque almost
pressé(e) in a hurry; citron
  pressé(m.) fresh lemon juice (lit.
  squeezed lemon)
pression(f.) pressure, draught (beer)
prévu(e) predicted
prier to beseech
prière de (you are) requested to
printemps(m.) spring
prise de courant(f.) power-point
prix(m.) price, prize
problème(m.) problem
prochain(e) next
proche nearby
professeur(m.) teacher
profession(f.) profession
professionnel(le) professional
profiter de to take advantage of
promotion(f.) special offer
propre clean
province(f.) province(s)
provinciaux (m.pl.) people from the
  provinces
PTT Post Office
puis then
puis-je? may I?, can I?
puisque since, as
pull(over)(m.) pullover
purée(f.) mashed potato

quai(m.) platform
qualité(f.) quality
quand when
quart(m.) quarter
quartier(m.) district
quatre four

que(m.) that, than
quel(le)? which?, what?
quelque(s) some (a few); quelque
  chose something;
  quelquefois sometimes
qu'est-ce que? what?
qui who, which
quitter to leave
quoi? what?

radis(m.) radish
raisin(m.) grapes
rangement(m.) storage
râper to grate
rapide rapid
raquette(f.) racquet
rasoir(m.) razor
recommander to recommend
recommencer to start again
reconnaître to recognise
reconstruction(f.) reconstruction
réceptionniste (m. and f.) receptionist
reçu(e) received (from recevoir)
réduction(f.) reduction
réfrigérateur(m.) refrigerator
regagner get back to
regarder to look at
région(f.) region
en règle in order
régler to settle up, pay
remercier to thank
remparts (m. pl.) ramparts
rénal(e) renal, kidney-
(se) rencontrer to meet (each other)
rendez-vous(m.) meeting, appointment
rendre to render, give up; se rendre
  à to get oneself to (a place)
renseignement(m.) (piece of)
  information
rentrée(f.) the start of work after the
  holidays
rentrer to go back, to go home
repartir to leave again
reportage(m.) report
reprendre to take back, to take up again
RER(m.) rapid underground train
  service between the centre of Paris and
  the suburbs
réservation(f.) reservation
résidence(f.) residence
responsable de responsible for
ressembler à to resemble
restaurant(m.) restaurant
restauré(e) restored
rester to stay, to remain
retard(m.) delay
retenir to retain, to hold back
retour(m.) return
retourner to return
retraite(f.) retirement
réunion(f.) meeting; la
  Réunion French island off Africa
réussir to succeed
revenir to come back
revoir to see again; au revoir good-bye
rez-de-chaussée(m.) ground floor

rillettes (f. pl.) potted mince, usually pork
rive(f.) bank (of river)
riz(m.) rice
robe(f.) dress
romain(e) Roman
rose(f.) rose; (adj.) pink
rouge red
rouler to roll, to move (of cars)
Roumanie(f.) Rumania
route(f.) road
Royaume-Uni(m.) United Kingdom
rue(f.) street
Russie(f.) Russia

sable(m.) sand
sac(m.) bag
saignant(e) bleeding, rare (of meat)
je sais see savoir
saison(f.) season
salade(f.) lettuce, salad
salaire(m.) pay
salé(e) salted
salle(f.) (public) room; salle à manger(f.) dining-room; salle d'eau(f.) shower-room; salle de bains(f.) bathroom; salle de séjour(f.) sitting-room
salon(m.) sitting-room
salutation(f.) greeting
samedi Saturday
sandwich(m.) sandwich
sans without
sardine(f.) sardine
saucisse(f.) sausage
saucisson(m.) salami
sauf except (for)
savoir to know (a fact or how to do something); je sais nager I can swim
savon(m.) soap
science(f.) science, knowledge
se (to) himself, herself, oneself, itself
sec, (sèche) dry
second(e) second (adj.); seconde(f.) second; secondaire secondary
secours(m.) help
secrétaire (m. and f.) secretary
sécurité(f.) security, safety
sel(m.) salt
semaine(f.) week
se sentir to feel (oneself)
séparer to separate
sept seven
septembre September
serveuse(f.) waitress
service(m.) service
serviette(f.) serviette, towel, brief-case; serviette de toilette(f.) hand-towel
servir de to serve as
seul(e) alone
seulement only
shampooing(m.) shampoo
short(m.) shorts
si if, yes (in contradiction)
siècle(m.) century

s'il vous plaît please
simple simple, straightforward; simplement simply
sinon otherwise
situé(e) situated
six six
ski(m.) ski, skiing
slip(m.) pants
snack-bar(m.) snack-bar
SNCF(f.) French Railways
social(e) social
soeur(f.) sister
soif thirst; avoir soif to be thirsty
soir(m.) evening, in the evening
soldes(m.) sale(s)
soleil(m.) sun
sorbet(m.) sorbet, water ice
sortie(f.) exit; sortir to go out
soudain sudden, suddenly
souffrir to suffer
soupe(f.) soup
sous under; sous-développé(e) under-developed
soutenir to sustain
soutien-gorge(m.) bra
souvenir(m.) souvenir, memory
souvent often
stage(m.) course
station de métro(f.) underground station
stationnement(m.) parking
stationner to park
station-service(f.) service-station
stea(c)k(m.) steak
studio(m.) bed-sit
succès(m.) success
succession(f.) succession
sucette(f.) lollipop
sucre(m.) sugar; sucré(e) sweet
sud(m.) south
Suède(f.) Sweden
Suisse(f.) Switzerland; petit suisse(m.) small cream cheese
supérieur(e) better, superior, upper
supermarché(m.) supermarket
suppositoire(m.) suppository
sur on
sûr(e) sure; sûrement, bien sûr certainly
surtout especially
sus, en sus on top, in addition
syndicat d'initiative(m.) tourist office

ta see ton, ta, tes
tabac(m.) tobacco, tobacconist's shop
table(f.) table
taille(f.) size, waist
taisez-vous shut up
tard late
tarte(f.) tart
tasse(f.) cup
taverne(f.) tavern
taxi(m.) taxi
Tchécoslovaquie(f.) Czechoslovakia
te (to) you, (to) yourself
technicien(ne)(m. and f.) technician

téléphone(m.) telephone
téléphoner to telephone
tellement so (much)
temps(m.) time, weather
tendu(e) tense
tenir to hold
tennis(m.) tennis
tenue(f.) outfit, clothes
terminer to finish
terrasse(f.) terrace
terrine(f.) coarse pâté
thé(m.) tea
théâtre(m.) theatre
ticket(m.) ticket
timbre(m.) stamp
tirer to pull
toi you, yourself
toilette(f.), faire sa toilette to wash and dress; les toilettes lavatory
tomate(f.) tomato
tomber to fall
ton(m.) tone, colour
ton, ta, tes your
toujours still, always
tour(f.) tower; (m.) walk, drive
touriste (m. and f.) tourist
touristique touristic
tournée(f.) round, trip round
tourner to turn
Toussaint(f.) All Saints' Day
tout(e), tous all; tout à l'heure a little while ago, shortly; à tout à l'heure see you later; tout de suite immediately; tout droit straight ahead; tout le monde everybody; tous les deux both of them; tous les soirs every evening
train(m.) train
transport(m.) (means of) transport; transporter to transport
travail(m.) job, work
travailler to work
travailleur(m.) worker
traverser to cross
très very
triperie(f.) tripe
trois three
troisième third
trop too; trop de monde too many people
troupe(f.) troupe
trouver to find; se trouver to find oneself, to be situated
TTC all taxes included
Turquie(f.) Turkey

un(e) a, one
uniquement only
université(f.) university
urgence(f.) urgency, emergency
utiliser to use

va, vas see aller

vacances (f. pl.) holiday(s)
vache(f.) cow
valise(f.) suitcase
vanille(f.) vanilla
varié(e) varied, various
il vaut it is worth, it costs
veau(m.) veal
vélo(m.) bicycle
vendeur(m.), vendeuse(f.) sales assistant
vendredi Friday
venir to come
vent(m.) wind
vente(f.) sale
ventre(m.) stomach
vérité(f.) truth
verre(m.) glass
vers towards
vert(e) green
veste(f.) jacket
vestiaire(m.) clothing, cloakroom
vêtement(m.) garment
veux, veut want, wants (from vouloir); je veux bien yes please
viande(f.) meat
vie(f.) life, cost of living
vieux, (vieille) old
village(m.) village
ville(f.) town
vin(m.) wine
visiter to visit
il vit he lives (from vivre)
vite quickly
vivre to live
vodka(f.) vodka
voici here is, here are
voie(f.) track
voilà here is, there is, there you are
voilier(m.) sailing-boat, yacht
voir to see
voisin(e)(m. and f.) neighbour
voiture(f.) car; en voiture by car; voiture-lit(f.) sleeper (train)
vol(m.) flight
volaille(f.) poultry
voler to fly, to steal
votre, vos your
je voudrais I'd like
vous voulez you want
voyage(m.) journey; voyager to travel; voyageur(m.) traveller
vrai(e) true, real; vraiment really

wagon-lit(m.) sleeping-car
WC(m.) (pronounced vé-cé) toilet
week-end(m.) week-end

y there, to it
Yougoslavie(f.) Yugoslavia

zéro zero
zeste(m.) zest (of lemon)

Index

Breakthrough Language Packs
Complete self-study courses

Each Breakthrough Language pack is designed as a complete self-study course using audio cassettes and a course book. Each pack contains:

* Three 60 minute audio cassettes
* The course book

Breakthrough Language Packs available

Breakthrough French	ISBN 0-333-48191-7
Breakthrough German	ISBN 0-333-48187-9
Breakthrough Italian	ISBN 0-333-48179-8
Breakthrough Spanish	ISBN 0-333-48183-6
Breakthrough Greek	ISBN 0-333-48714-1
Breakthrough Further French	ISBN 0-333-48193-3
Breakthrough Further German	ISBN 0-333-48189-5
Breakthrough Further Spanish	ISBN 0-333-48185-2

Companion Language Grammars

Companion French Grammar
Chris Beswick,
Head of Modern Languages,
Shena Simon Sixth Form College, Manchester
> 0-333-48079-1   144 pages

Companion German Grammar
Isabel Willshaw, formerly lecturer in German,
Ealing College of Higher Education
> 0-333-48180-1   176 pages

Companion Spanish Grammar
Sandra Truscott,
Adult education tutor in Spanish
> 0-333-48181-X   128 pages

These basic pocket grammars, designed for easy reference by travellers and students on non-examination courses, cover the most important rules for speaking and understanding everyday French, German and Spanish.

Contents include:
* Clear explanations of grammatical points with examples of the use of each item in common situations
* 'Try it yourself' and 'learn by heart' sections with a range of activities to test the most important points
* A grammar glossary to familiarize the reader with terms such as pronouns, direct objects, auxiliary verbs etc
* Verb tables
* An index referring the user to an explanation of the particular grammatical point.

All these books are available at your local bookshop or newsagent, or can be ordered direct from the publisher. Indicate the number of copies required and fill in the form below.

Name _____
(Block letters please)

Address _____

_____

Macmillan Education Ltd, Houndmills, Basingstoke, Hants RG21 2XS